# AMERICAN COOKERY

# American Cookery

A NOVEL

*Laura Kalpakian*

St. Martin's Press   New York

This is a work of fiction. All of the characters, organizations, and events portrayed in this novel are either products of the author's imagination or are used fictitiously.

AMERICAN COOKERY. Copyright © 2006 by Laura Kalpakian. All rights reserved. Printed in the United States of America. No part of this book may be used or reproduced in any manner whatsoever without written permission except in the case of brief quotations embodied in critical articles or reviews. For information, address St. Martin's Press, 175 Fifth Avenue, New York, N.Y. 10010.

www.stmartins.com

"A Ballad for Ginny Brothers" appeared in *Prairie Schooner*, Autumn 2006.
A portion of part one, chapter one appeared in *Good Housekeeping*, August 2004, in "What to Bring to an American Picnic."

Book design by Maura Fadden Rosenthal/M space

Library of Congress Cataloging-in-Publication Data

Kalpakian, Laura.
    American cookery : a novel / Laura Kalpakian.—1st ed.
        p. cm.
    ISBN-13: 978-0-312-34811-3
    ISBN-10: 0-312-34811-8
    1. Cookery—Fiction.  2. Mormons—Fiction.  3. Domestic fiction.  I. Title.
    PS3561.A4168A83 2006
    813'.54—dc22

                                                            2006043426

First Edition: September 2006

10  9  8  7  6  5  4  3  2  1

THIS BOOK IS DEDICATED TO

HELEN KALPAKIAN
1901–1987

AND

LILA JOHNSON LUTZ
1905–1990

SPECIAL THANKS to James Beard and Julia Child, great American cooks and writers. Their prose has inspired me, and their enthusiasm has ignited my own, and their books have brightened my kitchens.

# Contents

Tell me what you eat: I will tell you what you are.

—Jean-Anthelme Brillat-Savarin, 1824

I raised to my lips a spoonful of the tea in which I had soaked a morsel of the cake. No sooner had the warm liquid mixed with the crumbs touched my palate than a shudder ran through me and I stopped, intent upon the extraordinary thing that was happening to me . . . [W]hen from a long-distant past nothing subsists, after the people are dead, after the things are broken and scattered, taste and smell alone, more fragile but more enduring, more unsubstantial, more persistent, more faithful, remains poised a long time, like souls, remembering, waiting, hoping, amid the ruins of all the rest; and bear unflinchingly, in the tiny and almost impalpable drop of their essence, the vast structure of recollection.

—Marcel Proust, *Overture* to *Remembrance of Things Past,* 1913

BOOK ONE

# ZION

# Green Goddess

## 1926

## CHAPTER ONE

THE DOUGLASS WOMEN HAD A LONG TRADITION OF trouble. They had been known to borrow trouble as well as money and time. They often fed the many on a few beans and a hambone, on loaves and fishes. They wielded ten-pound fry pans and hoisted ten-gallon stockpots. Their instincts were to preside, to direct, and, when necessary, to defend. Woe unto the shiftless, the no-account stragglers, the thoughtless and thankless, the whiners and the weak. In that family, if you felt the surge of a strong tide, an all-but-lunar tug, it was always the women; they pulled people in their wake. Their men sometimes resisted, sometimes got distracted, misled by weaker, more pliable women, by religion, or drink, or get-rich-quick schemes, by great obsessions like Eden's father's Timetables, or great disasters like her husband's Westerns, sauced with dreams and debt. Sometimes these men gave up and made their exits. Some stewed in their own discontent. Some took braying refuge in a notion of patriarchy and the rights bestowed by an all-knowing God on wise men who were to be obeyed by submissive women who knew their place. The Douglass women just never did know their place.

So when little Eden Douglass, hauled into the Fourth Street School office for a serious schoolyard infraction, and about to be sent home in disgrace, asked the principal to call her aunt, Mrs. Afton Lance, or her grandmother, Mrs. Ruth Douglass, rather than her mother, Kitty, the principal blanched. Mr. Snow said he would call whomever he wished. He picked up the telephone by its long neck, put the receiver to his ear, and rang Miss Moody, St. Elmo's operator and chief gossip.

"Who are you calling?" Eden asked, more curious than truly humbled. "My aunt or my grandmother?" Mr. Snow glared at her, gave her a quick tongue lashing. Intuitively Eden knew what Mr. Snow wanted from her, so she feigned tears.

His sense of superiority thus happily underscored, Mr. Snow said he would call Afton Lance. "You must leave. Go out into the hall and sit in the Miscreant's Chair by the door."

Shoulders hunched, Eden shuffled out to the hall and sat down on the hard wooden chair outside the office door. Fans turned slowly, churning the smell of stale bread from a hundred lunch buckets, shoe rubber, long-spilled milk, and unwashed linoleum. In the high-ceilinged hall, the lights were off and the doors at either end were open to keep the building cool in the September heat. Eden pulled one knee up to her chest and rested her chin there, a posture forbidden to girls. She scratched at a flea bite through the hole in her black stocking. Eden Louise Douglass had short straight hair, thick, lusterless, dusty, unevenly cropped just below her ears. She wore a gingham dress, a hand-me-down from Bessie and Alma Lance, the blue and white faded equally into gray from drying in the hot California sun. She hummed under her breath the very songs that had gotten her into trouble, "Hot Tamale Molly" and "Keep Your Skirts Down, Mary Ann," and songs about creeping into tents late at night, songs she heard all the time on the Victrola at home, songs that everyone was singing in 1926.

A teacher had overheard Eden singing in the schoolyard and snatched her elbow, marched her to the principal's office. Though naturally the teacher could not repeat the offending lyrics, she had alluded to their general nature, and Mr. Snow had declared that Eden's mother should be called in and apprised of her daughter's crime, and the girl sent home in disgrace.

But Kitty Douglass was unreliable, and Eden knew this. Unpredictable. Kitty might laugh off the offense, and call the principal a pumpsucker, or, if she had been at the Bowers Tonic, she might . . . well, there was no telling. Eden had asked him to call her aunt or her grandmother because she knew what they would do. They would wash her mouth out with soap. No question. She would be in serious trouble, quickly punished, and it would be over. She was glad he'd called Afton instead of her grandmother. Ruth Douglass would be working at the Pilgrim Restaurant, the interruption unwelcome. At Afton's house—after Eden had her mouth washed out with soap—Afton would give her a honey and banana sandwich. Eden hankered after one of those. Her own lunch bucket held the remains of a cold fried-mush patty left over from last night's dinner.

Eden looked up from the scab on her knee to see Afton Lance framed, silhouetted by the sunlight in the arched double doors at the end of the hall. She pushed the baby buggy into the hall. She was never without a child clinging to her hand or her hem, and she always smelled of starch, a whiff of rosemary on her hands and breath. Her thick, dark hair was wound neatly atop her head. A solid, skirted figure, she wore her church hat, at odds with her weekday housedress. Her firm step echoed. She stopped in front of her niece and inquired after Eden's crimes.

"I didn't think the songs were so bad," Eden said in her own defense as she stood up. "I didn't think they were bad at all."

"What you think does not matter. What does the principal think?"

Afton dealt with Mr. Snow out of Eden's hearing. She had sent three of her children through this school, Lucius, Bessie, and Alma. Two were still here, Junior and Sam. The toddler in the buggy, Constance, would be a student here in due time. Afton was pregnant with a son, Douglass, who would be born six months later, in March 1927, and the last of her eight children was born in 1931. She was a legend in her own way. The interview with Mr. Snow was brief.

Leaving the school, Eden and her aunt walked side by side in silence while the baby Connie babbled in her buggy. For a woman as talkative as Afton Lance, silence was a sure indicator of the seriousness of the offense. They were halfway home when Afton asked, "What does your father think of these songs, Eden?"

"I don't know. Does he think of them?"

Afton gave a combined snort and shrug, a gesture so eloquent and singular that everyone of her acquaintance, from the youngest child to the oldest church Elder, braced for consequences.

Eden braced, but she defended her father just the same. "Pa mostly thinks about his Great Timetable."

"He'll never finish. How can he? History goes on, don't it?"

"But he's at it all the time. Almost every night after work he goes to the library. He can draw the charts at home, but he has to read in the library."

He goes to the library, thought Afton, because it is a remembered heaven. As a boy, a young man, Gideon had shown such scholarly promise and then had squandered his chances when he rejected the offer to attend a Gentile college. He could not imperil his Mormon faith, he had said. His very soul. Well, he imperiled his very soul now, didn't he? What else could you call it? Living with Kitty in sloth nigh unto sin. Afton wanted to pity her brother, but pity without action was unworthy of a Saint. Instead, she took up the redemption of her brother's children with an energy that bordered on vengeance.

Eden's grandmother Ruth was equally appalled by Gideon's fate and his wife. However, Ruth's steely nature did not admit of enthusiasm, even in the matter of rescuing. And redemption? Ruth did not think in such terms. Afton and Ruth differed on many things, including the Church and family: Ruth had long since bowed out of being an observant Mormon, and had found her own large family a burden. Afton unquestioningly adhered to the Saints and all their teachings. Afton enjoyed the noise and tumult of a large family. Still, they agreed that hapless Gideon and godless Kitty were beyond help or hope. But the children? Something must be done.

Afton and Ruth concentrated their rescuing efforts on Eden Louise. They saw her as one of their own. Her two siblings resembled their mother, fat, blue eyed, pink as little piglets, spiritless, and easily amused. But Eden Louise had the dark hair, the green eyes, the sallow coloring of the Douglasses. Moreover, she had the spirit, the smile, and the intelligence of her father's eldest sister, Eden, who had died in a train wreck in 1911. She had been named for this lost girl, this lost Eden. Of all Ruth's children and grandchildren, Eden Louise was the favored, the beloved. Her mother, her aunt, and her grandmother all competed, not so much for Eden's love—she could love all three—as for her loyalty. Each wished to shape her into a particular vision of what it meant to be a woman. Ruth valued independence and respectability, two values often at odds. Afton valued the energetic fulfilling of obligation and adhering to the Mormon religion. Kitty valued the fanciful and took her religion from the Saturday matinees at the Dream Theatre, from risqué, romantic novels; Kitty often confused the word with the deed, especially if the word was put to music, and could be hummed.

Once back at Afton's, Eden had her mouth washed out with soap. Crying and coughing, Eden spat into the sink and took a towel, wiped it all over her face, streaking the dust.

"Now, let's go into the kitchen," said Afton, the disagreeable duty done. "I made you a honey and banana sandwich. You eat it, and then Connie and

I will walk you home. It's time we talked to your mother. A serious talk. Another one."

The two regarded each other, the first-grader and the Mormon matron. They both knew that if Afton walked Eden home, they might well find Kitty Douglass the worse for wear, happily numbed by Bowers Tonic—once a medicinal compound originated by Nana Bowers, the matriarch of St. Elmo's premier black family. Now, in these dire times of Prohibition, Bowers Magic Bitters Tonic had evolved into bootleg hooch manufactured and sold out of the back room of the Bowers Barbershop, and in the balcony of the Dream Theatre. They knew, too, that they might find Kitty still not fully dressed. They would certainly find her wreathed in cigarette smoke, reading a cheap novel, the Victrola playing one of the very songs that had gotten Eden into trouble. They would probably find the toddler Ernest roaming the house, a nasty smell emitting from his unchanged pants, and four-year-old Ada unsupervised. They knew the dishes would be unwashed, the beds unmade, the floor sticky, and the dog, Buster, scratching at fleas. And they knew for certain that when Afton actually beheld these dreadful sights, she would be compelled to act in some dire and redemptive fashion.

"Do I have to go home just now?" asked Eden. "Couldn't I stay? I'm still hungry. Maybe we could bake."

"Someone needs to tell your mother what happened today in school. Will that someone be you?" The question sounded biblical.

Eden's shoulders slumped.

"A sin of omission is still a sin."

"They were just songs," said Eden. "I didn't kick or hit anyone. I wasn't mean."

"Of course not. You're not a mean child. You are a very sweet child. You are the image of our own dear Eden."

"Eden Douglass REGRET," replied the girl. This was the name on the gravestone in the St. Elmo Cemetery, as though Regret were Eden Douglass's real name, her true name. The thought made her prickly under her arms and behind the knees.

"Will you tell your parents what happened then?"

It was no good lying to Afton. You might make up a story after the fact and hand it to her, all buttery with falsehood, but that wouldn't work now. "I'll tell Pa," Eden offered. "Let him tell Ma."

"I see," said Afton, making her own plans. "Very well then. You eat your sandwich while I put Connie down for her nap."

The wretchedness at school, the taste of soap all but forgotten, Eden sat at the table, swinging her legs, savoring the honey and bananas, still humming "The Sheik of Araby." Light filtered through the dusty windows and the pepper trees outside and rustled over the dish towels drying on a string across the kitchen window, among the childish drawings pinned to the walls along with the array of ribbons Afton's baking and canning had won at St. Elmo's Citrus Exposition since 1914. The old dog, Chester, lay against the door, content with dog dreams. A fragrance wafted, emanating from the stove: a great squat enterprise with an oven, a separate water heater, and a plate warmer. From a speckled enamel stockpot on the back burner there rose wisps of scent. What was in that pot and the smell it gave off depended wholly on the leftovers that were then transformed into soup or the basis for sauce or gravy, for something to soften the baby's bread in. That smell defined Afton Lance as much as the scent of starch in her clothes and sprigs of rosemary she kept by the bathroom sink for breath freshener.

Afton returned, and tied on an apron, tossed one to her niece. "Well, let's bake something nice for everyone."

"What?"

"Well, we'll just have a rummage in the cupboard and the icebox, and we'll see what we come up with. We'll see what's at hand. The good cook wastes nothing, uses everything—and not just everything in the kitchen, but here, and here." Afton touched the top of her head and her heart.

Eden smiled. All was forgiven.

"There is a recipe for everything in life."

"What if you don't have what you need to make it?"

"Then you adapt."

"What's that mean?"

Afton considered, though she was not a pensive person. "That means you invent. A recipe is a license for invention. You take what you have and turn it into what you want. It requires imagination. Not your mother's sort of imagination. The good kind."

Eden wasn't about to ask after the bad kind.

Afton had on hand stale cake, milk, eggs, brown sugar, and a few overripe bananas. "Banana cream pie," Afton announced, setting Eden to work at the kitchen table with a rolling pin over the cake crumbs in a bag. Afton heated the milk and went to work on the eggs, flour, and brown sugar. Bits flew out of the bowl under her strong rhythmic beats. "You know, when I was a girl, my mother would never let any of us, not even the girls, work at the Pilgrim Restaurant. She used to say we had better things to do than to stuff people's guts, that education was your ticket out of the kitchen. I said to her, Well, Mother, people have to eat, don't they? Why should the kitchen be any less worthy an undertaking in God's eyes than, say, teaching school or lawyering, or the like? God is as happy to see a small task well done as a great masterpiece achieved."

"Is that in the Book of Mormon?" asked Eden.

"Somewhere." It was in fact her own bit of wisdom, and as such might as well be Scripture in this house.

Under her direction, Eden mixed the crumbs and some melted butter and pressed the mixture all over the sides and bottom of the deep dish. Eden poured the heated milk into the sugar and egg mixture while Afton's wire whisk, a tool of her own devising that her husband, Tom, had made for her, beat in a steady cadence. Then the whole went back into the pan. Afton drew a chair up to the stove and turned the heat on low. "There, now, Eden, your job is to be certain this don't burn, nor the eggs scramble. That's the trick of it. The skill. Keep your eyes on it and your hand moving. While you're at it, I'll teach you some good songs. Some useful songs you need never fear to sing."

Eden had not feared to sing "Keep Your Skirts Down, Mary Ann," but she did not say this. She just kept stirring and joined in as Afton warbled in her tuneless contralto, "Shall the Youth of Zion Falter" and "Welcome, Welcome, Sabbath Morning" and a few other Mormon anthems, including Eden's favorite, "Now Let Us Rejoice." Afton taught everything by example.

They heard Connie fuss, and Afton went to fetch her, setting her finally on the kitchen floor with some pans and a spoon to bang. She came to the stove. "Very nice work. You haven't let the eggs scramble nor the milk burn. You have the makings of a fine cook, Eden Louise." Afton brought to the most ordinary undertaking a sense of importance.

While Eden blended vanilla, cinnamon, and fresh grated nutmeg into the creamy mixture, Afton laid the brown overripe bananas on the bottom where no one would see them, then blanketed them with the custard and layered the attractive bananas on top. "You see the logic of it?"

"The good-looking bananas are on top," said Eden. "No one sees the brown ones."

"How smart you are, Eden!" Eden flushed at the compliment. "Now, before we put this in the pie cooler and keep it from those pesky flies, let's add a bit of inspiration. You know what that is, don't you?"

"Like when God gave the golden tablets to Joseph Smith?" Eden smiled, proud of herself. She went every Sunday to church with her father.

"What God gave to Joseph Smith was divine and timeless. This is orange peel." She handed her an orange and the heavy grater.

The damp, fresh peel flew up and tickled Eden's nose with its bright scent. "Can we have some pie now?"

"No indeed. We wait for the other children to get home from school. The shared gift twice blesses the giver. You know I'm right."

Eden did not contest this. No one did. Afton Lance was always right. Even when she was wrong, she was right.

"Now let's clean up. Chores are obliged of the faithful."

At Eden's house, chores were obliged only of the unwary or the desperate, but she did not say so.

Before the other children returned from school, Eden had the opportunity to play in the Lances' treehouse, which she seldom had to herself, always sharing with her Lance cousins. This afternoon it was a pirate ship where Captain Eden stood on deck overlooking the empty seas. Leggy red geraniums leaned against the back step like beggars, and shrubs of thyme and rosemary and weedy mint straggled nearby. Grass lay flattened from the feet of the six Lance children, but in this shaggy pepper tree Tom Lance had built a fine treehouse, well wrought like everything else Tom Lance ever made. Tom Lance worked for the railroad. Most of St. Elmo did; the railroad gave St. Elmo, California, its reason for being. But Tom Lance could support his large family on the railroad's meager wages, because Afton managed everything, and Tom, a silent, diffident man, did anything she asked of him.

The Lance children tromped in from school, dutifully putting their empty lunch buckets in the sink. The eldest, Lucius, at twelve was the image of his father without the scar on his nose. Bessie and Alma, sisters who could have been twins, fought over some imagined slight. The younger boys, Junior and Samuel, went to Fourth Street School with Eden, and teased her for her schoolyard singing.

"That's enough of that," said Afton. "It don't do to dwell on another's sorrow."

Eden gave them both a little sneer. They went to wash their hands at their mother's insistence, and Afton left to change the toddler, Connie. "I'll be right there," Afton called from the bedroom. "No fingers in the pie!"

Eden chose her chair, eye to eye with the pie. She regarded the pie with some pride. "I helped to make this," Eden announced with an air of unquenchable superiority as the other children jostled and fought for their places.

Junior scoffed, "Yeah and you got 'spelled, too. I seen the whole thing on the schoolyard."

"Just for this afternoon. I had a funner time than you any day."

"Why didn't you have 'em call your own ma? Why call ours? You must of known she would beat you."

"No one beats me."

"That's because your own pa ain't willing, and your ma ain't able." Tom Junior jabbed Eden's ribs. "Your ma is drunk. Sure as sin, she's drunk."

"Shut up, you pumpsucker."

"Ma!" Junior called out. "Ma! Eden called me a pumpsucker!"

Before Eden could retaliate, Afton breezed back into the kitchen, baby Connie hoisted on her hip. She chastised Eden for vulgarity, reminding her—in the immortal words of Ruth Douglass—that vulgarity was worse than sin. Sin could be atoned for. "Now," said Afton, "let us pray."

When Eden was ready to leave, Afton stood on the porch, baby Connie in her arms. She picked up the baby's hand. "Wave bye-bye, Connie. Wave bye-bye to Eden." Connie waved.

Afton gave Eden a kiss on the cheek and sent her homeward, calling out, "Goodbye Eden, goodbye precious girl," but only after she had larded on her recommendations, her admonitions, her ongoing cautions: to sing the good clean songs of the Mormon Church, and remember that the youth of Zion never faltered, that a clean mind was the angels' delight, the path to the Celestial Kingdom was littered with the lyrics of unseemly songs, on and on, invoking always a teaspoon of the Book of Mormon, a quarter cup of the the Doctrine and Covenants, a tablespoon perhaps of the Church's collective wisdom, and a quart of her own unwavering certitude.

## Afton Lance's Back Burner

*from the time of her marriage in 1911 till her death in 1965*

Fill a kettle or stockpot with water. Into this put any bones or leftovers with meat, chicken, beef, pork. It can be cooked or not. It can be a cut of meat too tough for anything else, or a chicken too old. Add a peeled onion. Few cloves of garlic. Add some peppercorns and bay leaves, some sprigs of rosemary and thyme, and a handful of fresh parsley. You can put in, too, any other greens, chard, spinach, or celery or carrots, any green onion tops, really any vegetable too tired or not fit to serve. You needn't tell anyone. Put on the lid. Bring to boil. Reduce heat, put lid to the side so steam escapes, and let simmer for a few hours at least. A day. Stir now and then. Strain. Use for soups, sauces, gravies, for poaching eggs or boiling beans, for keeping the well happy and nursing the sick back to health.

## THE SAINT

Afton Lance had a heart as capacious as her mind was narrow. At seventeen she fell in love with Tom Lance, married him in 1911, and never looked backward or inward if she could help it.

Tom and Afton Lance raised their eight children, though that didn't seem to be enough for Afton. The beds in their house never got cold. She took in her grandchildren and raised them, too, when her own offspring died or screwed up.

Lucius died in combat in 1942. Connie died of cancer in 1962.

Junior, Douglass, and William screwed up.

But Afton Lance would never renounce wrongdoers, naysayers, sinners amongst the Saints. She never gave up. She would never retreat, never say, *Never darken my door!* Her children wished she would. Her grandchildren wished she would. Eden Louise wished she would. But Afton Lance would keep on telling them, all of them, how wrong they were, how right she was.

Bessie, Afton's eldest, stolid, gloomy, and easily bored, discovered at seventeen that between her legs she had, unbeknownst to her all this time, a whole new wonderful country to be explored with handsome Nephi Hansen. Their eldest was born some six months after their hasty marriage. This was the only hasty thing Bessie ever did.

Afton's daughter Alma, named for the Book of Alma in the Book of Mormon, had more spirit. In the tradition of headstrong Douglass women, she ran off and married an Arkie Baptist, Walter Epps. His family came to California to pick fruit. For a time they lived in a car in the very groves where they worked. Alma brought Walter to her parents' house one Sunday for dinner. Walter wore a tie, too tight at the collar, and he could hardly eat. After he left, Afton told her daughter, Arkies are poor white trash, and Baptists, little better than A-rabs.

At least Walter wasn't a Jew. Connie Lance married a divorced Jew. Victor Levy came to the marriage with two children by his first wife, also Jewish. Victor Levy was the first person to join the Lance clan to have a university degree. He was much respected in St. Elmo. So Afton found it hard to fault him, except for his being Jewish and too old for Connie. Thirty-six to her nineteen.

What did Connie know at nineteen? Nothing. (She knew she wanted to get away from her parents and the Mormon Church; she knew that at nineteen.)

Afton even disapproved of the unoffending Eloise Travers, who married her son Samuel. Of the Lance sons, Samuel was the only one to have followed his parents' example of unremitting hard work. However, Samuel took a light line on the Church. He became a sheriff, way out in the desert. Far away from his mother.

Afton's youngest son, William, spent time in prison for fraud, forgery, and larceny.

At least her son Douglass followed the expectations of the faith and went on a two-year mission to Belfast. If the Protestants of Belfast were hostile to the Catholics, why should they be cordial to the Mormons? Douglass was stoned in the streets. Felled by stones and abject loneliness, Douglass Lance, that youth of Zion, faltered, fell in love with the first redheaded Irish girl who would look at him. He left the mission field and fetched up with the girl, eventually in Boston. He did not see his parents for eighteen years. He'd been married twice more by then.

Thomas Lance Junior was a decorated World War II veteran who fought in the European Theater of Operations. But later, returning home after the war, Junior grew surly, sullen, jealous, and bitter, and he took to drink. In 1961 he and his French Catholic wife rocked St. Elmo with scandal. Both fled. In different directions. Their three daughters went to live with Tom and Afton, who raised them till Afton died in 1965.

However, the son whose loss left a hole in Afton's heart was Lucius. The best, the brightest, whom God did not protect. Lucius died at Guadalcanal, and Afton Lance questioned God's will for the first time in her life. She questioned, too, her own inexorable correctness, her right to be right. This spasm of doubt was brief, but intense.

At the time of his death, Lucius was married to a pretty Mormon girl named Ellieanne, and they had two little sons, Micah and Jonah. Within months of Lucius's death in combat, Ellieanne took up with another man. She wanted to marry him and leave. Afton made Ellianne sign adoption papers renouncing all her rights to the boys on behalf of their grandparents. (A needless caution; she never showed back up in anyone's life.) Afton and Tom raised Micah and Jonah like their own sons.

Then, in 1962—the same year Connie Lance Levy died of cancer—Micah Lance married Helen Yamashita, daughter of a respectable Japanese family. Micah would not listen to Afton's tirade that the Japanese had killed his father in the first place. Afton had to sit beside Tom in the front pew of Helen Yamashita's church and watch Micah marry the enemy.

For a Saint, Afton Lance did a lot of unforgiving.

## CHAPTER TWO

THE GATE SQUEALED PITIFULLY AS EDEN PUSHED IT open and walked around the back. No one used the front door, except perhaps the Church's ward teachers on their once-monthly visits, the occasional salesman, and, of course, bill collectors. Eden lived with her family in a rented unrepaired clapboard in an untidy neighborhood. There was a peach tree in the back with a swing hanging from a bough. Laundry flapped on the clothesline, often for days, before Kitty brought it in. Eden stepped into a small back porch that had a deep double sink for the washing. The screen door slammed behind her. "I'm home, Ma."

In the kitchen she found her four-year-old sister, Ada, her round pink face smeared with red jam. A moth lay embalmed in the dish of pallid white margarine, and a loaf of bread withered almost audibly in the afternoon heat. The jam knife had fallen to the floor, and ants were inching up the table leg toward the pool of sticky stuff. Flies buzzed in endless circles, and the dog, Buster, looked up without interest. Buster would bestir himself only for Gideon.

"In here, duck!" called Kitty from the bedroom.

Eden Louise found her mother as she had expected. Kitty wore underwear and a loose wrapper. She sprawled in the bed and the baby climbed around her. She had a novel in one hand and a fag in the other. Her bobbed hair flew out around her head in a wiry, hennaed halo. Eden leaned against her father's desk, on which were the endless charts and blueprints of his Great Timetable. Drafts of the Great Timetable, rolls of them, were stacked in the corners and the wardrobe, and spilling out of the trunk that Kitty had brought from Liverpool. The charts pinned to the wall rustled in the breeze.

"Why the long sour puss? Bad day at school? Never mind. Come on, over here." Kitty threw the novel to the floor and plumped up the pillows beside her. She put Ernest at the end of the bed. She opened her arms to Eden.

Eden got into the bed beside her mother, pulled into an embrace redolent of cigarette smoke and intimate sweat, a wisp of talc, a whiff of Bowers Tonic. She relaxed against the thick soft cushions of her mother's flesh while Kitty chided and teased her in an abstract fashion, half humming "I Was a Good Little Girl," a tune from her old music hall days on the Liverpool stage. Eden smiled and hummed along. She was warm and sleepy and comfortable and loved. She could feel loved at Afton's, but she could never feel warm and sleepy and comfortable.

"Why are you late?" Kitty asked at the end of the singsong chorus.

"Sam and Junior invited me to Aunt Afton's. Afton made a pie."

Kitty's face brightened. "A bit of Afton's pie with a cup of tea. Now, that would answer, wouldn't it? A little of what you fancy does you good. What kind?"

"Banana cream pie. A little orange."

"Oh, heavenly! Afton send any home with you, did she?"

Eden shook her head.

"You should ask next time, duck. Ask if she can spare some for the starving Armenians."

"We're not starving Armenians."

"Yes, but if we was, she'd send it. She'd bloody slather it on if we was far away and living in dreadful peril. As it is, for her own flesh and blood, Afton Lance won't lift a hand."

"She came here and cleaned a couple of weeks ago," Eden offered, remembering the powerful presence of Condy's Disinfectant, which lingered for days.

"Is that the same thing?"

Eden had to admit it was not.

The baby clambered back over the bedclothes and fell across Kitty's lap. He smelled bad. "Oh, Ernest, I love you! But you are a nasty, nasty boy!" Kitty swung her feet off the bed and picked Ernest up under one arm. Eden followed as she carted the baby to the back porch, peeling off his dirty diaper, dropping it in a nearby pail with other such dirty diapers, and sticking his pink and brown bottom under the faucet, while he howled at the cold splash.

"Now, Miss Victorine St. John would not be washing this baby's bottom if she was me. No, she was caught in a web of passion with a Duke," Kitty declared.

"Is he her true love?" True love happened in all of Ma's novels.

"Of course! It wasn't his fault, nor hers neither, that he was a Duke, and she was born but a poor common girl. But she was ever a lady, and don't you forget it. He fell in love with her blue eyes and her spotless virtue, and her talent, ducky. Oh, she could sing, could Victorine."

" 'Piccadilly John with His Little Glass Eye'? Like you, Ma? 'Gone Where They Don't Play Billiards'?"

Kitty laid Ernest on the floor and wrapped the clean diaper around his bottom. Then he got up and wobbled toward the kitchen. His wet feet made muddy footprints on the linoleum, before he bumped into Ada and fell onto the long-suffering dog. "Well, Victorine was never on the music hall stage as was I, the Lark of Liverpool, me and all my family. My poor dear dead mama and papa and my little sister died of peenumonya from wearing damp tights."

Kitty sighed, as she always did when she recalled her music hall days as the Lark of Liverpool, her successes at the Empire, and she grew soulful at any reference to her late, lamented parents, or the little sister who seemed never to have had a name. Kitty had converted to the Latter-day Saints as a young woman in Liverpool, but once in St. Elmo, she lived as though she had never gone under the waters of baptism. No total immersion.

Kitty looked outside at the steep shadows cast by the peach tree and frowned. "I would of been up and out of bed long before this if you'd of come at three. You know how I worries when you don't come home." This was not true. She had scarcely noticed. She started humming "Hot Tamale Molly." "Is your pa going to the library after work? Did he say?"

"How do I know what he's doing?"

Expertly striking a wooden match, Kitty lit the gas burner under the kettle, blew out the match, and reached for the sturdy ceramic teapot, brown with a chip off the lip. "Well, there's time for tea, isn't there?"

There was always time for tea in Kitty's house, though the Word of Wisdom forbade Latter-day Saints tea, coffee, and naturally anything alcoholic. Kitty was fond of declaring that the Word of Wisdom, the Doctrine and

Covenants, the very Book of Mormon itself were nothing but the rantings of shameless pumpsuckers. These were painful words to Gideon, who believed in the Mormon Church, and in its wisdom. As Kitty routinely outraged his church and his family, Gideon clung the closer to his faith, and his scholarly undertakings on behalf of that faith. However, he, too, had stumbled on the rocky path of virtue: Gideon drank hot sugared tea, morning and night, grateful no doubt for that small comfort. Thirteen years of marriage had worn him down.

In fact, by 1926, Gideon Douglass seemed to understand what had happened to his life, even to accept it. He knew he was powerless against the tides that had brought him here. He had been tricked into marriage by the tears of a dishonored girl. The old ruse. No child was born then, but a year or so later there was a boy, a lovely little boy. Kitty called him Tootsie, and when he died in 1919 of the Spanish influenza, something inside her shattered forever. Gideon could hardly remember the boy any longer. Gideon could hardly remember the time when Kitty's pink lips could come together in a little pout and move him to a rush of love and gratitude. That time had so long passed he could have calibrated it on his Great Timetable. Gideon was working toward the present, without knowing he would never find it, that as he reached toward the present, it would become the past.

As some men seek the anonymous consolation of the saloon, Gideon Douglass sought the anonymous consolation of the city's Carnegie Library. There, he read and made notes toward the Great Timetable. In three long columns, all beginning with Adam and Eve, Gideon synchronized secular history, biblical history, and the events on the North American continent as described in the Book of Mormon. The charts were long, on blue paper, and calibrated to one-sixteenth of an inch. Each time he found something new to put on the Timetable, he had to start all over again.

Tall, powerfully built, broad shouldered, but hopelessly bookish and half blind, Gideon Douglass had none of his sister Afton's indomitable bustle, none of his mother's intelligent reserve, though these were the expectations that had gotten him the job in the front office of Insurance with Assurance. He was Ruth Douglass's son, after all; she was the city's most successful woman, and her Pilgrim Restaurant was renowned afar. But Gideon had proved unfit for the demands of the front office. He now filed papers in the back room. He feared a further demotion, out of the back room, out of the back door, out of a job altogether.

Buster jumped up and ran out of the kitchen, through the back porch, and out the screen door, barking joyfully when Gideon finally came home. Gideon lavished affection on the hound. "Good old Buster! Here, boy. Good old boy! Good dog, Buster. Yes, you are." But when he stepped into the kitchen, Gideon greeted his wife and children haphazardly. He looked over at the cold stove, the dishes slumping in the sink. The moth stuck in the pale margarine, ants marauding through the jam, his wife reading at the table, his children playing on the floor. He took his glasses off and cleaned them, a reflexive gesture when he could not bear to see. He asked, as though inquiring after a sick relative, "How is supper?"

The question seemed to surprise Kitty. She rambled over to the icebox, and poked about. "Let's see if there's any mush left over to fry. Alas, no. Alas."

"How about those eggs and toasts you always call Frogs in a Bucket?" Eden suggested. "How about some Bubble and Squeak?"

Kitty poked through the small shelves, which emitted a tired vegetative odor. "No eggs. No cabbage. No meat. Not even enough for Resurrection Pie."

"The Resurrection shouldn't be used to describe..." Gideon faltered, "something you eat."

"Well, *la di dah,*" sang Kitty. "Let's all eat chicken à la king, 'cept you have to be royal to eat it. If you're not royal, it'll stick in your craw. Or, well, we could all just take the trolley to dear old Ruth's fine old restaurant. Yes, I say, let's don our Sunday best and sashay into the Pilgrim Restaurant, where the fine folks go! Where the ladies of Silk Stocking Row all have feathers in their smart cloche hats, and the gents have gold watches in their pockets! Let's go to the Pilgrim, where the cook calls hisself Napoleon, no less, and the Chinese waiters bow and scrape and calls us sir and madam. Oh! Thanks awfully, yes, indeed, and I'll have the lamb chops and a rasher of fried tomatoes. Hummingbird Delight, for dessert, yes, Hummingbird Delight."

"What's Hummingbird Delight, Ma?"

"Just the food of the gods, all shiny green and pink." She paused. "A little watermelon, a little lime, and a lovely bit of cream on top. Ambroysal. Oh! And if you wasn't too busy, Ruth," Kitty rolled her eyes to heaven, "I'll have some of them figs that heathen Chinee Napoleon has named after his own self. The food of the gods if I must say so. Figs keeps you regular."

Gideon silently absorbed these backhanded reflections on his failures as a provider. Ruth Douglass was the proprietor of St. Elmo's most distinguished restaurant, and lived on Silk Stocking Row, but her son Gideon loped woefully along, barely evading creditors, just making do. When at last Kitty came to the end of her line of invective dressed up as play-acting, he inquired again after supper. He was hungry.

"A man deserves a hot meal at the end of the day," said Gideon.

"*La di dah*," retorted Kitty, but she was humbled. Eden could tell. From the icebox Kitty drew out a half-bottle of milk and put it on the table beside the slightly stale bread.

Gideon sat down heavily. "I have the patriarchal blessings of the Church and all I can get at home is bread stuffed down into a mug of milk?"

Kitty ignored the implicit blame, shame, and irony.

"I could go to Mrs. Patterson's," said Eden, "get some beans and meat and tortillas. I love Mrs. Patterson's food."

"Mrs. Patterson's beans and meat give me gas," said Gideon.

"Farting is good for you," Kitty replied, "releases evil vapors."

"I could quick dash over to Bojo's and bring something home," said Eden. "It's not far."

"Why must we always rely on others?" Gideon asked, not unreasonably. "The bread man, the milkman, they come to the house. The grocery boy will deliver. The—"

"If you don't like the Mexicans, then give Eden some money and put her on the trolley and send her over to China Flats to Kee's and buy dinner from him."

Eden jumped up from her chair, palm out for money. China Flats, Mr. Kee's neighborhood, was like a foreign country to Eden, though she went there often enough. Walking into the ill-lit precincts of Mr. Kee's store, Eden always felt like an adventurer. At Kee's there were red dragons over the doors, and shelves with strange concoctions in jars, and exotic smells that Eden loved and could not name. At Kee's, Chinese customers chattered in their own singsong tongue, and they brought their bowls to their lips and shoveled the food in with sticks. The Japanese of St. Elmo had a community, but the Chinese clung more closely together, more guarded, less civic. The men had come to St. Elmo with the railroad, finished building the terminus in the late 1880s, and stayed on, bringing wives from China or San Francisco, congregating on their own turf, keeping their own language and customs, poor, proud, and apart from St. Elmo proper.

"The Chinese are an educated people in their own way," said Gideon in his scholarly fashion, "but they're still heathens and their food is unreliable."

"Unreliable?" demanded Kitty. "What's that mean? Unreliable?"

A Saint at church last Sunday had remarked to Gideon that they had seen his daughter Eden on the trolley returning from Kee's with a bag of food, and the Saint had wanted to advise Gideon that the Chinese cooked their dogs. Gideon did not want to say this, so instead he replied, "Eden should not be going to China Flats. Certainly not alone. Respectable girls don't," he added.

"Respectable girls can go anywhere they likes. Don't make me laugh!" And then Kitty proceeded to laugh raucously before her face slumped into a scowl.

The question of supper, Eden sensed, was about to escalate into a full-tilt quarrel that would end in tears and recriminations, Ma weeping and powerless, Pa stoic and powerless. Everyone hungry. Eden and Ada would end up pawing through the icebox, and the cupboard. Her parents were glowering at each other and the baby had started to cry.

"Gimme some money, Pa. I'll go to Mrs. Patterson's. She's right nearby. Gimme a quarter."

Gideon looked at her blankly, then at Kitty, who frowned. With an offended air, Kitty announced that the last time she'd been there, Mrs. Patterson had told her that a pail of beans and meat-and-burlap-wrapped tortillas would cost forty cents from now on. "Forty cents! Don't look at me like I got money. You're the breadwinner, or so you're always telling me."

"Please, Kitty, dear. Where is some money? I gave you household money just the other day. Don't you know where it is?"

Kitty could not answer, or would not say.

Gideon, Kitty, and Eden began the familiar family scrounge through the drawers and assorted pockets, looking underneath chairs and down the sides of cushions, Eden crawling on her hands and knees around the area where her father tossed his pants when he took them off at night. She brought twenty-seven cents back into the kitchen. Gideon finally contributed his stash from under the inkwell, and gave it to Eden before retreating into the bedroom, where his Great Timetable beckoned. Eden bolted from the house just as the phone jingled.

# Kitty's Resurrection Pie

Take your leftovers, whatever they be, and mince well. Beat up an egg or two and pour over the whole, mixing well. Put all in a baking dish of some sort. Slice some already cooked taters and place on top. Salt and pepper well. Bake till bubbling.

### THE CONVERT

Resurrection Pie was a great treat in Kitty's Liverpool youth, as it presupposed there was something to resurrect, leftovers from some other meal. Mostly she ate bread with a margarine substitute concocted of the unthinkable. She ate bread and drippings when she had the lucky chance, or on rare occasions, she licked a bit of fried fish and mustard from the penny papers used to wrap them. These were sold out of a shop near squalid Ramsey Court, where Kitty Tindall lived with her mother and her stepfather, a Liverpool dock hand. Most of their children died of consumption, or typhoid. Consumption took longer. They all shared the flat with a lodger, bedbugs, fleas, rats, and roaches for company, gin and domestic abuse for entertainment.

Kitty was never the Lark of Liverpool. That was a lie. There was no family on the stage, nor a sister who died from wearing damp tights. Kitty was the bastard child of a man who quickly went to sea, never heard from again. The pivotal moment of her life came with literacy; she stayed in school long enough to learn to read. Once she could read, whole vistas opened to her. She was certain that the world of the romantic novels she loved must surely exist just beyond her sight, perhaps, certainly beyond her touch, but not beyond her imagination. In a life where everything was wan, gray, shabby, cold, and weak, Kitty's imagination was robust and opulent.

Robust and opulent too were the music halls and they were not beyond her sight or touch. Kitty delighted in the halls, to sit in the audience and revel in these great communal baths of sweat and smoke, beer, gin, of laughter, ribald palaver, and music. She dreamed of singing herself, of the nightly applause of hundreds, of opening her heart and her voice to raucous, adoring crowds who would always go wild with admiration as the Lark of Liverpool sang their best-beloved songs and did little Marie Lloyd—like turns on the stage. However, Kitty had no talent, or drive.

Still, every spare penny she could wrest from her stepfather, or save from her own meager wages, she spent on the halls, and she went with any lad she could entice into taking her. And if the lad asked for a little price at the end of the evening, well, small payment and perhaps a little pleasure. But the profound pleasure was on the stage. The brightness! The fancy! The shiny singsong patina that performers could give to drab experience!

Even experience as drab as hers.

Kitty Tindall worked as a buttonholer in a corset factory. She had risen from sweep-up girl, work she had first begun in 1906 at the age of twelve.

Some three or four years later, on her way to buttonholing in the corset factory, Kitty saw some Mormon missionaries on the streets of Liverpool. A handsome young man and an older man, taciturn, bearded, and intense, both of them handing out leaflets. The crowd pelted them with refuse. A leaflet blew against Kitty's shoe and she read it. She was literate, after all. The little paper told the dramatic story of a Restored Gospel and the forces of Good and Evil, the Nephites and the Lamanites battling to the very death, the Battle of Cumorah in what was now mere upstate New York, but had once been the site of great deeds and great drama. The Mormons promised believers a birthright and a place in the Celestial Kingdom, which sounded very nice indeed. A place unlike Ramsay Court. There was a meeting of anyone interested the following Tuesday evening. The Liverpool Saints welcomed all.

Kitty attended that meeting and thoroughly enjoyed the Liverpool Saints, their wonderful stories of Jesus on the North American continent and of pioneers like the Handcart Brigade, so staunch in their faith, they walked from Iowa to Zion in 1856. She also enjoyed the bread and butter and cake they served at the meeting. Alas, there was no tea. With her halo of bright auburn hair, her blue eyes, her eagerness to please, the Saints were delighted to welcome her. Kitty's dramatic renunciation of her wretched former life, her repudiation of her sins before she'd accepted the True Gospel, held them all in thrall—including the young missionary who had personally seen to her conversion.

However, Kitty hadn't reckoned on total immersion. Before she was baptized into Sainthood in a pond near the city, Kitty Tindall's body had never been under water. Going under the waters of baptism scared the hell out of her.

In 1911 the Latter-day Saints were still trying to populate Zion, and European converts to the faith were encouraged to emigrate. So Kitty Tindall sailed to America, albeit third class. The Liverpool Saints made sure she went. The young missionary was forever compromised.

GLORIA TRUJILLO PATTERSON DID A TIDY LITTLE business out of the back of her kitchen. Informally she sold small pails of spiced beans and meat, along with burlap-wrapped warm tortillas. Gloria Patterson did not parade her success. She and her husband, Benjamin Franklin Patterson, continued to live in their ramshackle house not far from Eden's neighborhood. Originally, they had had some acreage, too, and Mr. Patterson had once traded in horses. The horses were gone, though the rundown stable housed their new car. Chickens pecked about, and a fat sow and pink piglets were kept behind the stable, discreetly out of civic view. There were laws against hogs in the city, as there were laws against unlicensed businesses. Gloria Patterson's customers always went to the back door. There was no need to knock. It was always open.

Stepping into Gloria's kitchen, Eden salivated. The scents rose like gnats at sunset and swarmed in the close kitchen, hot, swimming in rich odors, spicy with cumin and coriander, chopped jalapeños, and the beans simmering eternally on the back burner. Long, bright banners of strung dried peppers hung from hooks in the ceiling, and the onions in their papery cloaks filled one whole bin. A sack of beans stood upright on the floor, and a great dollop of lard, white as snow, sat in a bowl beside the stove. Three massive cast iron fry pans warmed slowly. She smiled to hear the unmistakable rhythm of Gloria Patterson's life: the *scrape-scrape* of the heavy pestle, as she worked her peculiar magic over a large, open mortar.

Mrs. Patterson looked up from her mortar and pestle and greeted Eden warmly. She was a tiny woman, skin the color of nutmeg, with broad, broken features and droopy eyes. Her smile altered her misaligned features. Her nose and jaw had been broken in a childhood stampede accident, and they had healed improperly. She was shrewd and ugly, but all her children, four sons, three daughters, were stunning beauties: black hair, cream-colored skin, flashing blue eyes, brilliant smiles. She dusted off her hands, which were as strong as a man's. She was always sweating from the peppers more than from the heat. She took her kerchief and mopped her forehead and her smashed nose.

"Sorry, Eden," she said, "*nada* tonight. You are too late. Everything is gone for today. It's . . ." Mrs. Patterson looked over to her husband, Ben, who was reading the paper. Ben Patterson was still handsome, though corpulent and bald now. Eden had never seen Gloria Patterson wear anything but a dirty apron over a shapeless housedress. But Mr. Patterson always wore a suit, a bow tie, a paper collar, a starched, ironed shirt, and a vest that strained over his immense belly. Ben drew out his pocketwatch and announced it was nearing seven.

"You see? *Nada*. But here," she handed Eden something fried and crispy, dusted with cinnamon and sugar, "if you must go home with bad news, there should be something for the messenger."

Only Eden couldn't go home. She didn't dare show up with nothing. She couldn't take the trolley to Mr. Kee's, too late and the nickel would eat into her funds, so she started walking toward New Town, where her grandmother's restaurant was, but she was certainly not going there. In fact, Eden did some careful skirting, out of the line of vision of the Pilgrim in case Ruth should be looking out the window.

Down the street and across from the Pilgrim was Bowers Block, a solid brick edifice, two stories tall, narrow windows evenly spaced across the second floor, with offices leased to lawyers and a painless dentist. One served as an accounting office for the Bowers family's many undertakings. The street-level shops offered Miss Louella's Hats of Style, a drugstore and soda fountain, a German jeweler, and other shops that old Nana Bowers leased to all sorts of people. But most of the Bowers Block shops were leased to Nana Bowers's own varied offspring: generations of Bowerses and their various in-laws, relatives, and friends had had jobs there from the time they were children. The boys started out sweeping the barbershop where the Bowers men did a brisk business in their illegal Tonic out of the back. (At least it was illegal in 1926; it didn't start out that way. It was medicinal.) The girls began working early on, washing dishes, helping in the kitchen of Bojo's, a small eatery, nothing to compete with the Pilgrim. The name was a contraction of Bowers and Johnson. The food was filling, well cooked, reasonable; you could eat really well there if you liked things fried or pickled. Mabel Johnson would fry or pickle anything that couldn't run outrun her. Best of all, Bojo's had a little bowl of hot spiced almonds on every table, and the same could not be said for the Pilgrim.

A bell tinkled over the door as Eden entered. The place was nearly empty, save for the thin, dark-haired woman wearing a hat and eating alone at a table by the window. She was always there eating alone when Eden made her supper-time forays to Bojo's.

Eden dashed to a table and plucked a handful of spiced almonds out of the bowl and popped them into her mouth. The cayenne and pepper gave her a tremendous jolt and she was red-faced by the time Mabel Johnson came out from the kitchen.

"Your grandmother send you for some of my recipes?" Mabel asked good-naturedly. "She fear the competition?" She took a glass and poured some water, handed it to Eden. "Those almonds bite back. You should do them one at a time. You should ask next time."

"Yes, ma'am. Sorry." Eden gulped the water. "My ma sent me. Wanna know if we could buy some supper and I could take it home."

From a darkened corner came a snort and a laugh, and Eden turned to see Nana Bowers. Nana Bowers was fierce, so old as to be a relic, a ghost, already long dead, except she was most definitely alive and ferociously opinionated. She had known St. Elmo from the very beginning. She was among the city's earliest settlers in 1854, when she had come here as the slave of Madison Whickham, the famous Mormon scout.

"Don't your ma know how to cook?" asked the old lady, flexing her lips over near-toothless gums. Her tiny eyes, clear, despite her eighty-eight years, squinted at Eden. She put on her glasses. "I know you. Ruth Douglass's child."

"Granddaughter," said Eden. "My mother is Kitty Douglass."

"Don't tell me what I already know." Nana Bowers had coal-black skin and her thin hair frizzed out gray around her face, escaping from an inadequate hairnet. She had a gold tooth and a cane. She'd been known to use the cane on her smart-mouthed grandchildren, great-grandchildren, probably the great-great. Even Nana Bowers had lost track of the generations. "Didn't your mother never learn nothing?"

"My ma says why should she learn to cook when there's other people who do it so well," replied Eden in a burst of inspiration, "people like you."

"Yes, well, there's people who'll breathe and think for you, too, if you let 'em."

Eden went on, "My ma says Bojo's fried okra is just the food of the gods, better than anything at the Pilgrim."

"You're quick," said Mabel with a laugh.

Just then Mabel's little daughter Sojourner came out of the kitchen. She was holding the cat. She was a coffee-colored girl, perhaps ten, with neat pigtails and a shy manner. She nodded to Eden. "Saw you get 'spelled from school today."

Mabel Bowers regarded Eden with alarm.

"I wasn't 'spelled. The principal only called me in to say I'm so smart, I don't need school on Tuesdays. I can do any old thing I want on Tuesdays."

"Maybe you'll learn to cook," cackled the old lady from her corner.

Sojourner gave Eden a conspiratorial nod and addressed the old lady. "Eden was singing a song so bad, the teacher 'bout burst when she heard it. Something about the Sheik, Nana. About him creeping into folks' tents." Sojourner began humming "The Sheik of Araby" softly.

"Trash!" cried Nana Bowers, bringing down her cane. "All that trash at the Dream Theatre. All that huffing and puffing and girls swooning at the feet of sheiks and rajahs, all that senseless scum that takes folks away from their God-given duties and fills 'em full of lust. Yes, lust!"

The old lady ranted on. Sojourner must have known what would set her off. Sojourner was giggling, and Mabel shot her daughter a warning look. But when the old lady's spew of invective reached to Ernest March, the star of *The Green Goddess,* Eden felt compelled to defend him. Ernest March was a sort of god to Kitty, more than Jesus or Joseph Smith, or Brigham Young or Moses. Eden shared her mother's adulation for the suave actor. She made the mistake of interrupting Nana Bowers's tirade to maintain that Ernest March was a gentleman.

"Hush," snapped Nana Bowers. "What know ye of corruption? Nothin'. From that Dream Theatre corruption oozes out and corrupts everyone it touches. Corrupting."

"What's corruption?"

"Just agree with her," counseled Sojourner in a low voice.

"Yes, ma'am, corruption," said Eden, thrilling to the feel of the wonderfully wicked word. She turned to Mabel. "You got anything left I can buy and take home?" She put her forty cents on the counter.

Mabel Johnson clucked. "You gonna feed five people for forty cents?"

Eden offered guilelessly, "Mrs. Patterson can feed us all five for forty cents."

Mabel's brow creased. There was an unstated competition between the Bowers and Patterson clans to supply those in St. Elmo too lazy to cook their own dinners. In a town dominated by Mormons and Methodists, there were more customers than might have been imagined.

"Ruth Douglass never put her children to work," volunteered Nana from her corner, finished for the moment with one flurry of invective, embarking on a new one. "Ruth Douglass never let her young'ns work the restaurant, thought they was too good to work there. That was her mistake. Look what it brung her. Woe. All her children, 'cept Afton, brung woe or mischief. One's bad as the other." She brought down her cane again. "Young folks need to work, early on and often. Work hard. Keep 'em working. Wear 'em out. After a day of hard work, let 'em fall down dog tired and they won't find mischief, and mischief won't find them. I kep' all mine nearby. Kep' an eye on them. Know what they're doing, what they're thinking, and that includes your worthless son, Mabel." She hurled grim predictions for Mabel's son, one after the other.

"Now, Nana," Mabel soothed, but she shot a harsh look to Sojourner for having riled the old lady, and Sojourner ducked for the kitchen.

The solitary customer, the woman sitting at the table by the window, pushed her chair back and brought her check to the till. She seemed to totter in her shoes, so thin was she, and to Eden she looked as grim as old Nana Bowers, though she wasn't old. She wore a brown dress of stiff material with a spray of fake violets pinned to her shoulder; some were discolored, randomly paled by the sun. She had a straight nose, thin lips, and behind her narrow glasses, her gaze was suspicious. Her hat perched on her head in the shape of a mushroom and of roughly the same color.

"How was your supper, Miss Merton?" asked Mabel.

"Greasy as usual." She glared at Eden rather than step around her, and Eden moved. Miss Merton took her change and counted it back exactly, confirming with Mabel the amount. The bell tinkled as she wobbled out.

"If she don't like it," said Nana from the table, using her cane emphatically, "why don't Winifred Merton go eat at the Pilgrim?" She snorted in a way that reminded Eden of Afton Lance, derision and with a little pity sprinkled in.

"I'll tell you why," said Mabel. "Because she wouldn't dare dish out to Ruth

Douglass all the moaning and complaining she ladles on us. Ruth Douglass wouldn't tolerate it, but Winifred Merton knows we have to. She eats here alone, ever' night, and nothin' is ever right. Something or another's wrong ever' damn day. Winifred Merton is one of those people never made a joyful noise in all their lives, not so much as a fart. Sojourner!" she called. "Get in here and get these dishes, get 'em washed so we can all go home. Turn 'round the Open sign. You, Eden, come with me."

Mabel led Eden into the kitchen. "I'm gonna be extra good to you tonight, Eden." She pulled a large fry pan from the back of the stove and forked out a couple of pork chops, placing them in an empty pie tin. "I'm gonna give you the last two Shake that Thing Pork Chops."

"Why do you call 'em that?" asked Eden.

Mabel did not reply. "I can't bear to see children in want. I don't know why your mother don't lift a hand for her family."

"She thinks she's Victorine St. John."

Mabel scoffed. "Well, she might think she's Queen of England, but that don't make it so. Anyway, you are a good little girl, Eden. Smart, like everyone says." Mabel held the fry pan over the chops and scraped out a blanket of gorgeous bronzed sauce, fragrant with orange and a piquant whiff of something else beneath. She covered this tin with another and in another she put some greens at the bottom, three baked potatoes, and a chunk of Emotional Cornbread. That's what everyone called it. The recipe was Nana Bowers's. The name came from one of her sons, who had once declared Nana's cornbread wasn't a food, it was an emotion.

"Can't we have some more cornbread? You can't serve it up tomorrow, can you?"

"No, but I can grind it up and fry chicken in it." Still, Mabel put another piece in.

"No fried okra?"

"All gone." Mabel tied the two plates up in a small tablecloth and told Eden to hold it from beneath. "You walking home?"

"Yes."

"Well, this oughta be warmed up again before it's eaten, but I don't suppose you'll do that."

"I don't suppose we will. Thanks, Mrs. Johnson. I'll bring the tins back tomorrow."

Eden reached home as the last mauve fingers of sunset etched the dry sky. She burst through the back door expecting a hero's welcome, but sensed immediately that her mother's mood had curdled. Gideon used a sort of code with his eyebrows to indicate that Eden was in trouble. But his eyebrows weren't equal to communicating specifics.

"I'm late 'cause I had to go to Bojo's. Everything was gone at Mrs. Patterson's," she explained, putting the parcel on the table and untying the ends. The melded flavors floated out as she lifted the moist cornbread from the top, broke off a piece, and popped it between her lips. Kitty swatted her hand reflexively.

"There's only two pork chops. We have to divvy them," said Eden, taking her place beside Ada, who was fussing and whining. Ernest in his high chair banged happily with a spoon.

"We should pray," said Gideon. "Give thanks."

"Thanks to Mabel Johnson and Bojo's," said Eden.

"To God. O God, the Eternal Father—"

"Keep it short," said Kitty. "We're starving."

They ate wordlessly, spoons pinging on the plates, gulps and chewing, a lack of manners that Eden well knew would never have been tolerated at Afton's or her grandmother's house.

Finally, their hungers tempered if not assuaged, their fingers greasy, Gideon remarked that those were the best pork chops that had ever crossed his lips. "I wish there'd been ten pork chops. I could have eaten every one."

Kitty ignored him. "A little birdie told me Miss Eden Louise Douglass got sent home from school today. Only you didn't come home, did you now? It wasn't Sam and Junior Lance said come on home with us. Liar. It was the principal of Fourth Street School sends you home in disgrace."

Eden quit licking her spoon. Ada began to choke and cry.

"Swill some milk, Ada, and shut up," said Kitty. She returned her baleful attention to Eden. "Afton rings me on the box, me, right after you leaves for Gloria's, and gives me an earful, and I has to sit here and bloody listen to her. She goes at me like it was me sung the dirty songs. And with that operator, Miss Moody, hearing every bloody word. Withered slut. I wanted to tell Afton to eat coal and shit cinders. Miss Moody, too."

"Did you?" asked Gideon, strangling slightly.

"I no sooner gets off the squawker with Afton than Ruth rings me up, taking time away from her precious Pilgrim, to tell me how I shame the name of Douglass. As if I sung the dirty songs myself. But you done it, Eden. Shame on you, Miss Eden Louise Dirty Song Douglass." Kitty folded her heavy arms over her broad breasts. Her eyes narrowed.

"It wasn't like that," said Eden.

"The Douglasses been against me forever. They blame me. Me, innocent as ever I can be, and ignorant of what you done, Eden. And worse—a mother's woe—my own thankless child called Afton Lance instead of me, your own dear mum. God's Nostrils! I been betrayed by my own child! Don't say it ain't so. It's so. Talk about shame."

"I told Mr. Snow to call you, Ma! Honest," Eden lied without a qualm. Kitty, her anger once ignited, could wreak a lot of havoc, and Gideon wouldn't stop her. "Ask him. You just ask Mr. Snow yourself! And I didn't sing anything dirty, Ma. It wasn't dirty songs at all, just the 'Sheik of Araby.'" And with mention of the sheik, there came to Eden the image of old lady Bowers beating her cane against corruption and lust. The Dream Theatre. Eden smiled: Ernest March would save her now, just as surely as if she were tied to the railroad tracks, kicking her little heels, and he the handsome hero dashing to her rescue. "You want to know the real reason I got into trouble, Ma? I stood up for Ernest March. I did! Josie McGahey called Ernest March a dago wop. Maisie Fletcher said so too. I beat them up. Both of them. What is a dago wop, Ma?" Eden knew exactly what a dago wop was, one of the many epithets of race, religion, caste, class, or value hurled randomly at anyone at the Fourth Street School who was not a Mormon or a Methodist and white besides.

"How dare her! Ernest March?"

"Yes, Ma. Maisie Fletcher's father said it. He's the manager of the Dream Theatre and he said he'd met Ernest March and he was a dago wop."

"That little slut," said Kitty.

"Kitty, please," Gideon remonstrated. "Maisie Fletcher is a little girl. She can't be a slut."

"But she'll grow up to be one," Kitty snapped. "How could Ernest March be a dago wop? Look at him. There's nothing low or vile about Ernest March. He's a gentleman. Probably a prince. Oh, just think of him as the Raja in *Green Goddess*! We seen that picture so many times!"

"Oh yes, Ma! And Blanche Randall as Alice Crespin! The Raja tells her, 'I, the Raja, am the king of all the world. You are mine, body and so-ulle!'" From the title cards of silent films, Eden Louise Douglass had learned to read, if only imperfectly. Inspired to new heights of falsehood, Eden went on, "And guess what else, Ma? Ernest March and Blanche Randall are coming to St. Elmo!" Blanche Randall was Ernest March's usual leading lady, a great beauty with masses of golden hair and a tiny kissable bee-stung mouth. "You know how sometimes the stars and bigwigs come out from Los Angeles to St. Elmo to see if ordinary people like their films. They come on the train, or sometimes a chauffeured livery man drives them in a Pierce-Arrow, like Victorine and the Duke, and they come to sit in the Dream Theatre like ordinary mortals and see if we love them, if we applaud. He's coming to St. Elmo. Soon. An Ernest March preview, Ma!"

Kitty laughed and blubbered kisses on the baby's tummy. She had named her son Ernest for the love of Ernest March.

"Maybe Ernest March will come up to the balcony where we always sit, Ma!"

"He'll breathe the same air!" Kitty sighed, all thought of shame vanished. "Ernest! Ernest! Ernest, I love you!" The baby crowed with delight and spit up his supper. Kitty wiped the spit-up from Ernest's chin with his own shirt. Ada watched with pink indifference. Eden, spared her mother's wrath, got up and cleared the dishes, put them in the sink, and turned on the tap.

"I think the baby needs a bath," said Gideon.

When no one agreed with him, he took off his glasses, cleaned them, put the wires back over his ears. He retreated to the bedroom. He sat at his desk, unfurled his charts. From the kitchen he could hear Eden and Kitty warbling together, "Poor Butterfly." He picked up his pen, his precisely gauged ruler, the better to calibrate the course of human events down to the tiniest slivers of time, our finite moment on this earth.

# Shake That Thing Pork Chops

These pork chops put people in a good mood. Sojourner herself parted with this recipe, gave it to Eden, who eventually put them on the menu at the Café Eden. In about 1961, Sojourner's married daughter, Sonoma, changed the name of these pork chops, calling them Dedicated to the One I Love Pork Chops.

The recipe below is for two people.

Heat up your big cast iron fry pan with some oil. When hot, toss in one clove garlic chopped up. Brown and remove.

Take your two good-sized pork loin chops, room temp, rinsed and patted dry. Dust them and then rub them over with a mixture of a bit of salt and pepper, a whisper of ground coriander. Put these in your pan and fry on a high heat. Once they are seared and have good color, turn them over, let them brown for a bit, though not cooked all the way through. Add to this pan ³/₄ cup to one cup of thick-cut home-made orange marmalade, cover. Lower heat slightly. Cook through. Timing will depend on the thickness of your chops. You should use thick chops so the sauce has a chance to melt and swathe the meat in color and richness.

Best if homemade marmalade and not super sweet. If you find it's too sweet, add a dash of vinegar or mustard to the sauce after you remove the chops. This sauce will not need thickening. As the marmalade heats with the chops, it's thick enough as is. With the pan juices, scrape all together and serve atop the chops with mashed potatoes.

Savor these chops and shake that thing.

### NAOMI AND THE APOSTLE

It was a famous story known to every child at Fourth Street School, how Madison Whickham, Apostle of the Mormon Church and legendary scout, founded St. Elmo, California, in 1854. He brought some one hundred twenty souls to this outpost, including two of his thirteen wives and six of his own slaves. Madison was the first of the Whickhams to turn everything he touched to profit. But Nana Bowers bested him. Her real name was Naomi.

One afternoon in 1856—and under circumstances that changed with who was telling the tale—Naomi declared herself a free woman and no man's slave. Madison got out the whip to teach her something about disobedience. Madison's thirteenth wife reminded the Apostle that the circuit judge was coming through day after tomorrow. St. Elmo was such a new settlement, there was no hotel, so the circuit judge, or any other visiting dignitary, lodged overnight with the Apostle. There would be a trial the next day. Then all the slaves could watch Naomi's punishment. In the meantime, if Madison whipped her, she couldn't work, and she might require tending.

Judge Emerson arrived in St. Elmo at sunset. Sitting down to the evening meal with the Apostle and his family, the judge realized sadly there would be no alcohol with dinner, and no cigars afterward. Still, the food was excellent. Cornbread, hot, salted hashed potatoes gleaming with ham fat, buttered corn, crispy fried okra, and some stewed rabbit. For dessert there was apricot cobbler, rounded half-moons of rosy fruit bobbing in a crumbled crust. The judge declared himself well satisfied and asked if Mrs. Whickham had done the fine cooking. Both Mrs. Whickhams said no.

Judge Emerson colored, coughed. He had thought one of these women must surely be Madison's sister. Or sister-in-law. Or some other female relative. The judge made a short, negative speech bearing upon those twin relics of barbarism, slavery and polygamy. The Apostle argued freedom of religion. The evening grew tense and the atmosphere between the judge and the Apostle heated. Their voices carried into the velvety night.

As the judge was outnumbered by the Mormons, and unlikely to change their minds, he rose and said he would retire. But first, so fine was the dinner, the judge wished to convey his compliments to the cook. To his surprise, young Naomi came out of the kitchen. Judge Emerson offered fulsome compliments to Naomi's skill, especially in view of her youth. She was not yet eighteen.

Court was held the following morning in the main meeting room of the Mormon Fort. The first case was against the slave, Naomi, for disobedience. Bearded and regal, Madison Whickham looked like a man who knew righteousness biblically. He described Naomi's disobedience, her ingratitude. Naomi stood accused but unbowed.

Judge Emerson, in the interests of probity, heard the whole case out. Then he swiftly brought down his gavel and declared that in California there could be no slaves, and thus no disobedient slave deserving of a whipping. Naomi and the five others were not chattels but free citizens with no need to buy their freedom. They were free men and women. The Apostle protested his pecuniary loss, good money he had paid for slaves. Judge Emerson called all six Negroes before the bench and told them that henceforth Mr. Whickham, Apostle or not, had to pay wages. Nor could the Apostle compel their religion, though he had had them all baptized Mormon. The judge told them, Your religion, your labor, your lives are your own. That is the law in the state of California. Moreover, the judge continued, the state of California was content that there should be one man and one wife before the law, and did not recognize polygamy either. The judge was certain Mr. Whickham recognized California's sovereignty over, say, the word of Brigham Young, President of the Church in Utah, which was not a state.

That year Naomi married Elijah Bowers, one of the five other former slaves. They married right after they had each been baptized in the church of their choice, which as yet had no building, and no name, but it was not Mormon; they knew that. Elijah and Naomi Bowers had ten children and founded a dynasty. Nana Bowers became her own St. Elmo legend, famous for her grit, her intelligence, her responsiveness to opportunity, and, not least, her cooking.

In 1930, the NAACP held a luncheon in Los Angeles to commemorate eighty years of California's statehood. The guest of honor was ninety-two-year-old Naomi Bowers, who got a standing ovation on the arm of her great-great grandson. She sat between the guest speakers, none other than W. E. B.

Du Bois and the Dean of Women at Howard University. W. E. B. Du Bois himself told this august gathering the story of Naomi and the Apostle. He gave her a framed plaque commemorating her bravery in the past. He exhorted his audience to vigilance and bravery in the future. He said the fight was not over, but the cornbread was delicious.

THE FAMILY OF GIDEON DOUGLASS, HOWEVER THEY might scrape by—creditors at the door, overdue bills in the mailbox—paid two regular tithes. One on Saturday. One on Sunday. Gideon paid his tithing to the Church before he paid his rent, never deviating from the injunction that the first tenth of the true Saint's earnings belonged to the Lord, which is to say the Church. Additionally, every Sunday morning, Gideon put a nickel in the collection plate. He gave Eden a penny to do the same. Of the family, only Eden went to church with him, riding the trolley, holding his hand. Gideon accepted Eden's Sunday company with unspoken gratitude. He could not bear to go to church alone. The Saints distrusted the singular of anything; connection and comfort were inextricably mixed. Any adult, single, widowed, solo for any reason, was subject to their bland anathema.

On Saturday mornings Eden took that same trolley with her mother to another variety of religious experience. In the church of the Dream Theatre, Eden absorbed moral standards every bit as codified as in the

Mormon Church, and for Eden, more vivid. In the church of the Dream Theatre, the code of conduct required that you be true and, above all, valiant. It helped to be beautiful, of course, but beauty without valor was a poor thing.

Saturday matinees brought a flush to Kitty's plump cheeks. She wore an actual frock, as she called it, a blue dress with filmy flounces in layers, a neat cloche hat, and stockings rolled stylishly just above the knee. She tied Eden's hair with an enormous bow at a rakish angle; Eden shined up her own Mary Janes. Before they left home to catch the trolley, Kitty sometimes took a nip of Tonic, or bought an underhanded bottle from one of the Bowers family who ran an undeclared Saturday afternoon bootleg business in the theatre balcony. But it never soured her. On Saturdays Kitty was full of cheery *la di dah*. She and Eden went for the early matinee and usually stayed to see the picture twice. On leaving the theatre at last, they walked out of the Dream and into the dusty heat of a California railroad town. And yet, they both felt somehow ennobled; they savored the crisp intimation that adventures lay ahead from which they would emerge victorious, their courage intact, their values uncompromised, their future sweet and clean, that life would reward them for valor, for staying steadfast and true.

The Dream Theatre was as different from the prim, ungarnished Latter-day Saint church as could be imagined. Hugely ornate, even from the outside, the Dream Theatre reeked of Mediterranean fantasy—blue and yellow and green—with Moorish arches, ceramic flourishes, seagoing Neptunes, nymphs (breasts suitably covered behind large shells) all cavorting around the doors, which were themselves wave shaped. The very brass handles were sea urchins. The ticket booth was sculpted from a wave, and inside, the foyer with its dark wood, deep blue carpets, gleaming chandeliers, and ornate balustrades up to the balcony, spoke eloquently of a world emphatically not St. Elmo, California. And inside the darkened hall, gilt and blue velvet, richly polished mahogany and brass all suggested some sunken galleon listing peacefully beneath the waves.

When Kitty and Eden arrived, the ticket lady had barely taken her place in the booth. The ticket taker, his smart cap and gold-braided uniform gleaming, had just opened the Neptunian doors. The attractive girls at the food counter were stacking sandwiches on sparkling, tiered glass trays. Together Kitty and Eden sashayed in and then made a dash up the stairs to the balcony, past the sign that said COLORED ONLY. The staff had long since quit trying to tell them anything to the contrary.

Kitty and Eden made their way to their favorite seats in the front row of the balcony. They arrived so early that the theatre mice could be heard scampering back into their hiding places. The interior was lit only by wall sconces, and their eyes adjusted slowly from the bright sunlight outside. The blue seats, worn into half-moon patterns by a thousand bottoms, each rubbing off a bit of velvet nub, sighed with pneumatic bliss when Kitty sat down. High and alone in the suffocating semi-darkness, Kitty would open her arms to the empty space below her, to the stage, as though she stood on the proscenium, communing with her private past, her spectral audience.

Overhead fans moved sluggishly, and currents of unrefreshed air stirred, redolent of old smoke, antique sweat, dried orange peel, and dust. Far below them, in the orchestra pit in front of the screen, they could hear the clipped footsteps of Miss McBrean, the Dream Theatre pianist, who accompanied all the silent films. They could hear the rustle of her music as she set it on the grand piano, and the squeal of the hinges as she lifted its large wing. Miss McBrean trilled briefly on the keys, warming up, practicing bits and pieces of the music she would play when the silent picture began. Eden loved this part. It was like their own private concert, and Eden applauded. Miss McBrean, on hearing the appreciation from the dusky balcony, played with unconventional flourish, speeding up "The Last Rose of Summer," slowing down "The Entertainer." Eden clapped after every piece. Miss McBrean would turn her long face, her blue eyes to the balcony, and make a slight, formal bow.

Kitty sighed and turned to her daughter. "Let the Saints say what they will about the Temple, and going under the waters of baptism for the dead, duck. This here's the temple, and don't no one ever die or get old and ugly here, and if that ain't life everlasting, I don't know what is."

THERE WAS NO CLAPPING ON SUNDAY. THE CHURCH OF JESUS CHRIST OF Latter-day Saints, a building of unvarnished plainness, hard pews, no fans, had only an out-of-tune upright piano to accompany the singing. Sister Bledsoe, who pounded out hymns, encouraged the congregation to sing to drown out her execrable playing. She smiled through the whole service. So did everyone else. The Church of Jesus Christ of Latter-day Saints was a large collective quilt of happy correctness that smothered people painlessly in its warmth, so benign, so embracing that you felt churlish if you fought them. Sitting between her father and Tom or Afton Lance, Eden breathed in the smell of their sweat and the damp crush of their bodies. Sometimes it was so hot that the hymn book bled blue on her fingers. On those days Afton would bring little paper fans, and hand them to the ladies around her. Eden, too. Made Eden feel quite grown-up and pleased with herself. Gideon taught Sunday school to high school students and came away pleased with himself.

After church, Gideon and Eden caught a ride with Tom and Afton Lance in their big Franklin sedan. Gideon always protested, no there wasn't enough room. Afton pooh-poohed these objections, and they all climbed in. In the backseat, Eden sat on her father's lap. Bessie and Alma sat between the volatile Junior and Sam. Lucius, the eldest son, had the best place of all, the place of honor, riding on the running board. Eden so envied Lucius, so longed to be old enough to hang on beside Tom, the driver. Eden wanted to be the one waving, calling out as they rode through St. Elmo, greeting everyone they passed. Lucius got to reach down and toot the horn whenever he liked. Tom let him. Afton told him to stop, though everyone knew she didn't mean it. They were happy. All of them.

There was no running board at the Lances' kitchen table, so they all crowded in, Tom silent, of course, but delighted, holding Connie, soon to be ousted from babyhood; Afton was near term with her new baby. Lucius kept Junior and Sam from sparring, and Bessie and Alma peeled and mashed potatoes. Ruth joined them and corrected Eden's placement of the silverware as she set the table.

Eden Louise was one of the very few people who could draw from Ruth Douglass a brightened eye, a genuine expression of affection. For Ruth, allowing herself to love Eden openly, as she had never loved anyone else, brought satisfactions she had long denied. On Eden she lavished laughter, generosity, and tenderness she had stifled. Eden, for her part, accepted all this favoritism as though she deserved it. If someone once gives you this confidence in your youth, no one can ever take it from you.

Ruth was pained to discover that Eden had learned to read from going to the silent movies with feckless Kitty. She had picked it up from the title cards. Ruth had discovered that Eden could read just the month before, when she'd taken Eden on her restaurant shopping rounds at the open air New Market. From clear across the small plaza, Eden had pointed to Mr. Yamashita's vegetable stand and cried out its name, "Green Goddess!" Mr. Yamashita had named it in honor of the Ernest March silent film, which he, too, had enjoyed. Mr. Yamashita recommended to Ruth the ingredients for the newly fashionable Green Goddess salad dressing. His brother had sent him the recipe from a San Francisco hotel. Yes, yes, Ruth listened haphazardly to Mr. Yamashita, while she asked Eden what else she could read. Eden read cards on each of the bins, confusing *bear* with *pear*, stumbling on *potato* and *squash*, and stumped finally by *onion*. Mr. Yamashita remarked how remarkable it was that Eden could read. Ruth said she got it from the Douglasses and Mr. Yamashita did not contradict.

In Afton's crowded kitchen, Ruth composed herself and watched Eden critically. "No, Eden, the fork stands alone. Remember what I told you," Ruth said.

"The fork stands alone! The fork stands alone!" Eden began to sing to the tune of "The Farmer in the Dell," and the baby Connie joined in happily.

Ruth hushed them both. Noisy children annoyed her. She turned to her son. "Now that Eden Louise can read, you should take care she doesn't wallow in that trash that Kitty keeps around. You should see to it she reads good books, Gideon."

"That's what I say," Afton offered from the stove.

"I've told Pa I want to read *Ben-Hur*. I seen the movie so many times with Ma. I adore Ramon Novarro almost much as Ernest March," Eden said. "And that chariot race! If I could read that book, I'd could see that race in my head. Over and over!"

"*Ben-Hur* is too much," Ruth snapped. "You should take her to the library with you, Gideon. After work." Ruth frowned to see him remove his glasses and clean them zealously. Ruth Douglass had prospered in this world not only by virtue of her cooking skills, but by a shrewd appraisal of the opposition. Any opposition. "You are still working, aren't you, Gideon? Insurance with Assurance."

At last Gideon hooked his glasses back over his ears. "It may be with Assurance, but it's Insurance without me."

Afton turned from the stove and exchanged a look with Ruth, then smacked Junior's hand as he reached to take a warm sourdough biscuit from the bowl. "When did this happen?"

"Oh, I don't know. Soon. Not long ago. I'll find something else. Fear not." His attempt at confidence wavered, then seemingly gusted into the maw of the oven when Afton opened it.

Tom put the toddler Connie down, moved to the stove, and, using a towel to protect his hands, took the roast from the oven. He carved the pork loin roast, the slices studded with lemon, rosemary, and peppercorns. Bessie and Alma helped their mother serve up great heaps of beets and mashed potatoes, corn salad, tomatoes. Eden took her place beside her grandmother and sat primly, her green eyes alight. Tom and Afton took their places, and Eden bowed her head and sat through Tom's laconic prayer. It was the only time Tom Lance could be counted on to speak. Before this communion of Saints around the table, the bright colors, the steam, if there was anything divine, Eden thought, it was the food.

"I'll get another job," Gideon said without being asked. He passed the sourdough biscuits to Tom and asked for one of the little jars of jam. Peach. "I'm going to start looking in earnest, soon as I finish up with the Old Testament."

"What has the Old Testament to do with your working?" asked Ruth, her mouth pinched in a manner that boded ill for Gideon. She sharply corrected

Junior's manners, a move that Afton seconded. They both snapped at Alma. But clearly, their ire was directed at Gideon.

"My Great Timetable. Soon as I finish up the Old Testament. I still have the New—"

"And what of the rent?" demanded Ruth. "What of feeding, clothing, and caring for your family?"

"We're not hungry," he said.

"I am," said Eden. "I'm always hungry."

Afton laughed. "That's true! You always are."

Ruth smiled down at the sweet face of her granddaughter. She touched Eden's dark hair. Ruth was not much given to reflection, and when the odd contemplative moment came upon her, she was always surprised. Such a moment came to her now and resolved itself in her mind as a plan. A plan not without compromises, but on the whole, the notion had merit. If Gideon had no job and could not pay the rent, what if he and his family moved in with her? Ruth lived alone in the large home where she had raised her own children, a house on St. Elmo's old, exclusive Silk Stocking Row. True, Ruth would have to relinquish, or least diminish her privacy. And true, Ruth had never relished a big family or children underfoot. Her own children had often seemed to her an unruly tribe of small people with upturned faces, open mouths, and outstretched, dirty, demanding hands. And then, when they grew up, they were willful and rebellious and thankless. She regarded Afton and the large Lance brood. Afton Lance was a happy woman. Had Ruth missed something? Ruth preferred not to speculate on something she could not change. She mulled over a bit of potato and decided that Gideon was unemployed and hopeless. Of Kitty, less said, soonest mended. If the family moved in to Ruth's big house, at least Ada and Ernest, poor little mites, would have clean clothes, be well fed and taught their manners. And Eden? Ruth could put good books into her hands instead of the trash that Kitty read. She could shape the woman Eden would become. She could rescue Eden Louise from her father's weakness and her mother's sloth. But could Ruth endure living with the wretched Kitty? She stifled a shudder and looked again at Eden, stuffing food between her lips as if she might not eat again. And probably today, she wouldn't. Ruth placed her large, capable hand over Eden's small one. "Slow down."

SILK STOCKING ROW, THOUGH DEEPLY SHADED AND LINED WITH LEONINE palms, was no longer fashionable. The houses were all pointy prim Victorians with dark interiors, wide stairwells, dust-collecting woodwork, and beveled mirrors. For the Douglass children, however, Ruth's house was wonderfully large after the cramped old clapboard. They played endless games of hide-and-seek in rooms darkened with heavy draperies; they hid beneath tasseled dust ruffles and under great somber pieces of furniture. Eden, Ada, and Ernest each had a separate bed; separate rooms, even. Eden was grateful not to share the bed with her little sister, since Ada hadn't yet outgrown the cheerful ease of peeing in the night and not waking up.

Gideon Douglass had a study, no more than a cool room off the kitchen, but his own. Here he worked on his Great Timetable, undisturbed by the necessity of earning a living. After February 1927, when he and his family moved in with Ruth, Gideon never again worked in St. Elmo.

With no job, Gideon could not give Kitty money for the Dream Theatre. She sulked and stormed and wept, accused Gideon of abandoning her, giving up his family for his bleeding Great goddamned Timetable. She hated living with Ruth. Though, she had to admit, the big bathroom with its deep, claw-footed tub was an absolute haven on hot afternoons. She filled it with cold water, scented it with a dab of eau de cologne, and, like a great pink Venus, eased her ample flesh into it, novel in one hand, Japanese fan in the other, and a surreptitious flask of Bowers Tonic nearby.

There were indeed compromises all around. Buster, the dog, had to go live with Afton. Ruth did not like dogs. Or cats. Or bad manners, unwashed clothes, unmade beds, or dirty shoes. There was no pinning your hem up, no painting over a hole in your stocking with black ink. There was no running to Gloria Patterson's for a pail of hot beans and meat, burlap-wrapped tortillas, no jaunts to Bojo's for crispy fried anything and cornbread, no taking the trolley to China Flats for Mr. Kee's strange concoctions. There was certainly no Resurrection Pie. No mush. No stuffing stale bread into a glass of warm milk and calling it supper.

Ruth often brought home some of Napoleon's fine fare from the Pilgrim. Everything he created was wonderful, often exotic. Who else in St. Elmo, California, would make a sauce for chicken with sherry, sauteed mushrooms, and tiny flecks of tarragon? Eden recognized, even as a child, that something sumptuous had transpired on her tongue. This was not food you could bolt. Later in life Eden would spend years trying to recapture Napoleon's flavors and textures, so powerfully did they remain in memory.

Ruth compromised, too. Even with Kitty. Ruth tolerated her drinking tea, but Bowers Tonic was forbidden, which meant she had to be more astute about hiding it. As for the smoking, Ruth forbade cigarettes. Finally she agreed that

Kitty could smoke only on the back porch, where Ruth placed a big can with water in the bottom for the fag ends of her cigarettes. Kitty must not flick them over the rail. St. Elmo was dry and fires started easily.

Then one evening, after they had lived there for about a month, Ruth asked if Kitty would like a job at the Pilgrim. They all sat in the heavy-hued, half-paneled dining room, starched napkins, no elbows on the table, chewing with their mouths closed.

"You won't find me scraping no one's plates," Kitty said, lifting a forkful of Ruth's savory stuffing into her mouth, chewing, her lips ostentatiously pressed together, smiling as she gulped. She couldn't help it. The combination of almonds and raisins and oranges was too divine. The food of the gods.

Ruth bit back the observation that Kitty was renowned for her unscraped plates. "I wouldn't dream of having you scrape plates. I'm thinking of making you cashier."

"That's your job."

"I'm getting old."

"You said it." Kitty toyed with a split biscuit, trying to make it talk to Eden.

"Can you make change, Kitty? Count back the customer's money?"

"I am a lady and an artiste what has never sullied her hands with money."

"I'd pay you."

She put the biscuit down and wiped her fingers. "My own to-keep money?"

"Yes," said Ruth, though she extracted from Kitty a promise not to taint the Pilgrim or her person with foul substances like cigarettes and Bowers Tonic.

For her job Kitty got dressed every day, in a real frock, new ones she bought with her own money. A new cloche, too. New shoes and stockings. Garters. She took up many little vanities. The marcel iron, nail paint and lip paint with names like Coral Passion and Rose Romance. Rouge brightened her cheeks and Coty Powder softened her face. From the Japanese vendor in the New Market she bought a paper parasol and carried it with her as she walked to work, to protect her peaches-and-cream English complexion, she explained, from the California sun.

The family saw a good deal less of Kitty. Ruth scheduled her to be cashier at dinnertime, so she didn't come home until after the Pilgrim had closed up, usually between eight and nine on a weeknight. She stayed up late reading novels in the bathtub and couldn't rouse herself in the morning. The care and feeding, the very cognizance of her family gradually fell away from Kitty Douglass, and into other, more competent hands. Ruth's. The house on Silk Stocking Row echoed less often with "Hot Tamale Molly" and more with the sounds of Miss McBrean teaching Eden Louise to play the piano, "The Last Rose of Summer," "Take a Pair of Sparkling Eyes," and others of her Dream Theatre repertoire.

Each time Eden returned home to her grandmother's house, she first ran halfway up the stairwell and breathed deeply. This was the place where scents from the kitchen collected, lingered, cavorted, like diaphanous good-time guests, reluctant to dissipate. She always tried to guess what was cooking before she barreled into the kitchen.

There Ruth sat, a figure in black with a single long green apple peel falling from her knife onto damp gray newsprint in her lap. Eden would always remember her just like that, calm, with useful work, her hands moving skillfully, her severe serenity thawing only when she looked up to see Eden.

"Ham and applesauce?" Eden walked into Ruth's open arms.

"Yes indeed. You can set the table now," Ruth said, righting the big bow in Eden's neat hair. "Set the table, and then you can stand on a chair and stir the applesauce."

"The whole house smells wonderful!"

"It would, except Kitty is smoking on the back porch," said Ruth in a voice calculated to carry.

Kitty dropped the butt of her cigarette in a can of water and sashayed inside. "Why can a man smoke and a woman can't? I ask you. We can vote. We can smoke. Ain't that right, Eden?"

Eden made a neutral reply. She knew how near the surface was this generally festering quarrel.

"Smoking is bad for you, bad for everyone," said Ruth, rising, going to the oven. "Man or woman, it makes you stink."

"Well *la di dah,* won't I be the judge of how I smell?" Kitty lifted one heavy arm and sniffed underneath. "Evening in Paris, if you must know."

Ruth turned her back on Kitty and opened the oven door; she bent, holding towels on either side of the broad shallow pan, and brought the ham out and set it on the wooden table. The ham wore a sticky brown sugar and mustard jacket with clove buttons, and there were quartered tangerines, bronzed and gleaming, all around it. A rare look of unalloyed pleasure crossed Ruth's features. She smiled. "Now, that is a beautiful ham."

"It is," Eden concurred. "A beauty."

Kitty lounged, leaning back, her elbows on the counter, and she regarded the ham as if it were horseflesh destined for the glue factory. "If all I had for beauty was a ham, I'd kill myself. Yes, I would. I'd know my life was over. If I was ever to say that about a ham, that it was beautiful, I'd hang myself. May

God strike me dead if I ever say a ham is beautiful." Kitty flounced toward the door.

Little beads of perspiration collected along Ruth's upper lip as she struggled to control her ire. "Finish setting the table, Eden," said Ruth.

"Come along, Eden," said Kitty.

*Shall the Youth of Zion Falter?* Eden Louise Douglass had to make her choice, and she knew it. She turned to the kitchen dresser where wooden spoons stood like splintered lilies in a cracked vase. She opened the drawer and poked among the silverware.

Kitty left the room singing "The Man Who Broke the Bank at Monte Carlo."

# Afton's Pork Loin Roast

*Adapted for Café Eden, Skagit Valley, Washington*

Take your boneless pork loin roast of any size and rub down lightly with salt and pepper. Poke holes all along the fatty side. Take one lemon and grate the zest off of it. Mix this with some peppercorns and rosemary stripped from the tough twigs. Stuff this mixture down the little holes. Then squeeze the juice of the lemon over the roast. Chop up the lemon and reserve to scatter around the baking dish. In your big cast iron fry pan, heat some oil and sear your meat quickly for good color. Place the pork loin in a baking dish with the chopped lemon and bake at 350 till done, basting now and then. Can substitute a bit of thyme instead of the lemon zest. Use the pan juices for the gravy base, adding a little water or wine, beating in a bit of flour for thickening.

Or:

Cut a small pork loin roast in half lengthwise if it hasn't already come like that. Slice one whole lime thin and lay across one half. In between slices put one whole chili pepper. On top of this sprinkle some of your very fine-chopped garlic. On top of this lay some fresh mint leaves. A little salt. Put halves together and tie at three or four places. Do the same quick sear as above.

Bake at 350, till done, depends on the size. Baste a couple of times with pan juices. Place on serving platter, snip strings, cover with foil and let sit while you quickly caramelize your pearl onions.

Afton's method for the pearl onions: in advance throw them into a pot of boiling water for a few minutes only. Drain, rinse in cold water. Cut off each end and pop out of their jackets. Tedious, but worth it. Put in a small bowl with a little salt and pepper and cover with white vinegar.

In the pan you used for searing, heat a bit more oil. When hot, dump in the onions and vinegar. Stand back. Move all around the pan with a spatula, and toss in about 3 tablespoons brown sugar. Stir till all are coated. Put them around the roast, garnish with sprigs of mint and serve.

# SNAPSHOT

## THE PILGRIMS

Ruth Douglass was a well-known figure in St. Elmo with her straw hat pinned to the gray hair knotted atop her head. Her hat pin was her sole adornment. Tall, spare, severely clad, a woman once handsome perhaps, Ruth had matured into formidable. She had arrived in St. Elmo, California, in 1900, a widow trailing a pack of fatherless children, shackled to the truth by lies, and dependent on the charity of her odious brother-in-law, Art Whickham.

In her bid for freedom from servitude to others, Ruth called upon her skills as a cook. She was not then a fine cook, nor did she especially enjoy the work, but she had excellent instincts, unwavering strength, and an innate sense of propriety, though little charm. Once she had founded the Pilgrim Restaurant, Ruth overcharged her customers, balanced her books, paid her staff well, and kept her standards impeccably high.

So when in about 1915 she advertised in the St. Elmo paper for a new cook, few people applied. And indeed, those few were found wanting. It was something of a surprise to Ruth to be approached one morning by a Chinese man who sought the job. When she asked his name, he said he was called Napoleon, that he had learned to cook in the kitchen of the French Legation in Shanghai, China. He was willing to be tested. He would cook this day, all day, for no wages, and let Mrs. Douglass judge his skills. Napoleon's demeanor—serious, reserved, proud—matched Ruth's own. Another employer might have inquired what brought him to a railroad town like St. Elmo, but Ruth forbore. She wasn't interested in his past. Could he cook to her standards?

Napoleon proved himself that day, and every day after for the next twenty years. Napoleon could read and speak English, French, and Chinese. He had a secretive manner, he was taciturn and humorless, but what did Ruth care? She had not hired him for his charm. Such were his talents that the Pilgrim's reputation extended from Los Angeles to the Mexican border. People were known to get off the train in St. Elmo and then resume their journeys after they had eaten at the Pilgrim Restaurant. Napoleon stayed with the Pilgrim till the end. Then he vanished. For those twenty years he created magic that no one had ever asked him to write down.

After hiring Napoleon, Ruth left the restaurant kitchen in his capable hands and took her place behind the till as cashier. She greeted customers, led them to their tables, made obligatory small talk, and made change when they paid their bills. She passed their compliments along to Napoleon and his staff.

The staff was increasingly Chinese. As jobs at the Pilgrim fell empty, Napoleon suggested that Mrs. Douglass hire his cousins. They may or may not have been related to him. Certainly, once they came into the kitchen, he ruled over them like the emperor he was named for. From Ruth's point of view they proved entirely adequate. Morever, she was secretly amused at the consternation of St. Elmo civic worthies who told her that paying high wages to the Chinese set a dangerous precedent.

The success of the Pilgrim was exceptional, but not her greatest achievement. Ruth Douglass had arranged her life so that she answered to no one, certainly to no man. That was a feat few women could claim. If indeed there is a recipe for everything, Ruth had created independence out of unlikely ingredients. And if it had cost her more than she had intended to pay, she did not say so.

## CHAPTER FIVE

A LADY WITH HER OWN MONEY COULD DO AS SHE liked. The job gave Kitty Douglass more than money, more even than independence. As the Pilgrim cashier, Kitty found a whole new venue for her theatrical talents: an audience, which was its own sort of tonic.

Naturally, all the men who came into the Pilgrim were gallant to her, telling her, as they were taking a toothpick for their trouble, My my, what a fine evening it was, Mrs. Douglass, or, How becoming is that color on you, Mrs. Douglass, or, My my, how can you continue to look so perfectly fresh after a long day on your feet, Mrs. Douglass? All their wives were jealous old prunes.

When these conversations included customers' compliments for Napoleon, Kitty blushed, shrugged, and indicated that her own fair hands had wrought the marvelous meal they'd just eaten. No, alas, she could not part with the recipe for those famous Figs Napoleon; one of her ancestors had brought it back from the Spanish and Indian War with a curse should it ever be divulged outside the family.

To the talented Napoleon, Kitty never mentioned the customers' praise. Napoleon and his cousins—if they were his cousins—resented Kitty's high-handed assumptions of her own importance. Long skilled in the arts of compromise, the Chinese staff kept mute and united against her, biding their time.

And then there came the day in 1928 for which Kitty Douglass had preened and dreamed. Word percolated through the Dream Theatre manager, Mr. Fletcher, a regular Pilgrim customer, that the Monday night preview would be *Gold of the Yukon,* starring Ernest March and John Kent as two brothers who get gold fever, leave for the Yukon, and fall in love with the same girl, the beautiful Blanche Randall. Film stars and bigwigs often came incognito to St. Elmo, just sixty miles east of Los Angeles, pretending to be ordinary people in an ordinary audience. Except that every fourth person in St. Elmo knew two of the other three, so incognito was not possible.

Kitty begged and pleaded with Ruth to be let off for Monday evening to go to the Dream Theatre. She wept and cried. Ruth was inflexible. If Kitty was not standing behind that cash drawer at 5:00 P.M., exactly as she was supposed to be, she would lose the job altogether.

So there Kitty stood, sullen, nibbling on a nail, refusing to lift her hand to any task while the Chinese waiters scurried about making last-minute adjustments on the white-clad tables. St. Elmo was a workingman's town, and people ate early. But the first group through the frosted glass doors that evening were not St. Elmo worthies and their overupholstered wives. From her stand at the cash register and through the curtained window, Kitty glimpsed a chauffeur jumping out to open doors of a sleek, polished car. A Pierce-Arrow. Beautiful women and well-dressed men emerged. The women wore clothes so gauzy and colorful that they looked like hummingbirds, and Kitty thought of the dessert she had read about in some tropical novel, or perhaps just imagined, Hummingbird Delight. The women wore layers of green and pink; they were studded with pearls and wearing white leather gloves that you just knew were soft as butter, their lips pursed and pink and ready for romance. Blanche Randall pushed open the Pilgrim door and sauntered in.

Kitty gave a furtive tug across her own bosom and a touch to her hennaed hair and licked her lips. Behind Miss Randall were a couple of portly men and two more beautiful women. In walked blond John Kent, who had played Major Crespin in *The Green Goddess.* Kitty would have known him anywhere, though she was shocked that he looked neither dashing nor stirring in person. Only blond and dull with a heavy jaw. Following the lumbering Mr. Kent, there entered into the Pilgrim none other than Ernest March.

Kitty's heart pounded and her palms burst into sweat and she felt the blood descend in a rushing torrent from her head and there was a joyous little tingle between her legs. She watched as the headwaiter showed them to the Pilgrim's best table, and she could hear the Chinese chatter from the kitchen. She thought she might faint or cry or both. Kitty moved, in what she hoped was a graceful fashion, from behind the cash register into the kitchen. She went to the sink and turned on the cold water, put a little splash on the back of her neck. "Tell me everything they order," she said to the waiter.

His lip curled. "Nothing. Nothing for you."

Kitty went to Napoleon. "What have they ordered?"

"Now?" he replied in his oddly stilted English with its wisp still of the French Legation in Shanghai. "Now they have asked for glasses and a pitcher of our famous water so they may empty their hip flasks into them." The bead of his unswerving gaze shut her up.

Cursing him beneath her breath, Kitty went through the swinging doors back into the dining room. She picked up the little glass of toothpicks and took them to the table, offering them around as though they were made from pieces of the True Cross.

"No, thank you," said one of the corpulent men.

"The Green Goddess." Kitty cleared her throat and tried again: "The Green Goddess salad dressing is really very nice. Better than nice. Excellent. This is the only restaurant south of San Francisco that has Green Goddess. Named for the wonderful picture which I seen many's the time, and which is"—she saw the waiter coming with the pitcher of water—"emblazoned on my heart."

The waiter shoved her aside, poured their water. The hip flasks came out. Their glasses turned a glorious amber, and Kitty retreated to the cash register to watch. Surely Ernest March would notice her. Would speak to her. In the meantime, her gaze darted between Ernest March and Blanche Randall, to see if true love bloomed between them in St. Elmo as it did on the silent screen.

But here, with Ernest March so close by that Blanche Randall could have breathed in the air he breathed out, Blanche Randall scarcely looked at him. Here was Ernest March beside her *in the flesh*—the phrase made Kitty queasy with pleasure—and Blanche Randall hardly noticed. How could Blanche Randall be bestowing herself, her purring laughter, her knowing smile, the light of her blue eyes, on the balding fat man to her right? He had a big mole by the side of his nose and his eyebrows were shaggy as bear fur. In all those silent pictures Kitty had imagined Miss Randall's laughter trilling, thrilling, but here, in the Pilgrim, Blanche had a raw laugh, especially as she downed glass after glass of dilute bootlegged whiskey.

Monday was a slow night at the Pilgrim, and a good thing, too, since the waiters showered these customers with service. The diners continued to color their water with whiskey all through the meal; they became louder and more raucous.

Ernest March said almost nothing, seemed, in fact, oblivious to his companions. He ate in a curiously old-fashioned way, concentrating on the food, savoring, sometimes nodding to himself. The others ate haphazardly, the women doting on the other men, the other men bringing heavy-laden forks to their lips as though stoking expensive furnaces. They roistered in exaggerated merriment. None of this concerned Ernest March. He paid them little mind. He genuinely enjoyed the meal, eating everything, and looking much pleased.

He ordered the Figs Napoleon for dessert, and when it arrived—an amber pool of honey and butter with shining black figs sliding down the slopes of pale ice cream—he rolled his eyes. He grinned, shook out his napkin, and patted his lips. Kitty longed to change places with that starched foursquare piece of linen, and she vowed to snatch it before the waiters did. Ernest ate, eyes closed, dreamy with delight, sliding his beautiful lips along the curves of the spoon.

His mouth was more voluptuous than Kitty remembered from the silent screen. His lips hovered somewhere between romantic resignation and a smoldering command to kiss. Ernest March was a darkly handsome man with thick, crisp, curly hair, probably unruly, save that it had been greased slick and shiny as a helmet and lay close to his skull. He had perfectly arched, expressive brows, and his eyes were dark wells, a lustrous brown, framed by slightly hooded eyes with astonishingly long lashes. His nose was straight, high, and set off the rest of his clean features. He had a mustache, also thick and curling and gleaming. He had a strong chin and dark jaw. Was he unshaven? No. Just heavily, darkly bearded. He was altogether darker than Kitty had realized, not as dark as he had been as the rajah in *The Green Goddess*. He had played that role in what amounted to blackface, but he was indeed swarthy as the pirate in 1923's *Captain of Her Heart*. Ernest March was also not nearly as big or strapping as Kitty had imagined. He seemed rather slight, really, but perhaps that was the proximity of the paunchy man to his left.

Ernest March finished the figs and ice cream, motioned gracefully to the waiter to signal its excellence. His plate was cleared, and he seemed thoughtful, the quiet confidence, Kitty surmised, of a brave man, a man of charm and sophistication. He raised his eyes and smiled at Kitty Douglass. Then he glanced at his fashionable gold wristwatch, reminding the rest of them that the picture was due to start and they wanted to see the locals' reactions.

"Bunch of rubes," said Blanche Randall. "Who gives a damn?" She rose and stumbled slightly against the fat man as she rose. He supported her elbow and passed his hand down over her buttocks.

The paunchy man with gleaming jowls reached into a leather wallet and flung a bunch of bills onto the table. The money soaked in the small watery puddles on the cloth.

The waiter had not yet presented the bill, and he looked perplexed, performed a kind of sign language to his cousin: Someone must speak to them, to say the bill had not yet been tallied up, they must wait. The cousin looked over at Kitty, then shrugged. After all, whatever was not the bill, was the tip. And if the money was insufficient, it was the cashier's responsibility, not theirs.

Kitty herself saw all this, but was struck dumb, speechless with emotions she had no words for. She watched, trembling, as the men put on their hats, and women gathered up their glamorous cloaks and dug into sequined handbags looking for compacts. They powdered their noses. And just then, as they were all about to disappear through the frosted glass doors and out of her life forever, Ernest March came back to the cashier, took a toothpick from her little glass. Held it up in a jaunty fashion, and nodded.

"Wait!" Kitty called as he turned back to the door. "I . . . have seen every picture you have ever made. Many times. Many many. Ten times. Twenty. I . . ."

"Fine. Very kind."

"No, really. I am your great admirer. Your greatest admirer."

"Excellent. Very kind."

Kitty pinged a key, and on the equivalent of A-flat, the cash register coughed open its maw, and she found an old receipt. She rummaged on the stand below and found a stub of pencil. "Sign this, will you? Please."

"Fine. Excellent. Too kind. Please to tell the kitchen that the figs was . . ." Words failed him. "The figs—pleased to tell the figs are the food of the gods." He took his fingers and kissed the air, blew it toward her. She held up both her hands to catch it. He scribbled, then looked up. "And how are you called?"

"What?"

"Your name, Dear Lady. What eez your name?"

"Kitty."

He wrote across the top, *For Chitty with all god wishes.* "And now, till next time I come to your beeyoutiful town again, arrivederci."

She watched him through the window, walking slightly apart from his companions, his posture erect where theirs was shambling. She nearly ran after him. Her shoulders shook, and tears streaked her face. Ernest March had spoken to her in the flesh, spoken, and she had not told him that she loved him. She had not told him that she had named her own son after him, called the boy Ernest so she should have the pleasure, all her life, of repeating over and over, *Ernest, Ernest, Ernest, I love you.*

# Figs Napoleon with Leaves of Thyme

*Pilgrim Restaurant, St. Elmo, California (sans liqueur during Prohibition)*
*Café Eden, Skagit County, Washington*

Use small fresh figs, black. A pint box of them. Wash but do not peel them. Cut them perhaps $^2/_3$ of the way down. In a shallow pan, melt four tablespoons of unsalted butter. Add to this $^1/_3$ to $^1/_2$ cup of honey. Bring to a boil, stirring. Lower heat, add perhaps 12 figs, turning constantly, coating them, till they relax, release, open and go glossy. Have at hand maybe 2 tablespoons good brandy, Amaretto or Cointreau. Stir in till just warmed through. Remove from heat. Cover. Best if served immediately. However, if they have gone cold, warm gently.

In a good-sized plate, put a scoop of homemade (or premium) vanilla ice cream, ladle figs and honey around it in a kind of moat. Sprinkle around the outside the tiny torn-off leaves of thyme.

Excellent. Simple. Lovely. So lovely, you might almost believe these to be leaves of time itself.

# SNAPSHOT

## SHANGHAI, 1893

His mother roused him, early, before dawn. She made a sign for silence. Wan threads of moonlight lit the room where young and old snored, snuffled, shifted their sweating limbs. She held her breath—so did he—when his grandfather rolled over, grunted, then farted and fell back to sleep.

Once outside, his mother pulled him by the hand through steamy streets and narrow alleys, littered, lumped with rot, refuse, and excrement. Lean dogs prowled. His mother shooed them away. The air was thick with heat and moisture, beading like sweat on shanty and sampan alike. The reek of decay and low-lying smoke from braziers hung over their heads and snaked at their feet.

But even this early, working Shanghai roused. Coolies wearing only tattered cotton trousers stooped under the weight of bamboo yokes from which hung water buckets. Vendors began their cries, pot and crockery menders, beancake sellers, vegetable sellers, each sing-song call unique. Beggars and mendicants stirred in the streets. The boy could tell the beggars by their scars and mutilations. In the paling light emaciated ricksha runners hoisted their fares, corpulent men who were ending nights of revelry, and bound for the sanctity of the British Settlement.

Hurry up, his mother told him, tugging his arm. Hurry up. She was a tiny woman, and he was just a boy. Eight years old. Small for his age. Underfed.

They walked south, far from Soochow creek and crossed the wide pleasant thoroughfare, Bubbling Well Road, lined with leafy trees and extravagant mansions. She kept a tight hold on his hand. She walked with her head down, as they passed into the avenues of the French Concession and finally the rue du Consulat. They ducked swiftly into a narrow passage between high stone walls. Along the top, jagged shards of glass gleamed and sparkled. Hurry up, she told him, tugging his arm.

She came at last to a gate left slightly open, and she squeezed through it. He followed. They moved soundlessly through a vast garden, where arbors dripped with heavy flowers, and perfumes stagnated overhead. The boy was charmed. Before them a four-story palace rose up, windows reflecting the dawn. His mother led him down some steps into a well where there was a door.

A stout Chinese woman opened the door. She wore black. Western dress with a high white collar and her bulk tightly corseted. Very strange to see Chinese so fat and in these clothes. She wore a white cap on oiled black hair that was streaked with gray. A gold chain looped across her bosom to a tiny watch in a pocket. She took it out, opened and then snapped it shut. You are late, she said.

Humble pardon, Auntie, said his mother.

They followed her clicking shoes through a huge room where pans clanged, grinders sounded, and strange smells wafted overhead. Hot water hissed from a pipe. The boy had never seen such a thing, nor a room so large. He gawked. Chinese working here glanced at them only briefly, kept to their tasks.

Auntie led the boy and his mother to a smaller room with shelves from floor to ceiling, with racks from which hung strange tools, and stacks of drawers with porcelain knobs. A cat sat in window. Auntie regarded the boy critically.

His mother turned to him, knelt. You will stay here for a while with Auntie. I will come back for you, but I am leaving Shanghai, going on a journey. I am going to find your father.

The stout woman scoffed and said to the boy: Your father is dead. To his mother she said: They send men carrying dynamite into holes they dig into mountains. So let the Chinese be blown up. They send them to their deaths in deserts where their bones dry and their spirits will never come home. All to build a railroad? Any man who leaves China for such a life deserves such a death.

Please, Auntie, murmured his mother.

If he lives, he has a new woman.

Please, Auntie, his mother said again. She rose and put her arm on the boy's shoulder.

You think such men remember their wives in China? Their ancestors? They become American. Like mongrels.

His mother's face was smooth and tragic. She was still young. She was strong. She looked like the boy. She said to the boy: Your father did not choose to leave us. He was taken. But I know now where to find him. I have a letter. His mother touched a string around her neck that held a small cotton sack. Paper crinkled inside.

You cannot read, said the stout lady.

The letter has been read to me. I know every word.

In the kitchen, a short, sharp, warning cry sounded. Auntie excused herself and told them to wait. The boy saw a man stride into the kitchen. He had pale white skin, pale blue eyes, and bushy red whiskers, black coat, black long legs; the boy thought he looked like a beetle. He clapped his hands in a commanding manner, and spoke to Auntie in a guttural voice, a gibberish language.

Who is that man? the boy asked his mother.

Foreigners, she replied. Barbarians. These are the barbarian French. Better than the barbarian British. Or the barbarian American. Auntie is Number One Housekeeper here. She will teach you to serve them. As she serves them. You will work here in this kitchen.

No. I will go with you.

You will work here, she said again. You will never be hungry here. She knelt and smoothed his hair back from his face. His face was like her face. She said: Stay here till I return for you. I will bring your father. You will never be hungry here. You will grow. Get fat, like Auntie, she whispered, with a smile.

She rose and faced the fat woman who had returned to them. The barbarian had left the kitchen.

He must obey, said Auntie. I beat him if he does not obey.

He will. He is very smart, Auntie. He is a most smart boy.

What are they doing? asked the boy pointing to the kitchen.

Auntie smacked his hand. Ask no questions! Do as you are bid. Come.

The boy was frightened. He flung his arms tightly around his mother.

His mother removed his hands, his arms. She said: You remember what I told you?

You will return for me. You will bring my father. The boy understood now.

Yes. I will think of you every day I am gone. As your father thinks of us.

I do not remember my father. I do not care about him. I want to stay with you.

You will stay here, work with Auntie, learn everything that Auntie can teach you.

I want to come with you.

No. Alone I will be more swift. I will see you again. Soon. But every day you must think of me. You must wake every day and say *St. Elmo, California*. You must say it like that. In their language. English.

The boy repeated the strange formation on his tongue: *St. Elmo, California*.

That is where I am going. That is what this letter says. The railroad your father built through the desert ends in St. Elmo, California. Your father says there are many Chinese in St. Elmo so he will not be lonely while he waits for me.

The boy did not know what *lonely* meant. He had no concept of the word. Not then.

The boy said to his mother: If you do not come for me, I will come to you.

PART TWO

# Home
# Cooking

1936

GIDEON GROUND THE GEARS OF THE PILGRIM DELIV-ery truck as it clunked and rumbled into Fairwell, Idaho, Gideon at the wheel, Kitty beside him, their three children and all their worldly goods in the back. Fairwell, Idaho, was a city set high in the mountains, the northern Idaho panhandle, the hills once studded with silver mines. Silver Street, such as it was, led into town, past the cemetery.

Fairwell had the air of both having seen and still waiting for Better Days. Silver Street had sidewalks, but some stores had wooden planks from the door across open ditches. Though it was 1936, there were still troughs for horses, and indeed a few patient mules were tied nearby. The truck throttled past the inevitable unvarnished Mormon church, the brick high school, the combined courthouse and jail made of stone, a civic entity second only to the railroad station. The Buck's Head Hotel had double doors and a sign in the front, MIND WHERE YOU SPIT. THANK YOU. THE MANAGEMENT. There were saloons, now styling themselves bars, the butcher, the baker, the barbershop, food market, feed and tack stores, garages, a brick bank, storefront mining and land offices, the Fairwell *Enterprise*, and the tiny inglorious Bijou Picture Palace. Boarded up.

"Picture palace, my arse." Kitty set about rolling herself another fag.

On the Pilgrim delivery truck, blankets and bedrolls were tied to the running board, and a mattress was strapped to the passenger's side. On the journey from St. Elmo to Fairwell, the family had slept by the side of the road, Kitty and Gideon on the mattress, Eden, Ada, and Ernest on the ground. They had eaten little beyond bread and jam after they finished off the bacon sandwiches and cold potatoes Afton Lance packed for them. They were cranky, hungry, dirty, and uncertain, especially since Fairwell, Idaho, did not, in August 1936, look like the place Mason Douglass had promised his older brother. Mason Douglass had said to Gideon, "The mountains up here ring with precious metals! Wealth to be had for the asking! High times for the Sunstone Silver Mine!" Mason Douglass was the president and founder of the Sunstone Silver Mine. They were here at Mason's shiny behest.

Sitting in the back of the truck, Eden, sixteen, Ada, fourteen, and Ernest, twelve, rocked with the truck's clank and motion. Other than the bedding, a few pots and pans, a box of household goods, and cardboard suitcases, the contents suggested less a new beginning and rather what they had lost forever. Little Ernest sat on a box of baby clothes belonging to the long-gone Tootsie, which Kitty had insisted on bringing. The drafts and rolls of Gideon's Great Timetable were tied and stashed in tubes that made hollow sounds as they bounced. Gideon had abandoned the endeavor, though, like Kitty, he could not bear to leave it behind. The truck shuddered to a halt in front of a dreary-looking eatery with steamy windows.

"Well, here's the Paris Chop House," said Gideon. "Mason said he'd meet us here."

"Paris my arse," said Kitty. "This is a fool's errand, at the behest of a knave."

Mason Douglass, a chubby, self-satisfied man of about forty, brash and full of bonhomie, bought his brother's family dinner at the Paris Chop House. After all Mason had urged Gideon to leave California for Fairwell, Idaho, where Mason's glowing prospects for his Sunstone Silver Mine and his assurances of a rosy future veined with silver meant that Gideon would have lucrative work.

However, over a greasy meal at the Paris Chop House, Mason did not refer to these delectable visions. As if to humble his older brother before continuing, Mason asked after the events that had forced them to leave St. Elmo, the string of disasters in which Gideon's ineptitude was much to blame. Mason asked first after poor Mother. Gideon said that Ruth was now living with Tom and Afton, that she was only slowly recovering from the stroke that had felled her two years before. He spoke in scholarly platitudes, evasions, and no one, not even Kitty, had the heart to interrupt, guffaw, or jeer.

As Eden listened she put her elbows on the table and her head in her hands. Ruth would never have allowed such a lapse in manners, but the stroke had deprived Ruth Douglass of speech and movement, though her mind was seemingly unimpaired. Stricken, Ruth was difficult, still proud, bitter and mute, neither quite alive nor quite dead, only utterly powerless. Unable to wield her own astute judgment, Ruth suffered to watch Gideon try to assume her responsibilities. With no head for bills or business, Gideon fumbled, foundered, and finally, in the course of some eighteen months, lost the Pilgrim and most of Ruth's savings, the achievements of almost forty years. They sold the Silk Stocking Row house to Art Whickham for the price he offered. Ruth Douglass's hard work, her skill and bravery, were all as though they had never been.

Tom and Afton took the debilitated Ruth to live with them and their eight children. Eden never saw her grandmother again.

As he finished his description of the St. Elmo debacle, Gideon drew a deep breath and said, "Well, Mason. We're here. I used every penny we had left to bring the family up here. I'm ready to go to work. Ready and able."

Mason grinned. "Well, Gideon, I brung you here to Idaho because there is wealth and high times up here, just for the asking."

"So," said Kitty, "we're asking. Where are they?"

Mason's reply was energetic, voluble, but the unseemly truth slowly emerged: Mason's Sunstone Silver Mine was as defunct as an outhouse in a world of indoor plumbing. Mason, in fact, was on his way out Idaho's back door, up into the great Canadian wilderness, the Northwest Territories. Mason concluded, "There are many opportunities for a man of vision in the Northwest Territories."

"Canada?" asked Gideon, cleaning his glasses. "Canada?"

"Snail Snot," said Kitty. "That's your true name."

"What?" said Mason.

"That was always my name for you, Mason. I always said you was like snail snot. Gideon never liked it, but it's true. You always leave a shiny trail of snot wherever you go. It looks like silver, but it's really a trail of snot, and now we followed it all the way up here and we're bloody stuck in it and I, for one, would like to know what the bleeding hell we're supposed to do."

\* \* \*

As with the inevitable accumulations of memorable slights, serious injuries, and serial rancor endemic to marriage, Kitty never let Gideon forget that he had brought them all to Idaho for nothing. And in the equally inevitable marital reflex, he went selectively deaf to go along with his being half blind. In his own defense he always reminded her that he had gotten a job almost immediately.

The Fairwell High School history teacher ran off that very night with a bank teller. In an act of larceny that rocked Fairwell to its Mormon roots, they took embezzled funds. This misguided pair (they were later caught, tried, and found guilty) provided Gideon Douglass with a job. Gideon took the teacher's place. Gideon certainly knew his history: Adam and Eve, through the begets and begats, the whole dramatic tale of the restoring of the Gospel to Joseph Smith, the tenure of Christ here on the North American continent, and the travails and triumphs of the Latter-day Saints. And American history, yes, Gideon had a grip on that, too. The school superintendent—who was also the Mormon bishop—gave him the job on the spot. Thus, Gideon Douglass could say of Fairwell, Idaho, as Brigham Young had declared looking over the great Salt Lake, *This is the place!* Gideon Douglass taught school, taught Sunday school, joined the twice weekly genealogy group. He was a Saint in a Mormon town and a happy man.

But Kitty was a lost woman. Her aimless hedonism degenerated into a kind of dementia. Kitty wore a chenille robe, winter and summer, day and night. She smelled of an elixir brewed of Chesterfields, perspiration, and eau de cologne, which she often sipped. Gin was hard to come by in a Mormon town, even when Prohibition was over. Some days Kitty didn't get out of bed. She cursed the Mormon religion and all the Douglasses, especially Ruth, Afton, and Mason. She denounced her children for thankless wretches and mourned poor Tootsie, who would have been good to her. Before her wrath and crying jags, her singing binges and rattling accusations, Ada and Ernest cowered or applauded or did whatever she wanted. But Eden wouldn't. Eden slammed the frail doors to keep her mother out, or went outside, tramped in the snow if necessary. Eden despised Kitty's flailing impotence. The old camaraderie, the communion Eden and Kitty had shared in the Dream Theatre, that was gone forever.

In the grip of these rampages, Kitty reserved special epithets for Gideon. Gideon had stuck her in a mining town, far from civilization, nothing but mountains and snow, a town so bleeding backwards, you couldn't buy a tortilla and a pot of beans if you was bloody starving. Gideon cared nothing for his wife and family. Gideon loved the Lost Tribes of Israel, the Founding bloody Fathers, the Egypshine Fayros.

But Gideon no longer worked on the Great Timetable. Once in Fairwell, he took up that great Mormon passion, genealogy, so that the Saints might baptize the dead, those who had been denied Joseph Smith's teachings. Gideon took scholarly pride in this work as well as religious enthusiasm. Occasionally, with other Fairwell Saints, he made pilgrimages to the temple in Salt Lake to undergo baptism for the dead, to give unto those souls who had missed it the dispensations of the Restored Gospel. Gideon's affection for his pioneer ancestors, especially those who had endured the hardships of the Handcart Brigade, fortified him against Kitty's rants. Her rages could be heard all over the drafty four-room house (five with the tiny bathroom) they rented from a near-bankrupt mining company.

Set on a steep hill among other tin-roofed houses, some of them empty, the neighborhood had few fences, no porches or sidewalks. Most of the year, shirts, pants, and sheets hung frozen, splayed and immobile on the clotheslines. Shared incinerators spiraled thin ropes of smoke in the yards. Shared outhouses remained, though the company had tacked on bathrooms to some of the houses. Their house had partition rather than walls, spaces of about a foot between the ceiling and the partition, so that the heat from the big stove in the kitchen would rise and float into the rest of the house. That was the theory, and though heat may rise, it failed to fall into the two frigid bedrooms. Winters, they all but froze. Eden and Ada slept together for warmth. Ernest kept a cot in the kitchen, summers he slept on the sofa. The sofa was the first thing Gideon had bought with his small, reliable teacher's pay. The radio second, thinking it would cheer Kitty. Later, with another paycheck, Gideon proudly bought a round-bellied electric washer with a wringer and had it delivered, proud as if it were a prancing racehorse. He thought Eden would be pleased with the washer, because with Kitty's defection, household maintenance fell to Eden.

To be the eldest daughter, the capable one, in a family of daydreaming bunglers is hell. Gideon was hopeless. Ernest was lazy. Ada was incompetent. Eden began to understand and abhor the messy, pungent, wretched round of necessity that attached itself to human life. The eating, peeing, perspiring, the sloughing, dripping, defecating, the smoking, the monthly blood, the hairballs clogging drains, the eternal snot-filled hankies, the hacking coughs, the long underwear and mothy woolens all winter, the Sears catalog beside the toilet, the pages torn gently out, or the Fairwell *Enterprise*. Their backsides went black unless Eden remembered to buy toilet paper. As for the daily cooking, keeping these bodies knit to their souls, that too fell to Eden. Mostly she kept mush on the stove since it required only oats and water, milk; it could easily be sweetened and eaten hot or cold. She fell back on her mother's old standard of bread torn up and stuffed into a glass, or in their case, an old jam jar full of milk.

Once she stepped outside that rented house, however, Miss Eden Louise Douglass was someone else entirely. Miss Eden Louise Douglass was the smartest girl in Fairwell High. She knew how to play the piano. She knew how to type. She was a good driver. She was very pretty. She had her grandmother's build, tall, broad-shouldered, dark hair, green eyes, and good skin. She had cut her hair short, though it refused to curl. Her features were not as spare as Ruth's, and there was a softness about her; she was rounded and curvy, and alluring, as Emjay Gates well knew. Emjay Gates was in love with her, and she accepted his adulation, which in certain intense, intimate moments rose to engorged adoration.

Eden had ambition. She declared she would one day write for a great daily newspaper. Martha Gelhorn and Dorothy Thompson—those fearless women correspondents traveling around the world—replaced Ernest March and Blanche Randall in Eden's pantheon of heroes. She resolved to have a life of adventure and achievement and travel. For a beginning—she would need experience, after all—Eden presented herself to the editor of the Fairwell *Enterprise,* looking for a part-time job.

Mr. Redbourne said, "I don't hire high school girls."

"I can type," Eden persisted. "Fast. I can answer the telephone."

The editor leaned back in his chair, looking across the street at the beckoning doors of the Buck's Head Hotel. Prohibition past, the bar was now open. Ned Redbourne enjoyed the Buck's Head all-male bonhomie. "What will your father say?"

"I'm not asking my father. Why should you?"

"Well, most Mormon girls . . ." He raised his eyebrows.

"Are you running a church or a newspaper, Mr. Redbourne?"

"I'll pay you half what I pay that guy over there." He nodded to a man typing at a back desk.

"I'll take it."

The *Enterprise* was only a four-page rag twice weekly, but its small offices reeked of the pleasures of print, of ink, oil, molten metal, wooden floors, cheap paper, and cigarette smoke, of typewriter ribbons and wool worn too long. The radiators were noisy and inefficient. Eden wrote up the obits as people brought their sad information into the office. Three months later Redbourne gave her the title of society editor, though no more money. Society in Fairwell was mostly who was marrying whom. These notices had about them the same distressing monotony as the obits, the names recurring constantly. Fairwell was a lot smaller than St. Elmo, and there were only Mormons and miners.

Eden came to the *Enterprise* office every day after school. Ned Redbourne and his other writer took the opportunity to step out to the Buck's Head and leave the office in her capable hands. She typed out her obits at a huge typewriter; its carriage, swinging back and forth with the bell, kept up a pleasant rhythm.

From her desk, Eden could look up over the typewriter and out the window to Silver Street steeping in the long shadows cast by the mountains during the short afternoons. She had the strange sense of seeing a photographic negative, black-and-white, sky, the color of pillow ticking, the snow on either side of Silver, black, dirty at the ragged edges like the petticoats of beggars. Vehicles of every sort chugged through the March slush. People bent against the wind in dun-colored coats and hats.

The bell above the door jangled and Eden looked over to see a woman too old to be getting married herself, too young to have a daughter getting married. Eden figured she was bringing in an obit for a parent, and she put on her most sober, compassionate face. "May I help you?"

"Eden." The woman smiled shyly. "You so favor your father's people."

"Thank you. Aren't you Sister Thorsen from church?"

"Margaret. Yes." Margaret Thorsen had a fine, high, untroubled forehead, her hair pulled severely away from her face, the simplicity accentuating her great blue eyes. Her smooth skin was a little gray, like most of Fairwell, but oddly, as she unbuttoned her heavy coat, she wore a bright yellow wool scarf that cast a sunny glow over the sepia-colored office.

"What can I do for you?" Eden asked, taking up her pencil and paper.

"I come here with sumthin for your father, for your family I mean. I thought I'd give it to you, and you could take it home." She placed on Eden's desk an oblong loaf wrapped in a cheerful red-and-white-checked cloth, tied up with string, the knot a bow. The scent announced itself: gingerbread. "I sometimes bring my sourdough gingerbread to our genealogy meetings, and your pa does so enjoy it. I thought maybe you'd all like some. He's so 'preciative of every little kindness. I thought maybe I'd just 'stend that kindness to all of you."

"Thank you." Eden's stomach rumbled at the spicy aroma. As soon as Sister Thorsen left, she intended to open it up. Maybe eat the whole thing.

"I brung it here because it wouldn't be seemly, of course, for me to go to the high school and give it to Gid—to Brother Douglass, and I didn't want your mother thinking I believed she couldn't feed her own family. I don't know how she would of took it."

I don't either, thought Eden, though she could certainly have guessed it wouldn't be pleasant. Kitty's failures were well known, certainly among the Saints. Gideon insisted that Eden, Ernest, and Ada attend church with him every Sunday, but he never even made the effort with Kitty. Kitty's shortcomings could have humiliated a man less devout than Gideon. "I'm sure we'll all enjoy it, Sister Thorsen, thank you."

"And I wanted to meet you, too. Talk, I mean. Not just pass in church. Your pa is awful proud of you. He says you are the smartest person in Fairwell. He says you are a remarkable young lady and that the Douglass women are smarter than the men any day. I'm sure he's just teasing about that," she hastened to add, "but I know he is proud of you."

Eden had no idea her father had any such thoughts. When he was obliged to be home, Gideon closeted himself with student papers or long genealogical tables, and pens, keeping records of who begat whom and when. His own immediate family seemed of little interest to him.

"Of course a man smart as Gideon would have a smart daughter. He is just about the best man, and smart. I mean he knows everything 'bout history and his genealogy work is just sumthin to behold. You know of your father's genealogy work, of course."

Eden did, but only because she was in his Sunday school class, as was her sister, Ada. Ada always sat beside Melvin Brewster, though they both kept their gaze soulfully on the teacher. Even before a class of restless adolescents Gideon could re-create the struggles of the Saints. He waxed eloquent about the Handcart Brigade, those English, Welsh, and Scandinavian converts in 1856, some four thousand souls who had gotten as far as Iowa City and walked from there to Zion. He spoke as though this faith-testing, backbreaking trek had happened yesterday. Across Nebraska, waiting sometimes for whole herds of buffalo to thunder past. The converts were not allowed guns, so they watched the herds—meat on the hoof—trample past them. They pushed and pulled their carts up into Wyoming, through the Rocky Mountains. The handcarts were made of hickory or oak, with shafts of about six or seven feet, two wheels, and three wooden bars. They slung some bedding over the bars and carried all the families' earthly goods, their infants, their old, their sick and dying, westward. Eden always pictured harmoniums and fry pans strewn across the plains like signposts.

"My pa tells a good story," said Eden.

"Oh, it's not just a story," cried Sister Thorsen. "It's an inspiration. We have a common past, you know."

"I didn't."

"Your pa had a great-aunt in the Handcart Brigade. My great-grandmother come over with them, too. It give me some happiness to think our ancestors mighta known each other, mighta offered some comfort to one another on that journey when so many perished of hunger and fatigue, fell down in the traces, pulling carts through miles of heavy sand, under brutal suns and mountain snows. He makes it sound so real. Like the dead are with us still."

This gave Eden some pause, but Margaret Thorsen's brow remained untroubled, and Eden agreed that her father had a way with words in the classroom.

Sister Thorsen ignored the implied caveat. "Your pa says that our people, all our people, had good health and bad prospects, and that's why they left their native roots, and faced the unknown."

"Really?" said Eden, bored, and anxious to return to her obit. "I thought it was Joseph Smith, the Restored Gospel."

"That goes without saying," replied Sister Thorsen.

"Well, thank you for the gingerbread."

"It's sourdough gingerbread. You would never think of that, would you?"

Eden personally had no interest in sourdough whatever. Her only recollection of sourdough starter was a crock in Afton's kitchen with a smelly concoction from which Afton had made heavenly biscuits. "No, I certainly wouldn't think of it."

"Sourdough starter is the secret to my cakes, my reputation as a fine baker, though I do not mean to brag," Sister Thorsen added. "Most people wouldn't think of putting a half cup of sourdough starter in a cake, but it makes all the difference in the world. That starter has been in my family since 1856, when my great-grandmother come to Zion in the Handcart Brigade. They walked through broiling sun and blizzards," she said, as though repeating metric poetry. "Some set out too late in the summer and were caught in tragic snows. They died in droves, their backs to every Babylon, their eyes on a new Zion."

Eden recognized her father's favorite phrase. She had always thought it stupidly grandiose, but Margaret Thorsen's eyes lit, and Eden felt abashed for her.

"They had little to eat. They drank water from buffalo wallows and made fire of buffalo chips. If they was lucky. They woulda starved, no bread, no yeast, but for this sourdough starter. They don't make talking pictures of our people. They don't tell our stories like all that made-up stuff, because ours are true stories, and the true Restored Gospel of Jesus Christ on the North American continent. Our people perished and fought for the true faith. When my great-grandmother finally got to Zion, she had lost three children, and her husband died of a rattlesnake bite, but she had this recipe in her head—they can never take what's in your head—and this starter in her hand."

Eden wondered, with a stab of sympathy, if Sister Thorsen entertained some more tender emotion toward her father. How much happier he would have been married to someone like her. Pity for her parents overwhelmed Eden, an utterly new emotion; she had never thought of them as people who might have suffered in their own right. But her pity was seasoned with a pang of disloyalty, and a dash, too, of shame, though for whom, or what, she could not quite say.

When Sister Thorsen left, and with only a twinge of conscience, Eden untied the wrapper, broke off a piece of the sourdough gingerbread. Then another piece. The spice and tang of it contrasted with the soft texture and played upon the tongue. She took two more pieces. Then, she resolutely wrapped it back up and put it in the desk drawer, where its lovely scent would not tempt her as she returned to writing an obit for a life lived in the shadow of the mountains.

# Book Club Gingerbread

*Café Eden, c. 1980*

Eden could never replicate Sister Thorsen's Sourdough Gingerbread, or her starter, for that matter. However, she did eventually evolve an excellent gingerbread, very popular, especially in autumn, with the various book clubs that would gather at Café Eden for their monthly meetings. This cake is the perfect companion to fresh coffee or tea, and can be served with butter, whipped cream, or sour cream, at the reader's preference, and for those with a sweet tooth, even a bit of jam.

In a small bowl soak about a cup of raisins in a few tablespoons of good brandy or fruit liqueur. Stir now and then. Quickly blanch a cup, maybe a cup and a half, of toasted almonds, drain and slide them out of their skins. This way the pale almonds show up dramatically against the dark gingerbread.

In a bowl combine 2 cups flour, $\frac{1}{2}$ teaspoon soda, 1 teaspoon baking powder, and 1 tablespoon each: cinnamon, allspice, ground ginger, and fresh grated nutmeg. Add $\frac{1}{2}$ teaspoon ground cloves. In the food processor, or with a mixer, combine 1 cup brown sugar, $\frac{1}{2}$ cup butter softened to room temperature, 2 eggs, $\frac{1}{3}$ to a scant $\frac{1}{2}$ cup molasses, and $\frac{1}{3}$ cup buttermilk. When thoroughly combined, add your dry ingredients.

Turn into a bowl and add your almonds and your raisins, liqueur and all. Mix well.

Eden baked them in little individual tube pans for perfect singular servings to linger over. For the small tube pans bake at 350 for about 35 minutes. For a family it can be made in a large loaf pan or tube pan; bake at 350 for 50 to 60 minutes. Check with a toothpick or a slender knife. When cool, sprinkle with raw sugar for a golden effect.

This gingerbread goes with any good book.

## THE LOVERS

Gideon Douglass had never known true love. As a youth he had experienced chaste, high-minded romance with Miss Arlene McClure, his high school sweetheart, whom he surely would have married had his path not crossed with that of Kitty Tindall. With Kitty the romance was neither chaste nor high-minded, but the intensity stunned him. Though it passed. And once both the intensity and the amazement passed—and they seemed to have died together, vanished, eloped perhaps, but certainly they were gone by 1919, when Tootsie died—Gideon felt like a man stranded in his own life. There was no help for it. His situation could not be addressed or amended. Gideon Douglass was a man to whom things happened; he never exerted himself against anything. Kitty was equally weak, and so their marriage limped along, neither of them willing to admit to its chafe, constraints, or failures.

Even though Mason "Snail Snot" Douglass had brought his brother to Idaho at the bidding of one of his under-the-law schemes (one of the many; Mason ended his days, not surprisingly, as a lobbyist), Gideon was grateful to Mason. Without Mason, Gideon would have stayed in St. Elmo, where everyone knew him to be a failure.

In Fairwell he was not a failure. He was a pillar of the church, community, and school, a teacher loved by the students at Fairwell High and those in his Sunday school classes. He was a ward teacher, an Elder; he held priesthood and had all the blessings of the patriarchy that the Church could bestow. Twice a week in a Sunday school classroom, he presided over the meetings of the genealogy group. Twice a year, he made solemn pilgrimages with them to the great Mormon Temple in Salt Lake City, and went under the waters of baptism for the dead. Margaret Thorsen also went on these pilgrimages.

The passion that Gideon Douglass felt for Margaret Thorsen, and she for him, enriched the rest of his life. They were not reckless lovers. They were scrupulously careful. Scrupulously attentive to convention. But Gideon's face lit to see Margaret enter a room. And then, quickly, he would turn and let his smile, his happiness, beam on someone else, someone nearby. This is the way in which love ennobles and illuminates everything and everyone in its path. True love is prodigal.

Kitty had too much imagination to pay serious mind to anyone not in the pages of a novel. Kitty floated on her own little cushion of delusion, sauced, whenever possible, with alcohol. Kitty never guessed her husband loved another woman.

Brother Thorsen had too little imagination to believe his wife might love another man. Brother Thorsen never even noticed that after Gideon Douglass entered her life (at church, naturally, genealogy meetings), Margaret seemed to shed layers of care, to peel off the thick shellac of worry and fatigue that five children gave a woman, the crust that an endless round of hard work formed on her hands and hair and heart. Margaret Thorsen became beautiful, grew into the calm, clear-eyed, intelligent beauty she had always possessed, and that no one else had ever discovered.

Gideon's trysts with Margaret were fleeting and far between. They wrestled with guilt that their pilgrimages to the Salt Lake Temple afforded them guilty liaisons. They knew that the powers of the patriarchy notwithstanding, they were certainly sinners and no doubt bound for perdition. They often vowed to give each other up. And never did. Finally, they came to accept the irony of their love affair, though that isn't the term they would have used. Total immersion. That's what they felt for each other.

Twice a year they went to the Temple and under the waters of baptism for the dead—the poor, benighted dead, helpless against the True Gospel and hauled into the Celestial Kingdom from whatever nether-hamlet they might have been hiding in—and with these dead, Gideon and Margaret came alive. Despite the proximity of the other Fairwell Saints, they managed to share an afternoon hotel room, to shed their temple underwear, to walk the city's streets, to be in love.

Gideon, the scholar, questioned the validity of their Temple work; they were two unrepentant sinners, after all. These thoughts troubled him, so he evaded them. Despite his pronouncements to the contrary, for the most part Gideon Douglass kept his back to Zion while his eyes searched for any tiny Babylon he could find with Margaret Thorsen. If he could swiftly press Margaret's hand as they hung up their winter coats in the Sunday school classroom, that was Babylon enough. Love is prodigal.

## CHAPTER TWO

THOUGH INVOKING THE PATRIARCHAL ENDOWMENTS
had never worked with Kitty, Gideon had hopes that
Eden might respond. After all, Eden had been raised a
good Mormon girl—as opposed to Kitty, who had converted at an opportune moment. The notion of the patriarchy was central to the faith, repeatedly stated in the
Doctrine and Covenants, the Book of Mormon, and the
Bible, and it ought to be obeyed by the faithful. Gideon
believed, and he was prepared to insist, that the father
was the rock on whom the home is founded; he should
be heeded, nay, flatly obeyed in all things.

Having taken a good, swift dose of biblical inspiration and inflection, Gideon came into the kitchen one
Saturday afternoon and found Eden reading the *Enterprise* at the rickety table. "Your hours at the *Enterprise*
come between you and the home," he declared. "You
should be more attentive to the welfare of your brother
and sister. My welfare," he added. "I am the rock on
which the family is founded. Besides, I am the breadwinner."

Eden looked up from the page, curious, as if her father had suddenly spouted Swahili.

"Man cannot live on mush alone. It behooves a man to come home to a hot meal from his labors."

Eden went back to reading. "It's Saturday, Pa. You are not just home from your labors."

"Well, I am the rock on which the family is founded, and I'm hungry, Eden."

"The pan of mush is on the stove. There's a half bottle of milk in the icebox. There's some bread, and the dripping can on the stove is full of fat. Fry something up if you want."

"Horses eat oats and water. People deserve something better. Don't you think, Eden?" He softened the patriarchal tone: "People have to eat."

"What won't fatten will fill."

"Don't you get hungry?"

"Of course. Who doesn't?"

"I mean for real food. For home cooking."

"We have home cooking, Pa. It just depends on whose home, and who's cooking."

"Like your grandmother's ham and applesauce," Gideon mused, sitting across from her. "Turkey sometimes, too. Her stuffing. You remember, with the oranges and the almonds and the raisins. Like Afton's house. Afton's corn salad, her—"

"Those days are gone, Pa." The *Enterprise* stuck to a sticky spot on the oil-cloth. Eden tugged, and a bit of newsprint remained behind.

"They don't have to be."

"Oh, Pa. What do you want from me?"

"A little ambition. A little imagination."

"I have ambition. I have imagination, and that's why I don't stand at the stove and stuff other people's guts."

"It's not an ignoble undertaking, cooking. Just think of your grandmother. Think of the Pilgrim and what she achieved. Of course we can't bring back those who have gone to that country from whence no traveler returns, though we will all be reunited in the Celestial Kingdom." Gideon always spoke of death this way, as though quoting from a colorful brochure description of prime real estate. "But we don't have to wait for a land of milk and honey, do we? You come from a family of fine cooks."

"Really?" Eden nodded toward the bedroom partition. They could hear Kitty snoring.

"Is the tea still hot?"

Eden replied with an abstract *hmmm.* Gideon poured himself a cup of tea, and one for Eden. He laced them with milk from a bottle in the icebox and sat down across from his daughter. Eden folded up the *Enterprise* and readied herself for something akin to a scolding. Gideon always tiptoed into his scoldings by asking questions, by coaxing from the miscreant, be it a student or a daughter, answers that led to a sense of the error of their ways.

"The Douglass women are renowned for their good cooking."

"I thought that it was their get up and go," Eden said. "I want to get up and go and have a life not chained to the stove and the washer." If Ruth had sat opposite her, Ruth would have smiled, silently applauded, endorsed Eden's ringing statement. But Ruth was not there. Eden suddenly registered that chilling intimation of adulthood: the whispered insinuation, *It might not matter what you want at all.*

Gideon took off his glasses and cleaned them. "A girl like you, with all your talents! Why, I wouldn't be s'prised if you was a better cook even than your grandmother. Better than Afton."

"Oh, Pa." Flattery was working where the patriarchy failed.

Gideon reached into his pocket and drew out a ten-dollar bill, pushed it across the table to her. "Take the truck. Go into Fairwell and get us some provisions. Good ones. The best unto the finest. Do it up, just like Afton mighta done it. Make it," he put his glasses back on, "just like the old hymn, 'Now Let Us Rejoice'!"

To write down a recipe is to attempt the impossible: to revel in the pleasures of the season or the moment, and then to pick up the pen and preserve that moment for some other season. To write the words that will convey your skill to another hand, to reach across time into a new present when the cook herself has become the past. To create a small testament to both hunger and fulfillment. Eden bought provisions with the ten dollars Gideon gave her, but she couldn't think what to do with them. She wished she had asked Ruth to write down her successes. She wished Afton had written things down. And while she was at it, she wished Napoleon had written down his secrets. She salivated at the thought of his Figs Napoleon, but Fairwell, Idaho, was not the land of figs and honey. No, Eden was on her own, paddling around in the shallow shoals of memory and imagination.

She had a mound of peeled, sliced green apples and tossed them in a big saucepan with . . . what? Brown sugar. Yes. What else? She remembered the cinnamon stick because Ruth had always let her fish it out, suck on it once it cooled. Scent coiled up from the stove. Even if the proportions were not altogether correct, Eden told herself, the smell was almost the same. She fired up the oven, then poked the taters. She had learned some time ago, and the proverbial hard way, that if you do not poke your taters with a fork before you bake them, they will explode. Useful knowledge. Not splendid, but useful.

Fragrance from the kitchen slithered along the shafts between the roof and the room partitions, and presently Ernest came in, sniffing the air. He had incurious blue eyes and his mother's pink complexion and comely features. In early adolescence he had not yet grown into his hands and feet, which were huge. "What's in the oven, Eden?"

"Ham. Taters."

"Tangerine ham, like Grandma used to make? With all the little bright sticky stuff on it?"

"Yes. Well, maybe not tangerine. Not like Grandma's, exactly. But ham."

"Is that applesauce you're stirring?"

"It is."

"When do we eat? I'm hungry. Hungrier than I been in a long time."

She pointed at the sink, dishes, pots, pans afloat in greasy water.

"The dishes are dirty," said Ernest.

"Wash 'em. You got hands. You should have washed 'em yesterday."

"That's not men's work. I'm a man."

"Well, you're going to grow old a hungry man if you don't do those dishes. And do them right, too. No grease. Do them the way you're supposed to. Like Grandma taught me. Glassware first, dishes and silver next, greasy pots and pans last."

"We don't have any glassware."

"We have jam jars. Same thing." Eden returned her attention to the applesauce pan. "Now get to it, if you want to eat."

The old water gargled down the drain as Ernest began splashing around. He turned on the hot water tap, and the heater in the corner ignited noisily like a drunk roused from a dream of falling. Steam mixed with the smell from the stove and the oven as he sloshed the cups and dishes around and laid them on the drainboard. In the old kettle water could be heard boiling, bubbling away, as though sharing anticipation.

Ada came in next, making the same sniffing noises and the same inquiry. Ada was only two years Eden's junior, but they had never shared the giggling confidences of sisters. They were more like distant relatives with some common chromosomal thread. Where Eden had inherited and cultivated her grandmother's pride and conviction of her own worth—this mental finery aided and abetted by people who agreed that she was destined for great things—Ada was dim and sweet. Ada, like her father, was a devout Mormon. She had taken the good girl's oath in the church's Mutual Improvement Association for young people, vowing she would never kiss a boy unless they were engaged. Eden had scoffed at this. Eden had many times kissed the adoring Emjay Gates—and a great deal more, if the truth were told, which it did not need to be. She felt herself superior in this regard, too. A woman.

Ada asked what was in the oven and Eden retorted, "If you want to eat, you can set the table. You have to clean it off first. Wipe it down and don't just brush the crumbs on the floor. I want it done right. Sweep the floor, too." She knew she sounded like Afton Lance, but she couldn't help herself.

Her father came in, a sheaf of student essays in one hand and a pen in the other. His fingers were inky. "Oh, Eden, amen! The Lord looks well on a good meal." He took his place at the table while Ada worked around him, the brush of the broom softly counterpointing Ernest's banging of the pots.

"Well, Pa, I'm sorry but you can't eat yet. Your hands are dirty. You have to wash them. You have to put your papers away."

Gideon had a table in the living room that served as his desk. He left his papers there, then went to the little bathroom just off the kitchen, and emerged with clean, cold hands. He had splashed his stubbled jaw. Saturday was the only day he didn't shave. He returned to the kitchen and sat down at the patriarchal head of the small table. "I knew you could do this, Eden."

"You haven't tasted anything yet, Pa."

"But I have faith. I am a man of faith."

Kitty wandered in and leaned in the door frame, clutching her pale chenille robe. "I have never smelled anything so ambroysal." She had little flecks of sleep still in her eyes. A half-smoked Chesterfield was tucked behind her ear.

"Ambrosial, Ma," Eden corrected her, sounding just like Ruth. "The word is *ambrosial*."

"How true, ducky. When do we eat?"

Eden looked at the four of them, stolid Ernest, undemanding Ada, her poor, mismated parents. She felt the stirrings of maturity, in which a young person begins to see people as themselves, and not simply as they impinge on, thwart, or reward your own needs. Eden thought she might actually accomplish something here. Something beyond stuffing the family guts. Some kind of event or connection that might have significance beyond this Saturday evening in November, 1937. People need to eat. Well then, as Afton might have said, so be it. Eden spoke cheerfully but firmly: "You go wash up and put on a dress, Ma. Just like you used to do at the Pilgrim."

"I can eat without being dressed."

"Not today you can't, Ma. Not anymore. You got to put on some clothes. You got to get out of bed. You got to quit wallowing in a sink of iniquity." It was a stupid phrase, Eden thought, really more like something Kitty herself would repeat from a novel, or that Afton might repeat from a hymn.

"Sinks of iniquity! *La di dah!*" Kitty lifted her chin in an offended manner.

"Things are going to change, Ma. You're going to get dressed today. And tomorrow. And the day after that. Now, go put on a dress. One of your pretty frocks. Like you used to wear when you worked at the Pilgrim."

"Stockings, too? I always wore silk stockings, you know. The garters used to drive your pa into a state of sexchual frenzy." Then she added in a low voice, "Do you wear garters when you and Emjay go out on Saturday night, Eden? Have you bestowed on him the Final Favor?"

Eden hushed her instantly. "Go brush your hair, Ma. Wash your face and then you can come have dinner."

"Oh my! I gets to join the Elect? How very kind, your ladyship."

"If you wallow, you get cold mush, Ma. But there's ham for the rest of us. Look, Ada's set the table all nice. And there'll be ham for sandwiches tomorrow. And ham to have with eggs and taters tomorrow for breakfast. Resurrection Pie after that."

"Resurrection Pie was always my favorite," said Ernest. "I miss it."

Kitty looked at her son as though seeing him for the first time in years, noticed with some pleasure that he had her fair coloring, her blue eyes. "You do, ducky? Really?"

"We all do, Ma," said Ernest solemnly. "You could make it again. You should."

"Yours was best, Ma," said Eden. "It could be again."

"Go on, dear," said Gideon. "Get yourself prettied up. Lovely as you always were. Are. We'll wait."

Kitty smiled and said she would be right back.

"Ada," Eden said to her sister, "you go comb your hair, too. And, Ernest, you need to take off that dirty shirt. Put on a clean shirt."

"I save my clean shirt for Sunday."

"Well, if you want to eat on Saturday, you had better put it on."

"I can't wipe my mouth with my sleeve on my Sunday shirt."

"My point exactly," Eden retorted, startled to hear what she knew was her own adult voice.

"You are the image of your grandmother," her father said. "And Afton herself couldn't have done no better."

"Thanks, Pa."

Ernest returned in his Sunday shirt. Ada's straight hair was neatly parted and combed, and she had rubbed the dust from her shoes. Ada took her place and sat on her hands. The oilcloth was clean and dry. The tin plates were clean, tin spoons and forks beside each. They had to share the two knives. There were salt and pepper in the little tin shakers, and sugar in the small bowl, new sugar, no crumbs or specks in it. A slab of fresh yellow butter, not white margarine, on a saucer. There was a pot of hot tea, and milk in a little cream pitcher, and a communal scrap of flannel for a napkin.

When Kitty came back, her hennaed hair slicked down, though still awry, she was brushing off her skirt. She wore shoes and stockings. Everyone said how lovely she looked. Gideon said he could not remember such a delight to the eye as the way she looked now. Kitty flushed and focused.

"For this meal," Gideon said, "I'd like to give thanks. To say grace." He waited, perhaps for some riposte from Kitty, but she bowed her head. "O God, the Eternal Father," Gideon began.

Eden peeked between her fingers as he droned on. In all the years that followed, when she wanted to think of the best moment her family had ever had together, or ever would, Eden would remember this meal. We are linked, Eden thought, and I am part of them, fond of them. Perhaps not proud of them, but pleased. And happy that I have created something that made them happy. It was an evanescent moment, she knew that, perishable and perishing even as they lived it. It could not be preserved.

Eden rose and put the applesauce pan on the table, taking the lid off so as to let the fragrance tease and please while she fished out the stick of cinnamon with a fork. She handed it to Ernest like a trophy. Then she took the potatoes out of the oven and gave one to each. She plucked the biscuits off the sheet; they were so hard, they rang when she put them on the tin plate. Never mind, they were hot. She covered them up with a small towel. With another towel, Eden withdrew from the oven her replica of her grandmother's Christmas pie. It smelled divine and received a round of genuine applause, though the top crust looked rather thick and a little rugged. Lastly, Eden brought the ham out of the oven, just like she'd seen Ruth do. The ham wore a jacket of brown sugar with a few cloves for buttons. Quartered oranges and onions rolled golden, in the amber drippings gleaming in the bottom of the pan. Her family let out a collective sigh of anticipation, admiration as Eden picked up the knife, and slid it down through the fat jacket and the clove buttons. A pale pink slice curved away.

"Now, look at that, duck," said Kitty. "That is a beautiful ham."

# Christmas Pie (Cranberry Apricot Pie)

*A Holiday Specialty of the House, Café Eden*

Chop coarsely about 2½ cups of dried apricots. Put them in a big bowl and splash with good brandy, perhaps ¼ cup. Mix. Let them rest for a while. Half hour anyway.

To this big bowl add about 3½ cups of cranberries that you have just washed and drained. (They can be slightly damp.) Your cranberries must not be pale and wan. They need to be fresh and bright. The jewellike colors are one of the pleasures of this pie.

Add to this 1 cup of brown sugar. Stir till well moistened. Leave, returning now and then to mix well. When the sugar has dissolved, add 2 tablespoons of boxed tapioca. Mix well. The tapioca keeps the pie firm.

Put your pastry down in the pie plate and pour this mixture into it. Take 1 tablespoon cold butter and cut it up. Dab over the fruit. Cover your pie with the top crust and cut a couple of slits in it. Bake at 450 for 15 minutes. Reduce heat to 350 and bake for 30 to 35 minutes. Cool slightly before serving. Can be served warm or cold with whipped cream or without.

The apricots remain chewy and the cranberries will burst with a little surprise in your mouth.

A FAREWELL IN FAIRWELL

In November 1951, Gideon Douglass died in the shadow of the mountains.

Eden returned to Idaho in the company of her brother, Ernest, and his wife, Annie. Eden's grief was tinged with guilt, and tainted with regret. For years Gideon had written her letters, written to Ernest, too, hoping that they would again find their faith and return to the Church.

So now they left Los Angeles and returned to Fairwell, but not to the Church. Eden, Ernest, and Annie had taken an airplane from Los Angeles, changing planes three times, bumpy, noisy, wretched rides, all of them. Landing at the Spokane airfield was not the end of the journey. They stayed overnight in a Spokane hotel and took the train early the next morning. Only the morning train stopped in Fairwell. In the town's silver heyday, trains stopped there three times a day for ore. Hard to believe, Eden thought, that that railroads had blasted once through mountains, so eager were they for Fairwell's silver. The only people who alighted at the Fairwell station with the Douglasses were a few hunters and a handful of commercial travelers.

Brother Thorsen was there to meet them. Margaret had sent him, figuring they would certainly come, if not that day, then the next. Brother Thorsen had sad news: They were too late. Gideon had died the day before. Pneumonia. Ada and her husband, Melvin, had been with him. Kitty was too distraught. Brother Thorsen directed them to his 1948 Dodge. He said Kitty was not taking it well.

Fairwell had not prospered in the years since Eden and Ernest had last seen it. Annie Douglass had never seen it. To Annie, Fairwell was as strange as Neptune. In Brother Thorsen's Dodge they passed the cemetery, the church and courthouse, the school. Silver Street was checkered with boarded-up storefronts, all in the shadow of the still defunct mines. The *Enterprise* office was shuttered, and no other newspaper took its place. The Bucks's Head Hotel still stood. The Dodge climbed the unpaved road, up the hill to the lonely squalor of their old neighborhood. Gaunt dogs, roaming free, barked as they passed.

Near the Douglass home there were many cars and trucks haphazardly parked. The windows, dewy with perspiration, blared with light. Brother Thorsen remarked that Fairwell's Saints had turned out for Gideon Douglass. He again offered his condolences, and they thanked him.

Stepping out of the car, Eden took a deep breath of cold mountain air before plunging into the old family stew bobbing with religion, remorse, bubbling with obligation and evasion.

Ada and Melvin Brewster greeted the trio from Los Angeles with some reserve. They had never met Annie. Ada and Melvin both wore glasses, and they held their mouths pursed in exactly the same expression, giving them more the look of brother and sister, rather than husband and wife. Perhaps six children, and one on the way, and a decade sorting mail in the post office did that to you. Ada looked like Ernest with the stuffing kicked out, depleted rather than distraught. She had Kitty's pale skin and round face.

Kitty sat on the quilt-covered couch, clutching her cardigan with one hand and with the other tapping her lips, like someone struggling with a logarithm. She stared at the blank television. It had displaced the radio in the place of honor where it sat like a squat, one-eyed god. On top of it, on a doily stiff with dust, was a rabbit-ear antenna and a peacock feather in a Coke bottle. How like Kitty, Eden thought, to have somehow found a peacock feather in Fairwell.

Kitty looked surprised but not delighted that Eden, Ernest, and Annie had come. She smelled of Evening in Paris and Chesterfields.

Kitty whispered to Eden, I been a selfish brute, duck. But I'm going to change, and everything will be different and new. And don't you listen to Melvin. There's been a mistake, duck. Pa's not that sick.

Then Kitty returned her gaze on the door as though surely Gideon would come through it at last, these people would leave, the emergency would be over, and she and Gideon could go back to the old unsatisfying marriage that had sustained and vexed them both for nearly forty years.

The Saints asked questions of Eden, Annie, and Ernest, shocked to hear that Annie had her own business, that she catered meals at movie locations in the San Fernando Valley. Their disapproval registered, audible, visible, tangible. Then Ernest remarked that he owned a TV repair shop, and they crowded nearer to him, describing their TVs' various symptoms. Eden felt woozy, sticky with perspiration in a house that had never been warm.

A woman with a calm face and red-rimmed eyes brought out Kitty's old chipped-spout teapot and a clean cup and saucer. Melvin Brewster reprimanded her for encouraging Kitty to break the Word of Wisdom.

The woman replied quietly, Sister Douglass deserves her small comforts. It's not every day you lose a man like Gideon Douglass.

Eden suddenly recognized Margaret Thorsen, much aged, thin graying hair, her skin dry, pale, and crinkled with time. Her blue eyes were still large and clear. Eden spontaneously hugged her.

Your pa was always real proud of you, Eden, said Margaret. When you joined the WACs, he said you was defending your country and he wouldn't hear no word spoken against you or any WAC. When you was graduated from wherever it was, someplace in California, where was it?

UCLA, said Eden. Just last year.

He said you would be the one to make something of yourself. You work in a bank now, isn't that right?

Yes. Columbia First National in Los Angeles.

Do you do foreclosures?

No, Eden lied.

Are you married? asked a nearby matron.

No.

Sister Thorsen took Eden's arm and steered her into the kitchen before whispers of *She's an old maid!* could circuit through the crowd. She asked if Eden would like a cup of tea.

Eden would have preferred a stiff shot of brandy, but she agreed to the tea. The kitchen was crowded with Relief Society ladies. The small table by the window sagged under the weight of the Saints' generosity, piled with baked goods, small shapely loaves, pies, stout casserole dishes, and canned goods gleaming in Mason jars, carrots, beets, and squash. Odors utterly foreign to this house roiled through the kitchen: bread and cake, and pot roast baking, dueled with the strong smell of ammonia and vinegar. A squealing sound pealed out as a woman cleaned the window with vinegar and a wet newspaper.

Sister Thorsen, leading Eden, sailed through the gathering, out the back door. She and Eden stood shivering under the single bulb on the unheated back porch. The old wringer washing machine eavesdropped on their short conversation.

Your father was a good man, Sister Thorsen said, dabbing her eyes. A great man. Kitty don't know, never did know what she had in Gideon, never valued him. But I must tell you the truth, Eden: Gideon's sights were not on this world. He has left your poor mother penniless. I mean that.

I send them money every month, said Eden, ever since I got the job at the bank. Ernest and Annie send money, too.

There may be a pittance in the bank. I don't know, but it don't matter. Kitty's never so much as signed a check. She don't know how. Gideon did all that. Gideon . . . well, he left off paying the pension fund a while ago. There's no pension for Kitty, not even the widow's mite. The Saints and the school board are collecting money for the funeral. Enough to bury him.

There's no insurance?

He did not believe in paying against mortality, the certain fate of all. There's nothing.

You mean Ma is destitute?

Margaret Thorsen's blue eyes clouded and she frowned.

You mean there's nothing? No money at all?

That's what I said. I don't have a lot of time to talk. No one should know that I told you. No one knows that I know. But I want you to know, for a sure fact, that it troubled Gideon, at the end, that he hadn't provided for your mother.

Eden looked out the dirty window. She thought of her father's bungling away everything her grandmother had worked for. She thought of his grand ambitions to reconcile history, the Bible, and the Restored Gospel, his conscientious charting of the generations, his dedication to the past and indifference to the present. His love for the past had encroached on all their lives. He had failed at life, in Eden's estimation. Not in life, perhaps, but certainly at it. And then as wind rattled the panes of the curtainless window and snaked through the ill-fitting doorjamb, Eden feared for herself. I am thirty-one, she thought. Can it be that I might fail at living, though I will surely not fail to die?

I brung you out here to tell you a simple truth, Eden. I know it would be Gideon's wish, too. Do not leave your mother here in Fairwell. I do not admire Kitty, I am pained to say, but no one oughta be left to the mercies of Ada and Melvin Brewster. Melvin has only harsh words for Kitty. He sees none of her good points, her little charms. He has a cruel streak. Ada won't fight him. Do not leave Kitty here. Your father wouldn't have wanted her beat down. You have to take your mother back to California with you. You understand?

We can't take her to California! She'd have to live with one of us. With

Ernest and Annie, Eden added, grateful that they had a big house in the San Fernando Valley, and she had only a small apartment just off Venice Boulevard.

Kitty will be left to someone's mercies, Eden. You just see to it that it ain't Melvin Brewster's. You leave her here, they will destroy her. She don't deserve that. I'm telling you this in a confidence. You understand?

Yes.

Good. Now just remember you didn't hear this from me.

Yes.

Eden followed Margaret back into the kitchen, then she ducked into the cold bathroom, pulled on the string for the lightbulb overhead, and stared into the tiny mirror. Her face. The Douglass face. All that genealogy accosted her.

Was Afton right? she wondered. Is life like a recipe? Do you start with what's on hand—your father's studious cast of mind, your mother's capacity for delusion, your grandmother's energy, the family impulse for lies recast as diplomacy—and adapt all that to what history hands you? All those ingredients, are they stirred over time, chopped, slopped, boiled, simmered, frothed with circumstances, and then somehow shaped and formed into something that is recognizably your own life? What is a recipe, after all, but a license for invention? For making judgments based on taste, imagination, and impulse? What's at hand to be shaped into what is wanted.

A small boy banged on the bathroom door, announcing he'd do it in his pants if she didn't get out of there. Eden laughed. Then she remembered the occasion.

In the kitchen, Margaret Thorsen handed Eden a plate heaped with pot roast and potatoes in gravy. She said, Do not forget what I told you. Do not forget him, I beg you.

Just then Brother Thorsen came through the kitchen door. He looked at his wife, suddenly perplexed. He looked at Eden.

I won't forget, said Eden.

Brother Thorsen frowned. Forget what?

Their backs to every Babylon—said Eden—their eyes on a new Zion.

# PART THREE

# Tarte Tatin

1943

## CHAPTER ONE

THE *QUEEN MARY,* THAT LUXURY FLAGSHIP, HAD
given up her glamour for dull, gray-green camouflage, a
wartime sacrifice. As New York harbor fell behind the
horizon, the ship moved slowly out into steely seas, braving
German submarines taking troops to the European Theater of Operations. Cabins that might once have rung with
crystal decanters and the voices of sophisticated ladies had
been converted; tiers of military bunks, three or four of
them on either side, lined the walls. Eight WACs were billeted in the tiny space, along with all their gear and duffel
bags stowed in, under, and on top of every possible bit of
space. Corporal Eden Douglass found herself in the
middle bunk, looking up the bulge of Dottie Lofgren's bottom in the bunk above. The ship began to pitch and heave
and roll. So did her stomach. Overhead, Dottie groaned,
and nearby another WAC moaned. Faye Cole retched.
Eden got off her bunk and clambered for the door. She refused to be seasick, but there were limits of endurance.

She could not go very far. They were only forty
WACs on a ship carrying thousands of GIs, the women

very much confined, kept separate from the men. Eden moved swiftly down the narrow hall, similar sounds of retching and distress coming from the other cabins. Once on deck, cold air whipped her face and the wind blew right through her olive-drab uniform, nipping right through the wool, all the way down to her khaki-colored underwear.

She was making the journey her mother had made more than thirty years before, only in reverse. Eden was on her way to England, a WAC in the United States Army, part of a whole generation on the move. Eden's generation, uprooted, would never be the same. They were pulled, the men and women, from the old comforts and routines and cast into circumstances they could not have imagined. Some were sent to Operation Overlord, the Allied invasion of Europe, against the Nazis, some into the Pacific against the Japanese, their lives forever altered. Some would never come back. Some would never recover. Some would never discuss. Everyone had to do their part, but the young were called upon to do more. The gray Atlantic and the war lay before Eden, the only certainties.

An urgent voice came over the speakers ordering everyone on the *Queen Mary* back to their bunks and officers to the captain's quarters. A German sub had been detected nearby. Immediately, the engines were shut down. Radios were turned off. All activity was to cease immediately. Not so much as a cup could drop, or a toilet flush, or an oath be uttered, not so much as a cough or a sneeze till the all clear was given. Eden returned to the crowded stateroom where even the groans had ceased. She lay in her bunk, for hours, hearing nothing but her own heartbeat, realizing for the first time that her training had been preparing her for the possibility of death. Well, she thought, at least I am free of the switchboard.

CHICAGO PARK HOTEL, HOW MAY WE HELP YOU?

That was the phrase Eden Douglass had said a thousand times a day. Certainly it felt like a thousand times a day, as she sat at the hotel PBX switchboard, wearing a headset. The Chicago Park was a fine hotel, though the PBX operators worked in a drafty back room; their supervisor, a Mr. Lenski, seemed to sweat the smell of salami.

The Chicago Park was not what Eden had dreamed of. She had come to Chicago with high hopes that, despite her best efforts, had gone unfulfilled. Or maybe they weren't her best efforts. Maybe she simply didn't know where to put her time and effort and energy. If life was indeed like a recipe—a license for invention, what's on hand shaped into what's wanted—Eden wanted badly to invent something new. She had neither fulfilled her dream of writing for a newspaper nor fallen in love. The men she met and dated were nice enough, but no one stirred her. Not as she wanted to be stirred, "Body and Soul," just like the song.

To Eden the post–Pearl Harbor burst of patriotism seemed like a personal as well as a national alarm. Time to shake out of the old and unsatisfactory *Chicago Park Hotel, how may we help you?* and take steps in a new direction. She was more restless than ever at the PBX, but not until she read in the newspaper of the creation of the Women's Army Auxiliary Corps did she know what she would actually do. The WAACs called for volunteers. The WAACs offered training and travel, a chance for adventure and to take part in some significant experience beyond *Chicago Park Hotel, how may we help you?*

At the end of her shift, one autumn evening, Eden took off her headset and her name tag. She swiveled in her chair and jumped off. "I'm leaving, Lenski," she said to the day manager. She lifted her coat from a hook. "I'm going to see my folks in Idaho for Christmas, and then I'm joining the Women's Army Aux-iliary Corps."

Mr. Lenski made a rude remark about women's auxiliary positions in the army, on their backs, legs apart. Then he added, "You need to give notice."

"Not if I don't want the job back. So long."

Lenski laughed. "You'll be back, begging me for a job."

"Tell it to the Marines," Eden retorted with the attitude she had learned from her three roommates, also PBX operators, with whom she shared two rooms and a kitchenette. The four shared the bathroom with the whole second floor of the old house they lived in, now carved into rentals. Eden's roommates were tough, energetic girls who had good health, but bad prospects on the prairies of Nebraska and in steel towns like Gary, Indiana. They came to Chicago for the urban adventures, the chance to evade what fate would other-wise assign them.

These were the very reasons why Eden had come to Chicago. Eden Doug-lass had bolted Fairwell mere weeks before she was to be married to Emjay Gates, the young man on whom she had bestowed the Final Favor. In the back-seat of his father's car, Emjay Gates had assured Eden (his breath, his tongue hot on her nipple) that this was not sin, that it was all right if they got married.

It was all right, but it wasn't great. The pressures to marry Emjay were in-exorable, slow, but final as some geologic process that would root her there in Fairwell, unmoving as the mountains whose veins were drained of silver. She had before her the example of her sister, Ada, knocked up, married swiftly to

Melvin Brewster, mother to a mewling baby. Surely some larger life was possible.

Obliquely, Ruth Douglass confirmed Eden's conviction. Ruth did so, almost literally, with her dying breath. She died in 1940 while living with Tom and Afton in St. Elmo. Her will stipulated that her entire estate, still valued at one thousand dollars, was left to Eden Louise, not a penny for anyone else—not even Afton, who had cared for her for so many years. This money whispered to Eden in Ruth's own voice, *Take this money and the train out of Fairwell, and test yourself, if you don't want to be or become Eden Louise REGRET.*

Eden heeded this voice, packed, left a note for her parents, and one night took the train out of Fairwell. The next one was going east to Chicago. She rented a bed at the YWCA and applied for work she wanted to do. However, her experience, society editor of the Fairwell *Enterprise,* did not amount to sterling credentials in Chicago. The great daily papers were not looking for the next Helen Kirkpatrick or Dorothy Thompson. They were not looking to hire women at all.

She took a job briefly slinging hash, but she hated being at the beck and call of any guy with a three-cent tip. Another girl staying at the YWCA heard the Chicago Park Hotel was hiring if you could operate a PBX switchboard. Eden could not, but she lied to Mr. Lenski. Moreover, she lied using Kitty's music hall accent, along with a completely false story about being from an English theatrical family whose tour had been canceled in Manitoba. Ah, audience expectation! To Mr. Lenski's Chicago ear, any English accent sounded classy. As soon as she actually learned to operate the PBX, Eden dropped the exaggerated accent.

Putting Chicago behind her forever, Eden packed her few things and took the train west to Fairwell in December 1943. She sat by the window and watched the vast snowy plains, imagining the train tracks like perfect black stitching across the white landscape. As the elevations rose, and the engine pulled them up through the mountains, into the west, Eden's spirits unaccountably rose as well.

"Oh, duck!" cried Kitty when Eden stepped off the train at the Fairwell station. "You do just look too fashionable for words!"

"Behold," said Gideon, embracing his daughter, "the Return of the Prodigal!"

He waxed eloquent invoking the Prodigal as they returned to the house with partitions instead of walls. Ada and Melvin were there with their two little children and the baby. Ada had set the table for the family reunion, and brought the meat loaf and creamed beans. At dinner Eden took the moment to announce that after Christmas, she planned to join the WAACs. Kitty and Gideon didn't even know what the WAACs were, but Melvin Brewster did.

"Women can't be soldiers."

"That's not true," said Eden. "WAACs train just like men. Women everywhere are taking up jobs they never did before. There's a war on, in case you hadn't noticed. Ernest joined the navy right after Pearl Harbor," she added. "I'm joining up. What about you, Melvin? What are you doing for the war effort?"

"Melvin's a father," said Ada as the baby set up a cry.

"Women can't be soldiers. They can only be the whores of soldiers."

"Melvin!" cried Ada.

Gideon frowned deeply, but Kitty giggled.

"What's a whore?" asked Ada's eldest, a boy of about five.

Melvin rose and told his wife to gather up the children, and though Gideon tried to mollify him, he would hear none of it. To his wife's tearful dismay, Melvin declared that the Brewsters would not sit down with sinners, never mind the war. They would not return to this house till Eden had left.

"Well, *la di dah,*" said Kitty. "I been waiting for years for him to say he won't come back. Now, duck, Eden, don't fret over Melvin. Look at it this way, more dessert for us."

"And what's for dessert, Ma? Hummingbird Delight?"

"Oh, don't I just wish, Eden! We don't have no food of the gods. Sister Thorsen brought by some of her Sourdough Gingerbread. She said she knows you fancy it. So do I. But alas, lookie here, will you? Someone has already cut into and had a piece. Tut-tut. Sinners indeed."

Eden slept in the room she had once shared with Ada, only now her father had moved his desk there. Long charts, genealogical tables were pinned to the walls and rustled in the night like ghosts. There were books on low shelves and a desk, kept painfully neat. Above it illustrations of the Handcart Brigade had been cut from a church magazine and framed. A gift, he told her, from Sister Thorsen.

The day after her arrival, Eden took off her nice clothes, tied a bandana around her head, picked up the broom, the brush, and carpet beater, and went to work: rescuing the dirty laundry from where it fell, washing, bleaching, starching, and ironing everything within an inch of its life. The smell of starch and Condy's Disinfectant reminded her of Afton, to whom she wrote with her plans to join the WAACs.

*December 1943*

*Eden, dear*

How good it is to have your letter in hand, to know you are well and happy and how blessed are your dear parents to have you home this Christmas. My pride in you, in your [several spellings crossed out] choice to serve your country knows only the bounds of Christian humility. You will join the ranks of our family that have served when called. Let people say what they will of the WAACs, Tom and I suport you, just as we suport all our soldiers. Samuel is in the Pacific on a destroyer. Junior with the army in Europe. Some have served and called and paid the highest price, Eden. Our Lucius died this year. August 10th at Guadalcanal in the service of his country and his God.

I know you will marvel that I am so long in sending you this sad news, but, Eden, my heart was [scribbled out] broke to be to writing these words. Even now, as you can see, my hand yet trembles with the pen. I tried to write you. I honest did try. I would of writen to Gideon, but each time I put those words to paper I feel our loss afresh. Bessie and Alma offered to do the sad duty, and write, but my dear Tom told them, no, no girls, Mother must do this when she is able and not before. They don't make them like Tom Lance anymore. They threw out the mold after that man.

But you see here, now at last, these months later, I can write. My hand may tremble, my heart breaketh, but the Lord hath returned to me some strength.

Lucius died a hero's death. He left two little sons, Micah and Jonah who are my delight, who the Lord hath given to me in place of my own dear son. They live here with us. Lucius's worthless wife, that Ellianne took up with another man not six weeks after Lucius Lance fell. She wanted to marry this man, if reason don't strike you dead at the thought of it, leastways she wanted to run off with him. Her and him didn't want no little boys underfoot for what no good things they had in mind.

But I shall not dwell upon the retched. No. Mine eyes look afresh and afar to victory and peace and the return of all of you. I will not dwell upon my losses, but rejoice in the Lord, knowing that the Celestial Kingdom now has Lucius and in the knowledge that we will all one day be reunited.

My dear girl, you give our love to Gideon, to Kitty too if she'll have it.

My prayers will follow you always Eden.

*I am your loving aunt,*

*Afton Lance*

For Christmas dinner Eden used her parents' ration cards to buy a chicken. She tried to re-create her grandmother's famous stuffing, bread, almonds, oranges, raisins, but memory and imagination were thwarted by scarcity. What she came up with was not the same, but gratifying, and her parents were lavish in their praise. It was a fine, snowy Idaho Christmas. Kitty, warmed by brandy that Eden had brought from Chicago, waxed on about the wonderful Christmases of her Liverpool youth, great joints of meat, flaming plum puddings, all steamy and warm with currants, and oh! the surprise of finding one of the little silver charms baked inside. Eden's Christmas pie was very close to those remembered splendors, but no silver charms, alas. Still, Kitty wanted another piece. Gideon listened as though he had not heard these stories every Christmas for thirty years. Her father's good nature, Eden thought, was a gift in itself.

THE WAAC RECRUITER IN DOWNTOWN SPOKANE, WASHINGTON, WAS A middle-aged civilian with a weak chin. He played with his pencil in an annoying fashion, turning it end to end while he regarded the forms and Eden Louise Douglass appraisingly. He evaluated her height, five feet nine, her weight, 130 pounds, broad shoulders, narrow waist, firm breasts, good hips and strong long legs, dark hair, green eyes. He asked her to smile. Good teeth. "It says here you are a high school graduate."

"Yes."

"It says here you can type a hundred words a minute. Is that true?"

It wasn't, but she said yes. She could do ninety. "I've been typing since I was twelve."

"And shorthand, too."

"Yes." She had taken a night school shorthand class in Chicago, thinking it would be useful for the reporter she intended to be. "I have press experience. I worked for years for a newspaper. I'd like to be in the press corps."

"How fast can you take shorthand?"

"As fast as you can talk."

He nodded gravely. "You can operate a PBX switchboard? A hotel switchboard."

"Not well," she lied, unwilling to be answering the phone for the army or anyone else. Her PBX days gave Eden an aversion to the telephone that lasted her whole life.

"Can you cook?"

"No.

He frowned and asked, "Can you drive?"

"I can grind the gears of any old truck and move it up a mountain road. I've been driving since I was twelve."

"You've been doing a lot of things since you were twelve." He kept his pencil moving end to end, his stubby fingers sliding down it. "Why do you wish to join the Women's Army Auxiliary Corps?"

"Serve my country. See the world."

He smiled. "Welcome to the war, Private Douglass."

# Ruth Douglass's California Stuffing for Turkey

Spread your raw almonds in a single layer on a cookie sheet. Place in the center rack of your oven and toast at about 300 for twenty minutes, turning frequently with a spatula. Allow to cool before using or placing in an airtight container in fridge. They will make little noises as they cool.

Slice thin 2 medium or 1 big onion. Melt 4 tablespoons of butter and brown your onions till soft and golden.

Meanwhile, over a big bowl tear up your stale bread into small pieces. When the onions are done, add them to the bread. Then add and mix well after each addition at least a cup of toasted almonds, 1 big can (juice and all) of pineapple chunks. Have a couple of firm fresh oranges and scrape the skin against a cheese grater into the stuffing. Then take the orange slices, cut in half, de-seed, and put them in the mixture. You can use canned mandarin oranges if you must. Kumquats are very nice and colorful if you can find them. Add 1 cup or several good-sized handfuls of raisins.

To this add some salt and pepper and chopped parsley. Should you need more liquid (your butter will come from the onions and some juice from the pineapple), use fruit juice or dry vermouth.

Stuff your turkey and roast as usual, basting frequently with butter and a bit of oil till you have pan juices to baste with. This recipe can, of course, be altered to mood, or to what you have in the house. It's the texture of the almonds, the tang of the fruit, and the softened sweet raisins, that make it especially memorable. For Eden, her children and their children, this was the taste of Christmas, Thanksgiving, a scent that breached time.

### THE SOLDIER

In the army Eden Douglass learned skills that would serve her all her life: to be organized, efficient, resourceful, and responsible, to pack her entire life, including Kotex, winter and summer uniforms and shoes into a single duffel bag. She learned to take the measure of men, especially those who thought a woman would be a sap for any compliment. She learned stand up for herself, for what she wanted—or didn't want. She learned to ignore the sneers, cat-calls that the sight of a woman in uniform often elicited. She learned to march, to carry herself with military bearing. But she never did learn to smoke.

Basic training at Fort Des Moines, Iowa, found Eden, and a hundred others, marching, moving, sleeping when she could, sweating, swearing, peeing in some privacy when she was fortunate, and showering in lukewarm water every morning, and stuffing her mouth with greasy food that tasted like fuel. She slept in a double-deck bunk in barracks and woke at 5:45 to a bugle.

By day she marched in ice, snow, rain, mud, and slush; she took her turn at KP and survived minute inspections. At night she and other inductees watched endless replays, newsreel clips of Pearl Harbor, Guadalcanal, and the Blitz, German bombs falling on British cities, night after night, bombs and firebombs and sirens, and people waking in the morning to find whole neighborhoods charred rubble. They watched propaganda films prohibiting idle talk that could cost lives, and films instilling the fear of VD, extolling the condom.

Fourteen weeks later, in uniform, Eden marched with her unit while an army band played "Stars and Stripes Forever." She was part of a corps, pro-moted to corporal. In June 1943 the Women's Army Auxiliary Corps became the Women's Army Corps. No more "auxiliary." The name change required that they reenlist, and Eden was among the first. Offered the chance to volun-teer for an overseas assignment, she did that, too.

Eden, Dottie Lofgren, and Faye Cole, two friends from her basic train-ing group, were assigned to a school for army administration that was set up at the Denton State Teacher's College in Texas. These accommodations were luxurious: The young soldiers lived only two or three to a dorm room, and they ate in the college cafeteria, no army chow, no KP.

The college library at Denton allowed the WACs to check out books. Eden was a frequent customer. The wizened librarian always saluted Eden The librarian said that after the war, Eden should return, study, and get her degree.

But After the War was too far away to think about.

## CHAPTER TWO

*Dear Ma,*

Ma, I am having tea at the Ritz in London, and of course I am
thinking of you.

There is an old couple not three tables away, the man is
wearing a tweed coat, a little threadbare, but still nice
material, and his wife, a faded beauty, has a voile dress, blue,
with silk violets at the shoulder. Maybe they are Victorine and
the Duke now that they are older.

The waiters are all in starched black and white, very polite,
even nicer than the old Pilgrim. Clean white tablecloths, and
vases on each table with a single flower. All around the room
there are palm trees in pots, and even a small orchestra playing
the kinds of songs Miss McBrean always favored. In fact, they
just finished up "Humoresque," just like she taught me.

There's uniformed Aussies and Canadians here, and
probably some Poles, or at least other lingos I can't make out.
Even so, Ma, here at the Ritz, you could still pretend there is
no war. No buzz bombs, no cities in ruins, no rationing.
Especially you, Ma. You can pretend anything.

Please tell Pa I am writing this V-mail note with the pen
he gave me for Christmas.

What can I tell you that the censors won't black out? My life here is full of surprises. I am working long hours and the food is terrible. I probably shouldn't complain, but all their cooking is boiled, tasteless, and soggy. They serve a gray kidney stew with gray bread and white margarine and tin pitchers of tea made the night before. You can taste the tin. They put canned milk in it and you can tasted the tin there too. But the sweets are good. And, I have my friends, Dottie and Faye, so I guess it's like you always say, Ma, I'm just as happy as if I had sense.

"Miss Dole?"

Eden looked up from her small sheets of paper to see an American lieutenant. His shoulders were wet and he gave off a damp-wool smell. The military hat in his hand dripped.

"Sorry," he said, seeing that his hat had dripped on the rug. "It's raining like mad."

"It's always raining like mad." Faye Cole had arranged this outing, tea at the Ritz, with her latest flame, Frank Willing. She brought Eden only because Frank had said he would have a friend with him. "Are you Lieutenant Willing?"

His features eased into a smile. "No. I'm Logan Smith."

"Well then, we're even. I'm not Miss Dole, either. You got her name wrong. She's Faye Cole. I'm Eden Douglass."

"Eden. What a beautiful name." He seemed momentarily to bask in her name, as if it were a place that afforded him respite. He smiled and nodded toward the small orchestra framed by potted palms. "Debussy. They play very well. Too bad it's not something more upbeat."

He had a deep, measured voice, light brown hair, and fair skin with faded freckles. His face was well planed, with half-hooded blue eyes behind his glasses, animated by intelligence, but his manner was reserved and not at all pushy, openly hostile, or brash, as were so many of the men she'd met since she had joined the WACs. She could not imagine these men in their own towns or cities. Under the duress of war, they had been homogenized into fighting units, everyone uprooted and thrust together, crowding into England, whose resources were already taxed and whose women had been a long time alone. The English said that the trouble with Yanks was that they were overpaid, oversexed, and over here. Yanks retorted that the trouble with the English was that they were underpaid, undersexed, and under Eisenhower.

"Do you like music?" she asked.

"I do. My mother's very musical."

"My mother's musical, too." Though probably not like yours, she thought privately.

"Are we supposed to meet here, do you think?"

Eden could not help smiling. "I think we are supposed to meet. I think that Faye has set this up."

"Frank will be along directly. He's making a phone call. What do they say here? He's ringing someone up."

She sought some polite way of saying that Faye was in the toilet. "Well, why don't you sit down and wait?"

She wasn't going to call him Lieutenant Smith, and he certainly wasn't going to call her Corporal Douglass. Though there was an official ruling against enlisted WACs dating officers, it was not enforced. WACs had their pick of men, from GIs to generals: dates every night if they wanted them, mostly with men who wanted to drink and grapple, or vice versa. Oddly, Eden found herself following the old Mormon precept of safety in numbers. Lots of people meant less groping.

She was serving with the Eighth Army Air Force HQ on the grounds of an old estate, a manor near the small village of Bushey, Hertfordshire. The WACs called it the Castle, though it was not one. The house dated from the eighteenth century, a sprawling manor that had once been the hub of vast acreage, a farm, and tenants. With the British men gone to fight, their women worked the farm. The WACs and American GIs were housed in hastily built barracks on opposite sides of the manor grounds. The male officers were billeted in the grand old house itself.

Still, to the WACs, it was the Castle, and it had an endless supply of bicycles and an endless supply of men for pub outings and parties. Eden Douglass had never danced so much in all her life. In pubs, well-meaning locals, mostly old people, taught Eden and her friends to shoot darts, to drink beer. Dottie taught her how to ride a bike. The old groundskeeper, Arthur Jobson, taught her how to drive a motorcycle. He declared Eden was a natural on a motorcycle, though the lessons were cut short by petrol rationing. But for the bicycle, Eden and her friends needed only their own bodies and high spirits. As they wheeled through narrow twisting lanes, the landscape—tiny and tidy and picketed—seemed to Eden oddly disorienting, a tremendously foreshortened perspective for a girl from Idaho and California whose American experience included Chicago, Iowa, and Texas.

Bushey was only some twenty miles north of London, and the underground station was within cycling distance of the barracks. Whenever possible, Eden took the underground into the city, sometimes with Dottie and Faye, or a couple of GIs. She had more social life than she knew what to do with. She also had more responsibility.

Each night Eden fell into bed, exhausted, then alert at 5 A.M. The skills she had thought to use in working for a newspaper, typing and shorthand, were very much valued as secretary to Colonel Bancroft, known in the WAC barracks as Colonel Bedcrotch. Bedcrotch was a man in his forties, West Point, who had clearly confused the WACs with a sexual picnic. He expected the WACs in his office to respond to his every order, including nonmilitary directives like fondling bottoms and stealing kisses. Eden learned evasion tactics, to move swiftly out of his vicinity. She and the WACs who worked for Colonel Bedcrotch regarded him as a sort of enemy sub to be outwitted rather than sunk outright.

At least Bedcrotch's office was in a sitting room of the old manor house and actually had a fireplace, coal piled on, and the place kept warm. In this Eden fared better than Dottie and Faye, who worked deep in the manor house cellar in cryptography. The WACs' orders were absolute: no discussion whatever of their work. Not with anyone. When she emerged from HQ at the end of her shift, Eden sometimes felt she had whitewashed her brain clean of everything she might have read or thought or typed or transcribed. Except for making a joke of Bedcrotch's pathetic attentions, she never mentioned her work once she left the manor house and crossed the broad, damp park to the barracks. Not to anyone. No one did, even in the barracks, or among friends. It was as though she crossed a moat between her life and her work.

"Do you mind if I smoke?" Logan Smith asked, offering her one. Eden declined. "I guess we're the escorts for Frank and Faye, so they don't get into trouble."

"Oh, I think if Faye gets into trouble, she's perfectly capable of getting herself out."

Faye Cole was just the most exciting person Eden had ever known. Faye cut her own swath through life, and she didn't care who knew it. Eden Douglass, Faye Cole, and Dottie Lofgren were an odd but bonded trio. Dottie was the daughter of a Presbyterian minister from Wichita, Kansas. A thoughtful, slow-moving Norwegian girl, strikingly blond, Dottie was cautious in all things, except for riding a bicycle. On a bike she was fearless.

Faye Cole, by contrast, had been independent since she was ten. She had confided to Dottie and Eden that she had joined the WACs to escape the family firm, a bordello in New Orleans run by her grandmother. Her mother and two aunts worked there, Granny, too, when necessary. Faye was short, round, full, fleshy, coarse, and sexy, high-spirited. She knew how to make the most of her looks, to attract men. She had had more lovers than she could count on the fingers of two hands. That she was smart, she kept under wraps. Faye knew everything there was to know about not getting pregnant. She was an education to Dottie and Eden. Her nickname was Shortcake. How Faye had met Frank Willing, Eden did not know.

"Don't let me interrupt you, please," said Lieutenant Smith. "Finish your letter."

"Oh, it's just a note to my mother. There's so little we can say, you know, that I feel badly that I write most often with complaints. About the food," she added, realizing that this letter, too, had complained about the food. "I can't talk about my work or even where I'm living. Just as well. They'd worry if they knew that we hear buzz bombs every night."

"You're at Bushey?" he asked, lighting up. "That's only twenty miles from London, isn't it? You must surely feel the bombardment."

"Oh yes. It shakes us. Night and day. It's worse at night. I don't know why it should be, but it is."

"Can you sleep through them yet?"

"No. I hear the whine, the ticking, and I wake up instantly. We all do, everyone in our barracks. We lie there, and when the ticking stops, we count to ten and we listen for it to detonate and hope it's not right over our heads, hope it's a long way off. If you count to eleven, then either it's a dud, or you're going to be dead."

"Can you go back to sleep?"

"Yes. Some of the other girls can't, but I can."

"Well, you are fortunate, Miss Douglass—"

"Eden, please."

"Eden." He savored the name again. "So what can you tell your mother when you write to her?"

"That I am having tea at the Ritz. It would please her. She's English, from Liverpool originally."

"What brought her to America?"

"Religion. She converted to the Mormon Church and emigrated."

"I've never known a Mormon."

"You still don't." Articulating her lapse was somehow freeing, like taking off a heavy, moth-eaten coat she had long outgrown.

"Forgive me. I don't mean to ask such prying questions."

"Nothing to forgive."

"Questioning is a reflex for me, I'm afraid. I'm a lawyer in civilian life."

"I've never known a lawyer."

"I'm a Democrat, too. There, now I've broken all the social rules. Never talk about religion or politics."

Eden laughed, folded her unfinished letter, and put it in her pocket. "I'm a Democrat, too, so I don't mind breaking a few social rules."

Faye burst upon them, introducing herself to Logan, whom she had never met, waxing on about the Ritz's loo, a word she was fond of. Her favorite part of the HQ manor house was the loo. Any of them. "They have rose-painted porcelain sinks!" she exclaimed just as Lieutenant Willing joined them.

"It's all set," he said, winking at Faye. "We're booked at the hotel as Mr. and Mrs. Smith, baby. No offense, Logan."

"None taken."

Frank shook Eden's hand. "I'm Frank, and I'm Willing."

"Hey!" Faye interjected. "Don't forget who's buttering your bread!"

Frank Willing laughed. He had a bluff sort of energy about him that seemed Faye's match. "I see you've met my friend, the Philadelphia lawyer. Watch out! They're slick."

"How is a Philadelphia lawyer any different from another?"

"You've never heard that expression?"

Eden had not.

Faye laughed. "She's from Idaho."

Logan smiled. "The Wild West?"

"Well, Fairwell, Idaho, is not very wild anymore. Fifty years ago it had veins of silver."

"When you come from Philadelphia," Logan said, his speech unhurried, "even Pittsburgh seems wild. My father will be happy to know I've met a real westerner. He's a chip off the old Teddy Roosevelt block. All that generation of easterners believed in the Wild West."

Tea arrived on a silver tray, with a ceramic pot and a silver creamer. Eden was charmed. There was even a small bowl of sugar. This was the Ritz, after all. The cakes and small sandwiches, lovely, delicate, seemed to Eden like the sort of food Victorine St. John might have served to dolls. But the company was fine, Faye and Frank in fine spirits, anticipating their assignation. Faye had not bothered to tell Eden she was planning to go to a hotel and leave her alone with Lieutenant Smith. Eden sat across from Lieutenant Smith, watched his measured responses, his diffident, easy manners, listened to him explain in a droll self-deprecating fashion how his father's great friend Owen Wister had written the Wild West classic *The Virginian,* a book Eden had heard of but never read.

"With that book Owen Wister invented the notion of the Code of the West, the noble cowboy. It sold a hundred thousand copies the first year."

"They made a movie of it, didn't they? Did it have Ernest March in it?"

"The talkie in 1929 had Gary Cooper," Logan said.

"Does Owen Wister look like Gary Cooper?" asked Faye.

"Not at all. When I was a boy, I'd go to lunch with Mr. Wister and my father at the Philadelphia Club, which was always dark, even on the brightest day, all oak paneling and velvet drapes and deferential waiters, and I'd look at him and think, How on earth could you have written all that Wild West stuff? The lone cowboy with the wind in his face and his untutored morality? All that optimism! Owen Wister himself was," Logan paused, "melancholy."

"Is *The Virginian* a good book?" asked Eden.

"Depends on what your standards are. By Philadelphia standards, of course it was good. Excellent, in fact. Nothing risqué. All very manly. Owen Wister is from one of the old Philly families and could not write a vulgar word if his life hung in the balance. So the book lacks vulgarity, but it lacks, too, a certain energy that I'd expect out of the west. For my seventh birthday, Mr. Wister personally gave me an inscribed copy of his book, and said to me, 'See that you grow up like the Virginian, Logan, and keep to his code!'" Logan laughed affectionately at the memory.

"What was his code?" Eden sipped her tea.

"Well, it's pretty inflexible, but I always wondered how Mr. Wister knew it at all. He had only gone west, to Wyoming, in the 1890s for his health. Back then, if your family happened to have a boy who was sickly or weak, or not up to snuff, well, send him to Montana or Wyoming. Make a man of him." Logan paused, as though adjudicating. "I don't know if they sent them to Idaho."

Did he wink at her? Eden thought maybe an evening with Logan Smith— minus Faye—could be very entertaining. She saw the gold wedding band on his finger, of course, but there was no harm in taking in a film, walking around London. Despite the uniform, something about Logan Smith made Eden forget the war. Perhaps because he hadn't that air of nervous hunger that she sensed in so many other men, men whose hunger or need or dread made them treat women voraciously. Logan Smith, by contrast, exuded a sense of calm, even ease and thoughtfulness. How unlikely, she thought, genuinely enjoying herself, that I should be having tea at the Ritz with these people, Americans, yes, but people I would ordinarily never have known. Even the orchestra had gone more uptempo, "It Had to Be You." She wished Logan Smith would ask her to dance, but no one was dancing. She brought her cup to her lips, and fragrant steam wafted up as she smiled.

Her smile paled as the ticking of a buzz bomb filled the Ritz, fell over the potted palms and plated silver. The china rattled. Eden saw that the man in tweed held a bite of cake between his lips without moving. His wife, in her blue voile, composed her features, poised her knife and fork without moving. The waiter, balancing a tray of cups on his way to the kitchen, stopped. The orchestra quit playing in midmeasure. All conversation, all laughter, all movement suspended. Across the table, Logan Smith held Eden's gaze as firmly as if he held her face in his hands. She did not look away, nor did he.

The ticking drew nearer, nearer yet, then stopped. *One,* Eden breathed without moving her lips or her eyes, *Two, Three, Four,* all the way to a wordless *Ten* when the bomb detonated. The ground shook. But it was distant. They were not hit. Not then. Not that kind of bomb, anyway.

# Asparagus Tea Sandwiches

Choose fresh asparagus that are firm but not too fat. Cut stalks to a uniform length, perhaps six to eight inches. Tie in a bundle and steam swiftly. They should retain their color. Do not let them get altogether limp. Drain. Pat dry or they will sog through your bread.

Take your white bread and cut the crusts off. Roll them out flat with a rolling pin and butter sparingly. Put your asparagus spears in center and fold over in triangles, so that you have uniform edges. Press the ends together. Stack. Cover and put in fridge till butter hardens. Serve with paper-thin slices of lemon and fresh chopped green onion.

### THE PHILADELPHIA LAWYER

Francis Logan Smith was a Philadelphia lawyer all his life. As his father was. And his grandfather. He knew what it was to belong and yet not belong. To be part of a set of assumptions and yet never be wholly able to share them, to move in grooves smoothed for him, and yet find them splintery, chafing. He was a serious man by nature, made the more serious by these circumstances.

Logan stepped into the firm and the role expected of him after university and law school. He had gone to Penn, like all the men of the Smith family since 1866. As a lawyer, Logan gave his clients meritorious service, kept their discretions, made unimpassioned decisions. He was the sort of civic-minded Philadelphia lawyer who serves on boards, submits to insufferable tedium and long-winded colleagues in the name of civic service and the Greater Good. He actually believed in a Greater Good. He practiced civic service.

Philadelphia was a small world, and Logan Smith was part of the smaller elite: a self-enclosed social entity that had kept its privileges intact along with the assumptions on which those privileges rested. The Philadelphia elite and all it stood for survived the Civil War, survived the advent of new money, and railroads. Indeed, the Main Line helped to preserve this elite. It even survived the Depression. Everything was as it ever had been: the Smiths socializing with the Wisters, the Butlers, the Biddles, the Peppers.

Except that Logan's father, James Edward Smith, was a born boat-rocker. In 1916, James Edward Smith married a Catholic girl. Convent-educated by the Sisters of St. Joseph, gently reared, Mary Logan enchanted him with her red hair, blue eyes, a bewitching smile, and a love of music that she passed to her only son, Francis Logan, who was born in 1917. Old Protestant Philadelphia snubbed Mary, for which she cared nothing. James could not be so easily ignored. He was a member of the Philadelphia Bar Association, of the Philadelphia Club and others, of select boards and coteries.

Then, in the 1930s, James Edward Smith rocked Old Philadelphia's boat even more profoundly. He supported Roosevelt, endorsed the New Deal and the Democrats. This declaration effectively ended any association with the Peppers, and the other staid-unto-rabid Republicans of their circle. Many of the best Philadelphia families withdrew their legal work from the Smith family firm.

Logan Smith was restless in the family firm, but, unlike his father, he was no boat-rocker. Besides, what alternative had he? That life in the law firm proceeded at a geologic pace was, by Philadelphia standards, in its favor. To set up his own practice and chase ambulances through ethnic neighborhoods, like those lawyers with second-rate degrees? He could not imagine grasping, lunging for a living. And he had a wife to think of. Frances. Frances and Francis. They made a good pair. Everyone said so. They had known each other all their lives. Francis and Frances married in 1942, just before Logan shipped out for Officer Candidate School.

Francis Logan Smith admired his father. He adored his mother. He liked his wife. But he had never been in love until that day at the Ritz when the buzz bombs ticked overhead and the music stopped.

THEY HAD NOTHING IN COMMON UNTIL LOGAN bought an umbrella from a street vendor. They shared the umbrella as they left the Ritz and walked all over Piccadilly, Trafalgar, Mayfair, Leicester Square, Green Park, Pall Mall. Buzz bombs continued through that afternoon and evening. Sirens began their wailing counterpoint far off and grew louder, and as night fell, huge spotlights pierced the sky as Eden and Logan walked through London, arm in arm under the shared umbrella. Every pub and restaurant, every theatre and music hall, was filled with military men from all over the world. They milled in the streets and around every kiosk, undeterred by the rain, or the sirens, Americans, Australians, New Zealanders, Canadians, remnants of the Polish army, the Free French, the Dutch, whose countries had been summarily overrun four years before.

Eden and Logan passed whole blocks of flats, homes that had been blitzed, cordoned off, abandoned while life went on. There were homes from which the fronts had been sheared away completely, and lay in rubble still spilling out into the streets; from one, the loo hung precariously, connected only by its plumbing, the clawfoot tub askew, the bedsprings atop rubble; clothes still hung in the closet, the stove upended, the poor dog barking. The combination of homely domestic life and utter destruction appalled Eden. "I wonder what happens to these lives," she said. "I wonder what happens to everyone."

Logan tilted the umbrella against the rain and to shelter Eden from the sight. "They do the best they can," he said. "It's only Americans who expect their lives to be one long happy, unclouded path to success. Think how long Europeans have been living with war."

Eden wished she had some of her father's historical sense.

They ate that night in Duque's, a small French restaurant in Soho that Eden and Dottie and Faye had discovered on one of their forays to the capital. M. Duque was married to a breezy, jovial Englishwoman, whose daughters were in the WRENS, and she had treated the three WACs with special aplomb. Susan Duque recognized Eden, pleased to see she'd come with a young man.

She gave them a small table set apart from others and recommended the day's special, a simple stew. "Indecent the kind of provisions we get these days. Take my word for it. You want the special. Now, if only you'd have made a reservation, I would have saved you the last two pieces of my famous Tarte Tatin. It may be wartime, but we still have English apples. English apples and French know-how." Mrs. Duque lifted her chin. "I can still make an English apple sing, no matter the restrictions."

The meal was solid fare, well cooked, imaginative by English standards, wonderful by military standards. Logan and Eden went on talking, though nothing could be said of their work save that they did it. Logan was an information attaché on General Canning's staff. He was suited to the work for several reasons: From the time he was a boy he had built radios, and his legal training helped him to draft bulletins in appropriate language that would offer nothing to the enemy. He was quick with codes. The present could not be discussed, and no one looked very far into the future, so that left the past.

Eden made Logan laugh with tales of her past, of the feckless, the deluded, the devout among Douglasses, of the Dream Theatre, the Pilgrim Restaurant and the Fairwell *Enterprise,* of Afton washing her mouth out with soap for singing "Hot Tamale Molly," Gideon's Great Timetable, and Kitty's insistence on her Lark of Liverpool past.

"I was shocked, really, when Dottie and Faye and I went to the Empire and I knew so many of the songs! It was like an experience I'd already had. Only now, I know she made it up."

"The music hall?"

"No, the music hall is real enough. The rest of it, the Lark of Liverpool, the little sister dying of the damp tights. All that color and music and opulence. Now that I've lived here for a while, I think she probably came from the slums of Liverpool."

"Will you go there and find out?"

"Why? To prove she lied about her past? I wouldn't do that."

Logan leaned in to the candle to light his cigarette. "You won't ask her?"

"No. Why should I?"

"You don't want to know the truth?"

"She doesn't think of it as a lie. She thinks of it as fiction. Wouldn't you rather be the Lark of Liverpool than just another Mormon convert who washed up on the shores of Zion?"

"I wish I were related to someone who called herself the Lark of Liverpool."

"I'm glad you find my family amusing," she said, enjoying his warmth, his mirth. "I always thought they were pretty dull."

"Not at all. For really dull, you'd have to go to Philadelphia. People pride themselves on dull. It's considered a mark of good breeding. Philadelphia is the laughingstock of the east for our blue laws. Till just ten years ago movie houses were closed on Sunday, and you couldn't play baseball or football till after two P.M. It was against the law. And not just the law of the land. For Catholics, there's no midnight mass in Philadelphia because the cardinal is a teetotaler and fears that all the Irish upstarts will go to mass, have a cup of Christmas cheer, and sing in the streets. Which they wouldn't. Not in Philadelphia. No," he gave her a warm smile, "to be a true Philadelphian, and I am one, you must have Syng silver on the table, and a maiden aunt's youthful sampler on the back parlor wall. You cannot be arty or too musical, and you can break a sweat only in sports, say, cricket or skating or rowing. I'm very dull company, I think, for a girl from Idaho and California."

"I've never played cricket or gone skating or rowed a boat."

"Yes, but you can sing 'Hot Tamale Molly.'"

"Well, I won't sing now."

"Later."

"Okay. Later."

"Mrs. Duque," he asked her when she came for their plates, "do you know the words to 'Hot Tamale Molly'?"

"Used to. Used to know a lot of things I've forgotten." She gave a sly wink. "But not my way with an apple. Haven't forgotten that. Here's the pitiful pudding," she said, putting bowls in front of them, "rice pudding with treacle sauce. Next time you must make a reservation and you can have my Tarte Tatin."

"Next time we will," said Logan. "Won't we?" Did he wink at her again? "Coffee, Eden?"

"Yes, please."

Mrs. Duque left them and Eden tasted the undistinguished rice pudding. Eden said, "Maybe we could pretend this is Figs Napoleon."

"As in the Emperor?"

"In a manner of speaking," she said, suddenly embarrassed; *pretend* was not a word befitting a WAC. Soldiers don't pretend. But she went on to describe her grandmother's restaurant, and the Pilgrim cook, Napoleon, how he had named himself after the Emperor, and could in fact create pastries worthy of the name, and had learned his techniques in the kitchen of the French Legation in Shanghai. "How or why he came to St. Elmo, California, I have no idea. But his cooking was legendary, and what he could do with a simple fig! Sometimes he'd put them over ice cream, or over meringue. The meringue just dissolves in your mouth and then you have the fruit in its syrup."

"What syrup?" Logan's cigarette smoke floated into the candlelight between them.

"I don't know."

"I'm going to imagine with you," said Logan. "That we are in your grandmother's restaurant, and Napoleon has made us Figs Napoleon, and that you and I are longtime friends and know each other well."

"St. Elmo, California, is a dry, dusty railroad town," said Eden, moved by his sincerity.

"And Philadelphia is a stultifying cloister, all very Anglophile and distinguished by dullness. Even the food. But, it's the life I know. The life I will return to. If I live to return to it."

Eden's lips closed around her spoon. Might as well get this over with. "Tell me about your wife."

The sirens sounded again. "Come, come into the cellar," Mme. Duque encouraged her guests as she hastened through the place and checked the blackout curtains. "You'll be safer there."

"Shall we?" asked Logan as the patrons of the small café followed Mrs. Duque.

"I'm feeling lucky," said Eden, who guessed that her real and immediate dangers could not be foretold with a siren.

Logan nodded. He took off his glasses and smiled. Without them, Eden thought he looked younger than he was, and she wondered what impossible chain of circumstance had brought her here to London, to sit out an air raid across from this man from a world she could scarcely imagine.

"Your wife," she said again.

"Frances and I are sentimental cousins, and ours was a sentimental union. Our circumstances are so similar, we could have been related. She's like all the girls I've ever known. I'm like all the men she's ever known. Frances's family has a summer place in Maine very near my family's summer place. Our families both live in Chestnut Hill. Her father is in insurance. Mine is a lawyer. Our mothers are members of the garden club. She went to Europe twice before she was twelve. So did I. We've had the same Catholic education, except that hers was at a girls' school and mine was at a boys'. At the end of that, she went on to Chestnut Hill College, more Catholic education, and I went to Penn. Penn could hardly turn me down, my family being what it is. And so, like a lot of people in our set, when the war came, we realized we were in love and dispensed with the big wedding and the long engagement. We had maybe a week together before I went to OCS."

"Have you seen her since?"

"Once. A couple of days. Just before I shipped out."

"Do you have her picture?"

He found his wallet and opened it to a studio portrait of an attractive young woman with fragile features, upswept hair, and a sweet expression.

"She's very pretty," said Eden.

"She is, and she's a fine girl, but we shouldn't have raced into such a union. It's not like me anyway. Lawyers are famously not an impetuous bunch," he said, considering the photograph. "Everyone was getting married quickly. I should have known better."

"Why?"

"I should have known the war would change me. I'm not the same man I was two years ago. Of course I hate the killing and destruction, but without the war, I would have gone on the predetermined path that lay before me, living where my parents lived, and Frances's parents, doing the work my father did. If I live, I will no doubt go back to that, but I will never be the same. These past few years have changed me forever. And who knows what lies ahead?"

Eden watched the light play over his face, but she did not speak.

"You know what I'm talking about, don't you?"

"I think so."

"You think all the time about avoiding being wounded or killed, or doing something stupid, thoughtless, or sleep-deprived that would hand you, or the people who rely on you, over into the arms of death. This, the planning we're doing, is one thing," he spoke obliquely of the massive efforts for the invasion, "the execution will be quite another. So, after this, yes, I can still cherish what I knew, had at home, but I can see that even if it's valuable, it's narrow, confining, and claustrophobic. There are other ways to live. Only now, Frances ties me to all that."

"Isn't that what people want? To be tied to something? To be connected?"

"Perhaps, but getting married, that is, my marrying Frances, was like building a case on the wrong precedent. I was thinking: If I died, at least I'd have someone who would remember me, someone would remember that I had lived. I shouldn't have been thinking about if I die."

They heard the whine and the ticking, and they counted to ten. Somewhere, not too distant, the bomb fell. The walls rattled. The table shivered.

"I should have been thinking about if I live. If I die, what does it matter that Frances, or anyone else, will remember me?"

"I will remember you," she said, meeting his gaze directly.

He finished the rice pudding and lit up. "And I will remember you, Eden."

The all-clear siren sounded, and people emerged from the cellar and returned to their places. Mrs. Duque brought around the coffeepot and refreshed teacups as though nothing had happened. "Well, it's providential, that's what I say." She kept her voice low. "You never guess what I found in the larder, but two pieces of Tarte Tatin. Yes, the girls who do the washing up had set them aside for themselves. Not on my watch, dearie, I told them, not when we have soldiers out front. Americans."

"Oh, I'm full," said Eden.

"Don't be silly," Mrs. Duque clucked, *tut tut tut.* "My Tarte Tatin will make this evening memorable." She smiled knowingly. "More memorable."

Mrs. Duque's pride in her work was not misplaced: Her fashioning of apples cooked in butter and raw sugar, turned over into a short crust, the fruit coppery with caramel and rich with autumn, all this enchanted Eden. They ate very slowly, and the place had thinned considerably when Eden remembered the time.

"I have to catch the train back to Bushey," she said, collecting her things. "I can't miss the last one. Colonel Bedcrotch will have my tail in the wringer."

On the way to the train, she told him how Bedcrotch had gotten his name. Logan was appalled that a senior officer would be propositioning WACs.

"I can handle myself, and I can handle him too," said Eden, as they waited on the platform. Soldiers and a few civilians stood out of the rain, some squatting, their backs to the brick wall, smoking.

"Hey, Eden!"

She nodded in greeting to a couple of GIs she recognized from Bushey.

"You must have men asking you out all the time."

"All the girls do. It's not exactly love," she added.

"I can't remember when I last so enjoyed a day as I did today. I mean that truly. Years have passed since I had such a day."

"I feel the same way. Do you think it is Mrs. Duque's Tarte Tatin?"

"I think it's because you are the girl from the golden west. I think you are who Owen Wister had in mind when he believed the Wild West was good for people, that Westerners were uncluttered people, and inherently vivid."

Eden laughed. "I don't think that's so. I've known lots of dim and cluttered people. I'm related to them!"

"But you're not one of them." They heard the train's not-so-distant whistle. "Will you go out with me again, even if I'm married?"

Eden thought fleetingly of the train whistles of her childhood, those long woeful shrieks that rippled across the night, moving up Jesuit Pass, or through the Idaho mountains. Though her training as a WAC had instilled in her a sense of being truly American, Logan Smith gave her, for the first time, a sense of being rooted to a place, defined by a landscape.

The English train pulled in with a few brief blasts, and the men and women waiting, roused, turned up their collars and moved out of their shelters, despite the rain, to be able to get on swiftly once the train had stopped.

Logan opened the umbrella and put it in her hand. "Goodnight, Eden."

Eden smiled and stood on tiptoe—he was that much taller than she—and kissed him, not lingering, a swift, spontaneous kiss. "That wasn't goodbye," she said, waving as she ran toward the carriage. "There is such a thing as a kiss hello."

# Tarte Tatin

Perhaps a month after Eden Douglass and Logan Smith ate at Duque's in Soho, the place was bombed. Mr. and Mrs. Duque did not reopen. They vanished, and Eden never had the opportunity to ask Mrs. Duque about her expertise with an English apple. Years later, Eden struggled to re-create the flavor of apples basking in butter and sugar, the sensation of autumnal depths that lingered, long after your plate was clean. Her own recipe never quite measured up to her recollection of that first night she met Logan. Nonetheless, Café Eden's September specialties—apple pie and her famous Tarte Tatin—gathered applause from all who ate there.

For one pie: Your apples should not be tired and faded. Eden discovered the big awkward Gravensteins when she moved to Washington State in 1965. She liked them best for cooking, especially the ungainly ones not uniform enough for supermarkets. If you can't find Gravensteins, Granny Smiths or Jonagold apples will do. Any apples will do, except for a Delicious apple, which as an astute cook once remarked, was a contradiction in terms. Have your apples ready, peeled, cored, and quartered, 6 to 8 cups of them.

In a cast iron fry pan, on a high heat, melt 4 tablespoons unsalted butter and to this add 1 cup sugar. Stir with a wooden spoon till a rich, shining patina forms and the two combine to become one thing: caramel. Lift and tilt your pan to cover the bottom and sides. Remove from heat and quickly arrange the quartered apples artistically in the still-warm caramel. Slice the rest smaller and layer atop these.

Cut in small bits another 4 tablespoons butter and dot over apples. Bake at a preheated 400 for 35 minutes. Cool maybe 1 hour.

Make a short pastry crust, roll out and place over cooled apples, tucking the ends around, down inside the pan. Return to oven. Bake at 400 for another 30 to 35 minutes. Remove. Cool at least one hour. Run a knife along the inside and turn the tart upside down into a generous-sized plate. Lift slowly and it will wear the pastry crust like a collar.

Serve alone, or with whipped cream, but ice cream or crème fraîche are lovely too.

### THE CONSTRUCTS

Love lasts. That's what Eden told herself over and over. Love lasts, no matter what. Because if love didn't last, if love did not somehow insist and prevail, then why not simply slake your physical appetites with a man, and he with you? Why not satisfy your heart and your hungers with the equivalent of C rations and Hershey bars? In these years, Eden Douglass came to believe that triumph, tragedy, and, yes, love itself, might all be mere wordy constructs we drape over the physical, the inescapable mortal obligations of sex, sleep, eat, expel. But to cherish the construct was to give yourself reason to go on.

The construct itself could give you strength to revel in, or simply endure, every moment, every experience that shaped and pummeled you into the person you were, or would become. The person who, like everyone else, was finally finite, subject to death, decay, oblivion, and forgotten. She learned if you had any sense at all, you lived as though you would live forever. When you died, everything that comprised your life, your past, the people who had buoyed or duped you, they were all gone too. Eden was glad to be hungry or sleepy or have her feet ache and her head hurt, because she wasn't dead. She learned to work astutely on three hours of sleep and to quench hunger with C rations, food as canned fuel, to test herself against the elements, against the enemy, and a God who probably didn't care one way or the other.

# CHAPTER FOUR

SHE COULD NEVER CURE HIM OF SLEEPING WITH HIS watch on. Logan was an insomniac and lay awake, his arm around her, the watch near her ear, and sometimes it woke her. She lay there listening to their time slip away from them. She would turn in his arms.

"Did I snore?"

"Yes."

She laughed against his chest. Outside their hotel room, roistering Aussies were singing "Waltzing Matilda" and rollicking down the hall. "What time is it?"

"Never mind that. Tell me something I don't know about you."

"You first."

"All right. Let me think. There's nothing you don't know about me." He reached beside the bed for his cigarettes and lit one.

"There must be. Think."

"I've told you all my schoolboy pranks."

"All two of them."

"Dull boys grow up to be Philadelphia lawyers, baby. Get used to it."

Eden actually valued Logan's reserve, even what he called his lawyerly ways, a man who thought deeply, whose underlying strength lay in his willingness to hear all sides, to weigh and balance. Still, he had certainly plunged into this love affair. If wartime taught anything, it was that you could not turn away: not from what was demanded, and not from what was offered. It seemed to them both that so destined were they to be lovers that surely they would have met, even had there not been a war. Had Logan stayed in Philadelphia, never ventured beyond the Schuylkill, beyond Chestnut Hill, beyond Fairmount Park or Market Street, Eden would have found him somehow. For Eden, this man was the north star of her crowded firmament. She could navigate her life by his light.

"All right." He exhaled and stroked her hair. "When I made my first communion, I crunched on the wafer, and the whole church heard it. God heard it. I was in deep trouble. Your turn."

Eden nestled in closer to him. "I don't want to talk. I want to listen. Tell me about after the war. Tell me about our house and how our children will go to Chestnut Hill Academy, and go rowing on the river with you, and for walks in the Arboretum."

"After the war, I will go back to Philadelphia and tell Frances how things have changed, how I have changed. And while the social lightning bolts are flying, I'll just say I'm following in Father's footsteps."

"My mother used to sing an old music hall tune by that name."

"Sing it for me."

"Later. Finish your story."

"People will gossip and be shocked and say things like, Well, what can you expect but divorce from a family of Democrats, even if they are Catholics. My father won't be so bad, he only joined the Church to marry my mother. And my mother, despite her deep religious beliefs, she will come around. She always thought Frances was too conventional and pious. Frances's family will be hard to mollify. But Frances herself? She's a sensible girl, and I half expect she knows we weren't really in love. We were in war. Eventually, Frances and I will agree on a settlement, and she'll go to Reno for the divorce. I'll call you at your aunt's house, and you'll come to Philly. You'll get a job writing for one of the big daily papers, and we'll be together while we wait for the divorce to be final. Then we'll get married, and buy a house in Chestnut Hill. Of course," he added after due consideration, "we don't have to live in Chestnut Hill. We can live wherever you want."

"I'll live anywhere you are. After the war. Sounds lovely, doesn't it?"

Logan was silent for a time, unwilling to expand on After the War, even if the phrase comforted Eden. "I have a Christmas present for you."

"Christmas is a week away."

"I have an apartment for us. A flat, as they say. A friend, from Penn, his cousin has a little flat here in London, Great Russell Street, and he wrote me and told me I could use it. He's sent a letter to his landlady, a Mrs. Tanner, to give me the key."

"Where is the friend? Why isn't he using it?"

"He's in Scotland."

Eden listened to his watch tick. "He's training in Scotland, isn't he?" The Aussies had reached their room and the door had slammed shut. The hall was suddenly quiet. "When do you think it will be? The invasion."

"I don't know."

"They'll send you with the first troops, won't they?"

"They'll send me when they do. And they'll send you when they do, and there's not a damn thing we can do about it."

"If I hadn't fallen in love with you, I wouldn't be so afraid."

"If I hadn't fallen in love with you, I wouldn't be so brave."

"Oh, Logan, you always have the right words."

"We'll have our whole lives. And we'll have this Christmas. Look, my cousin's friend tells me his landlady loves the Yanks. He says Mrs. Tanner will kill us with kindness. He says the flat has a big clawfoot tub and a small kitchen. Just big enough for you to whip up some Resurrection Pie."

"You have to have leftovers for that."

"Frogs in a Bucket?"

"My mother's cooking is not something anyone wants to replicate."

"I have something else for you too."

She nuzzled into his neck, and stroked his chest, her hand swooping lower with each brush, lower till she found what she needed and wanted, and as he leaped to life in her hands and she rolled on top of him, she brought her lips to his ear. "This is what I want for now."


"You're a sap," said Faye, as they stood brushing their teeth in the makeshift sinks. The barracks bathrooms at Bushey did not have painted porcelain sinks with roses; they were more like tin buckets with gurgling drains. "Good-looking girl like you, all those smarts, why settle for a married man? Just because he's an officer?"

"I didn't ask to fall in love with him." Eden spat in the sink.

It was August, and the long English twilight was still descending. The

WACs at Bushey waited for orders. They could be moving to the Continent any day now that Paris was liberated.

"So ask to fall in love with someone else," snapped Faye. "I know these types. They'll say anything to get you into the sack. Like, oh, let me think now, how about this? After the War I'll get a divorce, and we'll get married. A direct translation?"

"Faye, we've been over all this before. I don't tell you not to sleep around. Don't tell me not to fall in love."

"You know what lingo he's really talking, don't you? Bang me, honey, eight to the bar. And when it's over, contrary to those sappy lyrics, I won't be seeing you."

"Hey, Shortcake," Eden retorted, "aren't you the one to be talking!"

"I'm short," said Faye, and this was true; she barely came to Eden's shoulder, "but I'm not stupid. How long since you heard from him?"

"Since his unit landed in Normandy."

"They're dying like flies. You know that."

"Logan is coming back to me. Logan's going to live. I'll invite you to the wedding."

Faye made a dismissive joke and gesture, which Eden ignored. Eden dried her face off and put her watch back on her wrist. On the back in tiny letters was engraved ELD & FLS, 1943. She smiled every time she put it on. The lighter she had given him for Christmas had the exact same letters engraved, only the initials were transposed. FLS & ELD. Ever since then, Eden had worn the watch to bed. When she woke in the night now, she tried to imagine it was Logan's heart beating nearby.

# True English Plum Pudding

*Café Eden, Skagit Valley, Washington, Christmas 1976*

This recipe is from Mrs. Julia Tanner, the Great Russell Street land-lady, Christmas 1943. This recipe had been in Mrs. Tanner's family since the 1890s. Mrs. Tanner had it from her mother, a cook in the Isle of Wight household of Queen Victoria. In 1976 the now very elderly Mrs. Tanner was delighted to get Eden's letter after thirty years; delighted to know her cooking and her recipe were so memorable. She sent the recipe as it is given below, but she did not remember Eden and Logan at all.

Ingredients 1/4 lb. finely chopped suet, 1 cup flour, 1 cup firm pack brown sugar, 1 tsp allspice, 1 tsp cinnamon, 1/2 tsp salt, 1 tsp baking soda, 1/2 tsp nutmeg, 1/4 tsp mace, 1 cup raisins, 1 cup currants, 1/2 cup chopped orange peel, 1/2 cup chopped citron peel, 1 cup chopped apple, 2 eggs, 1 cup day-old soft bread crumbs, 1/3 cup milk, 1/2 cup blanched almonds

Mix together suet, brown sugar and milk; add the eggs. Mix fruits, peels, citron and nuts with 1/4 cup flour. Mix and sift remaining flour with soda and spices and salt. Add fruit mixture, crumbs and sifted dry ingredients to suet mixture. Mix well and turn into a 2 qt. greased or oiled covered pudding mold. Steam on top of range 2 1/2 hrs. Serve with hard sauce. Serve warm.

### THE MESSENGER

A convoy of gray ships on a gray sea in a grim season, tossing wildly on the stormy Channel. Eden Douglass with a dozen other WACs and two WAC officers were the only women on board. The ship carried troops and supplies to support Americans fighting in the Ardennes Forest. Paris had been liberated in August, but the Germans were not yet beaten. This vast march of men, women, and materiel would be known as the Battle of the Bulge, and it would cost some seventy-six thousand American lives.

Eden was truly on her own. Dottie Lofgren and Faye Cole were sent elsewhere. She knew none of these WACs with whom she had been ordered to Charleroi, in southeast Belgium, an industrial and railroad city badly bombed, the citizens dour and disconsolate after years of German occupation. Eden, the WACs, and the officers were billeted in an old four-story home that had been looted long before and had served as quarters for waves of Germans, and then Americans. No heat. No hot water. One bathroom on the first floor. Eden bunked on the fourth floor.

But for all the cold and deprivation, Eden felt blessed. Logan Smith lived. Logan was serving with General Canning, not in her immediate vicinity, but near enough that the lovers could meet in Brussels. Not often. Not for long. But long enough to reassure each other that they were alive, that their love remained true and vital, that an Allied victory was assured. But when? They only knew about Now. They did not know when Then might come. Much could happen in between. Logan did not look well. But who did? Eden had lost twenty pounds, and she was often sick, chilled, her complexion gray as the Belgian sky.

American soldiers lived on a diet of C rations and powdered eggs, Australian mutton thick with grease. They shriveled inside their government-issue clothes. But at least they ate. Belgians could barely keep themselves alive. The refugees were starving.

Shifting caravans of refugees, long scraggling lines of the very old and the very young, moved east or west, depending on how the battle raged and who was winning at the moment. Their faces were haggard, gray, lips frozen; they clung to filthy coats and blankets. They fought over the garbage that American soldiers trucked to the dumps. They stood in the dumps when the American trucks were due to arrive and fought one another, clawed for scraps.

Eden saw this with her own eyes. In Charleroi, she saw perhaps more than other WACs who remained in clerical and cryptography positions. The army took Corporal Douglass at her word that she could drive anything over any kind of road.

She drove dump trucks and courier jeeps and supply and mail trucks. She drove motorcycles with messages and altered codes. She delivered. And in doing so, she saw things that would stay with her for the rest of her life, sights that defied not simply description but articulation. She did not speak of them, hoping that without words, the years would overtake them, grind them slowly from memory into dust.

Then one afternoon, a scavenging dog darted in front of the motorcycle the messenger Eden was driving. Eden swerved and went down with the bike, which slid, flipped over, and landed on her outstretched arm. Corporal Douglass was sent to a military hospital for WACs in Oxford, England. Eden's war was over.

Logan remained with army, General Canning's troops ordered east into Germany.

# PART FOUR

# Emotional Cornbread

1945

EDEN ROCKED ACROSS THE CONTINENT FOR DAYS AND days, sleeping, mouth open, to the train's insistent rhythms, and the incessant ticking of her wristwatch, the metronomic lulling broken by the occasional shrill whistle. Eden woke with a start to find someone new across from her. The cars were all packed, full of soldiers, some noisy and high-spirited, swapping stories, sharing cigarettes, candy bars, playing never-ending card games. Some, their young faces drawn, irretrievably aged, remained apart. Eden turned her face to the window, to see, by day, the plains stretch out, to see by night her own reflection. Finally the train climbed the long grade up Jesuit Pass, and the St. Elmo Valley unfolded below.

She was going to Tom and Afton's to await word from Logan. No matter how short the wait, it would certainly feel like a long time. The thought of Fairwell, Idaho, of the partitioned house, of Kitty, Gideon, and the delusions that sustained them—well, Eden wasn't equal to that prospect. Besides, she was determined to enjoy her time with Tom and Afton. Once she was married to a divorced

Catholic, Eden well knew, Afton would not be welcoming. Mrs. Logan Smith would not be welcome. Never mind, she told herself. I'm marrying Logan and anyone who doesn't like it can lump it. ELD & FLS. She fondled her watch.

The train whistle blew, and the locomotive slowed, pulling into St. Elmo's Moorish monstrosity of a station, smoke swirling, dissipating on the dry air. Deep sheltering arcades ran alongside the track, and these were thronged with people, usually in family clusters, some joyfully carrying flowers, some weeping in anticipation, all eyes scanning the windows of the train as it shuddered to a halt. In a flurry of turning locks, windows were raised and lowered, doors were flung open, and voices called out.

In these reuniting throngs, Eden saw no one of her own. She wore her uniform and the smart hat, her dark hair pinned away from her face, and she carried a suitcase that held her worldly goods. A military bag hung from her shoulder. She wandered inside the station, where the vast terminal rang with voices, and flat gonglike tones announced arrivals and departures. The high vaults were hung with bunting and a banner draped from end to end: WELCOME HOME VICTORIOUS MEN OF THE ARMED FORCES!

"What about the women of the armed services?" Eden remarked to a young sergeant standing beside her. "Surely the women were victorious, too."

He had a wad of gum in his jaw. "Don't take offense, sister. It don't mean nothing. It's like the men in 'All Men are Created Equal.' " He smiled, pleased with himself.

"I'm not your sister."

"Here! Eden Louise! Over here!"

Eden peered through the crowd to see a solid figure running, holding her hat to her head, calling her name. Afton's embrace was redolent of starch with a whiff of rosemary. Eden closed her eyes. Afton always smelled like starch and rosemary, and some heady and peculiar blend of affection and disapproval. *Home.*

"Oh, my, Eden, look at you! We're so proud of you! Did you recognize me?"

"Of course. You never change."

"Well, at my age, that's good to know. Yoo hoo!" Afton waved wildly to her husband and her sister, Lil. She steered Eden through the crowd, greeting every third person by name, and letting Eden's uniform redound to the credit of the Douglass women in general. "Look here, Lil! Tom! Here's Eden."

Tom Lance (like Afton) had grayed without fraying. They both wore glasses, wire-rimmed, which made their eyes look bigger. Tom still had his good nature and the scar across his nose, and his hands were more veined and weatherbeaten than any hands Eden could remember. Afton was unchanged by years, a new hat, perhaps, a dark blue Sunday suit, but the same bright eyes and volubility. Eden would not have recognized and scarcely remembered, her aunt Lil, but then Lil was not a memorable sort of person. Frail, pale, she resembled Afton minus the verve and girth and effervescence. Eden wasn't even sure how to greet Lil, an embrace might overwhelm her.

Into this vacuum Afton rushed with explanations, certain that she'd written Eden all about the death of Lil's second husband, a Mr. Walsh, apparently not much mourned, certainly not as much as Lil's first husband, Tom's brother Willie, who had died thirty years before. Widowed again, Lil had come to live with Afton, and Tom had built for her, separate from the house, her own little place so she could have her privacy. Lil was happy.

"Now, Eden," Afton hooked one arm into Lil's and one into Eden's, "the whole family is waiting to greet you. Yes, indeed, in your honor, we've gathered our tribe."

Eden had not reckoned on this; she hadn't had a bath in days, but there was no point in contradicting Afton's plans. "All I want to do right now is have a real bath, and sleep in a real bed."

"And eat, I hope. I've been cooking up a storm for you, Eden. We have killed the fatted calf for your return, more like the fatted turkey, and stuffed it, you know Mother's famous stuffing. And my famous pork loin roast. Oh, I couldn't let you come home and not make that! Corn salad with those pickled tomatoes I put up every summer. All your favorites. Three desserts, at least three, wouldn't be a party without three desserts! And everybody's bringing something. It will be a real Lance family reunion."

"Let me have your bag, Eden," said Tom. He flung it into the truck bed, where there was dirt and hay and feathers. They all four crowded into the cab, Eden at the window, and Tom coaxed the old motor to life. Afton reached into her bag and pulled out a sandwich wrapped in wax paper. She handed Eden a brown paper bag, sticky on the bottom, the homely waxed paper opened to honey, perfumed with banana.

Afton smiled and patted Eden's hand, as though the honey and banana sandwich was a kind of tribute, an unspoken bond. "The Lances know how to throw a hero's welcome, the soldier's return," she added. "And I won't hear no one claim the WACs aren't soldiers. I won't hear one thing against them who have sacrificed for the good of all. Some, the greatest sacrifice. Like Lucius."

For Eden, her cousin Lucius Lance would always be twelve and preserved in that fine and finite moment, riding on the running board, waving confidently to the world, honking the horn, grinning, and greeting the whole town. How Eden had envied him. She sought some word of comfort or understanding to offer Afton, but words seem to fail her. She patted Afton's hand.

The truck trundled eastward, moving toward the foothills, the narrow road bordered by citrus groves and alfalfa fields, grapes, tracts of farmland cordoned off by long rows of enormous eucalyptus trees serving as windbreaks. Eden smiled, cheered by the familiar dry wind and the mountains in the distance.

Lil asked after the time Eden had spent in Paris with Junior.

"It wasn't really time," said Eden. "Just an evening. That's all we had."

"Junior wrote us he was just so happy to see you, even just for that one day," Afton interjected, her momentary introspection vanished, her spirits restored. "He said it just brought old St. Elmo home to see his cousin. St. Elmo in Paris! Can you imagine, Lil?"

"No."

"Junior's got medals, Eden," said Afton. "Did you know that? Lots of them."

"He didn't talk about his medals when I saw him in Paris," she replied, not wishing to say that each of those medals had taken its toll on Tom Lance Junior; the long fight up the Italian peninsula, the fighting in France, had made of him a battle-scarred veteran. He smoked, he drank, he had a raucous mouth. He had not seen his family since the day he joined up. "Of all my family, Junior was the only one I ever saw during the war. During the war," Eden mused. "To say that sounds as strange now as After the War always sounded. How can that be? I always thought of After the War like that old song Ma used to sing, 'After the Ball.'"

"You're tired, dear. Finish your sandwich. You will get a nice long rest at our place."

"Eden never seen our new place," said Tom.

"Well, that's true! We moved there right after you and your family left for Idaho, and that thankless railroad let Tom go. Yes, they did. All those years of work and service, and no more loyalty than a cat. A dog'll stick with you, but a cat will curl up on any old door with a saucer of milk. I was undone. Undone. I don't mind saying so. How're we going to start over at our time of life, Tom and me? Tom, of course, took it better. We had Mother to look after, too. She was a burden. Beloved, but a burden. At least we didn't have all eight children at home, but there were plenty still." She pondered. "I disremember quite who."

"Enough," said Tom.

"So we took our savings and invested the whole in some acreage east of town, a small ranch was going cheap. There was still no electricity out there then. Now, of course, we have electricity and a telephone. We got cows and poultry, our own hogs and some beef. We had butter and milk and cream and eggs all through the war. Never mind that railroad." She patted Tom's arm as though the railroad's rebuff all those years ago still troubled him. "Tom made those citrus trees get up and sing with fruit. And the garden, we put that in. A victory garden before anyone even thought of war. Only the house wouldn't do. Too small. But Tom and the boys soon fixed that, added on the room, closed in the sleeping porch, and built a new high back porch, and a bathroom, too, with a fine tub. Oh, and Tom and all the boys redid the barn and chicken yard, and that little shed just off the kitchen for the washing. Nice big tub, a washer with electric wringer. No cranking. What do you think of that?"

"Imagine," said Lil.

"We moved William out of Mother's old room for you. That will be your room. William's our youngest, he's in high school now, but he'll have to share with the boys. You'll have to get used to boys, Eden. Boys everywhere!" Afton sounded happy. "Mouths to feed, clothes to wash, manners to mind. Micah and Jonah are my delight, those youngsters. Wonderful boys. Just like their father, our dear Lucius."

"Their mother never came back for them?" asked Eden.

"She was an s-l-u-t," said Lil. "If you know what I mean."

"Course she never came back! She don't dare show her face at my house." Afton folded her hands over her purse and raised her chin. "And good riddance. I know how to raise boys. Those boys are better off with us, a good LDS home, plenty of love and hard work."

A whole new generation to get their mouths washed out with soap, Eden thought. Afton's certitude was somehow dazzling. How could anyone be so correct? The war was over, yes, but for Afton Lance the Eternal Verities had never been in question, or in danger.

Afton's mouth pursed. "Well, I might as well tell you the other news. Alma run off and married a Baptist."

"And she didn't even have to," said Lil. "Their baby was born a whole year later."

"An Okie," Afton stated.

"An Arkie," Lil corrected her. "Even worse. From Arkansas. They come out here and picked fruit and lived in their car. It's true. Even Alma has to admit it's true."

"Almost everyone in California is from somewhere else," Eden observed.

"Walter Epps is an Arkie, but at least he's not foreign," said Lil.

Afton sighed. "Not like your poor brother's bride, Eden. What a shame. It just makes me so sad. Ernest is blinded by love, but he will rue it. I promise you. Love at first sight, he said. A USO dance. Married this Armenian girl three months later."

Lil said, "It takes two Jews to beat an Armenian."

"At least they're Christian," said Afton. "Not like some people we know."

"Apostolic, mumbo jumbo, worse than Catholics," said Lil with uncharacteristic fervor. "We met Annie and her parents."

"You did? You never wrote me that you'd met her."

Afton exchanged a look with Lil. "Well, your brother had some leave, just a day or so, and he telephoned and said he'd love to see us and could we come to Annie's parents' house in Beverly Hills and meet his new bride. We couldn't use the gas ration, of course, for something so frivolous, but we took the train, and Ernest come to collect us at Union Station. In a convertible! Yes!"

"A Cord," said Tom. "Handsome car."

"Annie's father bought it for her for a graduation gift. Not even a wedding gift, but graduation. Lil and I didn't know we were going to ride in a convertible. We got blowed to bits."

"What is Annie like?" asked Eden, who had seen only a picture of a petite dark-haired girl with a gardenia in her hair standing next to Ernest in his navy uniform.

"She's foreign," said Lil, "like the starving Armenians."

"Well, these people are not starving. I can tell you that! But the food was weird! Weird beyond words. Grape leaves. Yes, they use the leaves and roll them up with all sorts of things inside, and there was sticky syrupy dessert and something that tasted like roses. Yes. Flowers. We had to come home and have taters and eggs. Nice fried eggs on top of leftover mashed potatoes."

"The grape leaves affected my bowels," said Lil. "Tell Eden about the grease."

"Annie's mother kept going on, grease this and grease that, but it wasn't lard or drippings! It was Greece, the country. Like me and Lil had been there. Or knew or cared about it! The idea!"

"Tell her about the girl, Mother," suggested Tom gently, "about Annie."

"Annie is a very nice girl, I'm sure. Very capable," Afton folded her hands and stared ahead, "though foreign. She and her family all has their citizenship papers. She just graduated from UCLA. So she must be smart. And she is pretty. Though foreign. I told him, Ernest, it's very nice you have a college graduate in the family."

"Well, you have a college graduate, too, now," said Eden with an affable nudge to Afton's shoulder. "Junior's wife, Juliette. She graduated from the Sorbonne. In Paris. It's a French university," she added, seeing their brows crease. "Juliette's English is very good. Better than Junior's French, since he doesn't speak a word. She and Junior are so happy. Junior was just glowing. We only had that one night together in Paris, all four of us," she added stupidly. Eden gazed out the window, her hand over her wristwatch, ELD & FLS, 1943, remembering the little restaurant Juliette had brought them to, run by Normands. Juliette had said, "Normand rhymes with gourmand." Eden remembered their laughter and the food, Tarte Tatin for dessert. Junior and Juliette were absolutely besotted with each other; they couldn't keep their hands off each other. The sexy, irreverent Juliette loved everything American. Especially Tom. Eden had never heard anyone else call Junior Tom. Made him seem like someone else altogether. And so, perhaps, he was, Eden had thought as she had pressed up against Logan in that smoky Paris club, "Body and Soul," and all the other music rendered indelible by a jazzy quintet, a three-fingered guitarist who ate up the strings and cried out, *C'est chaud!* Oh yes, Logan and Paris and . . .

Tom coughed hard, snapping her reverie. "You say Junior's married a French girl?"


IN AFTON'S RANCH KITCHEN, THE SAME OLD ENAMELED POT ON THE BACK burner simmered. The scent greeted Eden like an old friend, then dispersed into the sweat and steam and busy ether of a kitchen teeming with women. The mothers jiggled babies in their arms. All the babies looked alike, despite their mothers showing off to Eden some truly marvelous nose, or crop of hair. Eden had the feeling of meeting people in a dream, where, quite without consequences, your mind puts faces you know on people you don't. Cousins? Spouses? In-laws of their in-laws? The news of Junior's marriage to the French girl circuited through the house like a tumbleweed afire. Eden inwardly cursed Junior for not telling her he had kept his family in the dark. Well, it was on him now. She couldn't be blamed.

Afton fought off saccharine condolences—*How could Junior have been so thankless? So thoughtless?*—by taking up the mashing of potatoes and whipping them.

"Junior is entitled to marry anyone he wants," declared Connie, the youngest of the Lance girls. Connie was only a scrawny child when Eden last saw her. Now, at twenty, she had the look of the Douglass women, broad-shouldered, dark-haired. Though she had a toddler in her arms and another child clinging to her skirt, she exuded disdain for everything around her. "Let go of me," she said to the bewildered boy. "Go play." She unloaded the toddler into the arms of someone's sister-in-law. She turned to Eden. "You want to get out of here?"

Eden followed Connie out the kitchen door. Amid the din of barking dogs and children slamming screen doors, playing tag, and quarreling, chickens pecked and clucked in the yard. Roosters strutted and crowed over the brainless gobble of the turkeys. Connie kept walking, down the front porch steps, beyond a deeply shaded area with dusty chairs. They turned a corner, just out of sight of the house, where lemon trees provided shade to rickety wicker chairs. The dirt around them was littered with butts. Eden laughed out loud.

Connie lit up and offered her a Lucky.

"Thanks. I don't smoke. I was laughing to see all these cigarettes. This must be where the family comes to break the Word of Wisdom. Does Afton pretend she doesn't know?"

"My mother? Pretend! My mother is the Cab Calloway of guilt."

The thought—Afton Lance in white tie and tails, prancing up and down, conducting the Big Band of Guilt—made Eden laugh again. She would have to remember that and tell Logan.

"Mother just makes pork roast to spite Victor."

"What?" said Eden as they sank into the chairs.

"Victor's not religious or anything, but it kind of makes him sick. It was the way he was raised. Being a Jew is like being a Mormon. Not just a religion, but a way of life. You can't escape." She frowned. "Victor's Jewish. Didn't you know that?"

"No, I didn't. I didn't even know you got married," Eden confessed. "No one told me."

"I'm not surprised. We eloped. We had to. You know Mother and Dad and the Jews. Victor's older than me. He has two children."

"Is he divorced?" asked Eden, hoping she would not be the first to conjure the specter of marrying a divorced man outside the faith.

"If he's Jewish, what did it matter that he was divorced and older than me?"

Eden conceded that any one of those things would have set Afton against him.

"Anyway, we eloped to Nevada. When we came home, I told Mother I was pregnant. So of course, Mother started telling everyone we'd eloped months before. It was really very funny watching her scramble to make me respectable even though I had married a Jew. But she wouldn't give us a reception. She had a party for Alma and Walter after they eloped. And Walter's a Baptist."

"So I hear."

"But not for me and Victor."

"That must have hurt you. Victor, too."

"We didn't care. Victor and I had our own reception. We rented the Elks Lodge for the afternoon. Victor paid for everything, for the whole party. Champagne. Everything. Even if it wasn't the wedding I dreamed of," Connie looked momentarily wistful, "it was a good party. Winifred Merton even wrote us up in the *Herald*."

Eden frowned, calling up from the distant past a vision of Bojo's and a solitary woman eating alone. "Who is Winifred Merton again?"

"The editor of the women's pages for the *Herald*." Connie scoffed, "She's been working there since Methuselah—oh, what the bride wore and who came to the afternoon tea and Methodist Ladies' League meets for charity. St. Elmo's finest just fawn all over Winifred Merton. Ordinarily, she wouldn't have lifted her gloved hand for someone like me, but for Victor, well, he is the managing editor, after all. She was there, all right, her little gold pencil in hand at the lovely reception for Mr. and Mrs. Victor Levy, who had romantically eloped some months before." Smoke spiraled form Connie's nostrils.

"Did your parents come?"

"I was hoping they wouldn't." Connie regarded Eden with desperate resignation. "I was hoping Mother would say, Never darken my door again. But she didn't. And if Mother came, the whole family came. It was awful. One side of the room, all Victor's cronies from the paper, swilling champagne, smoking cigarettes, and chomping away on those little cocktail weenies. On the other side, all the Saints standing around with their lemonade in one hand, sweating in their temple underwear, and waiting for the conversion of the Jews in these latter days. You know what they're like."

"I do. I know they take it in with the air they breathe. You can't change them."

"Seven months later, our little daughter was born. Right on time." Connie stubbed out the last of her cigarette under her shoe, and ineffectually waved the smoke away from her troubled brown eyes. "The baby's all right, but she's too young to be very interesting. And my stepchildren are little beasts. Victor's first wife didn't want them. Sometimes I think he married me just to have someone at home for his first two children."

Connie Levy had the look of someone who has missed the first act, and now only vaguely understands the second, and Eden could not help thinking that escaping Afton Lance only to inherit three children didn't seem like much of a bargain. "We should go in," she said.

Pitchers of water and lemonade stood at intervals down the length of the white cloth in the sunny, seldom-used dining room. Mismated dishes sparkled with color, bowls of bright pickled tomatoes, steamy greens, and plates of puffy sourdough biscuits beside great slabs of butter. They all took their seats, and Tom Lance said grace. The only time he could be counted on to talk.

Afton, like a domestic Eisenhower, instructed that Eden, the returning hero, should be served first. No one would think of disobeying. "And yes," Afton snapped, hearing a tiny scoff from the boys at the end of the table, "a woman can be a hero just as much as a man. I'll thank you to remember that, William. Eden has served her country well and truly as any man. I won't hear no different."

Up and down the table, voices spilled and babies fussed and the sounds of spoons on crockery counterpointed the occasional slurps and exclamations. The taste of Afton's pork roast brought to Eden those Sundays of her childhood, herself and father, her grandmother around the Lances' table. Eden's gaze went up and down as they passed the high, steaming platters hand over hand; she tried to align her cousins' faces, their adult features with the children she remembered, to sort out their spouses, their burping babies. All these lumps in the family stew. Of which, she thought, I am one. The thought did not displease her, especially as she knew her time here with them was finite: Once she married Logan and moved to Philadelphia, she might never see them again.

Along with dinner, on everyone's lips there were bits and broken-off pieces of Junior's runaway marriage to the French girl. Was it true that French girls were kissing any American they could get their hands on when the Americans rolled into Paris? Were they throwing themselves bodily? Did they all smoke cigarettes, even the children?

"Lots of people smoke cigarettes," Eden offered feebly.

"Well, not Junior. He's a Saint." Lil was firm on this.

"Is it true," asked William, "that French girls don't wear underwear or take baths?"

There was a gasp all around the table. Eden picked up her ribs dripping with sauce, and said, "These are the best ribs ever. This sauce is wonderful!"

"It's my mother's recipe," said Walter Epps, flushing. "She sent the ribs. To welcome you home."

"Well, that was very nice of your mother. Please thank her."

"Walter's mother is a generous woman. And a generous-minded woman," Alma announced, adding with a tinge of defiance, and a crisp nod to Afton, "Eden, I do not believe you have met my husband, Walter. Walter's family is originally from Arkansas."

Eden responded cordially, grateful to have evaded the question of French girls' underwear.

"My mother's barbecue is famous all over Arkansas," said Walter. "Famous all the way to Memphis."

"Well, it's like nothing I've ever tasted. But then I've never been to Arkansas. What does your mother put in it?"

"There is no recipe. She keeps it all up here." Walter touched his head sagely. "But I'm sure she would be pleased to write it down if you would like."

Alma Epps, having scored her point on behalf of her husband and his Arkansas family, turned solicitously to Eden. "So now that the war is over and you're home, what will you be doing?"

"Eden's getting married," said Afton with an assured smile. "All the girls get married."

In the manner of most cooks, Eden adapted Mrs. Sally Epps's recipe. It became Eden's famous sauce at the Café Eden. It can be yours, too.

This is never quite twice the same. Your sauce might depend on what's in the house, or, what isn't. The important thing is to balance the sweet and the sour, the tangy and the rich. You can use honey or maple syrup for sweetener, different kinds of mustard, but the trick each time is to make the balance. You have to taste often and adjust.

Begin with a couple of onions chopped fine and put into hot oil. Cook this with a lot of brown sugar on a medium heat for, say, 15 or 20 minutes. Stir pretty often. Add 2 or 3 cloves of chopped-up garlic. When your onions, sugar, and garlic mixture has turned brothy, thick and rich-looking, add some sort of fruit juice, whatever is on hand, though not orange juice. Your cider vinegar will provide tang. Add honey or sugar, ½ cup. Then use a potato masher on any old fruit, but it has to be really ripe. Watermelon is good. Peaches are excellent, though they have to be peeled. Apricots don't. Berries or strawberries are good. Grapes don't work because they shed their skins and have little pits. Add mashed fruit to the sauce. It should not boil.

Add then, one whole big bottle of ketchup. Rinse it out with cider vinegar, a cup or more, depending on taste. This sauce is a good way to empty out half-used ketchup bottles. Then add a good splotch of mustard. Salt and pepper. Stir well, taste. If you want your sauce to bite back, add a few tablespoons of red pepper flakes. Lower your heat, cook, stirring now and then till it turns the color of a red barn.

Excellent on ribs, chops, chicken. Can elevate a lowly hot dog to stardom.

## The Ox and the Horse

Annie Agajanian Douglass and Eden formed a bond that lasted all their long lives, more like sisters than sisters-in-law.

Annie's parents were Armenian refugees from Turkey who had lived in Greece. They had come to Los Angeles in 1923. Annie was born at sea. Vartan and Shushan Agajanian between them spoke seven languages, though Vartan's mastery of English was never complete.

From her father, Annie learned early on that people have to eat. This would scarcely bear noticing if he had not come from people who had not eaten. The term *Starving Armenians* was not one to be used in Vartan's presence. Not in any language. He rented a small shop in Santa Monica and opened a grocery store. He gave credit (with interest) and he prospered.

Vartan Agajanian's family lived simply, even frugally, while he took the profits from the grocery and invested in land throughout Los Angeles County. By the time Annie, his eldest daughter, was sixteen, he was a rich man. They had a home in Beverley Hills with landscaped gardens and a pool. Vartan closed the small Santa Monica shop and opened the first of several large grocery stores.

Annie Agajanian was small, vivacious, with dark, dancing eyes and a lovely smile. She graduated at the top of her class at Beverley Hills High and went on to study art history at UCLA.

She met Ernest Douglass, then in the navy, at a USO dance. For Ernest it was love at first sight. In his sailor uniform he towered over her; he wanted to protect her and ravish her in the same moment. Annie, for her part, was smitten by his eagerness to please, and she responded to his faith in their future. There was a rocklike certainty about Ernest, especially appealing in an uncertain time.

Annie had never met a Mormon. Ernest had never met an Armenian. They both had a lot to learn.

Ernest formally asked her father for her hand in marriage. Annie sat beside him. She wore a gardenia pinned in her hair in the fashion of the times. Vartan Agajanian asked after Ernest's religion. Though Vartan himself practiced the faith of the Armenian Apostolic Church, Annie had been raised a

Protestant. Ernest said he had been raised a Mormon, but that he practiced no religion and would gladly follow Annie's. Vartan assumed the Mormons must be something like the Methodists. Ernest let him think it.

Vartan asked if Ernest's parents approved of this marriage, and Ernest said they were thrilled. In truth, he did not tell Kitty and Gideon till months after he was married. And when he wrote to his parents, he did not mention her maiden name, or that she was foreign. Annie was indeed Ernest's foreign country; everything about her—from the scent of her gardenia, to the lilt in her voice, to the very vocabulary she used—took him to some gorgeous place far, far from Fairwell, Idaho, from St. Elmo, California, from anything he had ever known. Mysterious and foreign.

After a dinner of lamb and rice, or grape leaves wound tight as little cigars around some strange enchanting flavor, Ernest sat in the Agajanians' living room sipping foamy coffee in tiny cups. The cups were so fragile he feared his own strength when he touched one. He reveled in the sticky pastries they served, papery and delicate and hinting of honey and roses. He admired their Armenian food, but he knew nothing whatever of the thousands of years of Armenian culture, their pride in being the first Christian nation, even if they no longer had a nation. Ernest Douglass was utterly ignorant of Armenian art, the literature, the music, the churches. His sole acquaintance with Armenians was the phrase *Starving Armenians,* which he wisely forbore to use.

They were married by a navy chaplain. They had a three-month courtship and a two-day honeymoon in Santa Barbara. Then they drove Annie's Cord convertible back to Los Angeles. Ernest shipped out of Long Beach on the *Baroka Sea.* Annie got a job at an art gallery run by Armenians who had reason to be grateful to her father. She lived with her parents and waited for letters from her husband. When they arrived, she took them to her room to read, as much because his grammar was poor as for the sincere and voluble emotions they contained.

When Tom, Afton, and Lil came to her parents' home that Saturday afternoon, Annie gave no indication that she recognized their distrust, even their dismay. Annie recognized that she, too, had married into a foreign country. Ernest never even noticed the Lances' prickly response to his bride. He was in love.

Ernest Douglass was steadfast; it was his great virtue. And, his wife slowly discovered after the war, his great detriment as well. After the war, and despite all Annie's exhortations, Ernest refused to use the GI bill to get a university education, like thousands of other returning GIs. He learned TV repair from the equivalent of one of those schools advertised inside matchbooks. He opened a TV repair shop in a new shopping center not far from the Encino house Annie's parents bought for them and for the three children born to them in quick succession.

Once he had made his mind up to something, Ernest could not be stirred either to action or anxiety. His marriage to the brisk, intense Annie suffered as a result. Vartan Agajanian later described their marriage as the ox and the racehorse trying to pull the same cart. Annie was the racehorse, eager to go, to plunge forward into the competition. But the ox is content with the yoke. The ox is stronger.

Annie, the racehorse, remained married to Ernest, lived with him and with their children, but she unharnessed herself from the ox. Annie Agajanian was the best thing that ever happened to Ernest Douglass. In truth, she was the only thing that ever happened to him. But she was not content with the yoke. She started a business as far away from art history as can be imagined.

People need to eat. Annie Douglass catered meals at movie locations scattered throughout the San Fernando Valley. Her father's connections in the grocery business were helpful to her, but she prospered with her own hard work and long hours. Though she began with a few panel trucks that lumbered out from her central kitchen each morning before dawn, she soon had a fleet of trucks and contracts with the many movie-location ranches in the Valley. She called the business Oasis for reasons she never disclosed to her husband.

## CHAPTER TWO

SWIFTLY UPON HER RETURN TO ST. ELMO, EDEN'S life took on the quality of a Victor Herbert musical. The Parade of Prospective Grooms: fanfare, horns, and the chorus of chanting aunts and cousins, their friends, neighbors, in-laws, all but singing "Marry marry marry, 'tis better to marry than to burn!" Eden Louise Douglass was passed before the battalions of Prospective Grooms. Eyes right. Salute. Good men. Honorable. A few with medals. All with distinguished fighting records, Eden was assured. Though Eden politely declined to go to church, Afton, undaunted, brought LDS men home for Sunday lunches. These men, fair-haired, blue-eyed, some uncomfortable in civilian clothes, all decent, were eager to marry, settle down. But their unveiled appraisals reminded Eden of the WAC recruiter assessing her: height, weight, good bones, broad hips, broad shoulders, someone to share the old yoke, to plow through life with. She wanted to write to Logan, to tell him how maddening and amusing all this was, but she had to wait to hear from him first. She needed to get a letter from him to know where to write.

She refused to haunt the mailbox. Pride. And she slowly learned to keep her expression neutral when Afton would return from the mailbox out by the road with only a letter from her parents. An invitation from her brother's wife, Annie, to visit her in Los Angeles. A card or note from her WAC friends, an invitation to Dottie Lofgren's wedding in Wichita, Kansas. Faye wrote with news of her impromptu marriage to a guy from New York. No word came from Philadelphia.

One of the Prospective Grooms took Eden into town to do some errands. He sat at the soda fountain of the drugstore while Eden went to the telephone booth, pulled the squealing door shut behind her, and called Philadelphia Information. Looking for a Smith. The information operator actually laughed when she said this. Francis Smith? she continued. No. Logan? No. F. L.? No. A law firm with Smith in the name? A Smith with an address in Chestnut Hill? The operator hung up on her, and Eden remained in the stifling confines of the booth, staring at the round expectant dial on the phone.

The Parade of Prospective Grooms included young men who took her to the pictures. At the Dream Theatre, Eden started for the balcony. "We don't sit there," one man explained. "That's for the coloreds. You know, the Sons of the Lamanites."

"I never heard anything so stupid in all my life. My mother and I always sat in the balcony."

This ended this man's interest in her, but other young LDS men regarded the unbelieving Eden as a lost lamb and they took on the role of Shepherd. These were the most tedious of the Prospective Grooms.

By day Eden toiled on the Lances' ranch—hoeing, digging, planting, weeding, cleaning out corrals and barns, feeding the animals. Her hands coarsened, her skin darkened, she got strong and dirty and exhausted. The rows of tomato plants she had put in sprouted, grew tall enough to tie up, and little green tomatoes gleamed. Eden and Tom put in stakes at each end of the rows and draped cheesecloth over the plants to protect them from the birds and the ceaseless California sun. She hauled water in buckets and refreshed their roots. The ground dried again. And still, Eden had no word from her lover. She asked Tom to cut her hair short. As the thick dark hair fell to the porch and blew away in the dry wind, Eden felt the clip of the shears was a sort of penance, a rejection of the Prospective Grooms, like a vow of celibacy. She was drying up with the desert wind, dying a little each day.

Without purpose or direction, in these months Eden felt suspended, inanimate, watching her own life from a distance. Everyone around her talked of the GI Bill. Of college and jobs and opportunities. California was the place to be!

Eden listened to a lot of this talk at various meals—at her cousins' homes, their in-laws', their in-laws' cousins'—endless spreads of creamed spinach and pot roast, white sauce on white potatoes, bland fare, bland faces, bland pleasantries, smothering conformity. One particular Sunday, at her cousin Bessie's house, a Prospective Groom thought to charm her with talk of the Dodge he was buying and the Japs he had killed. Eden kept her eyes on her plate. From the other end of the table, she caught a low, rising drone.

Bessie's father-in-law, an old man who wore a napkin tucked into his collar, blathered, patriarchal grumbling against women in general, the WACs, all WACs were whores of Babylon who had put on uniforms in order to be camp followers, to know men biblically. The old man's harangue escalated, though his relatives tried to hush him.

Eden, sitting there, felt a slow heated flush color her neck, her face, to the very roots of her hair. She hated these narrow-minded Mormons. She hated St. Elmo. She hated that she had heard nothing from the man she had loved and known biblically. She had known Logan Smith in lust, love, and everything in between. She had loved Logan, had been loved; her love was every bit as sacred and satisfying as anything these people knew.

Eden turned to the Dodge-loving Jap hater beside her. She said, "So, you're a hero and I'm a whore? How did that happen?" She put her napkin down, excused herself to Bessie, and left.

She walked all the way to the Dream Theatre, paid her money, and went up into the balcony, not caring about the film, but breathing the stale, familiar air, redolent of smoke and sweat, illusion and fulfillment, the code of conduct that required that you be true and, above all, valiant. She would wait and be brave.

CANNING AFTON'S SUMMER IN A JAR WAS A PROCESS THAT ONCE INITI-ated, could not be halted, and though repetitive, was not mindless by any means. It required concentration, timing, commitment. Once begun, there was no possibility of escape.

This summer morning Afton and Eden worked in tandem, sweat darkening their underarms and beading on their foreheads. Steam swirled a fog over the whole kitchen, though the windows were open and the dry wind blew through. Two vats of boiling water bubbled away on the stove, one for the jars before they were filled, another to seal them shut. Across the oilcloth-covered table lay the filmy, slipped-off skins of tomatoes and the pulpy remains, along with garlic, peppercorns, strings of dried chilis, and rosemary.

"You mustn't pay any attention to that old fool who was at Bessie's the other day," said Afton, gingerly handling hot lids, zapping them quickly on the hot jars.

"You heard about that?" Eden slid the still-warm tomatoes out of their skins, pushing them down into the hot jar that already held the garlic, chili, and pepper.

"I hear everything. I know everything. Can't help it. It's just the way I am." Afton put the lid on the jar and moved it into the boiling water bath, and returned to the next one. "There are people who will refuse to believe that now it is a new world. After the war. Times have changed and we must change with them. Those of us who can change. Who are still alive to be able to change." Afton took the tongs and lowered another jar into the boiling water. She mopped her forehead with her arm, then gave a tremendous, typical harumph. "Lucius don't have that chance. And Junior? Here is Junior Lance, brave enough to fight his way up the whole I-talian peninsula, to liberate the I-talians, and liberate the Frogs and liberate everyone else that crosses his path, to wipe out the Nazis, but not brave enough to tell his parents he's married. I have three letters from Junior, and not one word of this French girl. Not one. It's an ill wind blowing through that marriage."

"He'll be home soon," Eden offered, dreading the direction the conversation was taking.

"Oh yes. So he will," Afton replied grimly. "You are brave, too, Eden. You've been through war as few women have. You followed orders then. Why can't you follow now what God is clearly telling you."

"And what's that?"

Modestly, Afton declined to put words in God's mouth. "No one wants to end up alone. Do you want to end up alone?"

"Of course not. I want to marry. One day. I want to have children."

"Then do it! Of course it's a new world, now, after the war, but God's commandments stay the same. God don't change. God wants us to do our duty and prove ourselves worthy to inherit in the Celestial Kingdom. A woman's duty is to marry and bring to earth all the little souls awaiting bodies and to be tested on this earth. I don't see why you haven't chosen one of the young men here. They're all so nice."

Eden didn't want these men, nice or not. Didn't want to spend her whole life raising children and pickling tomatoes, a slave to the needs of her garden, her man, and lots of dirty little faces looking at her beseechingly. She had enough of Ruth Douglass in her to want more than that. She wanted Logan

Smith. She wanted Philadelphia, Chestnut Hill, and all the pictures he had painted for her of their life there: rowing on the river on autumn mornings, summers in Maine, life in a city where she might yet even write for a newspaper. Eden chose her words carefully, keeping to the general and avoiding her own particular situation. "Surely there are ways for a woman to live that will let her love a man and have a family, but not give her life over entirely to serving others."

"There are ways for people to stand on their heads, but most don't," replied Afton. "There are ways to avoid your duty, to skulk and shirk."

Eden felt a bright flare of anger. She wanted to lash out, to say, I have done my duty for years, but I will marry when I damn well want to. And who I damn well want to.

"There are ways to do all sorts of things, Eden, but you can't expect to have the love and affection and goodwill of the people you disappoint."

"I'm sorry you're disappointed in me, but I must live my life the way I see fit."

"You have a strong streak of independence that does not bode well for a woman. Look lively. Timing is important. Get that next jar ready. These have to stay hot when they go in the vat. I do not speak merely of this life," Afton went on, "but the life after this one. The Celestial Kingdom. Unmarried people cannot fully participate in the afterlife God plans for us. You don't marry, you don't get into the Celestial Kingdom."

Eden groaned. Even in death the Church had people lined up two by two, just like the Ark. Of course, Mormons got to procreate in the Celestial Kingdom, so no wonder they had to be married. She suddenly felt overwhelmed, the steam in the kitchen and a sense of slithery umbilical cords tightening around her, long matrilineal cords, generations of babies connected at the breast, the sound of thousands of slurping infants draining their mothers dry. Everything Afton stood for. Kitty had escaped these bonds and obligations, but she had done so by ducking under the surface of life, and failing to engage with any but imaginary creatures. Eden couldn't live like that. Surely there had to be alternatives. Ruth Douglass had managed to live beyond these bonds and obligations. How? And then, fleetingly, Eden wondered, At what cost?

"There is a recipe for everything in life, and you should follow it." Afton hoisted the jars and then lowered them into the boiling water.

"You always told me that a recipe was just a license for invention, that you should use what's on hand, and some imagination, and see what you can make."

Afton wiped her hands on her apron and composed her features severely. "I only want what's best for you. Marry one of these fine, young men. Return to the

Church, the faith of your family. You will be rewarded. On earth as it is in heaven. I only want what's best for you." She consulted the flame beneath the canning vat. "These will process and boil now ten minutes. Make sure the water stays at a boil. It's ten ten. At ten twenty, hoist out this whole basket and set it on the counter. Let them cool and test the seal. This will be the last jar."

"But there's more tomatoes, and more vinegar and sugar heated up."

"Well, you finish them up then. My work is done here. Remember what I told you."

"Keep the lids hot and the jars hot and the vinegar warm and work fast."

"Remember what else I told you, too." And with that Afton scooped up the whole pile of tomato skins and put them in a bowl and went outside, the screen door banging. Eden could hear her calling to the chickens.

# Afton's Summer in a Jar

Toss your tomatoes briefly in boiling water, fetch them out with a slotted spoon in a few minutes when the skin starts to split. Place in a bowl to catch juices. (You can make a nice salad of these peeled tomatoes, too, while you're at it. When they're cool, slip them out of their skins and into a salad bowl. Dress with a bit of oil, wine vinegar, and some freshly cut mint and parsley. Set aside till suppertime.)

To pickle your tomatoes, use small jars, $\frac{1}{2}$ pint. Into each sterilized jar, place 1 clove of peeled garlic, some peppercorns, 1 or 2 red dried chili peppers. Then put in your tomatoes, pressing down. Work only with as many jars as you can do swiftly.

Heat equal parts red wine vinegar and water, 1 tsp pickling salt, and a bit of sugar. Bring to a boil so that sugar and salt are dissolved. Pour over tomatoes, leaving about $\frac{1}{4}$ inch headroom. In each jar, slide a sprig rosemary or thyme. Important to use herbs that have some stems and rigor to them. Otherwise they wilt and don't look good in the jars.

Cap with hot two-piece caps and process 10 minutes in boiling water, as per canning instructions. Remove carefully from hot water bath. Place the jars on a towel and leave until completely cool. Test the center of the lid. If there is no "give," your seal is fine and you can unscrew the ring and keep in a cool dark place. Wait at least three weeks before using these pickled tomatoes. Best opened in January when the savor of summer can be yours all over again. They are a pungent addition to any salad. They can also be added to a pot of stock from Afton's Back Burner for a fine winter soup. Preserved thus, they will keep for years.

### HEARTBURN

Logan was lost to her, and the ache of missing him affected her like persistent heartburn. Eden lay awake in the room that had been grandmother's. Despite the long days and hard work on the ranch, sleep eluded her. She endured the old elemental hungers of the flesh, all that sweet carnality of connection: Logan's hands and lips and body under her hands, her lips, her body. And now, restless, sleepless, Eden lay alone in the big bed, night after night, longing, hungry, wondering if Logan lay with his wife in Philadelphia.

Why had she left everything to Logan? Eden had never even asked for his address or Philadelphia phone number. She had trusted him. Why hadn't she just said, *Forget Philadelphia. Just come to California. To hell with scandal. Everyone in California is from somewhere else. You get to reinvent yourself in California. Everybody does. We could live in Los Angeles or San Francisco. No one would care that a divorced Catholic had married a lapsed Mormon. No one.*

And then there came upon her the awful specter that some freak accident had befallen him. That he was wounded. Or worse. That Frances Smith had gotten an awful telegram. Who would call Eden? Who would write her? How would she know? Was it easier to bear his being faithless than his being dead? What was it Faye had said? *Bang me, honey, eight to the bar. And when it's over, contrary to those sappy lyrics, I won't be seeing you.* Was Logan faithless? Had Eden been forsaken?

*Faithless* and *forsaken,* the very words had the ring of one of Kitty's silly novels. Highblown. Flyblown as old music-hall lyrics. Hackneyed as they might be, these words racketed round Eden's sleepless mind. Her favorite phrase, *After the War,* withered, transcended, elided into the old sad waltz that Kitty always sang, "After the Ball."

| | |
|---|---|
| *After the ball is over,* | *Many a heart is aching,* |
| *After the break of morn* | *If you could read them all;* |
| *After the dancers' leaving;* | *Many the hopes that have vanished* |
| *After the stars are gone;* | *After the ball.* |

After the end of the love affair? What now? What next? After the ball? After the war?

WITH SPARE PARTS AND IN HIS SPARE TIME, TOM Lance refurbished an abandoned 1929 Model A for Eden. "A girl needs wheels for independence," he said as he showed her how to hot-wire it. There was no key. The motor turned over and Tom added, "Now you're on your way."

"Where?" For Eden, the question was real. She had been here almost three months.

"Well, Connie called Mother and asked you to come to her house for dinner tonight. Afton can tell you how to get there. Afton can tell you how to get most anywhere or do most anything."

Eden drove the fumy, noisy old Ford up the paved driveway to Connie's home. So new, it had no front porch, few front windows, only a small, clipped lawn, a big driveway, and a two-car garage. It suggested a completely different domestic direction than any house Eden had been in.

Connie, wearing smart trousers, high heels, and a pointless little half apron, came to the door and led Eden to the kitchen, which had every convenience, a big electric stove, the MixMaster on the counter, the Formica counters gleaming. The refrigerator hummed happily. The table was laid for three. Place mats, no oilcloth. As different from Afton's house as could be imagined.

"You'll be happy to know that I haven't invited any young men for you to meet."

"Thanks. I've had my fill of Prospective Grooms."

"Mother just does not let up, does she?"

"It's her great strength," said Eden. "And her great weakness."

A broad but narrow kitchen window looked out to the back, a covered patio and a huge backyard. On the swingset children played, Connie's two stepchildren and her own toddler, Leah, who, she explained, were all in the care of a woman named Josefina.

"Just a few more touches," said Connie as she lifted a bright green wobbly square from a big dish and set it on a lettuce leaf on a salad plate. "Seven-Up Salad," she explained. "Lime. My favorite. Do you like Seven-Up Salad?"

"I've never had it."

"That proves you've been living with Mother. It's all too modern for her. So is chicken à la king. Do you like that?"

"I've never had that, either, though I've heard of it. My mother believed it was food for royalty."

"Here." Connie got out a spoon and scooped some chicken à la king from the baking dish and put it in a small bowl. "Have a quick taste." Connie grinned. "Great, isn't it?"

Eden prodded with her fork through chicken à la king, colorless meat in a lumpy white sauce, studded here and there with gray-green peas and little cubes of ultrasoft carrots. Poor deluded Ma, Eden thought. This pale slop? Worse than Resurrection Pie. "It's wonderful," Eden assured her cousin.

"I cut the recipe from the *Herald*. I'll give it to you." Connie went to the sliding glass door and called out to Josefina. "I couldn't live without Josefina. She fed the kids early and she'll put them to bed in a bit. Would you like a drink? Victor will have a gin and tonic when he comes home. Does that sound good?"

Good? It sounded civilized. Mature. Undemanding. Nonjudgmental. Just being in Connie's youthful presence affected Eden like tonic. The scent of the lime, the fizz from the carbonation tickled her nose, as she savored the gin and tonic.

They took their drinks out on the patio, and Connie lit up. Long yellow streaks of twilight bore down on the dry grass, and the wind caught and swirled the blue smoke from her cigarette. Beside her chair was an ashtray that looked to be on stilts.

"I'm pregnant again," she said, confounding Eden with her candor. Connie had the dark hair, the broad shoulders, the clear skin of the Douglass women, but her mouth trembled with impotent dejection, and her dark eyes looked into the distance. "I haven't told Victor yet. I don't want it, of course, but what can I do? Be more careful next time, I guess. I wonder how Mother stood it. Eight children. She never even seemed to notice there were so many of us."

"I think Afton likes a crowd. She'd be happy right there beside Jesus feeding the five hundred."

"She'd be telling Him how to cook the fish and how to bake the loaves."

"And she'd be right," said Eden.

"The lively tumult."

"The what?"

Connie shook her head. "A phrase Mother read somewhere. I remember her saying to me, Yes indeed, that's what I like, the lively tumult of a big family where nothing goes to waste. I was just a little girl, maybe ten, but I told her, I want to waste things! I'm sick of everything hand-me-down and picked over. I shocked Mother. Even then. I've been shocking her ever since."

"I wore your sisters' hand-me-downs, too," said Eden. "But I always loved the way Afton made simple tasks seem important. You could be a child and still be important."

"Mother makes people love her whether they want to or not. My stepchildren don't love me. I don't know why. I've tried to love them, but I really can't. I have to admit that. Not to Victor, of course. If I'd known Victor's first wife wasn't going to keep his children, I might have done things differently." Unhappiness hovered at Connie's mouth. "This isn't what I wanted at all."

"What did you want?"

She plumed out a wreath of smoke. "I wanted to write for a big daily newspaper. To see my byline at the top of column of print. I thought marrying Victor would be part of a life like that."

"That's what I want! Wanted." Eden stumbled. "Want. I wrote for the *Enterprise* in Idaho, obits and society. Boring, sure, but I saw my name in print. I always dreamed of being like Martha Gelhorn, or Dorothy Thompson, one of those fearless women writers who go after the story and damn the consequences."

"They were always my heroines!"

"I wanted to join the press corps, especially during the war." The phrase—*during the war*—still had an odd ring for Eden, as though a great gulf separated her from her own life. "The WACs were the next best thing to the press corps. At least there was some adventure."

"I've never been out of St. Elmo," said Connie, peeling a bit of tobacco from her tongue. "I won the award for the Best Girl Journalist in the City when I graduated, St. Elmo High, class of 1943. There was an awards luncheon for the honor students. That was where I met Victor, the managing editor of the *Herald*. He gave me the plaque, and shook my hand. I hardly noticed him. All I could think was, Martha Gelhorn, watch out! Here comes Connie Lance! The day after I graduated, I walked into the *Herald* and applied for a job. I was all ready to step into the newsroom and prove myself. What a fool I was." Connie blew out a smoke ring. "I really believed a girl could invade the newsroom."

"What happened?"

"They gave me a typing test and put me in the typing pool. But I took the job."

Josefina brought the children up for a good-night kiss, duly administered, and then she took them inside to bed. Connie informed her that her pay was on the counter; she could collect it on her way out.

"That Christmas, Victor invited me to the company Christmas party. There was a lot of stupid gossip because he was so much older, and my parents, well, you can imagine what they thought."

"I certainly can."

"I was hoping Mother would throw me out of the house for going to a Christmas party with a Jew. I would have left home, happily. But she didn't. No, she stood there while he pinned the corsage on me. She was thin-lipped and furious, and as we were leaving she said Merry Christmas."

"And Victor, how did he react?"

"You think he hasn't been through this before? He's Jewish! My parents are the worst of the lot, but he knew what to expect. I warned him. He didn't care. He was crazy about me, and he was a grown man and not some boy just learning how to kiss. He wanted to marry me. And I thought, Well, why not? What more can you ask?"

Eden said nothing, knowing she would not have settled her fate with that question. Eden had asked for more. Much more. And now she knew she risked getting nothing at all. She had given up on Logan, but the future remained opaque.

Victor Levy, on arriving home, was far more lively than he had been at Afton's. He was jovial and eager to please. He joined them on the patio, loosening his tie, lighting up, chuckling, offering bits of newsroom gossip. Eden found

Connie and Victor bracing, lively, and invigorating. They didn't talk about the family or the church, or what ailed the chickens or what to do with the alfalfa, about the St. Elmo High baseball team, or the Relief Society bake sale. Connie and Victor were restless and eager, not at all like Tom and Afton, whose world was perfectly picketed. Connie and Victor felt more like friends than relatives. They laughed till their eyes ran at Eden's stories of the Prospective Grooms, especially the one who had insisted on showing off all the dental work the army had done for him, right there in Afton's dining room.

"Well, Eden," Victor chortled, "when Afton Lance sets her mind to something, you might as well go along with it. Afton will win. She'll wear you down and win. If she is trotting out the Prospective Grooms, she'll have you married by the end of the year."

Eden considered this. "You two didn't go along with her. You got married. You got what you wanted. Why shouldn't I? I'll marry whoever I want," she added, though she hadn't meant to take quite that defiant a tone. Victor and Connie both looked at their glowing cigarettes, and that's when Eden realized that the whole Lance tribe, every cousin and in-law, guessed, knew that she was waiting for a man who would not be coming. That she had been jilted.

The timer rang and they went inside to eat at the Formica table with the place mats.

"Eden needs a job, Victor," said Connie with something of Afton's finality. "Eden could work for you. At the paper. She's had experience. She wrote for a paper in Idaho for years. You've had years of experience, haven't you?"

"Yes," she replied, surprised at Connie's brilliant idea. She told a rather inflated tale of her *Enterprise* life. Victor kept eating.

"She's a returning veteran," Connie went on. "You know, if my cousin Eden was a man, you would find a place for someone talented as she is. No matter who you had to let go."

"It's not that simple. You don't understand, honey."

"The *Herald* has a new building downtown, but they're still stuck in the Dark Ages. Isn't it time the old *Herald* had some new blood? Isn't it time for a change? Isn't it time Winifred Merton retired?"

Victor Levy coughed and took a great gulp of iced tea, and polished off the ice from his gin and tonic, crunching away. "Winifred Merton, retire? She's been the *Herald*'s society editor for . . . forever. Forty years. More! She was probably there, pecking away at the typewriter, when this valley was nothing but sagebrush and rabbits, before the Indians, before the Mexicans, before the Mormons got here in 1854! Winifred Merton will leave her desk in a coffin, and not before. And at that, they'll have to pry her fingers from the keys." His face grew red and puffy, and he took another bite.

"I didn't say fire her," Connie said.

"Fire her? Fire Winifred Merton? That's a good one. No—you'll pardon me, please, Eden—but it would not matter one goddamned bit if your cousin Eden were Pearl S. Buck come to St. Elmo and wanting a job, to put her Nobel Prize, framed, on the wall above her desk. I still couldn't move Winifred Merton. No one can. My predecessor tried." He made a face. "And I told you what happened to him."

"All right then. Let Winifred Merton stay."

"Yes, and let the planets stay in their orbits." He gave an unenthusiastic guffaw.

"Maybe Miss Merton needs an assistant," said Connie, "you know, a helper."

Connie—like Afton—would get her way quickly, or she would persist until she did. Victor Levy looked up from his plate and assessed Eden Louise Douglass, and though his was not the gaze of the Prospective Grooms, or of the WAC recruiter, Eden could all but hear the springs and traps of his mind working.

"Can you type?" he asked.

# 7-Up Salad

Connie Lance Levy adored 7-Up Salad. It was her signature dish. Different kinds of Jell-O made different colors; the judicious use of food coloring helped. She made a red, white, and blue version for the Fourth of July picnic, but this failed. In the heat, certainly the heat of a St. Elmo summer, 7-Up Salad melts and all the nubs and pineapple bits separate, and float apart in an unappealing mass.

This salad was a staple of postwar American cooking: easy to make, almost foolproof, colorful. The 7-Up, substituted for the liquid, had no perceptible effect or taste.

> 1 large pkg. Jell-O (choose any color)
>
> 1 small can crushed pineapple, drained
>
> 1 pint cottage cheese

Make the Jell-O, using the juice from the canned pineapple and 7-Up for your cold water. Add the pineapple and cottage cheese. Pour into a flat dish. Refrigerate overnight and cut in squares or diamonds and serve on a lettuce leaf.

# SNAPSHOT

### The Return of the Native

In 1962, Constance Lance Levy, age thirty-six, was diagnosed with cancer. Death took her so swiftly that neither of her parents even learned to pronounce the name of the cancer that killed her. She died within four months. In August. Afton, Tom, and Victor were with her at the very end. The last words they heard her say sounded like *This isn't fair.*

The funeral—Victor did not even protest Afton's wishes—was at the Church of Jesus Christ of Latter-day Saints.

Eden returned to St. Elmo for the funeral, but she went to the wrong LDS church. She had not known there was a new one built. She was directed by an obliging Saint who was sorry for her loss. The parking lot at the new LDS church was full. Eden wondered how many of these people were here for Connie, and how many came to support Afton. Saints greeted Eden, embraced her, spoke as if she had never left St. Elmo, as though she were still holding her father's hand.

Eden looked for Victor Levy, and found him alone, except for his children, pacing and smoking a cigarette on the sidewalk outside of the church. All four children looked like Victor; his children from his first marriage and his children by Connie were the image of their father. Connie had not left her imprint even on her son or her daughter.

Eden touched Victor's arm. He turned to her, and tears sprang to his eyes.

The children remained tense, brittle, and silent. Sixteen-year-old Aaron stood rooted beside his sister, eighteen-year-old Leah. Eden embraced each of them, even Connie's stepchildren, but none of them flinched or responded. Eden felt a sudden surge of resentment on Connie's behalf. Eden wanted these children to be sad. Eden was sad.

Victor was sad. Victor was beside himself. Bewildered. Victor wiped his eyes, and put his hand on Eden's shoulder. He said, Connie loved you, Eden. She admired you.

Connie was more like my sister than my cousin.

Alma Epps interrupted them: Mother wants you, Alma said to Eden. Mother wants you to sit with them. Alma patted Victor's arm, and said again that Mother wanted Eden.

So Eden followed Alma into the church, to the front pew. Behind her, the vast, the overwhelming Lance clan lined up, a sea of faces. Lil moved to one side so Eden could sit beside Afton.

Afton was sad. Her whole body trembled, but it was not in her nature to be bewildered. She held Eden's hand. She said, Connie was a lot like you. You might have been sisters instead of cousins.

We had the same dreams, said Eden.

And you made the same mistakes. You were both reckless, said Afton as the service began. There was a general flurry of hymn books. But Afton had chosen the hymns, and so had no need of the book. She did not release Eden's hand until she reached for a hanky for her tears.

After the service, people slowly made their way to the gym, where food was laid out on long tables underneath the hoops and the lights. The high gymnasium windows were open. A furnacelike wind blew in. In Connie's honor, many people brought 7-Up Salad. Oblong squares in a hundred pale colors dotted the tables, and they all melted in the heat, chunks of pineapple swimming in a nubbled pastel sea.

## CHAPTER FOUR

WHEN EDEN LOUISE DOUGLASS WENT TO WORK FOR the St. Elmo *Herald,* the women's pages of the nation's newspapers did not print articles about PMS, ADHD, STDs, or the health and fitness of anything so crass as the human body. They did not offer lead features about erectile dysfunction, or what to do if you found your son wearing women's clothes, or your husband cheating with a co-worker, or how to choose a therapist, or talk your daughter out of getting her bellybutton pierced. There were only two possibilities: Events and Recipes. Recipes were mostly variations on Seven-Up Salad, canned soup, canned tuna and cornflakes; dessert was anything with a maraschino cherry. As for Events, any delightful occasion dignified by the presence of Miss Winifred Merton, the sour social autocrat of St. Elmo, became an Event.

The *Herald* had moved into a new building downtown just before the war. Modern, vast, and airy, though not yet air-conditioned, it took up a whole city block. The presses were in the basement; they hummed and gnashed all night long. On the first floor you would find reception, the typing pool, the archives, a conference room, and the offices of people who did not get their hands dirty. The second floor was entirely given over to editorial, the newsroom. Except for Victor Levy's glassed-in cubicle, this was a vast sea of desks with typewriter tables at right angles to the desks. On these sat large, upright typewriters whose bells and keys provided a constant percussive symphony. The fluorescent lights were on night and day. When the reporters were bored, they would sharpen their pencils and play darts at the acoustic tiles in the ceiling. This floor rang all day (and late into the night when the sportswriters covered St. Elmo High football games) with the frantic work of the news. Phones ringing. Telex machines. Telegrams. Typewriter keys noisily chewed up cheap paper under the hands of reporters, and the copy boys called out, running up and down the employees' stairwell to the press room, long galleys of newsprint in their gritty hands.

In all this general frenzy of ink and cigarette smoke, shirtsleeve camaraderie, there were no women and only one lady, Miss Winifred Merton. She kept a single rose always by her typewriter. Her desk was at the very back of the newsroom, near the employees' stairwell.

Arriving daily at the newspaper, Winifred Merton did not use the employees' stairwell so near her desk. She took the elevator, got off, and stalked through cirrus clouds of cigarette smoke in the newsroom, past the men's desks, as though she were a gloved-and-hatted dinghy navigating treacherous shallows. Once at her desk, she removed her gloves, tucked up the little veil on her hat; she gave an evil look to the men in the newsroom and sat down at her typewriter. Imperious Winifred Merton, so skinny as to be buttless, breastless, her pallor accentuated by hair dyed the color of boot blacking. The sportswriters and city-desk men, the cop-beat writers and the wire-service writers, even the copy editors treated her with sarcastic deference that masked their begrudging fear. She was older than any of them. She had been there longer. She commanded fierce, unswerving loyalty among St. Elmo's social elite. Brides and grooms and mothers of the brides and grooms, social climbers and those in decline—the would-bes and the has-beens—slathered and clambered and lusted after her notice. So powerful was Miss Merton's column that her gushing description of a reception for a couple who had "eloped" months before could bestow unquenchable respectability upon children who had been conceived in the backseats of cars. Connie Levy could testify to this.

Miss Merton informed Victor Levy, in her dry, unyielding way, that she absolutely did not want an assistant, but the managing editor prevailed.

Defeat did not set well on Winifred Merton.

"Do not believe for one moment," she said to Eden on her first day, "that you will be inheriting my job."

"I don't. I only want—"

"No one cares what you want," said Miss Merton, her brows knitting over the rims of her tortoiseshell glasses. "You have gotten here by a family connection. I have gotten where I am by virtue of hard work and self-denial. I am not to be trifled with."

Janitors were moving the desks around, placing Eden's up against Miss Merton's. Miss Merton could look out upon the newsroom and beyond, out the great windows onto the world. Eden could look at Miss Merton and the wall. Who cares? Eden told herself. I'm here. I'm breathing ink and smoke. My name will be at the top of long gray columns of print.

"And don't imagine you will have a byline. Everything on this page is mine. You may be typing, but you will not be writing for the *Herald*. You will be working for me." Miss Merton pressed her brilliant red lips together, and sucked in her thin cheeks. "Is that clear? Moreover," she looked Eden up and down, "you will not be wearing trousers ever again."

"They're good for work. They protect—"

"They're not good if you intend to work for me. Trousers belong on men for a reason. That's why women don't wear them."

"What reason is that?"

"Men have something to put in them."

Behind her, Eden could hear the snickering in the newsroom. Even Miss Merton colored, but she demanded the janitor to get on with it and pointed Eden to her chair.

Eden rolled the coarse paper into the typewriter, and began a new life, dedicated to Events and Recipes, as assistant to the editor of the women's pages, Miss Winifred Merton.

Eden Douglass rented a tiny furnished second-story apartment with a kitchenette. The three small rooms had been hastily carved out of an old house not far from Silk Stocking Row, so tight was postwar housing. She returned the 1929 Model A to Tom Lance, and bought Annie's Cord convertible when Annie and Ernest were expecting their first child and wanted a more sedate car. Every morning Eden got into the snazzy convertible, tied a smart scarf around her dark hair, put on sophisticated sunglasses, and drove to the St. Elmo *Herald*.

Within months of Eden's arrival, Miss Merton learned to take advantage of her assistant. Miss Merton assumed almost total command of Events. If perchance two Events conflicted, Miss Merton went to the more socially desirable and sent Eden to innumerable Women's Assistance League luncheons, where she nearly passed out from boredom, cigarette smoke, and the clouds of Emeraude. Inevitably they served tousled greens with pinkish ooze atop that the menu described as French dressing. Chicken à la king was their standard dish, a thin brown film coagulating here and there where the cream had cooled and been reheated, the taste and texture such that the lumps either slid down Eden's throat with a sickening finality, or turned to talc under her teeth. She came to recognize this substance as undissolved cornstarch.

Worse than Events were the Recipes. Though the final edits and selections were Miss Merton's own, Eden had to tout and render exact instructions for her readers to broil grapefruit, to concoct salad dressings of equal parts of ketchup, mayo, and sweet pickle relish. Eden was obliged to exclaim over canned hams unzipped from their tins, rinsed, swathed in mayo, and served up as picnic fare. These, Miss Merton asserted, were the recipes the *Herald* readers wanted, asked for, everything easy and up-to-the-minute. Especially now that the war was over, and austerity a thing of the past, women wanted to know how to cook quickly, easily, with the least possible fuss. To get out to the golf course, or go shopping, or to put on their gloves, heels, and a hat, and go to an Event.

As Eden followed Miss Merton's instructions, she experienced an almost lunar opposite tug. She spent a lot of time in the Cord convertible, top down, driving around with the radio on, cruising in a desultory sort of way, looking for . . . she wasn't quite sure what, succumbing to a powerful nostalgia for what was not up-to-the-minute and easy. The old scents and textures of childhood delights: the stairwell at her grandmother's house, Afton's kitchen, Bojo's, Mr. Kee's store, delectable remembrances of Gloria Patterson's tin pails of beans and meat, her burlap-wrapped tortillas. All—save for Afton's kitchen—gone, the places shuttered, the people, well, who knew? As for the achievements of Napoleon, who had fed the citizens of this railroad town sauces of sherry and portobello mushrooms, who could poach a fish properly and serve it with a bright banner of parsley and pistachio sauce, these accomplishments had disappeared with Napoleon himself. Figs Napoleon and Green Goddess dressing were the stuff of legend. There was nothing like that left in St. Elmo. Even the building that had housed the Pilgrim Restaurant had succumbed to a quake in 1939.

It didn't bear thinking about.

Especially not on Saturday nights, when Eden had a standing date with a sportswriter. He took Eden out to dinner, usually at the Happy Horseshoe, where he spouted scores and plays and the statistics from long-ago games. He swathed his hamburger, his French fries, his meat loaf or rice or leathery steak in ketchup. Eden figured he could eat old shoelaces with enough ketchup. Going to bed with him after the Happy Horseshoe answered Eden's physical hungers but never touched her deeper needs or feelings. She felt quite certain that the old man in the next apartment kept his ear to the wall. This dampened Eden's enthusiasm for sleeping with the sportswriter, who, in any event, quickly finished his business. He seldom stayed the night.

Eden better enjoyed Friday nights, when the sportswriter covered high school football, and she went over to Connie and Victor's. Eden had plenty of family in St. Elmo, but she didn't make friends at the *Herald*. Except for herself and Miss Merton, women at the *Herald* worked in the typing pool. They resented Eden, especially since everyone knew she had gotten the job through Victor Levy, her cousin's husband.

She was leaving the Herald building around noon one day, bound for yet another Ladies' League luncheon, when in the crowded main lobby she accidentally bumped into a black woman. They both apologized, and then stared at each other.

"Eden Douglass?" said the woman.

"Sojourner Johnson?" said Eden.

They laughed and shook hands. Not yet thirty, Sojourner already had the look of her mother. That's how Eden had recognized her.

"Are you still making trouble?" asked Sojourner. "You were always good at that. My mother used to say you had a little devil in your eyes."

"I work here now."

"Really? Doing what?"

"Well, I write for the women's pages," Eden replied with some small pride.

"For old Miss Merton?" Sojourner made a face.

Eden cringed. "Yes, I'm afraid so."

"Writing up all those temptatious recipes, are you?"

"Yes, I'm afraid so."

"Come on out to Bojo's sometime, Eden."

"But it's gone."

"It's moved. We're out on Valley Farms Road. Way out."

The new Bojo's had been an old house, gutted and rebuilt as a restaurant far from the center of commerce, so far out that probably white people didn't come here very often. Eden parked the Cord in the shade of a huge old eucalpytus tree swaying over the dirt parking lot. A boy of about eight opened the door for her and said for a nickel he would watch her car. Eden smiled to remember Nana Bowers's injunction about keeping kids working. She gave the boy a nickel and walked up the steps to the long, deeply shaded porch.

Bojo's had an easy ambience, very different from the old café in St. Elmo's civic district. Her eyes had to adjust to the dim light; shutters were drawn against the heat. The floors were of well-worn wood and the booths deep, set off from one another, secretive. A couple of swamp coolers filled windows at either end, and their sluggish churning counterpointed the crack of billiard balls from the back room. Someone turned up the radio or the juke box, the music rhythmic and bluesy, infectious and unfamiliar. "Shake That Thing."

A boy of about twelve sat at an empty front table reading a thick schoolbook. He tucked it away and asked what he could do for her.

"I bet you're Sojourner's son, aren't you?"

"I am. Wallace Dawson."

"Well, Wallace, would you please tell your mother Eden Douglass has come to see her."

"Have a seat. I'll go get her." He gave her a menu.

Eden took a deep breath. "Do you still make fried okra here? I'll take an order of that, please. I'm starved. I'll eat anything that isn't broiled grapefruit or 7-Up Salad, or chicken à la king."

"Is that on the menu?" Wallace looked perplexed.

"No. Thank God. Oh, and do you still make Emotional Cornbread?"

The boy smiled. "We're the only place in St. Elmo you can get that emotional."

Fifteen minutes later Sojourner came out with a tray that held pitcher of iced tea, a plate of fried okra, a pan of Emotional Cornbread, and a pack of cigarettes.

"Salt 'em up and eat 'em hot," said Sojourner over the crack of billiard balls and the slurp of the swamp cooler. "Cold fried okra don't bear looking at. You came at a good time. I got time to talk. Tell me what you been doing. You can see what I been doing. Married young and never strayed too far from the family business, though the Whickhams forced us out of downtown. Bought the Bowers Building and doubled the rents after Nana died."

"I see you followed old Nana's advice about keeping your children working and close by."

"Oh yes. And I see you followed your grandmother's example."

"I did?"

"Making your own way. Beholden to no man."

"I wish that were true. I still have a lot to learn."

"Well, eat up, and tell me what you know so far."


ACTUALLY EDEN WAS MUCH BEHOLDEN TO VICTOR LEVY, BUT EVEN HE habitually cringed before Winifred Merton. One Friday night, eating dinner with Victor and Connie, Eden brought up the possibility of running a series of articles with recipes from an older St. Elmo, places like Bojo's that had their own recipes and traditions. Victor rolled his eyes and appealed to Connie to define for her cousin Eden the true meaning of the word: *impossible.* Winifred Merton would not have it, and Victor Levy would not press her.

All right. But on her own time, Eden began talking to people, collecting recipes and writing up feature stories about Sojourner Dawson and others. Eden called up Walter Epps and went to visit his mother, Sally, who parted with her Famous All the Way to Memphis Barbecue Sauce recipe, and the story that went with it. Eden prevailed on Afton Lance to write down some of her recipes. Afton declared she didn't have the time to write down what she always just kept in her head. Eden said, "Just talk. I'll take down what you say in shorthand, and type it up later." For these interviews, Eden took all her notes in the shorthand she had learned to be a great reporter. Granted, they were not the kind of notes that Martha Gelhorn took, but they were Eden's own. They took Eden beyond Miss Merton's girdled notion of how post-war women wanted to eat, wanted to cook, indeed, wanted to live.

Her greatest triumph Eden found in Zacateca's, a hole-in-the-wall place wedged between a pawnshop and a shoe repair on a back street where only Spanish was spoken. There were the usual dusty piñatas overhead and paintings of bullfights, portraits of Benito Juarez. The fans had not been oiled in a long time. But Eden perked up at the old remembered ribbon of scent. Eden asked if the place belonged to Gloria Patterson, who used to sell tortillas and beans from her back door.

"My mother never did that," said the waitress. Her hair was wound in a braid around her head and she had hard, bright blue eyes. Her skin was clear, though no longer fresh, and she was still sharply attractive. Her name tag said Lupe. "We had no permit. You want to see Zacateca's permits? They are in the kitchen."

"I'm not with the health department. I'm with the *Herald.* The newspaper."

"And?"

"Is Gloria Patterson still alive?"

"She is alive, but she talks to the dead."

"I'd like to talk to her. She'd remember me."

"Why would she remember you?"

"I'm Eden Douglass. I used to go to your house all the time. I remember your father, Ben."

Lupe softened. "Poor Papa. May he rest in peace. Okay, but no selling without a permit."

"That never happened," said Eden.

"And if Mama gets tired . . ."

"I will leave."

The afternoon sun beat down mercilessly as Eden stopped her car in front of a chain link fence that enclosed a scrappy lawn where a yapping mutt flung himself at her. The house was shuttered, darkened, the porch buckling under the weight of the bougainvillea. Cars up on jacks sat in the yard, and a handsome young man, perhaps seventeen, scooted out from underneath a Chevy and asked what she wanted.

"I'm looking for Gloria Patterson. Lupe gave me this address."

He took hold of the mutt, indicated she should open the gate and go around the back. Waist-high weeds brushed at her skirt as Eden followed the walk to the back where an old grape arbor, great twisted boughs the size of a man's arm, wrapped up and over the patio, creating a dense shade, the leaves overhead so thick, no sunlight could pierce them, and grapes forming in still-hard clusters. Long yellow ribbons of flypaper curled down from the rafters, studded with flies. A scraping sound, rhythmic, practiced, metronomical, came from the back, and for a single moment Eden closed her eyes, and might have reached up, taken her father's hand, so surely did that unchanging rhythm take her back in time. She opened her eyes to see a little walnut of a woman, a small table before her, working a mortar and pestle. The woman did not look up.

Mrs. Patterson had shrunk. All but her hands. They remained strong, sinewy. The mortar and pestle never faltered; she worked, *scrape, scrape,* as though she were keeping time for the cosmos, unrelenting, unchanging. Her hair was completely white, cut very short, almost as short as Eden's. Her still-misshapen nose seemed to have collapsed into her face, and her eyes were milky with cataracts.

Lupe opened the screen door and frowned to see Eden. She went to her mother and spoke in a low voice and in Spanish.

The mortar and pestle stopped. Mrs. Patterson motioned for Eden to come closer. She touched Eden's face, her hair; her fingers were so tough, Eden wondered that they could register anything tactile. Eden gave her name, and Mrs. Patterson broke into a great toothless grin. "Sit. Here. Near me." She said something in Spanish and then added, "Lupe, something cold to drink. A beer, yes, Eden? Or, are you Mormon like your father?"

"A beer would be great." Eden pulled up a rocker across from Mrs. Patterson and her little table. The rocker was scarred, the cushion unstuffed. Beneath her feet the earth of the unpaved yard was so hard packed after generations of feet that it was almost dustless. "I work for the newspaper, Mrs. Patterson. For the *Herald*. I'd like to write about how you came to be such a fine cook and fed all St. Elmo from your back door."

Lupe, returning with three cold beers, interrupted. "That didn't happen. Zacateca's, now that's our family's place."

"Is the food the same? Like what you used to . . ."

"You were a child," said Mrs. Patterson. "Nothing will ever be as it was then."

Eden was old enough to know this was true. That was why she was here. "You were a pioneer, Mrs. Patterson. People eat on the go all the time now. There's a place on Brigham Boulevard now where you drive in and stand at a window and order a hamburger for fifteen cents, and they put it in a bag. They have the hamburgers all wrapped up. It's fast, but it's not satisfying. What you cooked was magical."

Mrs. Patterson seemed pleased. Lupe looked suspicious.

"I'd like to publish your story, your recipes in the *Herald*. One day," she added.

A flurry of Spanish exchanged between Mrs. Patterson and Lupe. Finally, Lupe said, "The story, yes. The recipes no. People want to eat well, they must go to Zacateca's. You will put that in the paper?"

"Yes."

Gloria motioned for Eden to sit, to relax, to take the cold beer. "This is a good story, Eden. I was born Gloria Trujillo, the youngest, the only girl in a family of horse thieves. The Trujillos, they were the finest horse and cattle thieves in California. They were—" she nattered in Spanish to Lupe, nodded, closed her eyes.

With a dish towel, Lupe brushed at the hovering flies. "The Trujillos were princes of cattle thieves. Two generations. They knew every canyon, every arroyo, every ravine and creek and trail from San Gabriel to the desert, to San Gorgonio. They knew Jesuit Pass like that old Jesuit himself. No herd was safe from the Trujillos if they decided they wanted your horses, your cattle. Sometimes they would come into St. Elmo and raid the railroad stockyard. Very dangerous life. One of my mother's brothers was hanged in 1894 or '95. People used to say the Trujillo gang could steal your horse from under you, and you won't know nothing till your backside hits the ground. By then the Trujillos have the horses sold, and they are smoking somewhere, innocent as can be."

Lupe and Gloria both laughed out loud. "This is a good story," Gloria repeated.

"The Trujillos' little ranchito, their hideout, up in the—" Lupe nodded eastward toward the mountains. "No one ever found it."

"Almost no one." Mrs. Patterson's laughter spilled from toothless gums. "My parents had six sons, maybe seven. They were all before my time, grown men before I was born. Hard men. My brothers were swine. They are better to their horses than to their women, their children. They were not loyal sons to my father. They stole from him. I cannot prove this, but I believe it just the same. I am born late in my parents' lives. A surprise! Their only girl. A little gift, they said. They adored me, my parents. But life is hard for a little girl among such men as my brothers, and one day, I am perhaps five or six, I am caught in a stampede of horses my brothers are running. They do not warn me. My nose, my jaw . . ." She ran her leathery hands over her face. "Destroyed. My head, broken open. There is no doctor to go to. My parents think I am going to die. But they pray, and I live. I am not very smart after the accident. It takes me a long time to learn to talk again. My skull, see? And my face! But it makes no difference to my parents. I am their angel. Their sweetness of life." She said something in Spanish to Lupe and told Eden to wait.

Lupe went back into the kitchen, brought back out a tray with three more cold beers, steaming fresh tortillas, a mound of refried beans and some spiced meat, soft and studded with bright green jalapeños, and a bowl of sauce in which the chili peppers glistened like little yellow eyes. Golden tamales lay on another plate, side by side in smooth, ribbed corn husks.

"You eat, Eden." Gloria patted her knee. "I like to feed people My own guts are not so good these days, but I like to watch people eat. You too, Lupe. A story goes better if you are not hungry."

Eden thought to herself, I will remember that, as she took a warm tortilla and slathered beans and meat on it, dolloped the whole with the bright sauce, bit down, and broke into a sweat of remembrance. The cold beer tingled in her mouth like a round of applause above the sting of peppers.

"I can see my ranchito still." Gloria sighed. "My father builds in the *cañón* where no one knows. We have a good barn, but my brothers live in shacks with their cowardly women. The house of my parents, though, that is a good house. There, my mother teaches me how to cook. Not just the boil and fry of it, but the . . ."

"Instinct," Lupe supplied after five minutes lapsed in silence.

"Yes. Then one morning, two of my brothers ride up, with an extra horse, and tied over this horse, face down, there is a man, a boy really. Bleeding very bad. My brothers have caught him, found him spying on them in the ravine with the stolen cattle. And who is this boy? *Madre de Dios!* It is Ben Patterson, the worthless son of Judge Patterson."

"Poor Papa." Lupe sighed. "Just this once he does something right."

"May he rest in peace." Gloria made the sign of the cross.

"Truly, my papa was never smart," said Lupe thoughtfully, sipping her beer, "but he was handsome."

"He had blue eyes," said Gloria, leaning back in her rocker. "Golden hair. Blue eyes. Dimples. And such a mouth." Gloria brought her thin withered lips in a kiss. "And a beautiful smile. Even after my brothers broke his nose, he was so beautiful. Never has there been a beauty like Ben Patterson."

"Poor Papa," said Lupe again. "He was never very good at anything except riding a horse."

"How did he find your brothers?" asked Eden.

"Money." Gloria rocked and nodded, nodded and rocked. "One night Ben is drinking at the Ferris Hotel and a man there moans about how the Trujillos have stolen his cattle and ruined him. Ben casts doubt on his manhood. *'After all,'* says Ben Patterson, *'who are Trujillos? A bunch of Mexicans. If you can't get your cattle back from a bunch of Mexican horse thieves, what kind of white man are you?'*"

Gloria and Lupe both laughed. Clearly this was a story that had been told many times before.

"So there is a bet," continued Gloria. "Everyone is drinking. And finally it comes to three hundred dollars! Three hundred dollars says Ben Patterson can't find this man's cattle. Ben says he is one smart hombre, smarter than Mexicans. And he was true to his word, wasn't he?"

Gloria and Lupe both gave rippling laughs. Lupe had to wipe her eyes.

"He found the Trujillos' camp, didn't he?" Gloria went on. "He found the cattle and the hideout."

"But poor Papa. The Trujillo brothers found him, too."

"Of course they beat him, but they could not hang him without the consent of my father. So they tie him over the horse and bring him to ranchito. My father remembers the son Judge Patterson hanged in ninety-five. My father says, *'Judge Patterson's son will have the same fate my son suffered, but I do not want my daughter to watch a man hang. Take this gringo down the* cañón, *far from here, and hang him all the same.'* But, my mother says, *'Wait.'*"

Gloria Patterson leaned back, took a deep breath, and closed her eyes. Her shattered features composed themselves.

"Do you want to rest?" Lupe asked after she had been silent for while. "Mama?"

"Just for a moment. This is the best part."

Gloria Patterson and her daughters declined to part with any of her recipes and techniques. To taste these unique combinations, you can go to Zacateca's in St. Elmo, California. They have moved from the place between the pawnshop and the shoe repair. The new restaurant now fronts Caesar Chavez Boulevard. They are open from 7 A.M. till 9 P.M. Monday through Saturday and for lunch on Sundays. They do not take reservations. Get there early. But, if still you must wait outside, there is a deep awning for shade, and beautiful girls circulate with glasses of fresh hibiscus iced tea (free). You are guaranteed a fine time. A little heartburn perhaps, but worth it.

Eden, experimenting later in life with what she remembered of Mrs. Patterson's cooking, came up with the following to approximate what she used to buy at Gloria's back door. Her approximations never quite lived up to what she remembered. What does, when the salsa is nostalgia?

Use a cheap cut of meat, pork or beef, seasoned with the below combination, and braise it slowly till it falls off the bone. When done, put your meat in a large pan, and add to this 2 or 3 jalapeños (depending on your tastes) chopped fine, some red onion, chopped fine, and warm quickly on a low heat, stirring often. To this add a few chopped tomatoes and a combination, depending on your amounts, equal portion of coriander, cumin, chili powder, and a dash of cinnamon. A little salt too. Cover. Quickly fry up your corn tortillas, placing each in a warm oven as you finish. Serve with refried beans, salsa, and condiments of your choice, grated cheese, chopped green onion, sour cream, though these latter were never part of Gloria's tacos. The gift was not what you put on top, but what Gloria put inside.

# SNAPSHOT

## GLORIA AND THE METHODISTS

Señora Trujillo told her husband it was a sin to hang a man who could not speak. Señora Trujillo was a fine strapping woman, tough as an old leather harness, erect, purposeful, her gray hair braided and hanging down her back, tied with a leather thong. She said they must wait until the Patterson boy woke up. He might have some last words.

Fine, said her husband, returning to the corral where he was breaking a colt.

Señora Trujillo told her sons to put the Patterson boy in the barn and throw some water on him, to wake him.

Then can we hang him? they asked.

Leave me alone with this stupid gringo, she replied.

Benjamin Franklin Patterson slowly roused to painful consciousness. Señora Trujillo held his jaw, tilting his bloody face this way and that, looking into his mouth, checking out his teeth. He screamed and started to babble and yelp, to blither. It was only a bet! He would say nothing, tell nothing, tell no one! God, only let him live! Señora Trujillo told him in Spanish to shut up. He continued to pule and gibber and plead for his life.

His wrists and ankles were still bound. She washed the blood off his face from the broken nose and busted-up eyes and lips. She checked his skull for fractures. Her expert hands roamed over his body. He whimpered and cried and shrieked, and promised never to drink or bet again, and then, as Señora Trujillo unbuttoned his pants and his red flannel underwear, he screamed in a way that would have wrung the heart of heaven.

Gloria Trujillo, sixteen years old, heard these screams from the house where she was grinding, mortar and pestle, coriander, cumin, and chiles, coriander, cumin, and chiles. She kept to her task, never breaking her rhythm. *Scrape scrape.*

Señora Trujillo buttoned Ben's pants. She left him there and returned with her husband.

Señor and Señora Trujillo studied the blond gringo boy, who still babbled and wept. Señor Trujillo said this boy was the end of their lives. People would follow him, find him. Señor Trujillo wanted to hang him.

And if he is found hanged, they will destroy us, said Señora Trujillo. Her husband vowed they would bury him so no one would ever find his body.

181

All this time Benjamin Franklin Patterson blubbered and wailed. Snot and spit dribbled down his chin and every time he hiccuped, his broken ribs made him cry out in pain.

Señora Trujillo threw another bucket of water on Ben Patterson. To her husband she said, We are too old for this life. It is too dangerous for a man your age. Let our sons fend for themselves. Offer this boy the deal, Juan.

Here is the deal they offered Ben: He could marry their sixteen-year-old daughter, Gloria, afflicted and ugly and retarded as she was, or they could hang him.

As she left the barn, Señora Trujillo passed her two sons sitting in the shade of the live oaks, smoking, readying the rope to hang Ben Patterson. Their shoeless children played in the dirt; their dog-eyed wives brought out plates of badly cooked food. Señora Trujillo told her sons to find a chair, take it to the barn, and tie the stupid gringo boy to it.

She went into her own house, where she found Gloria at the long plank table, the grating sound of the mortar and pestle soothing, regular. Señora Trujillo smoothed her daughter's dark hair and smiled into her broken face, smashed nose, her droopy, red-rimmed eyes. She explained bluntly—she was a blunt woman—how she feared for Gloria.

When we die, she told her daughter, you will have no one to protect you. You will have no home of your own. Your brothers will not respect you. They will rob you, as I feel certain they have robbed their own father. You will be the slave, a drudge to their wives, coarse women, little better than whores. Señora Trujillo sighed. She was disappointed in her sons. For years I have been praying for a husband for you, Gloria. But who would marry you? Who would even see how sweet, how beautiful you are? With that nose? That smashed-in face? And now here is this stupid gringo boy, sent by God to answer a mother's prayers. Any husband, even a stupid gringo, is better than no husband. At least you will be married. Your father and I can die in peace.

Señora Trujillo told Gloria that the boy had been offered the deal; he had agreed to the marriage, but the choice was Gloria's. Altogether her own. If Gloria did not want to marry Benjamin Franklin Patterson, they would hang him, and no one would be the wiser.

Gloria stopped with her mortar and pestle only after her mother had finished speaking. She licked her finger and dabbed the bowl, tasting her spices.

Sensible of the gravity of the moment, she took off the flour sack she had tied across her skirt for an apron. She followed her mother out of the house, and through the yard, past her surly brothers and their curious dog-eyed wives, and into the barn where her father waited with Benjamin Franklin Patterson, who was tied to a chair.

Her father glowered and reiterated that it was her choice. She could marry him or not.

Gloria Trujillo approached Ben Patterson. His nose had been broken. Like hers. She touched it. He winced. She brushed the blond hair from his forehead and looked into his blue eyes, framed now in bruises that were beginning to swell and turn purple as beets. His lips were bloodied, broken, and swollen. He had a four-day stubble of beard. He was the most beautiful thing Gloria had ever seen, except for the china doll her father once brought her from Ensenada, Mexico. She said she would marry him.

It was done swiftly, the priest brought up to the ranchito, and in the meantime, the Trujillo brothers slaughtered one of the stolen cattle for Gloria's wedding feast.

When the priest, a Father Callahan, went back down the mountain into St. Elmo, he had a letter for Judge and Mrs. Patterson from their son, Ben. It made no mention of the bet in the Ferris Hotel. Ben wrote to his parents only that he had been riding and his horse had bolted and threw him, that he had been injured, and he was being cared for by a family who had rescued him from certain death. He had fallen in love at first sight with their beautiful daughter. He was a married man.

Some months later, in the fall of 1902, Mr. and Mrs. Benjamin Franklin Patterson rode into St. Elmo. Ben drove a carriage, gift of the bride's parents, drawn by a pair of fine, high-stepping horses that had been stolen from a ranch up near San Gabriel. The carriage had been stolen from farther afield. Tied to the back of the rig was a heifer so that Ben could collect his three hundred dollars. They went to the home of Judge and Mrs. Patterson.

In the Patterson family parlor the elder Mrs. Patterson wept openly. Ben sat beside Gloria, holding his hat. Gloria smiled her crooked smile. She was a bride, after all. The judge leaned on the mantelpiece. He gravely assured Ben that this was no real marriage and it could be undone.

Ben said he didn't think it could be undone. Father Callahan was a real priest.

Judge Patterson said that divorce was possible. Ben demurred.

Judge Patterson asked his son, Do you really want to marry into a family of Mexican horse thieves? What kind of white man are you? Moreover, the judge said, if Ben stayed with Gloria, the Pattersons would disown him. Would he keep this retarded girl over his own mother and father?

A girl who has been run over by horses is certainly equal to a bunch of Methodists. Gloria was ugly, but she was not retarded, and though years of physical pain had made her quiet, she was not easily bullied. Certainly, she was not stupid. Gloria rose to her feet, nudging Ben's elbow. He rose, too.

Gloria said, We have each other, that is enough. We are married in the eyes of God. I love this man. I will love him till the day I die. You will not change that. Nothing will.

Gloria Trujillo Patterson was as good as her word, and so was Ben, though his part of the bargain did not stipulate supporting her and their seven children. Ben went from job to job, faring poorly. Finally he shrugged off his failures, and looked to his wife, who, at some indeterminate date, began selling tortillas and meat and beans out of her kitchen, and the world beat a path to her back door.

IN THE SUMMER OF 1946 THE INCIDENT OF THE tainted shrimp inadvertently served at the Methodist Ladies' League annual charity Event was not mentioned in the women's pages of the St. Elmo *Herald*. Nor in what might be otherwise thought of as the men's pages, which is to say, the whole rest of the newspaper.

Still, everyone knew that ambulances had been called, that Miss Winifred Merton and perhaps thirty other civic worthies were rushed to the hospital where they had long tubes put down their noses, and their stomachs pumped in a sort of hallelujah chorus of gagging, vomit, and tears. Miss Merton, thin in the best of times, was especially stricken; shrimp was one of her favorites. Her doctor ordered her bed rest for ten days. Winifred Merton had missed work only once before, when the 1919 flu had felled her.

Into this breach rode Eden Louise Douglass, fearless and foolhardy.

*Herald* readers opened the women's pages on Monday to find a long feature story about Gloria Patterson, who was afflicted, but not retarded, and a young man who believed it was better to marry than to hang. At Zacateca's any *Herald* reader who brought in this article would get 10 percent off the bill.

All that week Eden Douglass polished and published her stories about Bojo's, about descendants of Mr. Kee who, though China Flats was long gone, had a small restaurant also known as the Red Dragon. They offered up the recipe for their delectable Carrot Ginger Soup for the *Herald*.

Eden published the recipe for Sally Epps's Famous All the Way to Memphis Barbecue Sauce and the story of the Eppses' westward trek from Arkansas to California, bedeviled by bankers, bad weather, and hunger. The Epps family had been driven by hunger since the original Eppses had fled Ireland in 1848, and ended up in Arkansas. Even Afton Lance had to admit to begrudging respect for the Eppses' courage when she read the story. And when she read her own recipes, and the family stories Eden had written down about them, Afton flushed with pride, and then disavowed any such emotion.

The *Herald*'s women's pages ran articles about St. Elmo's once-thriving community of Japanese greengrocers. Eden had sought out Mr. Yamashita, who had named his small store Green Goddess honoring the famous play, the famous film, and where she had once dazzled her grandmother with her reading. New Market was still there, no longer new. Green Goddess was gone, closed when Mr. Yamashita and all the St. Elmo Japanese community were marched into internment camps far to the north. Some returned, some didn't. Mrs. Yamashita declined to speak to Eden Douglass about Green Goddess or anything else.

All week long the phone at the *Herald*'s women's desk rang off the hook. Eden did not answer it. She knew it was Miss Merton. Bedridden, perhaps, but not prostrate.

Miss Merton called Victor Levy as well, and gave him a tongue lashing on behalf of his duty to the newspaper and to their readers, and instructions to fire Eden Douglass immediately. But the managing editor declined to do Miss Merton's bidding. His wife, Connie, had pointed out to him, quite correctly, that this was between Winifred Merton and Eden Douglass. And, when it was over, he would be rid of one or the other. This made sense to Victor.

On Friday afternoon Winifred Merton, thinner, grimmer after her ordeal, wobbled into the newsroom of the *Herald*. She got off the elevator, and as she made her way slowly through the vast room, typewriters fell silent. Eden had no view of the newsroom and was busy typing. Finally, her machine was the only one clattering away. A fearful pang seized her chest. She remembered the detonating buzz bombs in England during the war and she counted to ten.

Winifred Merton went to her own desk across from Eden's. She touched the rose that had long since withered in her absence. Shaking, she removed her gloves. "You must think yourself quite clever," she began. "You must think how very progressive you are! Applauding the cooking of the Negroes and Mexicans and Chinese in my pages, writing about Arkies, and Jap truck farmers, and your own family."

"They are the women's pages, Miss Merton. Not yours. Not mine," Eden said with more equanimity than she felt. She stood up for more gravity.

"I do not think you are clever. I advise you to get out. Now. While you still can."

"You can't fire me, Miss Merton."

"I am not firing you." Her voice was more steady than her hands. "Use those brains you are so proud of, Miss Douglass. Get out of this newsroom. Get out of this business. Get out of this town. Get married. Go to college. Do something, any-thing. Do. Go. *Be,* Miss Douglass! But get the hell out of here! Now! Before you are tied to complacent people who will never regard you with anything but pity. Even contempt. Get out before you are tied, inextricably, to the smuggery you so clearly detest. Do you really think in a few years' time you'll have earned this pa-per's respect? Do you think you'll be over there, with them?" She raised her bony finger and pointed to the men in the newsroom, the shirtsleeve brigade, wreathed in stale smoke. "Perhaps ten years' time? Twenty? Do you think that in 1966 your by-line will be atop a story that *isn't* about the Assistance League, a Recipe, or Event?" Miss Merton wheezed out a dry, unpracticed laugh. "You are a fool, but surely you're not so foolish as that. Do you really think that you are so fine a writer, that your gifts will take you out of this corner? That you will have a desk in the news-room? That you will write *for the world?*" she added, rasping and impassioned.

"Martha Gelhorn does. Dorothy Thompson—"

"Oh, shut up about Mrs. Ernest Hemingway. Mrs. Sinclair Lewis, you little fool. Use your mind! Use your eyes. Look at me! Ink is in my veins, I tell you! I breathed newsprint from the day I was born. My father owned the *Gazette,* the first newspaper this town ever had. My father brought the first printing press to St. Elmo. We came the same year the railroad was finished. We slept in the freight car with the press, that's how dedicated we were to the newspaper business. My father had been driven out of Missouri and Texas and Arizona by the competition, but here in St. Elmo, he knew, this was the place. He knew it like Brigham Young knew it, could say, *This is the place!* And it was! My father could set type so fast, his hands were just a blur. He taught me my letters so I could help him. My mother hated the newspaper business. She left him. She tried to take me with her, but I wouldn't go. I loved the newspaper, more than I loved my mother. More than I loved my father. Or any other man. I loved the sound of the press, and the clank of the type and the hot metal and the ink! I loved what the newspaper brought to this town, to any town. The blessings of a free press." Miss Merton was breathless now. She struck the desk with an impassioned fist. "I lived for that paper! Lived and breathed and had my being! I was writing for the newspaper when other girls were dressing up their dolls for tea parties." She advanced on Eden, shouting, "Do you know what I am talking about, Miss Douglass?"

"Yes." Eden did not look away.

Miss Merton backed off, breathing harshly. "And then my father died, and my worthless brother deserted me, and I had to close the *Gazette*. Then the owners of the *Herald* came to St. Elmo. They wanted my presses, my list of sub-scribers, and I sold it to them. But only on the condition that I would work at the *Herald*. And I do. Don't I?"

"Yes, Miss Merton."

"Have I not achieved my dreams, Miss Douglass? Am I not a success? Do I not daily revel in fulfillment? Answer me!"

But Eden could not.

"Do you really think that this is what I wanted to become? Do you think it was my ambition to chronicle who went where and what they wore, and how lovely was the entertainment, and the chicken à la king, the celery sticks and fruit punch, how Mr. and Mrs. Methodist are having a tea on Friday?" She gin-gerly plucked the dead rose from its vase and dropped it into the trash can. "Do you think I really give a damn? Have you no imagination? You, too, will be old one day, Miss Douglass. Will you be pathetic as I? Will you?"

Eden's lips would not part in reply, but she made an instinctive move to reach out to Winifred Merton, who stepped back against the wall, as though she were already a wraith and the wall would absorb her effortlessly. Suddenly, in the silence of the newsroom, Eden turned around to look at the men at their desks. Their faces were draped in a collective snicker.

"I don't know what I will be, Miss Merton. But I will not be here."

"Good. Good for you, Eden."

"Goodbye, Miss Merton."

"Goodbye, Eden. Good luck. I look for great things from you. Whatever you do."

Leaving her sheet of paper in the typewriter, Eden walked through the newsroom to the elevator, and waited there, her back turned to one dream, un-certain of the next. Before the elevator doors hissed open, Eden heard the chairs squeal, the keys tapping: All the real writers had gone back to work, their type-writer carriages crashing, bells ringing, when they came to the end of another line of deathless prose.

BOOK TWO

# BABYLON

PART ONE

# Sourdough
# Starter

1952

## CHAPTER ONE

*AFTER THE WAR.* BY 1952 EVEN THE PHRASE HAD come and gone, certainly in sunny Southern California, which was booming and building, gazing ahead into the future, impatient with and tired of the past. And this was true for Eden Douglass, too. The dream or vision or hope of Logan Smith had long since dissolved, as though decades separated them, not merely years. When she thought of Logan at all, he seemed to her as distant as a character in a book she had once read. By 1952 Eden had emerged into a new chapter of her life.

Columbia First National Bank required her tact, time, and intelligence, but her weekends and evenings, her money, and her life were her own. She rented a one-bedroom courtyard apartment just off Venice Boulevard in Los Angeles, less a city than series of interlinked ideas of what a city should be. She asked no one's permission to do as she wished. She was not called upon to soothe furrowed masculine brows, or kiss skinned childish knees, or wear dowdy clothes, because all the money had gone toward a washer, or a fridge, or a dinette set. Eden was not saddled with a mortgage and a lawn to mow, a fence to paint, or even a car payment. She still drove Annie's old Cord convertible, with its prewar sepia glamour, while her married friends drove thick-fendered sedans with bulbous trunks and great innocent headlights that reminded her of overfed fish.

She could have married any number of the returning vets who were also in UCLA's class of 1950. She earned a degree in business, and put all thought of Martha Gelhorn in the past. The most serious love affair she had was with an engineer, Ray, who had asked her to marry him. Ray landed a good job at Lockheed, and he would buy a house in Lakewood; he promised her a good life. She declined because she did not love him—though admittedly, she had said she loved him, many times, those Saturday nights they had thrashed around in her bed. She declined because Ray left her still hungry in the old "Body and Soul" way, in the way of old love songs, in the secret way that left you feeling enhanced, body and soul. When Afton Lance grumpily chided her for having lost her chance to marry, because she was waiting for an impossible man, Eden just smiled, put her arm around Afton's shoulder, and said, "Who knows what's possible?" Afton grumbled, but even she had no all-knowing retort.

So when Eden Douglass fell in love—and this was no metaphor, she really did fall—she was surprised at the swiftness, certainty, and intensity. She might have recognized the very moment she fell in love, save that she was facedown in a puddle of mud and coffee and she had badly burned her hand. It would have been horribly comic if it weren't so painful, so prescient, the pratfall of the heart.


Eden Douglass hoisted a huge coffeepot with two pot holders from the burner in a ramshackle cookshack. Early that Saturday morning she had answered Annie's frantic call for help, filling in for one of Annie's Oasis staff who simply didn't show up. Eden carried the pot out the door of the cookshack and across the sparse and balding sunlit grass of an old picnic area at Greenwater Ranch, a movie location for Westerns. Cowboys, stuntmen, actors, wranglers, and crew were all eating lunch at a bevy of picnic tables scattered about in the shade of eucalyptus and live oaks. The air was full of flies and talk, coarse laughter and cigarette smoke, the smell of horses and dung drying in the sunlight.

Eden was crossing the wide yard toward the tables under the trees when suddenly from behind her she heard a distant *whoop,* and then the onrush, a thunder of hooves, and before she could so much as turn around, she felt a resounding *thwack!* on her backside. Eden stumbled, cried out, fell forward, and the coffeepot went flying, but not before she reached for it with her other hand and then cried out in pain, her palm against the hot metal, just before she went facedown into a pool of coffee and mud. The blow and the burn together knocked the wind out of her. Her nostrils filled with dirt; she couldn't breathe, and she couldn't see as she spluttered and choked, rose, fell back down. Blood streaming from a torn lip mingled with the coffee and mud and Eden coughed and spit, and then she felt an arm across her shoulders. A man knelt beside her, rolled her over, braced her against his knee, and held her in his arms.

"Son of a bitch! Goddammit! Son of a bitch!"

He brushed the hair and dirt and mud from her face. He swore again. She spit, dirt and blood and coffee grounds. She couldn't open her eyes. "My hand," she said, clutching her left wrist.

"Burned? Son of a bitch."

"Here, Matt," someone offered. "Here's a bandana."

"And here's some water."

Matt doused the bandana, and, still supporting her on his knee, he mopped her face, the dirt from her eyes, the blood from her nose and lips. "Can you open your eyes?"

She blinked against the grit still in her eyes and he wrung the water over them.

"It's nothing," said Eden, though it did not feel like nothing.

He brushed the dirt and water from her eyes with a touch that was urgent, but gentle. Still holding her braced against his body, he glanced up and asked, "Who did this?"

No one knew. Or at least, no one said.

"Whoever thought this was funny, get your horse, collect your pay, you're gone. I don't care who's the producer, this is still my property." He turned back to Eden. "You'll live, won't you? You're going to be all right."

Despite the shock and pain and having the wind knocked out of her, the blow to her head and her bleeding lip and nose, Eden thought this was true. She couldn't speak, but she would be all right. His embrace was firm. His lips were full, his chin was stubbled, and he had a thin, aquiline nose and an olive complexion. His eyes were dark.

"Promise me you'll live."

She spat out a wad of grit. "I promise I'll live."

And then, having been slapped on the ass by love or fate or happenstance, or whatever the name we give to the seemingly other-than-random accidents that shape our lives, Eden felt, deep in the solar plexus of her soul, the bowels of her being, some little spark ignite and glow. This spark—sometimes in beams, sometimes in flickers—shone for the rest of her life.

THE FOLLOWING MONDAY, AS EDEN DROVE THE CONVERTIBLE TO THE bank, she wore the casual scarf she always affected, to keep her short hair in place, and dark glasses. Only today the dark glasses barely concealed the abrasions across her face and bruises that ringed her eyes with a purple tinge turning to green. Her banged-up lips could not be covered. A woman more vain would not have gone out of the house. Her left hand, though not badly burned, was still swathed in bandages and quite painful. As she walked into the bank, across its marble floors lit from long rectangular windows, she collected stares, inquiries, expressions of shock and empathy. She had already decided to say that she fell off a horse, rather than that she had been slapped on the butt by a trick-riding stuntman.

Eden Douglass walked to her office, where a small nameplate sat on her desk. On the frosted glass door that separated her ante-office from the loan officer's cloister, Mr. Brock's name was painted in block letters. Secretaries got nameplates on their desks because they came and went. Secretaries, as Mr. Brock often teased her, got married, and left, and the bank wasted all that money they'd spent in training these girls to do this job.

A monkey could do this job, Eden often thought. All right, an exceptional monkey. Most monkeys didn't take shorthand. Eden was mildly annoyed that her taking shorthand seemed to matter more to the bank than her cum laude in business from UCLA. The bank also wanted to know if she could type. Yes, Eden could say in truth, she had been typing since she was twelve. Could she operate a PBX? No, she lied. She had vowed never again to wear a headset and repeat the same lines endlessly. As executive secretary to the loan officer, Walter Brock, her duties entitled her to protect him from tiresome details. He made the decisions. She typed the documents, screened his calls, logged appointments, and made excuses for him when necessary. She sometimes thought of herself as a guard dog in high heels.

Eden's desk, protectively placed between Mr. Brock's door and the vast expanse of the bank, looked out over the whole first floor. Columbia First National Bank, like a temple to money, had high ceilings. Gilded bars separated the tellers from the customers; the marble counters were complete with fountain pens; the inkstands were filled daily. High windows of stained glass portrayed ships and railroads, locomotives looming across cornucopias whose colors altered the sunlight and cast it down upon the marble floor in little pools of rose and gold and blue. The stained glass windows suggested wealth, all the fruits of progress from a hundred years of California statehood, 1850 to 1950: cattle, citrus groves, fishing, farming, films, railroads. From her desk Eden liked to watch long rectangular swaths of sunlight pouring in through the bank windows, shifting with the season and the time of day.

She had been here now almost two years. The job had promised security and promotions, though the latter had not come to pass. Perhaps she had misheard. Still, she was an exemplary secretary and had gotten one raise, her salary now $275 a month. This honor was bestowed formally upon her by the smiling bank president, the dough-faced Mr. Webber, while Mr. Brock and the spectrally thin Miss Franklin looked on. The little ceremony that afternoon was held in Mr. Webber's second-floor office, which smelled of cigars and furniture polish. His face flushing, Mr. Webber extolled Eden's intelligence, her dedication, her ability to turn out a perfect letter, with accurate figures and correct grammar! What a pleasure. Most secretaries didn't know how to write. Mr. Webber said only Miss Franklin could do better. Miss Franklin's narrow lips pursed into an apostrophe of a smile.

Miss Abigail Franklin was, in truth, possibly the single most-powerful person in the bank. Mr. Webber was unreliable after long boozy lunches, and in the afternoons Miss Franklin actually served as president. Mr. Webber relied on her for everything, her judgment, her acumen, her unswerving loyalty. Among the younger employees, this latter quality was the subject of muted mirth. They speculated that Miss Franklin, with her gray hair and string-bag mouth, had been in unrequited love with Webber for years. She made his life better, easier, happier. She even picked out Mrs. Webber's birthday and anniversary presents. She did all this for the magnificent sum of three hundred dollars a month. She was, Eden knew, Winifred Merton all over again. A fate Eden intended to evade.

There were other perils at the bank. Other fates Eden intended to evade. Rumor, innuendo, sexual hearsay, like nasty little snapping fish swam in the sunlight that poured in upon the marble floors. One of the perils of Eden's job was the hydra-handed Mr. Brock himself. Mr. Brock's name had been linked to those of several of the more attractive young tellers in the bank. His last secretary, Eden had heard round and about, had left in some haste and under a cloud that impugned her reputation without affecting his.

In his midforties, Walter Brock still had some of the bounce and all of the fierce competitiveness that had made him the California Collegiate Tennis

Champion in 1930. He still played tennis, but his urgent need to win was now expended primarily with women. He seemed to regard flirting as a sporting event, like, Eden thought, a sophisticated Colonel Bedcrotch. Mr. Brock didn't grope like Bedcrotch, but he was full of nonstop suggestive talk that he sugared up with a low tease in his voice. He sometimes took her out to lunch and sat too close to her in a booth.

"You really have no idea how intriguing you are, do you?" he said after they had ordered. He brought his hands together. His cuff links glinted and his smile as well. "I like that. A girl who doesn't know she's fascinating. I'd like to know you better. To know you well."

Eden thought, What kind of sap do you think I am, you vain, pigheaded louse? But she said, "Mr. Brock, please don't make me point out the obvious. You are a married man. You and I work together, but there really can't be anything else between us."

"But you'd like there to be, wouldn't you? You were a WAC. You must be always ready for adventure." His knee jostled hers. "How are you going to keep them down on the farm after they've seen Paree?"

Eden moved her leg. "I did my bit, that's all."

"Ah yes, all that glory and sacrifice, all that testing in battle and adversity! And who remembers it? I ask you. Look around."

"What's remembered here in Los Angeles is not the same as what's remembered in France or Germany or England or Japan."

He waved away the implied intellectuality of the comment. "At least please call me Walter. You'll do that, won't you, Eden? Forget the office and call me Walter?"

Eden called him Walter after that. However, she did not forget the office and nothing came of that lunch or his avowals of personal interest in her. Little came of his express instructions to close the frosted glass door when he wanted her to take a letter.

The Monday that she arrived at the bank bruised and bandaged, she had already shown Mr. Brock's ten o'clock appointment into his office and fetched the man a cup of coffee. "Good morning, Walter," she said when he came through her door.

"Good God!" he cried. "What happened to you! Were you in an accident?"

"In a manner of speaking. I fell off a horse."

He noticed her bandaged hand. "Can you still type?"

"If you mean, can I still do my job, of course." I could do your job, Eden thought, though she kept her expression benign and her gaze direct.

Just then there was an unexpected knock, and a man entered her small ante-office. He was not tall, but solid, and he bristled with a bright intensity. He wore a broad-shouldered jacket with wide lapels, neatly creased pants, and cowboy boots. The boots arrested her attention. Then she looked back at his face. His eyes were dark, his hair was crisp and curly, his nose was high and aquiline, thin, and his skin was pale with an olive cast. He had a voluptuous mouth, and his smile was magnanimous, inclusive, and without guile. "Eden Douglass?" he said.

"Yes."

He brought forth from behind his back a bouquet, gaudy, random, loosely bound, an armful of scarlet snapdragons, wild sunflowers, wilting California poppies. The stalks were roughly cut and tied with a blue ribbon. He set them on her desk, where they wafted up the briny, just-cut fragrance of fields, as though the vast cornucopias on the bank's stained glass windows had suddenly gathered in the ante-office.

"Picked them myself. This morning. I probably should have gone to the florist, but—" he gestured expansively and his teeth gleamed, "who wants flowers that have been refrigerated? I ask you. Excuse the intrusion, please, but I had to come by and apologize. That cowboy who smacked you on the . . . who smacked you, I've told Monogram Pictures, he can't work at Greenwater again. He showed bad judgment. Very bad judgment." He paused and his eyes seemed to light. "But not bad taste."

"Cowboy?" said Walter Brock.

"He's just a kid, Miss Douglass, a trick wrangler who didn't know his own strength. Said he couldn't help himself. He said you had a great ass, begging your pardon, and he couldn't help himself, but he was very sorry, and he never meant to hurt you. He was just showing off. Still, he won't work Greenwater again." He turned to Brock, shook hands briefly. "Matt March. I own the Greenwater Movie Ranch up at the north end of the Valley. You must know it. Anyone who watches Westerns knows us. Hopalong Cassidy, Gene Autry, Roy Rogers, Sons of the Sagebrush, Red Ryder, and all the B Westerns, Saturday morning serials, *The Three Mesquiteers,* they're all filmed out at my place—well, maybe not all. Lots. Lots of others, too. You like Westerns?" He turned his attention back to Eden without waiting for an answer. In the close confines of the ante-office, he seemed to carbonate the air around him. "The vet said he thought you'd be all right. What did the doctor say?"

"The vet?" asked Eden.

"You don't remember Les talking to you? He's not really a vet, I guess, but Les Doyle is one of the smartest stuntmen in the business. He knows animals.

He's the one who gave you the horse pill for pain till Annie could get you to the doctor. Of course, he broke it in half. Otherwise, you'd still be out cold."

"I don't remember."

"Les asked you if you were going to faint, and you said WACs don't faint. But you did pass out." Matt March turned to Walter Brock. "Not for long. Tough cookie, this girl." To Eden he said, "I called Annie this morning to find out how you were, and she told me where to find you. I thought I'd come by and apologize in person. And take you to lunch."

"It's not lunchtime," remarked Mr. Brock.

"No, and it's not 1975, either, but one day it will be." Matt turned away from Walter Brock and gave his full attention to Eden. His eyes were bright and full of promise. "Can I come back at noon? I know a great Italian restaurant. Pierino's. La Cienega. You know it? They just reopened in December. I can promise you a fine—"

"Miss Douglass is busy, Mr. March. Surely you can see that. In spite of the injuries she has suffered at your hands—"

"Oh, you misunderstand, Walter. It wasn't Mr. March's fault."

"Matt."

"Matt," Eden repeated carefully. She kept her gaze on his dark eyes. "I was helping out my sister-in-law, Annie. Oasis caters meals at movie locations. I was carrying a pot of hot coffee and a rider came up behind me. On a horse," she added pointlessly.

"And slapped you on the . . ." Walter Brock sputtered. He had not been able to so much as snag a kiss and a squeeze from this girl. His indignation sharpened with his sense of betrayal. "Is this the way you spend your time outside the bank?"

Eden buried her bruised face briefly in the enormous bouquet that she had just been handed. She said to Matt March, "I'll meet you at noon. Outside the bank."

Mr. Brock, visibly disgruntled, slammed his frosted glass door behind him.

"Only . . ." she faltered, "I look terrible. My face is a mess."

"You do not look terrible to me," Matt said, and there was not a false note in his voice. Eden felt herself smile, aware of every beleaguered muscle in her face. She said she had only an hour for lunch. "Time enough," said Matt.

PIERINO'S WAS CHIC: BLOND WOOD PANELING, BLOND WOOD TABLES EM-braced by great rounded banquettes of red vinyl. The floors were a tough blue tile that could stand up to stiletto heels, and the crowded foyer rang with low, sophisticated voices, men in suits, women in hats and gloves, their dresses tightly belted in the New Style, their cigarette smoke sinuous.

Eden Douglass blinked after the bright sunlight outside. She wished she had not come. She was certainly the only woman there with bruises the color of eggplant, with abrasions on her lips, her nose, her cheeks, her burned hand swathed. People stared. Matt March, his hand at her elbow, guided her through groups of people to the front. He did not have a reservation. He said he was Matt March. A undercurrent of irritation rumbled when the headwaiter showed him and Eden to a table almost immediately. Near the bar where they could hear the piano player. A jazzy "Bess, You Is My Woman Now" floated on the smoke.

"You must come here often," said Eden.

"I do. But that's not why I get such great service." He lit up, but he didn't glance at the menu. His beauty was marred only by dark circles under his eyes. "You like seafood? Good. We'll get the Rigatoni with Seafood and Pepper Sauce. It's the best. I mean, you only have an hour, so we just have the one course and dessert. The rigatoni is what my uncle always gets. Now, there's a man who knows fine food. High standards. That's why he fronted the money for this place in twenty-seven." Matt laughed, and lowered his voice. "That, and Old Pierino and his brother lived in the same garage apartment my father and uncle had lived in when they first got to L.A. It belonged to some Poggibonsi relative who specialized in collecting noisy crowds for union protests. The rent was cheap, and all you had to do was show up and chant slogans against capitalists. You know? That's what hurt him. Old Pierino, I mean. Him and his brother Paul. You know Paul Pierino?"

"Should I?"

"Set decorator? My uncle got him his first big job. *Gold of the Yukon*. Paul Pierino was the best. He doesn't work here anymore. He moved to Rome. He can work there."

"I remember *Gold of the Yukon*. At least I remember the avalanche and the train wreck."

"You like the movies, yes?"

"Yes. I go every week."

"Good. I couldn't be seen with a girl who didn't like movies. You go with a boyfriend?"

"With my mother usually. She's living with Annie and my brother. They need the break." In the six months that Kitty had lived with Annie and Ernest following Gideon's death, her needs, demands, her pouting and delusions were grinding their marriage into dust.

Matt grinned. "Good. I mean, it's good you go with your mother. That you take care of your mother. You like Westerns?"

"Yes."

"I love Westerns. Ever since I can remember. My father and uncle, they took me to Westerns when I was too little to hold down the theatre seat. My father gave me a signed first edition of *The Virginian*. You know that book? Great book. The best."

Eden resolved to go home that very night and reread Owen Wister's *The Virginian,* which Logan had given her. The classic Western written by a melancholy Philadelphian.

A handsome young man exuding bonhomie came up to their table, shook Matt's hand, and declared that anyone named March had a permanent reservation here.

"Eden," said Matt, "this is Frankie Pierino. Frankie, Eden Douglass."

"I had an accident," said Eden, gently touching her bruised face.

"Never mind," declared Frankie, "you're still beautiful. Matt always has the best taste in women. So what do you think of the remodel?"

"I've never been here before," admitted Eden, "though I've heard of the place, of course. Who hasn't?"

"I closed it down for a year," said Frankie, "and now, to look at it, you'd never guess my old man opened this place in twenty-seven, would you?"

"No," she replied, taking in the decor, "it's very modern."

"I sold the mural to pay for the remodel. You wouldn't believe what it was worth."

"No!" cried Matt. "The one by the guy they call L.A.'s Chagall."

"It was old-fashioned. I'm not." Frankie turned, hailed a waiter, and then he was off, shaking hands with Matt and, oddly, she thought, winking at Eden.

The waiter arrived and Matt gave him a fiver to give to the piano player. "Always pay the musicians," he told Eden. Then he ordered for them and peeled out another five-dollar bill, slipped it to the waiter, and added, "Choose us a bottle of wine, will you? Nice wine, prewar."

"I couldn't," said Eden. "I'm working."

"No," said Matt with a direct and unsubtle smile. "Now, you are having lunch with me. Later, you can return to the bank. Now, tell me how you came to be hoisting coffeepots for cowboys. I don't mean filling in last Saturday for Annie. I know she's married to your brother. I mean how did you come to be here on this earth, this time, this place, so I could meet you? I believe in these things. Destiny."

"Not random chance?"

"There is no random." He smoked and thought for a moment. "And not enough chance."

Her face hurt when she smiled. The jazz piano man lit into "Body and Soul."

The waiter brought the wine; the bottle had been hastily dusted, and the cork came out with a festive pop. He poured, and the aroma, rich, red, prewar, floated up and over her. They brought the dish, steaming, colorful with peppers and basil, the sauce punctuated with gray clams and purple mussels in their shells, and pink curling shrimp, the whole redolent of the sea, yellow lemons, and red peppers.

"I've never tasted anything like this," said Eden. "It's a sort of magic, isn't it?"

"The best cooking always is. That's what my uncle says. He does most of the cooking at home. My mother, some, but he loves to cook. I like to eat. I like women who like to eat. Appetite is good for you. One evening, soon, we'll have lots of time. We'll come back here for the four-course meal, but I don't like to rush the cook. You know how that is."

"Yes," she said, "I certainly do."

# Pierino's Rigatoni with Seafood and Pepper Sauce

*Pierino's Restaurant, La Cienega Boulevard, Los Angeles, California, 1927–81*
*Also a much requested item at the Café Eden*

These proportions for 1 pound pasta:

Two or so red bell peppers, perhaps 3 peeled garlic cloves, handful fresh basil, parsley, oregano, thyme, rosemary. Chop all. Should have some texture. Certainly not pureed. Heat olive oil in a cast iron fry pan and cook the above quickly on a high heat. Add 1 (big can) of crushed tomatoes and some red wine, reduce heat and simmer. (Or half a dozen chopped fresh tomatoes. If this, use extra salt.) Sprinkle with 1 teaspoon of crushed dried red peppers, a little salt and pepper. Simmer a bit, maybe 20 minutes, adding more vino if necessary. Cover.

Take 1 pound mixed seafood. You can find this at the fishmarket, usually frozen; mostly the rag ends of this and that, bits of scallop, octopus, squid, shrimp, clams, mussels. Thaw and rinse. You can add more of whatever you like, for color and texture. Fresh mussels and clams steamed in their shells add color, scent, and intrigue. But the mixed seafood is a good base, and not expensive.

In a broad fry pan put the juice of 2 lemons and perhaps ¹/₂ cup of dry vermouth, 1 tablespoon of butter or olive oil. Bring to a boil, reduce heat, and let cook down by perhaps a third. If you're steaming fresh clams or mussels, use this liquid; cover, till they open. Remove and add your seafood and toss, cook only as long as necessary; the pieces in the seafood combination are always small bits, so not long. Add to Pepper Sauce and mix well. Have your pasta cooked and ready. Toss the whole and serve immediately.

Excellent. A winter version without basil could use pizza seasoning or Italian seasoning, dry.

# SNAPSHOT

## The House of Un-Americans

In the postwar years, you were a real American and you kept your mouth shut. Consequences could be dire if you did not. If you had old-country ties, or had once evinced a youthful enthusiasm for left wing politics, or had shouted anticapitalist slogans with your comrades at strikes or marches, or even betrayed a sneaking sympathy for any of the above, your life could be ruined. Not by what you had done, but what you were rumored to have done.

Old Man Pierino's old-country ties, his loud loyalty to his old Socialist friends, doomed him. Late in 1949, Old Joe Pierino and his younger brother Paul, a well-regarded set decorator, were called before the Un-American Activities Committee where a producer, naming names, pointed the Red Finger at Paul, and insinuated sexual misaffiliations as well, Paul's many liasions with young men.

Blacklisted, Paul Pierino never worked in Hollywood again.

However, nothing was proved against the restaurateur, but the experience forever tarnished Joe Pierino's faith in America and undermined his health. After that he no longer believed that hard work and high standards would bring to a man the rewards of a life well spent.

But in 1926, Joe Pierino had great family recipes and great ambition. With the money borrowed from his old friend, the actor Ernest March, he opened his place on La Cienega. The exigencies of Prohibition required that the restaurant be divided. In the back room they served more than tea. This back room cost Pierino plenty to maintain—to have alcohol there at all, and to be certain he wouldn't be raided—but he managed. He managed; his wife did the cooking; his children helped out in the kitchen.

He managed even to limp through the Depression, though they closed off the whole back room so that the place would still look crowded when it was not. Pierino found a hungry artist to paint a mural on the new wall. The artist later became known as the Los Angeles Chagall. During the war, for any soldier in uniform, Joe offered dessert and a liqueur on the house.

After the war, when the committee was through with the Pierino brothers, and Paul had been publicly declared a pinko deviant, people were afraid to be seen at Joe's restaurant. Joe Pierino, for all his resilience and ingenuity, had no weapons against this. He was ruined not by what he had done, but by rumor and innuendo.

But his son Frankie was smooth, shrewd, and closemouthed. Frankie closed the place down, tore it apart, and reopened for the Christmas season in 1951. For twenty years Pierino's was a Los Angeles landmark, the sophisticated place to eat. Then, for ten years it was a cliché. The site is now a parking lot.

## CHAPTER TWO

MATT STOPPED AT SOME DISTANCE, AND KILLED THE
motor of the jeep. He bought a finger to his lips and
whispered to Eden, "Shhhh. Sound carries. Especially
over water."

In the distance she could see a single tree on a knoll
overlooking one end of the lake. The somber tree, a live
oak, had been blown into a peculiar flattened formation by
a century of winds. One sinister branch stretched out, dark
against the golden hillsides. From this branch there hung a
rope that rested around the neck of a man on horseback,
while other men, also on horseback, rattled around him,
their horses snorting. They spat in the dust. Their menac-
ing voices carried, though not altogether clearly, but you
could tell that the man with the rope around his neck
protested his innocence. Futilely. Someone asked if he had
any last words. Someone else told him to make it quick.
He spoke, scanning the rims of the nearby rolling hills,
hoping for rescue while he awaited the inevitable slap on
the horse's rump that would send his body spinning and
his soul out into the wild sky of morning.

"Cut!"

The cowboys turned their horses and rode away. The hanged man, who had never been in any danger of hanging, got off his horse and walked away. A kid, an experienced wrangler, came up to the horse, and put a boot-clad dummy on the horse's back; then the kid smacked the horse's behind. The dummy swung from the tree while the horse ran off into the distance.

"Cut!"

The wrangler rode after the horse. Everyone else sought some shade and lit up cigarettes.

"We can go down there now," Matt said to Eden as he started the engine.

It was Saturday, a week after the initial accident, and Eden's face, though healing, was still scratched, and her bruises had gone to green. Eden had used the injuries as an excuse to beg off her usual Saturday jaunt, taking Kitty to the movies. She accepted Matt March's offer of a tour of Greenwater. She had not mentioned Matt March to Kitty. Much less that he was the nephew of the great star of the silent screen. If Eden could still picture Ernest March—his dark eyes, his smoldering expression, his slicked-down hair, expressive brows, manicured mustache, voluptuous mouth, and thin, high nose—imagine how vivid he would yet be to Kitty.

Once Matt had told her at their Pierino's lunch that he was Ernest March's nephew, Eden could see elements of that famous face. Matt's, less sculpted, was more interesting. Eden had been astonished to learn that Ernest March was still alive and lived in the same house with the man who sat across from her. She was almost equally astonished to discover that Matt March—so knowing, experienced, and sophisticated—was two years younger than she.

Matt drove the jeep fearlessly, even recklessly, and Eden clung to the door as they plunged downhill. It was the same kind of threadbare, springless vehicle she remembered from the war. The jeep could go anywhere, and Greenwater Ranch was laced with rough dirt roads, many badly rutted, to transport men, animals, and equipment to the various locations scattered about the four hundred acres.

Stopping near the clusters of actors and animals, Matt left the motor running, took his clipboard, and jumped out. Signature Pictures was shooting *Rustler's Revenge,* a B Western. Along with other B Western companies, Signature had their offices in L.A., on what was known collectively as Poverty Row. They all did their location work at Greenwater.

Matt found the producer. "Let's see, I have here, the main street, close-up on the saloon, sheriff's office, dry goods store, and the rest are all interiors, right?"

"Chase scene."

"I have that. I just want to be certain of the town. Do you want to check the script?"

The producer snorted. "You don't think anyone really writes this shit, do you?"

Matt got back in the jeep and turned to Eden, as he released the brake. "What do you think, Eden? Does anyone really write this shit?"

EDEN GRIPPED THE DOOR TO HOLD ON AS MATT SWERVED TO AVOID A BOUL-der in the dirt road.

"I've lived here all my life, man and boy, with my father and mother, and my uncle," he said. "Well, my father died in forty-four, so it's just me and Ernesto and Mama now. My father and his brother never lived apart. Before moving out here in twenty-eight or so, we had a big house on West Adams, near downtown. I've seen pictures, but this is the only home I can remember."

"Greenwater must have been incredibly remote in those days. It's still really remote," she added.

"When my uncle bought this place, there was nothing here at the north end of the Valley. Jackrabbits and ramshackle ranchitos where people raised some cattle, chickens, and maybe some shacks with squatters, nothing but buzzards and eagles in the sky competing with the coyotes for the gophers on the ground. One day, so my father told the story, I was too little to remember it, we all four drove up here for a picnic. Stopped there by the lake and had the picnic in the shade of that tree overlooking the lake. The one they just hung the guy from. My father said it was like my uncle Ernesto had a seizure or a vision or something. My mother, devout Catholic that she is, thought the saints and angels had descended on poor Ernesto. Yes, it's true, Eden, I'm from a family of mackerel snappers."

"Don't worry. I'm from a family of Mormons."

Matt grinned broadly. "You believe in polygamy?"

"Plural marriage, they call it. And I don't believe in any of it. Finish your story."

"Well, whatever Ernesto experienced, that very day they drove all over till he found the owners of this property. These people lived in the ranch house—where the picnic area is now," he turned to her, "where you had your accident last week. Your fortunate accident."

"They say there are such things." Eden smiled.

"Ernesto gets out of the convertible, tells my parents he'll be right back. He knocked on their door, offered them eight thousand dollars in cash for the whole four hundred acres. And they took it. It happened just like that. My uncle was made of money in those days. After *The Green Goddess,* Ernesto was making three thousand dollars a week. He hired some famous L.A. architect to put all other projects aside—money talked, even then—to design and oversee the building of the hacienda, guest cabins, a barn for horses. There was going to be tennis courts and a polo ground and a pool, cattle, vineyards. It was all going to be just like the old country."

"You're from the old country?"

"I'm not. They are. Well, my father and uncle. My mother's from New York. Anyway, that old-country stuff, it's horseshit, if you'll pardon the expression."

"Nothing to pardon. I've been in the army."

Matt smiled, swerved. "It's all horseshit. They made it all up! If they want to believe it, who am I to say they can't? That's fine. Just don't ask me to pretend it's true. No, the truth is, why would they have come here if they were so fine and prosperous in the old country? The name is really Marchiani. I started school as Matt March, and I'll stay Matt March. No more Matteo Marchiani for me. I'm an American. Who wants to be carrying around some old-country moniker in America? In California? Someone else's old name?"

Eden remembered briefly how she had always feared that Eden Douglass REGRET might be her own real name. Now, she feared nothing. She felt strong and confident, excited and at peace in the same moment. Love. Matt March, with his thin, high nose, dark eyes, crisply curling hair, and his air of unquenchable enthusiasm, his confident charm—to say nothing of his cowboy boots—was the most attractive man Eden Douglass had ever met. Bar none. Love. He stirred in her the anticipatory tingle of desire and tenderness. His buoyancy was like a kite in whose dancing shadow she felt both sheltered and enlivened. She untied the scarf that bound her hair as they came over a rise, the surrounding green and golden hillsides splashed with coppery California poppies and wild sunflowers, and in the distance dry blue mountains rose up.

"I saw all of Ernest March's pictures," she said. "My mother took me to the Dream Theatre as regularly as other people might go to church. But I can't remember him in a Western."

"One. *Gold of the Yukon.*"

"Oh yes, the avalanche and the train wreck." She could see again the gray and granular image of snow and smoke, and herself as a child, clinging to Kitty in the old Dream Theatre, scared witless.

"The avalanche scene and the train wreck! They were spectacular! But the picture flopped. Ernesto and my father loved Westerns, but Ernesto never really had it in him, the walk or the physique, or any of that. It was his only real failure. He just wasn't a Western kind of guy."

"Like you," offered Eden.

"Like me," Matt agreed genially. "No, my uncle is Mr. Civilized. He still wears a suit, a vest, and a bow tie every day even though he doesn't leave the hacienda. My uncle loves opera. Good food. Wine. Doesn't smoke, though. Says it ruins the palate." Matt chuckled. "And no one can cook like he can. You should see him, though, he's hugely fat."

"My mother thought he was the most beautiful man who ever drew breath. She was in love with him. I mean that truthfully. She named my brother Ernest just so she could say, Ernest, I love you, over and over."

"I'll bet your father loved that."

Eden wondered briefly if Gideon had known that.

The frontier town lay before them. "The companies who film here, they can call it anything they want," said Matt as he pulled to a halt and they got out. "But I think of this town as Lariat. Only thing we don't have is a railroad. That's the only thing we need. Well, and a courthouse. That'll come. Be nice to have a small herd of buffalo."

"Here, in the town?"

"No," he waved vaguely to the north, "out there. I got room for them. Maybe a herd of mustangs, too. Nothing like horses and buffalo for a sense of freedom and power and spontaneity."

"On screen?"

"Anywhere."

They got out of the jeep and walked along planked sidewalks lined up parallel to troughs and hitching posts, passing in front of saloons, the barbershop, the blacksmith's barn, a dry goods store, a hotel, a few homes, and of course the obligatory bank to be robbed. There was a sheriff's office and jail to collect bad guys, but no courthouse in which to try them. The schoolhouse was located where the frontier street made an L-turn. At the end, a steepled church, harshly white, stood. Beyond that, neatly picketed headstones indicated a graveyard, where no one was buried. A crane, idle, sat nearby, and there were men setting up lights. Down the street a tiny tumbleweed rolled, like a lost child seeking its mother. Oddly, given the California light, the surrounding dry hills, Lariat reminded Eden of Fairwell, of what it might have been like when it was thriving and still had a future. All along the streets, there were buildings framed, unfinished.

"Is Lariat still under construction?" she asked.

"Of course! You always need construction. The town always needs to look like it's growing, not just static, a place content to have women with bonnets on the street." Matt scoffed. "This is a real frontier town. See, a lot of these sets have interiors. Look in the window. All these windows open. The curtains blow in the breeze." Matt put his hand on a porch post, gripped it. "Any other movie ranch, this post would rattle, but everything here is fully formed and sturdy. Fewer accidents for the stuntmen. And women. I'll have to introduce you to Les and Ginny Doyle. They are the best in the business. Ginny used to do a Suicide Drag. She invented the Suicide Drag! You know what that is?"

"I don't."

"Well, I can't begin to describe it. You'll just have to see her on horseback. She's a genius on horseback. A champion. Her horse is named Cody. All her horses are named Cody. Her mother was born into Buffalo Bill's Wild West Show. In London! An American Indian born in London. Isn't that something?"

"Hard to imagine."

"Prairie Fern was part of Buffalo Bill's show before she could walk. Now, I wish I'd seen that, don't you?"

"Yes, I do." Eden enjoyed being engulfed in his enthusiasm.

"Les and Ginny are just about my best friends. I don't have many real friends. I know a lot of people, but it's not the same. Les is the one who gave you the horse pill last week. Cut in half," he added. "We call him the vet. No one knows horses like Les Doyle. Unless maybe it's Ginny."

As they walked the wooden sidewalks, Matt pointed out his passion for detail. The guns in the gunsmith's window were painstaking reproductions of period pieces.

"Did you always love Westerns?" she asked.

"Hell yes. We all did. That is, not my mother. But my father, my uncle, me. My father, my uncle thought John Ford's *Iron Horse* was the greatest masterpiece in silent film, except for Buster Keaton's *The General,* of course."

"Of course," said Eden, who remembered it well, the train plunging into the river.

"Now me, I think John Ford is a god. I think *Stagecoach* is the best picture ever made. A hundred times better than *Gone with the Wind*. But," he shrugged and they turned around, walking back toward the jeep, "what can you do? If it was wine, people say, well, 1939 was a very good year. But one day, I'm going to make a Western that's even better than *Stagecoach*. Right now, I'm just following along after Signature Pictures, Monogram, and the rest of Poverty

Row. But it won't always be like that. I'm looking ahead. I got vision. You wait and see."

"I will," she replied.

"This town is going to be legendary one day. See, in my Western, I don't believe in all that lone-gunman stuff. The lone gunman, a man noble and alone, he's a myth. How can he be a real hero? How sorry can a man be with nothing, no one to care about? That's why *High Noon* worked so well. Zinnemann, the director, he had both. That's what made it so brilliant. The sheriff was on his own against Frank Miller, but he wasn't alone. You see the difference?"

"I never thought of it like that. The townspeople in *High Noon* were pretty cowardly, you have to admit that."

Matt held out two hands. "You have to balance these various elements, the land, the guy on his own, the greed, the loud stupidity, the people who want to make a life, and the guy who has something to protect, to live for. The real hero can never be fearless, but he can be brave. He has to exert himself against his fear. He has strength, but he has to recognize fatalism, too. You see?"

She didn't, but she liked hearing him talk about Westerns, the ones he had seen over and over, the ones he hoped to create himself, the ones they were shooting here now as they strolled Lariat's streets, dry wind chafing their lips and faces, ruffling their hair. Matt called out, waved to men on the lights and cranes for *Rustler's Revenge*.

Before they got back into the jeep, he looked fondly back. "My father started the movie ranch with the town. My father designed it. Some of these buildings, he and Ernesto, they put up with their own hands. They were all fine carpenters, my father, grandfather, devout Catholics, modest men. Well, Ernesto wasn't modest. My father had the vision though. I'm going to see it through. The Mexican village isn't finished yet, but do you want to see the fort?"

They drove on the dirt road encircling the frontier town and east toward the mountains, past rugged arroyos and enormous boulders clustered on the hillsides. They came in sight of the three-sided fort. The fort needed three sides so that actors dressed as Indians could be filmed as they raced around it, barechested and whooping on horseback. A little distance away was the fort's interior, looking broken off from the whole, oddly pathetic, all of it abandoned in the hazy midmorning sunlight.

"We can put the fort and the Indian village pretty close together because anyone needing the fort will probably need the Indian village, too. So you don't have to worry about the sound carrying." He smiled at her, taking his eyes off the road, and then swerved to avoid a rabbit darting across their path. "I had great summers here, Eden. My own horse, and four hundred acres to ride all over, playing cowboys and Indians."

"Which were you?"

"Both. I had the freedom of the place when I was a kid. No friends nearby, just me and the horse. Dancer. The old folks were used to living without me anyway, so as long as I was home for dinner, they didn't care what I did. How much trouble could I find out here?"

"You didn't live here?"

"Most of the year I was at school. St. Ignatius in Santa Barbara."

"How old were you?"

"Six."

"They sent you away to school when you were six!"

"I started school at Agua Verde Elementary, and came home the first week with head lice. My mother is a stickler for form, for everything being just so. She told my father and Ernesto, her son was never going back to school with a bunch of peasants. Who do you think lived way out here twenty-five years ago? Not movie stars! No, my mother insists I must have an education. She wanted me to be lawyer or a doctor, a senator, not another wop carpenter like my father, my grandfather, my uncle who turned actor. They sent me to St. Ignatius up in Santa Barbara. All that Catholic education, and I'm still basically just another damned carpenter in the family."

"She can't be disappointed in you."

"Of course she can. She's my mother. She invented suffering."

Matt gestured toward the Indian village, which lay before them in a shallow, treeless dish of land. Three tepees all exactly alike, one sadly fallen down. The sun was high and the shadows were pitiless. "Owning this land, Greenwater, means everything to my family," he said at last. "I tell you the truth, Eden, my mother can say what she wants about not living like peasants, but they are peasants about this land. They love it. They cling to it. They take the dirt to bed with them. That's between you and me. Don't ever tell them I said they were peasants."

"I'll never tell." I'll keep all my promises to you, she thought.

Matt considered the landscape, watched a hawk swoop down on a luckless field mouse. "You think about sound carrying, and you can just imagine how much fun they had making silent pictures. They say that Lesley Markowitz used to jump up and down and scream at the actors. They brought in string quartets for mood. You could make as much noise as you wanted. They could swear and sing, and laugh at the jokes. They could shout encouragement, tell the actors what to do while they're in the middle of doing it. Silent pictures must have been fun."

"What happened to Ernest March when sound came in?"

"Ernest March, my little chickadee, was finished. Talkies were the end of him. He didn't speak English! I mean, not very well. Still doesn't. He's still so self-conscious of his accent, he hardly talks at all. Without speech, his beauty, his talent . . ." Matt took his hands off the wheel and held them, palms up to the sky. "From three thousand a week to nothing in about a year. My mother's on her knees, bead-bumbling, fluttering the pages of her book of saints, looking for a saint for washed-up actors. You've got to remember, this was just about the same time as the Crash. I knew nothing of any of this. I'm off at St. Ignatius Catholic school, touting myself as the son of the great actor Ernest March—oh yes, I denied my own father, sorry to say. You want to see the bad guys' hideout and their cave?"

"Why is it only bad guys have caves and hideouts?"

"And black hats and dark horses. They're bad guys! The shack's on the way to the cave. It's a fake cave."

"Of course I want to see it. I want to see all of it."

Matt downshifted as they began a slow ascent. "When I look back at what happened to my uncle, I sometimes wonder why he didn't kill himself. His working life was over. They'd just finished building the big hacienda and the guest house, garages, and the barn. They had the hole dug by steam shovel for the pool. And there was not a damned dime. There never would be." Matt spoke with dark intensity. "My father and uncle filled that pool hole together. One shovel at a time. Ernesto planted a goddamned garden in on top of it."

He took a sharp curve, and Eden hung on to the door.

"The great Ernest March," Matt continued, "heartbreak of a million women, talks like a wop and can't speak no good English, and won't get his mug on-screen ever again. He'll never make another cent. My mother wrings her hands and looked to heaven. Which is what she does all the time anyway. My uncle sulks, cooks, and listens to opera. Finally, my father's had enough of prayer and pasta. The truth is, Ernesto was the beauty of the Marchiani family, but Nico, my father, was the smart one. My father says, Okay, there's no money, but there's the land. Let's go back to what we always did. We can build. What! Ernesto says to my father, Ernest March to pick up a hammer! By now Ernest March isn't the same guy who wore red flannel underwear, a toolbelt, and a straw boater. Ernest March is a great actor! A screen lover! A gentleman! Making more money than Ramon Novarro! Only not anymore. Get to work, says my father, and we'll build sets all over Greenwater's four hundred acres, and rent them out by the day. Good idea, yes? Take what you have in hand and make something of it."

"Like a recipe," she said. "My aunt always says you use the recipe to invent, alter it to suit what you have. You take what you have and turn it into what you want."

"That's what they did. My father got a huge map of the place and laid out where each set would be. He designed the town, the ranch house. They hired some local guys to help. It was brilliant. As long as there are Westerns, we're fine. Westerns will never go out of style. We got all we need right here, except for the railroad, the buffalo, and the herd of mustangs. The barn my uncle had built is still standing. Nothing in it now, of course, but we could have shelter and provisions for the animals. One of the guest houses got built, and that's right near the hacienda. Anyone who doesn't want to drive all the way back down to L.A. for a two-day shoot, they can stay there." Matt seemed momentarily thoughtful. "It would need a hell of a cleanup job, though." Matt smiled, and his earlier dark mood vanished. "I love this life. I couldn't wait to get back from the army and build this place up after the war."

"You fought? Where?"

"I didn't exactly fight, Eden. I won't lie to you. I know you said you were a WAC in the ETO, right there where the real fighting was going on. I respect that, and I wish I could match your war stories."

"I don't like war stories. I like love stories. And Westerns." She gave him a coy, knowing smile. "Anyway, what will you say when your kids ask, What did you do in the war, Daddy?"

"I was Captain Propaganda, kids!" Matt thumped his chest, coughed, and took out a cigarette. "I made ten-minute masterpieces for the army in D.C. Watch *Captain Propaganda Defeat the Evil Hun and Slant-eyed Jap! Loose Lips Sink Ships; Keep Your Condom On, Don't Bring VD Home.*" He gave a deprecating chuckle. "Even John Ford made a movie in 1942 called *Sex Hygiene.*"

"I probably saw that, too. They showed them all to the WACs, too."

"I tried like hell to get into the fight, get sent overseas, but the major who was supposed to be in charge of making these films didn't know shit from Shinola."

"And you did."

"I'd told everyone I was Ernest March's son! I was stuck with the lie. But I faked it. Pretty good, if I don't say so myself."

"Did Ernest March ever have a son?"

"He never married. Lots of women, of course. Maybe a few men, that's my own speculation. But he never married. He was comfortable living here with his brother, me, and Mama."

"So, in a manner of speaking, you were his son."

"Yes."

"And do you tell your children what you did in the war, Daddy?"

"No children. I'm not married." He cupped his hands, struck the match, and lit the cigarette. "How could I marry some poor girl when all I do is work? And bring her back here to live with my widowed mother and my fat old uncle? What kind of life is that? And this is where I live. Where I have to live and work."

"I see what you mean," she said thoughtfully.

The bad guys' shack was a lusterless lean-to, three-sided, with a tin roof, a pipe sticking out, and an outhouse complete with half-moon door. The cave, just up the road, was a bit of ingenious draping of dark tarps over a wooden frame set about with boulders. They got out of the jeep and walked around.

"It's all so much smaller than it looks on the screen."

"It has to be. That way the short men look taller, and the camera changes proportions of things anyway. This little hideout cabin, it's been in hundreds of movies. Literally hundreds." He held out his hand, and she took it. "Bad guys always come to a cabin like this, plot their revenge, and get in fights. The fights are all falling down on cue and sound effects. They do the galloping horses' hooves with coconut shells."

"Sounds like fun."

"It is. Do you ride?"

"Horses? No."

"Too bad. That's really the only way to see the place. You can go all the way up to the top over there," he pointed in a northerly direction, "and on a good day, a really clear day, you can see the ocean. I'm sure of it."

He pulled her to him. In his cowboy boots he was just taller than she. He touched her face, brushed her temples with his lips, and Eden again had the peculiar sensation of being both buoyed and sheltered in his arms. She closed her eyes and tilted her chin to be kissed, but his kiss was so gentle she scarcely felt it, then again and again.

"When these heal," his fingertips lightly patted the abrasions, "I'm going to kiss you the way you ought to be kissed."

"How do you know how I ought to be kissed?"

"I know. I've known it from the moment I saw you."

"Before or after I was facedown in the mud?"

"I just know when I'm not with you, you're all I can think about. I see your beautiful face, I long for the sound of your voice and the way your hair smells." He drew her into his embrace, and ran both hands through her short, dark hair. "But I've never yet had a woman wince when I kiss her, and I don't want you to be the first. I don't want you to wince at all."

"Shall I swoon like my mother used to swoon for Ernest March?"

"You'll do better than that."

Eden smiled, and the mending abrasions on her face tingled. "I'm sure I will."

"You want to see the ranch house? Then we'll go back and have lunch with everyone at the cookshack."

The jeep rattled down the dirt road. Matt explained that they needed a lot of empty space around the ranch house because sometimes they had to have cattle in the scene, or they needed fake crops, and besides, if two different companies were using Greenwater on any given day, anyone working at the Indian village would probably also be using the fort. But the town and the ranch set couldn't be too close together. "Sound carries. Way up here in the Valley, we're lucky we don't get planes overhead. Planes have put some location ranches out of business. Once we get the railroad built and bring in some old steam trains, Greenwater will be set up for every kind of Western there is. We'll have more work than we can handle."

"What then?"

"What do you mean?"

"What's the point of having more work than you can handle? You'll have to turn people away."

He grinned over at her, and the wind whipped his dark hair around. "I got big plans, Eden. I'm not always going to be the guy with the clipboard counting cowpies. I want you to know that. To believe it."

"I believe it."

"I'm looking ahead. Greenwater Pictures. One day Greenwater Pictures will make the best Westerns in the world. John Ford will weep. Look at everything I have to work with! Great land, authentic sets, good weather. I got water, the Agua Verde lake, and further up, in the winter anyway, there's a small stream. Plus, I know every wrangler and cowboy in the business. Even the singing cowboys, Sons of the Sagebrush—you know them? We'll go see their new picture. Tonight! You want to go tonight?"

"Sure. I want to go tonight. I love Westerns."

"And love stories."

"Yes."

"People never get tired of Westerns. When I see a bad Western, I want to throttle whoever did it. I hate to see those crummy exteriors, painted canvas backdrops, cardboard trains, rubber cactus. I want to tell them they're not being true, they're falsifying the story and the people who lived it, what it all means. Look at this land around us. It's mythic. No, Eden," his teeth flashed brilliantly, "Westerns are the only really American stories, and after John Ford, I'm the one who can tell them. Authentically. Ironic, huh? The wop, the son of immigrants, but I'm the one who can do it."

"Everyone is from somewhere else," said Eden. "Only the Indians are native."

"I'm including them. I'm going to tell everyone's story, Eden. I'm going to make Westerns even better than *Rio Grande* and *She Wore a Yellow Ribbon,* and *My Darling Clementine* and *High Noon.* I've got vision."

"What's stopping you?"

"Money. I'd need to build my own soundstage for interiors, and, well, the railroad, of course. The equipment, I can contract out for most of that. But I'd need interior sets. Too bad Paul Pierino isn't around. He was a great set decorator. A real genius." Matt steered the jeep downhill, bouncing as it zigzagged over the ruts.

They came in view of the three-sided ranch house, and he drove downhill, freewheeling. The jeep recoiled over rough terrain where small ragged sunflowers, wild mustard, and the burnished petals of California poppies stippled across the landscape, falling, crushed beneath their wheels, releasing a dusty exhale that evoked for Eden a powerful feeling of nostalgia, though for what she could not say. Eden knew that the ranch house, too, was a three-sided weatherworn fake, but it seemed to her familiar, as if her hands knew the very grain of the wood. The wooden porch, set high, was complete with rocker. There was an ancient live oak and a water pump with a trough in the yard. A windmill turned, creaking in the stiff, dry breeze. The barn was off to the side with a few other outbuildings, which Matt pointed out as chicken and hog pens and a smokehouse. An outhouse testified to authenticity.

"You see," said Matt, "there's a lot of movie sets won't have an outhouse. Too vulgar. Like the people who live here never have to pee! No bodily functions. How can a place like that be real? One of these Monogram Pictures guys said to me, I'll film here, but you got to take down the outhouse. I don't want audiences picturing the heroine, skirts hoisted and bent over the open hole. I told him: The outhouse stays. This is Greenwater! Not Knott's Berry Farm. Of course," he added with a wink, "the outhouse doesn't actually work, and if the actors have to pee, well, the boulders to the right are for the girls, and the boulders to the left are for the boys."

Eden herself needed to pee. But the bodily functions she endured at the moment were more complicated than that, a confusion in the flesh, turmoil of the heart. Her whole life had changed in a week. "The house looks as if it only just needs a family to move in," said Eden, "a woman to sit in the rocker, a man to walk up to the porch. . . ."

"A dog in the yard."

"Yes. A child to play there. Maybe a game that has a song to go with it."

"Another child to slam the door. A swing to hang from the tree over there," he added.

"Yes. Two children. If those people were suddenly to materialize, then you have the feeling this whole place would just come to life. It would be real, so real, they'd invite you to dinner. That they had lived here always, that they had work and good times and bad times, and laughter and tears, but they stayed together."

He drove the jeep twice around the three-sided house, in a circle, scattering rabbits and ground squirrels and routing a flock of noisy finches out of the live oak. Eden put her head back and let the sunlight drench her, arms overhead, eyes closed, mouth open in a moment of sheer undiminished joy, absolutely real, evoked by the fake house.

The following Sunday afternoon Matt March and Eden Douglass would bring a picnic to this place, and here, in the semishelter of the three-sided house with the sunflowers and the wild mustard to witness, they would make love for the first time.

For this picnic, Eden Louise Douglass did not want Matt March to think she was a ham sandwich kind of girl. She wanted this picnic to live in history of all picnics. She called Annie Douglass and asked for her advice. Annie had the perfect picnic solution. Picnic fare you could eat with your fingers. The blueberries and honeydew cool and moist. The chicken wings and drumsticks sweet and hot. You could lick your fingers. Or someone else could lick them.

### Annie's Delight to the Eye in Summer

In a blue or yellow or white bowl, cut small one honeydew melon and splash about with fresh blueberries. A pleasure to look at, much less taste.

### Annie's Sweet and Hot Picnic Chicken

In a small pan melt some butter and add some olive oil. To this generously sprinkle cayenne pepper, a little salt and pepper, a couple of dashes of ground allspice. Stir together. Lay your chicken wings or drumsticks in a single layer in baking dish. Pour this over them, and turn them over so they're coated. Bake at 350 for about an hour till well done, turning them over in the sauce at least once. Excellent and tangy, though messy.

# SNAPSHOT

## The Toga and the Talkies

Once there were two brothers, Ernesto and Nico Marchiani. Their father was a carpenter and a Socialist. When Italy entered World War I in May 1915, he knew that conscription would slurp up all the young men, and kill them for the profits of pigs, for kings, kaisers, and armament makers. He sent his sons to America. He knew he would never see them again, and he never did. But they lived.

Ernesto and Nico went first to New York, where they stayed through one winter only. They could not endure the cold. They went then to Los Angeles and stayed in the same garage apartment with the Poggibonsi cousin who needed bodies for his Socialist rallies.

In 1917 the Marchiani brothers made maybe three dollars a week. They wore overalls, tool belts, red flannel underwear in winter, and straw boaters. They built sets for Lesley Markowitz.

Lesley Markowitz is forgotten now (for that matter, so is Ernest March), but in the early days of silent film, Markowitz was fabulously creative, inventive, successful, and a renowned bully on the sets.

Nico and Ernesto and the other workmen were putting the finishing touches on the steps of the Roman Senate when Markowitz's flunky hustled them all off, saying, Time is money.

Some things do not change.

The workmen moved to the sidelines. With a flourish Lesley Markowitz arrived on the set, took his place while the actors were assembling. All was in readiness, save for the star. Where was the leading man? The flunky didn't know. The flunky picked up his megaphone and called out the star's name, knocking on dressing-room doors.

The toga-clad girl third from the end gave Ernesto the eye; he never wanted for women, even when he wore overalls.

Twenty minutes passed. Time is money. Markowitz was about to shit lead or piss bullets, whichever orifice opened up first. Just then, the star staggered out, falling-down drunk. He wobbled over to the steps of the Roman Senate, and burped.

Markowitz bolted from his seat, took the actor by the shoulder, tore off the toga, and left him naked. Then Markowitz turned, glowering, and, still holding the toga, looked around the set. Time is money. He saw Ernesto Marchiani on the sidelines. He said, Hey, you! Take off your clothes, put on this goddamn toga and get to work!

They darkened Ernesto's eyebrows, caked up his face with makeup, and shoved the toga-clad carpenter in front of the camera. They told him what he was supposed to be feeling, to be expressing. He didn't have to speak. He was a natural. For the next picture they put him in a loincloth, told him what to do, what to feel, what to emote. He did it. Nobody did it better. Ernest March broke hearts all over America, though his English was limited and heavily inflected. What did it matter? In film after film, he won the girl, and carried himself like the lover he was.

By 1919 he was earning $250 a week, and he had moved with his brother, Nico, and Nico's wife, Stella, to a big house on West Adams. By the time he made *The Green Goddess,* he was earning $3,000 a week and making as many as five pictures a year, mostly with the beautiful Blanche Randall, she of the bee-stung lips and foul tongue. They coolly detested each other. She thought Ernest a stupid wop, and he thought her a little whore. Nonetheless, they made theatres steam with their on-screen chemistry. Ernesto's screen allure was almost unrivaled save for John Gilbert's, Ramon Novarro's, and Valentino's.

When Valentino died in August 1926, Ernest March knew the competition was now down to himself, John Gilbert, and Ramon Novarro. He did not know that in dying Valentino would live forever as legend. He did not know that Ramon Novarro would have *Ben-Hur,* that John Gilbert would have Greta Garbo. That Ernest March would have nothing, that his name and face would crumble as time gnawed at the fragile film he graced.

He knew none of that. He, Nico, and Nico's wife, Stella, lived in a West Adams mansion. Nico spent his days playing the stockmarket with Ernesto's money. Stella spent her days doting all over her little son, Matt, the only one of three children to survive. Stella went to St. Agnes's every morning for mass. The March men wore Savile Row suits, English tailored shirts, 24-karat gold cuff links, and Italian handmade shoes.

They wore expensive clothes even when the family took Sunday drives for picnics in the country. Stella wore a smart cloche to hold her hair in place while she and little Matt rode in the back of the open roadster. One spring day they drove north. They found the knoll with its sweeping vista of the green-water lake, the surrounding hillsides.

Ernest March fell in love. For a man who never married, he made a profound commitment. Ernesto saw in Agua Verde a vision of his own small sovereign country: a vista of his own land, as far as his eye could see, that he would share with Nico, Stella, and Matt, where he could host enormous parties for visiting opera impresarios. He came, he saw, he built, pleased that he could create all this from the clickety-clack of celluloid ribbons rattling through the camera, rolling through the projector, wheels turning clickety-clatter, the rhythm as steady and insistent as a train on a track, noisy loops of longing and fulfillment, light dissipating into the smoky overhead darkness before concentrating its mesmerizing power on the white, silent screen.

At the premiere of the first talking picture, *The Jazz Singer*, crowds thronged the sidewalk, their hands and arms thrust out to Ernest March and Blanche Randall, who emerged, radiant, from the Tower Theatre. Once they were in the sleek car that Lesley Markowitz provided, Blanche Randall cursed, and lit up. Ernest March told the driver to take him to the Ambassador Hotel, where he spent the night whenever he was obliged to be in the city. Inevitably over a drink in the palm-tree-and-stuffed-monkey ambience of the Cocoanut Grove bar, he found an obliging girl to laugh, to dance, to go upstairs with him.

He returned home the next day. While he was making lunch in the hacienda kitchen, Ernesto confided to Nico and Stella that Mr. Al Jolson in his blackface was all very fine declaring, *You ain't heard nothin' yet*, but his signature tune, "Toot Toot Tootsie," was no *La Traviata*. Ernesto wiped his hands on his apron. He crossed the kitchen and put on *Aida*. He said *The Jazz Singer* was no *Ben-Hur*, no *Green Goddess*.

A few months later, Ernesto, Nico, and Stella made an overnight jaunt to the city to go to the matinee of a picture everyone was talking about. *Lights of New York* was a silly bagatelle about barbers and bootleggers. It, too, was no *Ben-Hur*. It was the fourth talking picture, but no one quite trusted sound; there were still title cards for the story and the dialogue.

Ernesto, Nico, and Stella sat in the middle of the darkened theatre while human voices crackled from the screen. The audience all around them gasped *ooh!* and *ahh!* Though on-screen, the language and the lips did not always match, and a hissing undercurrent, flecked with audible bumps, droned, still words—sound!—rolled out over and into the darkness. People talked among themselves, *Oh my, oh my! Didja hear that?*

And then someone down near the front stood up, turned around, and shouted: Shut up, damn you, so we can hear the damn picture!

Ernesto, Nico, and Stella flinched in unison. Hear the damn picture? How does one hear a picture? It is a moving picture, yes? Only now it is a talking picture.

The three left before *Lights of New York* ended. They drove to the Ambassador, where they were registered as Ernest March and party. Their rooms were like palaces, with fresh flowers and fruit in each. They each had a manicure, a pedicure; they changed into evening clothes and went to Pierino's on La Cienega for dinner, where they were treated like royalty. The best table.

After Pierino's they returned to the Ambassador, the Cocoanut Grove. The maître d' conducted them through the crowd. Just under the strains of the jazz orchestra, word telegraphed through the famous and the infamous: *Ernest March has arrived.* He ordered champagne and ice cream for himself and his party. Banana ice cream, served in crystal goblets and on beds of fresh mint. Someone sent over a bottle of French champagne with his compliments. People came to their table so Ernesto could sign napkins or a handkerchief. They asked when he would be in a talkie, and, since his English was imperfect, he flashed his smile that required no translation.

A beautiful girl wearing a backless dress with gold-beaded fringe smiled at him, a smile that also needed no translation. On the dance floor, Ernest's beauty next to hers, they were dazzling; people gave them room to swing, to swirl, applauded them. The orchestra played as long as they wished to dance. The trumpet player nearly gave himself a hernia.

The girl in the gold-beaded dress went upstairs with Ernest.

That night, even Nico and Stella made love. An extraordinary occasion indeed.

The girl was not there at breakfast. Ernest, Nico, and Stella ate in a leisurely fashion by the Ambassador's pool. The pool at Agua Verde had been dug, but not yet built. Ernesto and Nico swam for a bit, then changed into their street clothes, Ernesto and Nico dapper as ever, Stella's blue silk scarf setting off her olive complexion. Ernest March paid the hotel bill with a check, including a tip guaranteed to make him memorable. The manager rang a bell, and the three were escorted to their Locomobile with the fawning, extravagant gratitude of the masses.

That afternoon Ernest March went to the large kidney-shaped hole that was to be the Agua Verde swimming pool. He stumbled, slid down the dirt embankment into what would be the deep end, losing his balance, staggering and streaking his fine clothes with dirt. He sat there with a gun to his head for three hours until his brother found him.

## CHAPTER THREE

HER FINGERTIPS WERE BLUE WITH CARBON PAPER
stains, but everything was laid out perfectly in the folder
marked MARCH, MATT, GREENWATER PICTURES: the appli-
cations and collaterals, the net worths and net sums, the
taxes and copies of the deed, the title insurance, the portion of the four hundred acres being mortgaged to secure the loan that would launch Matt's dreams.

Every day that he could get away from Greenwater
in the late afternoon, Matt met Eden at her apartment
when she came home from the bank. Their time together was often spontaneous, unplanned. She loved to
see the Greenwater jeep parked there. Eden unlocked
her apartment door and went straight into Matt's arms.

They made love, they went to Pierino's. Maybe they
even worked on the loan application. They would go to
the movies, preferably Westerns, sit in the back row with
their popcorn, while Matt whispered what he would do
differently when he made his own Westerns. Or they
might get Chinese food in little cartons and climb into her
spacious bathtub, and feed each other with chopsticks

while Eden told him how Kitty used to make them all talk a spurious Chinese, no English allowed, when they bought their dinners from Mr. Kee's Red Dragon. That summer Matt March took Eden to places she would never have dreamed of. They went to parties at the homes of Poverty Row producers. They mingled with these same men, their wives and girlfriends, in bars and cafés near Sunset and Gower, in the vicinity of Poverty Row itself. They frequented a bar in the Valley, they whistled and applauded when the Sons of the Sagebrush performed there. They met often with Ginny and Les Doyle at their favorite place, a café where stuntmen gathered, where the cooking was plain, the waitresses sturdy, the beers cold, and Hank Williams was on the jukebox. Matt took Eden to a memorable dinner at the home of Juan and Marinda Reynolds, Juan a long-time stuntman who suffered from a terrible cough. Marinda was a fabulous cook, a slight, graying, impish woman with many stories of the Mexican Revolution and eating ice cream with Pancho Villa.

However, Matt never took Eden home to meet his family, and Eden never offered an occasion for Matt to meet her mother. Matt knew Annie, and that was enough. The time she had with Matt, Eden wanted to spend immersed in him, not having to explain, or worse, apologize for Kitty Douglass.

Matt slept beside Eden, never waking her when he had to leave the apartment in the wee hours; it was a long ride back to Greenwater, and work began just after first light. His warmth lingered with Eden for the whole day, body and soul. She loved him. He loved her. They spoke of their love often, sometimes wordlessly, with a caress, a glance, the very presence of their body warmth radiating. But Matt did not speak of marriage. Their talk of the future was for the loan to fund Matt's Greenwater dreams. Eden was determined to marry him, but she waited for him to propose.

In August, having checked and double-checked the loan application, Eden deemed it ready, and Matt called for an appointment with Walter Brock to request a loan. No mention was made of Eden's contribution: the figuring, refiguring, her knowledge of what the bank looked for, valued.

Walter Brock said he would put Matt's application before the bank's finance committee. Five days later Walter informed Eden that Columbia First National did not usually dabble about in . . . he sought the word . . . anything as flighty as B Westerns. But property? Greenwater was a fine property. The Valley was booming. The investment was sound. He handed the file back to Eden and asked her to make the call, and set up an appointment for Mr. March to come in and sign the documents and collect his money.

All business, Eden said into the phone, "Mr. March? Mr. Brock will meet you then, Thursday afternoon at two." She knew Walter Brock's habits. In the mornings he often brought with him the shadow of marital discord, which made him cranky. A few hours of work and flirting, a couple of martinis at lunch, and his testy attitude evaporated, replaced by his usual smarmy geniality. Matt shouted happily on his end, but Eden kept her demeanor absolutely neutral. When she put down the phone and turned around, Walter Brock was still standing in front of his frosted glass door.

"Bring me in some coffee, will you, Eden. You know how I like it. Same way I like my women. Hot. Sugared."

"Yes, Walter." Eden rose. She could be both crisp and acquiescent. Perhaps a month, six weeks before, Walter Brock had struck up a liaison with a young woman in escrow. He no longer took Eden to lunch, and his interest in her, mercifully, diminished to the occasional innuendo passing for wit, such as with the coffee.

For this Thursday afternoon, to celebrate Matt's loan, Eden had bought an African violet for her desk. She pulled out her desk drawer and checked her makeup in the mirror she kept there: no lipstick on the teeth, her complexion tanned and bright from weekend afternoons riding in the open jeep around Greenwater. Her eyes were alight, her short hair easily fluffed. She was so excited at Matt's prospects—inaugurating Greenwater Pictures with the prestigious backing of Columbia First National—she could feel herself perspiring. Glowing, Kitty always said. Sweat, perhaps, but the scent of Chanel No. 5 wafted up to her nose from between her breasts, beating with her heart even through her smart silk blouse.

She had discovered, in the few months of her affair with Matt March, a new appreciation for silk: silk blouses, silk slips, silk lingerie replaced the cotton she had worn all her life. A lacy garter belt held up her silk stockings. Eden no longer wore a girdle. Matt didn't like girdles. He said he liked to watch things move when she walked. He liked to pat her behind and feel the response of flesh, not rubber or elastic. She thought of tonight, their dinner at Pierino's and then . . . a little shudder of anticipation tingled through her. You are at the bank, she scolded herself, crossed her legs, and closed the desk drawer. She glanced at the wall clock above the file cabinets. One ten. She took Matt's file into Brock's office and laid it neatly on top of the blotter. One fifteen.

She kept busy, typewriter clacking, checking accounts and appointments. At quarter of two Matt March strode into the bank. Eden watched him cross the floor; he was not an especially big man, but he carried himself with such vitality (and the cowboy boots, the curling black hair, the brilliant smile didn't hurt either), such an air of exuberance and intensity that everyone in Columbia First National Bank seemed, in Eden's eyes, to pale in his wake. As he strode across the marble floor, through the pool of stained-glass sunlight, the tellers looked up, secretaries glanced his way; even the bankers themselves seemed responsive to his presence.

"Walter's not in yet," said Eden. "You're early."

"I'm nervous." He took the chair beside her desk.

"Don't be. Do you want to wait in his office or out here?"

"What do most people do?"

"You're not most people." She kept her expression bland as she spoke. Anyone in the bank could look through to her desk and see her face. Like looking out of a fishbowl, she thought. Or into one.

With his back to the fishbowl, Matt let anxiety play over his features. He cleared his throat. "I have you to thank, of course, for all the help with the forms, but more than that. You made me believe everything is possible. Everything."

Eden glanced up and saw Miss Abigail Franklin walk by. Miss Franklin seemed to swim past, to turn her head and give Eden a lemony smile. "You should go wait in Walter's office," Eden said to Matt. "We don't want people to . . ."

"To what?"

"To think that I have anything special to do with your loan."

"We don't want them to think we're in love?" His voice was low and urgent. "Why not? Who gives a damn?"

"Let's get the loan first. Then not give a damn." She rose and opened the frosted glass door between her small ante-office and Mr. Brock's spacious one. "Right this way, Mr. March. Mr. Brock will be here directly. Can I get you a cup of coffee?"

"I bet you say that to all the guys." He sat in the chair opposite Brock's desk, staring at the tennis trophies. Eden returned to her desk, closing the door behind her.

At 2:10 Walter Brock was not there. By 2:25 Eden's palms were damp, and the sweat she was popping had nothing to do with pleasurable tingle. She made a few phone calls inquiring if Mr. Brock was in another office. To no avail. She did not dare leave her little office to look for him. Suppose he walked in and found her gone? She did not dare go wait with Matt in Brock's office. She did not want Matt to see how worried she was. Had she possibly overlooked something? Was Walter detained by an accident? Every possible avenue, excuse, or flash of reasoning seemed stupefyingly trivial and, at the same time, hugely momentous.

Finally she saw Walter Brock enter through the bank's front doors. He and another man, a Mr. Simon, crossed through the oblong patches of stained-glass sunlight. Simon was Brock's 2:30 appointment. God's Nostrils! Eden swore inwardly. She rose, and blurted out, "Mr. March is waiting for you, Walter. Did you forget? He's been—"

"This won't take a minute," Walter said to Mr. Simon, ignoring Eden altogether. "Have a seat." He gestured toward the chair by Eden's desk. "She'll get you some coffee." And he vanished behind the frosted glass; there was a stir from inside Brock's office and a blur of voices.

"Java would be swell," said Mr. Simon.

Eden's office chair creaked woodenly as she sat back down. Suddenly overwhelmed by the conviction that there was something she'd forgotten, she clutched her desk. Something amiss. Something important. What was it? Like being in those dreams from which you wake out of breath but soothed to find yourself in your own bed, and not standing stark naked in front of all sorts of people—some you know, some you don't—no one quite with the kindness or courage to tell you you've forgotten to put on your clothes, sorry to say. But this was not a dream. She had forgotten something urgent. What was it? She nibbled a nail and shuffled mentally through the necessary documentation. Something done wrong? Left undone? Had she misread the old deed, title to the original Agua Verde? Was there some difficulty she'd missed on the document where Ernest March made a quitclaim deed for the the whole of Greenwater Ranch over to his nephew in 1946? Greenwater belonged to Matt March as his sole and separate property. Yes, but . . . what had she had missed? Something essential had slid past her altogether. Not the loan. Something else.

The frosted glass door opened, and Matt stepped out. His face was pale, his lips twisted in a hard seam, his dark eyes expressionless as two lumps of coal. He carried nothing. He said nothing, not even to Eden. He strode into the sunlit fishbowl of the bank.

"Right this way," said Walter to Mr. Simon. "What, no coffee?"

"What happened in there?" she demanded of Brock. "What happened to the money?"

"The loan?" Walter ushered Simon into his office. Eden followed. Brock picked up the file, MARCH, MATT, GREENWATER PICTURES, and handed it back to her. "This loan was denied."

"No, it wasn't. The finance committee—"

"Changed its mind. After more careful consideration, we did not feel that we could loan money out for, well, for cowboys and Indians. No, we decided against it." He paused, savoring for the moment the look on her face. "I act on behalf of the bank. As do you. Time is money."

Eden stood there, speechless. And then she saw the glint in his eye. And she knew what she had missed.

Eden turned around, clutching the file to her breast, but Matt March was nowhere to be seen. She put the file on her desk and dashed out into the vastness of the bank, aware vaguely, as she passed desks and the gilded bars of the tellers, that there was an element of the old naked dream: People were staring at her, a titter, a murmur, a bit of comeuppance. Eden had missed what everyone else had somehow known.

On Spring Street in the ferocious August sunlight, she looked up and down for Matt, for the sight of his back moving through the afternoon crowds; she saw him as he was about to turn the corner; she called out his name and she ran, high heels and all, she ran, calling his name. When finally he stopped, turned around, she flung herself at him, taking his shoulders in her hands. "Oh, Matt! I'm so sorry! It's not you! It's not Greenwater! That's not why! Matt!" She shook him. "Listen to me! Look at me! Talk to me!"

He brought his gaze down to her face. The pain and humiliation in his eyes was almost more than she could bear. He removed her hands from his shoulders. "I do not take it personally," he stated, the words each distinct as if he were spitting marbles. "I understand business. I am not a stupid wop."

"Oh, God, Matt. What did he say to you? That bastard. Listen to me . . . please." She seized his face in her hands, stroked his pale face. "It was my fault, Matt. Brock never intended to lend you the money. I didn't understand what was happening. I won't sleep with him. It's sordid. But it's true." She was crying now. "Walter Brock has been after me to go to bed with him since I came here. And I won't do it."

They stood like a little island in the sidewalk and people gave them a wide berth, looking over their shoulders as Matt stood like a stone, arms at his sides, and Eden wept and ranted on about sleeping with Walter Brock, or not sleeping with him, and his punishing her by humiliating Matt. "Don't you see, Matt? He knows how much I love you. How much I believe in you. And he wanted to hurt you, too. Oh, that snail-snotting son of a bitch! Oh, Matt, I'm so sorry."

Matt's eyes cleared. "About what?"

"About the loan. About Brock. About—"

"Forget Brock." His voice was clear and without passion. "Are you sorry about me? About loving me?"

"No. How could I be? I love you. I will always love you."

"Will you marry me?'

"What?"

"Will you marry me?"

"Yes! Yes I will!"

"Now. Today."

"It's late. We can't get married today."

"We can in Mexico. It's not late in Mexico. It's never late there. We'll get married in Mexico. If you want."

"Mexico?"

"Why should we wait? We're neither of us religious. We're old enough. My mother will be glad I'm married! Think of my poor old mother."

"I don't know your mother, Matt. I've never met her."

"And I've never met your mother. Who cares? We love each other. Why should we wait? We don't need permission. We listen to our hearts. My heart tells me you are the woman for me. Now. Always. If we're going to start a new life together, why shouldn't it be right now? If you don't want to marry me, then that's different."

"You are the man for me. Now. Always. Yes." Eden closed her eyes and he brought his mouth to hers and wrapped his hands around her back. Pressed against him, she balanced precariously on one high heel. Crowds parted around them.

He took her hand and started down the street.

"Wait. I have to go back."

"What? And work for that *bastardo*? No. To hell with him. With Columbia First Fucking National."

"I have to collect my things. The loan folder. We did all that work. I don't want to leave it there for Brock. This isn't the only bank. We'll get the loan somewhere else. Come with me."

He considered for one moment, then took her arm and they turned through the jostling crowds. Even the asphalt beneath her feet seemed to Eden to twinkle up at her, winking, somehow in unison and harmony. At the bank Matt pulled open the door and walked at her side across the broad expanse and through the blue and gold light spilling through the windows. Eden paused there, just for a moment, in the reflection of all that abundance; she longed to throw her arms up and shout that she and Matt March were getting married, that their success would shame Columbia! Voices dimmed, eyes followed them as they crossed the floor to her ante-office. She stepped in, dropped her nameplate in the trash, where it rattled metallically. She collected her purse from under the desk, took up the file, MARCH, MATT, GREENWATER PICTURES, and put it under her arm. "I'm ready," she said.

The frosted glass door opened. Walter Brock stepped out and seemed about to speak.

"I quit, Walter. Matt and I are getting married. Today." And on second thought, she picked up the African violet.

They drove the Cord convertible rather than Matt's Greenwater jeep to Mexico, in keeping with their romantic escape. They made one stop. Matt went to his bank and withdrew cash, $350. He figured he'd come home broke. He also knew they would never forget their wedding. Then they headed south, Matt at the wheel, driving too fast, the wind tousling their hair, the sunshine bathing them, the wind cooling them.

"I hope you're not going to feel like you missed out on a big wedding, all that."

"I never wanted that," Eden said truthfully. "Certainly not after working for Miss Merton, all those tedious weddings, what the bride wore and who attended her. That isn't what I want."

"What do you want?"

"You. I want to be loved by you. I want to love you all my life, body and soul."

"That's what I want, too."

Their route connected with Pacific Coast Highway at San Juan Capistrano. The road was a gray ribbon between the vast Pacific on one side, the Sante Fe tracks on the other. Matt told Eden of his boyhood train trips with his father and Ernesto to the Del Mar racetrack by the lagoon, and on to stay in the Hotel del Coronado.

"Before this moment," he reached out for her hand, "that was as happy as I can remember being."

They were married in Ensenada, a civil ceremony conducted by a Mexican justice of the peace whose back room, reserved for these solemn occasions, was stifling, airless in the August heat, and decorated with celluloid flowers and pictures of happy couples that Eden recognized as cut from *Life* magazine advertisements. The JP himself looked tired of all this happiness. He was perhaps fifty, his face hard and dry as a coconut shell, his hair just as wispy. He spoke from memory, in Spanish, and held up his index finger when Matt and Eden were supposed to say *sí*. His wife witnessed. In contrast to her husband, she winked and nodded and clapped, and cheered, her own small noisy congregation saluting their marriage.

If Miss Merton had cared to note it, the bride wore a lacy Mexican blouse, bought that afternoon, low on her shoulders, bright ribbons, red, blue, green, threaded through the lace and wrapping around her shoulders. Her full skirt had matching ribbons around the hem, and she was bare-legged in new sandals. She had an emerald pendant—to match her eyes—on a gold chain around her neck. Matt's wedding present to her.

Matt said the old Rosarito Beach Hotel was known for its glamour, and was the best place for a honeymoon. Eden did not ask how he knew this. She was content to be his new wife, to have a room with an ocean view and a wide sweep of beach. Wandering mariachis played all the time. In the dark, cool bar with its overhead fans, Matt prompted the bartender to create a new drink, which he called the Blue Eden. It turned their lips blue and left a salty tang when they kissed.

From their hotel room, they made the necessary phone calls. Matt rehearsed his by calling Signature and Monogram Pictures. Full of high spirits, he accepted their congratulations on his marriage. Then he had to kiss the bride, of course.

To call his mother, Stella, and Ernesto, Matt got up and put his pants on. He washed his face and combed his hair. Eden remembered him saying his mother was a stickler for form. He sat on the edge of the bed, his hand resting comfortably on Eden's hip as she curled next to him. He lit up and telephoned.

Matt offered up the news of his marriage enthusiastically, but having delivered that announcement, his subsequent conversation consisted of "No, Mama," or "Now, Mama," and protestations of his love for his mother and his uncle. When he hung up, he looked a little sheepish. "When we get home, they'll come around."

This was the first time Eden realized she would be living with Stella and Ernesto. She had not looked that far ahead. She did not do so now. Instead, they rolled around on the rumpled bed.

Eden called Annie, whose exuberance more than made up for Matt's family's subdued response. "Will you tell Ma?" Eden asked her. "She'll rattle on and want to know everything. I can't bear the thought of talking to her now."

"Okay, I'll take care of it, don't worry. It'll be a pleasure to tell Kitty something that will actually shake her up." Annie gave a rueful laugh. "But you'll have to tell her about Ernest March. Not me."

"Oh, later. I'll do that later. And, Afton, will you call her, too?"

"Oh God, Afton!" Annie gave a little shriek. "Sure, sure I'll do it. You forget all this family stuff. You two just go have a dance on the beach. And tell Matt he is one lucky guy."

The wedding picture of Mr. and Mrs. Matt March would not have suited Winifred Merton or the society pages, nor was Matt's mother amused. But it always made Eden smile. On a street in Ensenada, Matt and Eden in sombreros and serapes posed, Eden sitting on the back of an uncomplaining burro, Matt standing boldly by her side, in front of a piñata stall. The burro had a harness of bells and ribbons around his head and banner that said, viva mexico! The picture was in black-and-white, grainy grays, but seemed to Eden always drenched, awash in color and scent and sound, voices, laughter, honking cars around them. Her lips were slightly blue from the Blue Eden, her fingers were sticky from the sugary candy they had just eaten, little perfectly fashioned animals in pink and green and orange that melted, creating in her sweaty hand a colorful swath, like holding a tropical sunset in your palm.

# Blue Eden

Dampen the rim of your wide-mouth glass with a half slice of fresh lemon. Tip upside down in a dish of kosher salt and cover the rim. Throw in some ice cubes. Pour a shot of good tequila, or tequila liqueur. Two shots of Blue Curacao. Top off with fresh tonic. Stir well and plunge in a whole slice of lemon. Ponder before drinking.

Fine anytime. Best on a hot summer evening in the company of someone who will still kiss you even if your lips turn a little blue.

### A CATHOLIC EDUCATION

Unlike her mercurial son, Stella March was a force like gravity. She was devoted to dolor and looked darkly upon all change. Stella was solid, somber, a short, bullet-bodied woman whose darkly circled eyes her son had inherited. She never wore makeup, not even lipstick. Her lack of vanity was an act of contrition. Stella dressed always in black or gray, as though practicing for widowhood, which came to her in 1944. She had expected to suffer more when Nico died. She did suffer, of course, but she was of such a solemn and devout turn of mind that the step into grief was short.

She had met Nico Marchiani and his brother Ernesto at her family's apartment in New York City's Little Italy. Her brother Alberto brought them home one night for dinner. They ate with gusto. They talked and laughed. They worked the same construction site with Alberto. They shared the same Socialist politics. Stella's mother remarked on Ernesto's beauty.

Ernesto, for all his beauty, never drew Stella. It was always Nico for her, from the time she first met him. And when Nico's eyes rested on her skin, fine like marble, her dark, half-hooded eyes, and luxurious hair, he was instantly smitten. Stella remained a good Catholic girl and gave up only the smallest kiss so that Nico Marchiani would know she was serious. Stella was serious about everything. Even then. But she was also shy and wistful.

When the winter came, the Marchiani brothers couldn't endure New York, and there was word of a Poggibonsi cousin or neighbor or some such person who lived in Los Angeles. He could get them work. He had an apartment over his garage. They waited till spring and then the Marchianis took the train as far as Wichita and hitchhiked to Los Angeles from there.

Nico wrote often from California. Stella replied. He and his brother found good jobs working for Lesley Markowitz. Had Stella ever seen a Lesley Markowitz picture?

Stella then went to the theatre to see a Lesley Markowitz picture and wrote back she had not seen him or Ernesto in the film.

Nico replied they were not actors. They were building sets for Lesley Markowitz. Would she please take the train to Los Angeles and marry him? He loved her. He would be a good husband. Did she want him to write to her father?

Stella thought about this while she worked at the laundry not far from her family's apartment. She ironed there. Except for the heat in summer, Stella liked to iron. She found it soothing. And it was easy to see what you had accomplished. There was no ambiguity with the iron. She would marry him.

Once married to Nico, Stella thought Ernesto would move out, but no one suggested splitting up. When Ernesto's acting career started bringing in good money, they all three moved to West Adams. Stella, born and raised in New York, was a city girl always and loved this house. She could walk to St. Agnes's. Later, she did not love Agua Verde. Too quiet. No nearby church. No sounds from the streets. She suffered.

But suffering was part of life, and Stella accepted it. She knew suffering. In 1922 there had come a note from her priest in New York with the terrible news of a gas explosion in the building where her family lived. All gone. Of her two pregnancies, both were stillborn, but the third, Matteo, lived. She told God she was content with one child. She would not ask for more. Would not tax His patience, a vow which also seriously tempered her relations with Nico. Stella promised God that if Matteo lived, she would dedicate herself to the Church, give up her son to the Church. Stella gave up her son to the Church, sending him away to St. Ignatius when he was six years old.

Without the boy living in the Agua Verde hacienda, the three adults each kept to small, separate domains. Stella's was a dour Catholicism. Ernesto's was cooking, while Italian opera warbled from the Victrola he had set up in the kitchen. Nico played the stock market with Ernesto's money. While it lasted. Then, almost simultaneously, came the Crash and the talkies. No matter. Stella insisted the fees be paid to keep Matteo at St. Ignatius. He must never go to school with peasants. He must have a Catholic education.

And yet, for all the Jesuitical training, Matt did not grow up to be a good Catholic. He discovered girls early and enthusiastically. As a boy he liked confessing in order to shock the priest. As a man he had many girlfriends and his share of desultory affairs, trysts in women's apartments or hotels, or the backseats of luxurious automobiles. He did not bring these women home to the big hacienda, scantily furnished, echoing with emptiness. He did not introduce them to the old folks, his silent, obese uncle Ernesto, his grim, long-suffering, widowed mother. Sometimes Stella and Ernesto did not see Matt for days on end. Or, he might come home only to change clothes, have a quick meal with them, remaining always charming, then he was off again.

Where does he go? Stella used to ask Ernesto, who only shrugged his heavy shoulders in reply.

Stella did Matt's laundry, ironed his shirts, and the scent of the women Matt had been with rose from the heat of the iron, the scent of sex and smoky restaurants and cafés, of jazz clubs, and giddy laughter in the backseats of cars. Sometimes in his pockets there were tickets from losing horses at Santa Anita, and occasionally sand from unknown beaches and matchbooks from restaurants and clubs with mysterious names. Stella would have done Matt's penance for him, but he did not confess to her, to anyone, and she could not begin to imagine his sins.

## CHAPTER FOUR

From her Oasis office, Annie Douglass phoned the Marches' home and congratulated Ernesto on his nephew's marriage to Eden Douglass. She was calling, too, to invite Stella and Ernesto to a reception, to greet the newlyweds on their return from Mexico. Annie would host a small party at her Encino home. Ernesto listened, excused himself, and with a muffled exchange gave the phone to Stella.

Stella was polite but firm. Fine, the reception for the newlyweds—and Annie noticed there was just a little strangle over the word—who would be getting back from Mexico—another sad, significant pause—but it must be held here, at Agua Verde, Matt's family home. "You are Annie Douglass, yes, of Oasis, the caterers?" Stella asked. "Well then, it cannot make any difference to you. You are used to this. You bring everything here. We do not go out anymore, Ernesto and me. Our health, you know?"

Peace in the family seemed to Annie to be a thing worth preserving. She acquiesced to Stella's wishes,

242

which in fact had nothing to do with their health. Their health was fine. Stella and Ernesto wanted to be on their own turf when they endured this shock. Stella was especially distraught. Her only son, her only child, had married a non-Catholic, a woman Stella had never met, in a civil wedding. Worse, a civil wedding in Mexico.

Early on the morning of the reception, and well in advance of the Oasis caravan, Annie drove out to Greenwater alone. Once through the gate, she did not take her usual left turn toward the cookshack and picnic grounds, but drove her station wagon straight down the long, unpaved road toward the hacienda.

As often as she had worked at Greenwater, Annie had never seen the house, finished in 1928. There was a forlorn air to the place, though it was opulent, and set about with palm, magnolia, lemon, and avocado trees, and two stories of cream-colored stucco, red tile roof, all Moorish smooth arches with a long wooden balcony across the second floor. A heavy bougainvillea vine, alight with spiderwebs, rippled along the balustrade. All the windows and the French doors were brown with thick dirt; the shutters had dried and cracked. The drapes were worn, streaked with sun stains. The wide driveway ended at a flagstone path, much overgrown, and the broad shallow steps up to the porch were bordered on either side by overgrown untended hydrangeas; they too had bleached in the unforgiving light.

Ernesto answered Annie's knock. He said little. He wore a white apron over his suit. His enormous stomach bulged over his belt and his chins wobbled over his collar and bow tie. All that remained of his youthful beauty was his high nose, very like Matt's. His mouth was hidden under a brushed, gray mustache. The eyebrows, once so carefully sculpted, had grown bushy and wild. He was quite bald. At least, Annie thought, it's unlikely Kitty will recognize her old screen idol. Even the name might not ring with her, so often was Kitty afloat, awash in her own world of gin and fiction.

He led her through the house, back to kitchen. Their footsteps echoed on teak floors through all-but-empty halls. Annie was surprised to see the place so utterly unfurnished. The Marches had been living here twenty-five years. She had her second twinge of doubt about Eden's marriage. Her first was when she had talked to Afton, who had greeted the news of a Mexican civil ceremony to a Catholic man even more coldly than Annie had feared.

"The kitchen is yours. I am finish there." Ernesto smiled at her, and removed the apron. He was perfectly groomed.

The March kitchen was huge, with windows over the sink that overlooked a brilliant, graceful garden. The back door opened onto a sheltered patio with a fountain. Annie was stunned, speechless really, to see that the big table in the middle was already covered with a cornucopia of food. The table sparkled with five white ricotta tortes, each swirled with a great *M* in raspberry jam, and a small ring of melted jam around the cake. Two strawberry cheesecakes glowed pink in their chocolate-crumb-crust collars. Ernesto had made too bowls of portobello salad and an eggplant and olive caponata. There were marinated mushrooms and beans baked with artichoke sauce, and roasted red peppers wrapped around some savory cheeses, then baked, the red and gold of the peppers in a checkerboard pattern. "I do a little cooking of my own," Ernesto demurred, "but the caponata, that is Stella's. Bitter loves salt."


By three o'clock, Stella stood in the garden beside her brother-in-law. They waited in the lacy shade of a pink crepe myrtle, Stella looking as though she were about to be tied to that tree, blindfolded, and shot. Stella wore a gray voile dress that still smelled of the mothballs from which she had exhumed it the day before. Her gold cross gleamed against the gray and beside the corsage of white roses Annie had pinned to her shoulder.

"You are the mother of the groom." said Annie as she pinned it to the voile. She slathered on the flattery, all to no avail. Stella did not flinch or smile. She said thank you as one might thank the soldier who offers the doomed a blindfold for the eyes.

Ernesto, on the other hand, seemed pleased with his white rose boutonniere. His bow tie was correctly knotted; he wore a vest, a coat, a white shirt with gold cuff links.

But, like Stella, Ernesto was appalled as the Douglasses descended on Greenwater in hordes. Their qualms mounted as car after car came, disgorging huge families with fussy children, screaming babies, uncomfortable matrons and men ill at ease in Sunday suits, all of them hot, weary from the long drive from St. Elmo. Introduced to Eden's family, Ernesto and Stella both smiled as long as they could. Then they simply stared, their eyes haunted with misgiving.

In Italian, Stella mumbled, *"They have the look of people who have come for the free food."*

*"Look at them,"* he whispered. *"They are mongrels, these Douglasses."*

Of course, they weren't all Douglasses. Annie's parents were there, Vartan and Shushan Agajanian; their grandchildren all looked like Annie, dark, intense eyes, black hair, and strong features. Vartan and Shushan considered themselves cosmopolitan, and the very proximity of the bumptious Douglass

clan in such numbers made them bilious. They had come today on Eden's behalf, and because they knew their daughter Annie would need an ally among
the Douglasses.

A motley tribe, some Saints, some sinners. Eden's relatives gathered to welcome the bride and groom, to sample the strange food, to pass judgment. They
would forgo their own internecine feuds, at least for an afternoon.

Tom Lance, Jr., and his French wife wore their mutual dissatisfaction as visibly as combat medals; like tired soldiers, they smoked without speaking. Their
three bratty daughters, unsupervised, picked fights among themselves, and
when that activity paled, they ganged up on the other kids, pelting them with
the tomatoes from Ernesto's carefully tended plants in the garden he had
planted to hide the sight of the filled-in swimming pool.

The vegetable wars ended in tears and messed dresses, and one the Epps
boys got pushed into the fountain, his backside swatted, right there on the spot
by his mother, who sent him to sit in the wicker rocker to drip and cry.

Samuel Lance and his wife each held a crying baby and did little dances to
hush them while their other children played screaming tag amid the palms and
magnolias. Eden's cousin Bessie and her husband, Nephi, had long since outgrown the baby stage of their family life; they watched the antics of their own
unruly children with the stolidity of mules linked to their traces.

Connie Levy held fast to the hand of her youngest, Aaron, while Leah and
her stepchildren continued their quarrel just out of her reach. Leah stuck her
tongue out at her mother and ran away. Victor shot Connie a baleful look, and
she reminded him tartly that two of their children were not even hers. And yet,
in the middle of all this, Connie suffered a pang of déjà vu from her own wedding reception. She remembered the love and pride she had felt being Mrs. Victor Levy. Remembered that her people and the groom's people hardly spoke,
and never melded. Connie felt a pang of pity for Stella and Ernesto. The Mormons outnumbered them by the hundreds. Children, big and small, swooped
down upon the once-quiet garden like Goths intent on Rome.

Friends of Matt's stood in small uncomfortable knots, ill at ease, holding
their beers or wineglasses, as if fending off a posse. The Mormons cast them all
disapproving glances. Oasis waiters offered cold beers to the Sons of the Sagebrush, to Ginny and Les Doyle and Juan and Marinda Reynolds, and the other
stuntmen and Greenwater wranglers and cowboys. Spud Babbitt took two beers
when the waiter passed in case he didn't get back this way. Poverty Row showed
up for one of its own; both Monogram and Signature Pictures were well repre-
sented, but lost among the Saints.

Carrying heavy trays, waiters offered wine and lemonade. Alma and Walter Epps made a great show of declining wine, though their oldest boy managed to help himself. His cousins, Micah and Jonah Lance, teenagers, each snagged a glass of wine and felt like men of the world, as long as they stayed behind the magnolias and out of Afton's sight.

Afton, flanked by Tom and Lil—clear across the garden from Stella and Ernesto—clutched her lemonade in one hand, her hankie in the other. The sisters wore identical hats and gloves. Tom Lance chewed slowly on the strange hors d'oeuvres. He asked what foreigners had against real food. Lil wondered aloud if Mexican marriages were even legal.

Afton choked and sniffed back tears. "Eden has broken my heart. I loved that girl like my own daughter. And now she's coming back from a Mexican marriage to a Catholic."

"Now, Mother." Tom put his arm around Afton's shoulders. "Let's try and be happy for her. Least she's married. You was always worried she never would marry."

"Think about the Celestial Kingdom if it'll help." Lil patted her hand. "Least she can get in now." Lil paused. "Maybe."

Then at the other end of the garden they saw Kitty enter with her son, Ernest. Ernest wore a suit, though not easily or well. He towered over his mother, who fluttered on his arm, if anyone as heavy as Kitty could be said to flutter.

Afton and Lil remarked between themselves on Kitty's full floral dress (*too young for her*) in an apricot color that matched her hair (*henna*), cinched at her broad waist (*like putting a ribbon around a little piglet*), and the white rose corsage wilting at her shoulder. She wore salmon-colored gloves. A little Mamie Eisenhower hat with a veil clutched her hair. Afton and Lil managed to criticize her and pity her in the same moment, a feat requiring either constant practice or considerable imagination.

Annie had cued her husband that Matt's mother would also be wearing a white rose corsage, and Ernest Douglass stepped forward, and said, "Mrs. March, this is my mother, Eden's mother, Kitty."

Kitty held out her gloved hand. "As the mother of the bride, I am de-lighted to make your esteemed acquaintance."

Stella nodded curtly.

"I'm Eden's brother, Ernest."

Ernesto looked up, interested. "I am called Ernesto."

"I know," said Ernest, already tired.

"Dear lady," said Ernesto, taking Kitty's hand. "The mother of the bride. And how are you called?"

"What?"

"Your name, dear lady. What is your name?"

Kitty seemed a little flummoxed, so Ernest intervened, and repeated, "This is my mother, Eden's mother, Kitty Douglass. Shake his hand, Ma."

"De-lighted to make your esteemed acquaintance."

Ernest took Kitty's elbow and steered her toward the shade of the covered patio and, seeing Annie come out of the kitchen with a fresh dish for the table, sent her a glance encoded by years of marriage that Kitty had not recognized Ernest March. Not yet.

Just then a cheer rose up. Eden and Matt had arrived home!

Mr. and Mrs. Matt March came through the gate and into the garden, the sunlit magnolia trees, geraniums ringing the flagstone patio, the fountain splashing musically. Eden wore a wide bright band of gold on her left hand and the emerald pendant on her neck. A broad-brimmed new hat sheltered her face from the sun. She was radiant with happiness. The lacy Mexican blouse low on her shoulders showed white against her fresh new tan, and the smooth rise of her breasts. She wore a full skirt, and sandals; she was barelegged, as though she had just stepped off the beach at Baja. Matt grinning, kept an arm around her waist, sometimes slipping to her hip. With his other hand he flung his coat over his shoulder in the manner of a casually contented husband, though he clearly was surprised to see so many people he did not know.

Matt made his way to Stella, took his mother in his arms, and held her; Stella stroked his face, wept, and mumbled in Italian. "English, Mama," said Matt genially.

"I know, dear." Stella sniffed, waved her hanky. "It is the emotion, that's all."

"Mama, this is my wife, Eden." Matt beamed.

Stella drew Eden into a tearful embrace, kissed each cheek, and said, "Oh my dear, you're so much better-looking than his first wife."

"Oh, Mama!"

"It's true." Stella sighed and nodded at Matt. "She is better-looking."

Stella's remark circuited among the nearby guests while Eden recoiled, as though struck. She had the same sense of shock and seismic outrage as when the young stunt rider had ridden past her, slapping her behind. Only this time she wasn't facedown in the mud, though a roaring in her ears drowned out all sounds, but she saw Matt flushing crimson, and barely comprehended that the hugely fat man beside Stella was the gorgeous Ernest March. The faces of the

Douglasses all around her overwhelmed her; the adults were all stunned and silent, and all but the very youngest children seemed to realize they had missed something juicy. Eden winced seeing Afton glare at her from across the garden. Her tongue felt thick between her lips and she stupidly blurted out, "What does this mean, Matt?"

"Oh, princess! It's nothing."

"Have you lied to me?"

"Hey! It was nothing really. Nothing. You're the only girl I ever wanted to marry. That's the truth! As God is my witness, yes, and all these people," he waved to his new in-laws, their curious eyes on the newlyweds, "you're the only girl I ever wanted to marry!"

"But not the only one you did marry?"

He laughed uncomfortably. "Oh, Eden!"

An Oasis waiter came up with a tray of champagne glasses, but Eden brushed him away.

"Matt? Have you been married before?"

"I was going to tell you," he protested, using his hands like fans. "I should have told you. I'm sorry. I would have told you. I was going to tell you. Oh, Mama, why did you have to—"

"I didn't know you didn't tell her," said Stella with an innocence that a saint could not have bested.

"Are we married?" Eden asked. "Or are you . . ." The hapless irony of her situation assailed her: plural marriages.

"I'm divorced. It's true. There. I've said it. I was afraid you wouldn't marry me if I told you the truth. I love you, Eden." He turned to the crowd and shouted out, "I love her!"

"But you lied to me, Matt. Oh, Matt."

He brought his gaze down into Eden's green eyes. "I can explain," he said, taking her arm. "But not here."

He drew her through the crowded patio, into the kitchen, and up the broad stairs, into an unfurnished bedroom. Old rugs were bundled in the corner. The room was close, the windows long unopened.

"It lasted less than a year," he said. "It was the war. I told you. I was Captain Propaganda, and she was a girl I met in D.C. She was a secretary in the office. I thought I was going overseas to die and so did she. And then I didn't die. I didn't even go overseas. She fell in love with someone else who was going overseas to die. He didn't die either. I hardly even lived with her. She went to Reno for a divorce and married him. It was a stupid mistake, that's all."

Eden thought of the many times she had pictured Logan's wife getting a Reno divorce. "You might have mentioned it."

"I should have. I'm sorry. Everything was happening fast."

"It wasn't happening fast. Months. We've been together for months." Yet, in those months Eden had not mentioned Logan Smith, whom she could remember but not imagine. Even the memory was curiously static; with the tumult of the war years gone, Logan seemed isolated in the past. Matt was Eden's future, and in her heart she knew this, but she was still wincing, both from the humiliation and the revelation. "Is that why we went to Baja to get married, because you're married to someone else?"

"No! Never. I have the divorce papers around here. Somewhere. Listen, Eden, I wanted to get married in Mexico because you have to wait three days in California! I didn't want to wait. I wanted to marry you. Now. Look, I'm sorry I didn't tell you. I don't excuse myself. I'm sorry."

"You lied on the marriage license, too. You didn't put down that you were divorced."

"The forms were in Spanish, Sweetpea. The Mexicans don't care."

"They're still official. You signed them."

"I forgot, Eden. I'm sorry. Really, baby, it didn't mean anything. It was all, what, eight, nine years ago? It was the war. You know what that did to everyone? Everyone went a little crazy. We all thought we were going to die."

Logan Smith had married Frances because he thought he was going overseas to die, and once overseas he had met Eden, and yes, everyone went a little crazy. But Logan Smith, crazy or not, would not have lied to her. Except, she had to admit that he had lied. What else could you call it? He had never written. He had never come for her. The men she had loved after Logan, they blurred and diminished. Sex was like eating, you might physically crave what would simply keep you alive. But nourishment? Pleasure? Sustained imaginative exhilaration? Body and soul united and satisfied? There was no one like Matt March. There never had been. There never would be.

Eden walked to the window and turned the handle to open it. It opened reluctantly. Noise, voices from the party below floated up.

Matt came up behind her, but he did not touch her. "Sure, I've had women in my life, I never hid that from you. But I forgot everything, everyone else when I met you, when I fell in love with you. When I turned you over in my arms there in the dirt that day, everyone else paled into insignificance. I've told you that so many times. You must believe me."

Eden turned around. "I do believe you. I felt, feel the same about you. But now—"

"Now we're married. We'll always be together. I'm sorry I didn't tell you about the divorce. I promise I won't keep anything from you ever again. I love you and only you."

"Forsaking all others?"

"What?"

"Isn't that part of the bargain? Forsaking all others till death do us part?"

Matt gave his old laugh. "Who knows what he said in Spanish! I'd have agreed to an order of tamales to marry you."

"That's what I promised, Matt. Spanish or not. Forsaking all others."

"Yes, Eden, yes."

"For better or worse. Richer or poorer. Sickness and health?"

"Yes, all those things I promise. You're my wife. I love you. I will always love you. No matter what happens to us. You can believe that. Take it to the bank!"

"I don't work at the bank anymore. Are there going to be any more surprises?"

"Of course there will! There should be! Hey, life ought to be full of surprises! I like surprises. I like not always knowing what's going to happen every day. If I could live like that, day in, day out, no plans or dreams, or surprises, hey, I'd be the one working in a bank."

"I'm talking about illegitimate children. Old girlfriends showing up to claim their underwear. Old lovers under the bed?"

"None. I swear. You look under any bed you want, Eden. Anyway, I never brought my girlfriends here. You're the only girl I've even brought home. The only girl I wanted to marry. Ever." He brought his arms around her from behind; he kissed the back of her neck in the way that he knew best, and her knees went weak. "Come on, Sweetpea. Give me another chance. I said I'm sorry. Hey, what are you gonna do, Eden? Go to Mexico and divorce me?"

"I'll never divorce you, Matt. I'll never give you up, and I'll never give up on you." She gulped, but she meant it.

# Torte Liza

*Created by Ernesto March for the wedding of Eden Douglass and Matt March, 1952*
*Named for Liza Ruth March, served at her baptism, July 1953*
*Served also at the Café Eden in Skagit County, Washington*

Make your usual graham cracker crumb crust, but add to it ¼ cup toasted almonds that have been ground up fine. Mix with 1 tablespoon of sugar and 4 tablespoons of butter melted. Or, you could use amaretto cookies, and forget the sugar. Press around your springform pan. Bake 8 minutes at 350. Remove and cool.

Separate 6 eggs and beat the yolks well with ¾ cup sugar and a dash of salt. When well combined add to this a fifteen-ounce container of ricotta, 3 tablespoons of sour cream, 1 tablespoon flour, and 3 or 4 teaspoons of Orange Flower Water.

Beat your egg whites in a copper bowl till they hold stiff peaks. Slowly add this to ricotta mixture, taking care to keep up the volume.

Turn into your springform pan. Bake at 350 for about 35 to 45 minutes. Remove, run knife around edge. Cool before serving.

Serve on a platter surrounded with fresh raspberries or blueberries for color. For the letters that Ernesto put on top of the pale cake, he melted jam till it was thick and syrupy and used this.

### THE DOWRY

Eden March brought life to a house that had lain silent. She brought Green-water to its feet. She brought Matt into his element. She brought Stella and Ernesto out of their long torpor. She filled up holiday gatherings with her multitudes of Lance cousins and their tribes of kids. Connie and Victor and their children came often and stayed overnight. Annie and Ernest and their children loved driving around Greenwater with Matt. Even Afton could not hold out against Eden's happiness and Matt's charm.

On a less resoundingly happy note, Eden brought her widowed mother, Kitty, to live at Greenwater in November 1952.

Eden also brought the television set from her old apartment. Ernesto and Stella had resisted television. Ernesto had his opera records. Stella had her prayers. Matt was committed to the movies, the darkened theatre. But Eden plugged in the Admiral console with its ten-inch screen, and her brother put an antenna up on the high roof.

Strange things began to happen. As Matt watched television, Western series for kids, *Hopalong Cassidy, The Cisco Kid,* he started to think. Why, he asked Eden, did the television Westerns all have be for kids? Why couldn't there be something of John Ford quality on television, filmed right here in the town of Lariat?

And once the Admiral console's blue light wavered in a small patch over the floor, Ernesto delighted again in the Westerns he had always loved, except for singing cowboys Gene Autry and Roy Rogers. Ernesto would cover his ears when they sang. But he would listen to the Sons of the Sage-brush.

And perhaps most remarkably, there now came from the living room strange sounds, raspy unpracticed laughter. Stella laughing? Stella? Milton Berle could make a stone laugh. Stella ate lunch with *Sheriff John's Lunch Brigade,* charmed by the antics of a cartoon clown who emerged out of an ink bottle and ran around the desk, and a flapper who said Boop-oop-a-doop.

Is there a way to preserve our revels? A recipe for happiness, so that later, if necessary, you can reconcoct it? These early days of Eden's marriage were long and rich, the nights as well. The tousled unmade bed she shared with

Matt abounded with lust and laughter, with talks long into the night, and mornings that felt like, each one, a wholly new dawn.

And then in the summer of 1953 Eden also brought into the house, home from the hospital, a squalling six-pound, twelve-ounce morsel of humanity named Liza Ruth March.

With Liza's birth, Stella March shed her wary grimness, and her black and gray clothes. She wore bright colors, and reveled in Liza's every smile. Childless Ernesto became a doting grandfather. He took Liza out to the garden and told her the names of all his plants, as though introducing her. He parked her playpen in the kitchen and played Verdi and Puccini for her. Liza called them Nana and Babbo.

Liza called her grandmother Kitty Dadie, for reasons best known to her infant self. Kitty was not especially smitten with the baby. She would have been more interested had Eden and Matt named her Victorine. But they didn't.

Eden March was utterly unprepared for the maelstrom of emotion that assailed her with motherhood. She felt cosmically connected to the future, the past, the world, the very universe. She basked in the baby's uncritical adoration. The baby girl plunged her parents into a three-sided love affair, besotted as they were with each other and with Liza.

Matt constantly babbled baby talk to Liza. He shared the latest snapshots of his dark-eyed baby girl, tales of her achievements (like sprouting a new tooth) with anyone who would listen. His good friends like Les and Ginny Doyle, and Frankie Pierino, were tolerant. Others were flatly bored, but Matt didn't even notice. He showed Liza's pictures off to cameramen, actors and sidekicks, to the wranglers who looked after horses.

Matt walked the floor with Liza when she fussed at night and sang her songs. He told her stories of all the great things she would do. She would learn to ride in the English fashion. She would learn to play piano. She would be the best. She would go to Stanford. All the things Daddy would do for her. He would see that she had a horse. The best horse. The best teacher. He would buy the best piano. He would pay for Stanford. Liza would have everything she wanted.

Stella wanted her baptized Catholic, with Stella and Ernesto to stand as godparents.

Eden had no dormant loyalty to the Mormons. All three of her children were baptized Catholic. Liza in 1953. Stellina in 1955. Lastly, in 1960, their son, Nicolas Ernesto, the surprise child, the delight. With each Catholic baptism, Eden braced for Afton's vociferous opposition. She knew Afton Lance would erupt with indignation, and in this Eden was not mistaken. Afton never gave up, and Eden never gave in. They were the Douglass women, after all.

## CHAPTER FIVE

THE COTTAGE THAT HAD NEVER SHELTERED A GUEST became one of Eden's first undertakings after she moved to Greenwater. She set to work, opening windows, shooing out mice and spiders, washing from the walls and corners the dust of a quarter of a century. She painted and bought new furniture. By the fall of 1952 the place was ready to install Kitty Douglass, and it was time for Eden to relieve Ernest and Annie from the intolerable burden. Eden tried to brace Matt for what Kitty might do or say or demand, without admitting that her mother had all but destroyed the marriage of Annie and Ernest Douglass, brought them to the point where they fought and fretted and froze each other out. Eden did not want the same to happen to her marriage. Kitty wasn't malicious, just thoughtless, selfish, weak, and whining. Oh God, thought Eden three months after her marriage, give me strength for this.

Eden went alone to Encino to collect Kitty. Kitty was gloomy, Annie tight-lipped, Ernest sullenly oblivious all through the excruciating Sunday lunch. Their three children, Linda, Susan, and David, were antsy and subdued. Eden did her cheerful best, spoke brightly of her great plans with Matt, submitting their loan application to other banks, their hopes to finish the Mexican village, and build a soundstage on the property, to see Greenwater Pictures into being, but her own words sounded to her like pebbles dropping into a hollow bucket.

"I'll just keep Pa's Great Timetables, and the genealogy charts, if you don't mind, Ma," said Ernest as he took her suitcases out to Eden's car. "They're no good to you."

"They were no good to him either," Kitty sulked. She jammed her Mamie Eisenhower hat on her head, clutched her coat lapels, and stalked out to the Cord, heedless of the rain.

They pulled away from the house. "Here's a towel, Ma," said Eden. "You'll have to wipe up the moisture that gathers on the roof. The ragtop leaks. I guess I'll finally have to get rid of Annie's old convertible, much as I love it. Get something more matronly."

Kitty burst into tears and used the towel to mop her face. "You don't know what I've suffered in that house. I have been so unhappy! For a whole year!"

"Well, Ma," Eden kept her eyes on the road, "that makes six of you."

"What?" Kitty brought her face out of the towel.

"Annie, Ernest and Linda and Susan and David, that's five other people besides you who haven't been happy."

"Those children are brats. Annie doesn't even love them. Annie only cares about her business. Oasis. She's no better than her rug merchant father."

"He's not a rug merchant."

"I could make your ears ring with stories of that family. She made my life a misery."

"Ma, they bought you Coke by the case and Chesterfields by the carton. They got you dentures so you have teeth now. They gave you money to buy sweets from the Helms man every day his truck came down the street. They rationed the gin, but they didn't take it away from you, did they? They've been good to you for a whole year now since Pa died."

"You wouldn't understand. Her Nibs was just vicious to me. Vicious. And Ernest, my own son, he never stood up for me. He just left the house, went to work in that TV repair shop. He just watches TV with never a thought for my suffering."

"Ma, you make too much of your suffering."

"Fat lot you know." Kitty pouted and looked out the window.

They drove awhile in silence. "Please mop the roof of the car, Ma. Rain is getting in." Eden took a steep breath; she had been practicing for days to find just the right phrases. "We have to talk about some rules of the house."

"Whose house?"

"Mine. Ours. Matt's and mine." And our baby, she thought with a little interior whoop of joy. The child she was carrying filled Eden and Matt with hope, elation, and certainty. "You'll have your own little place, Ma, a guesthouse with your own television, separate from the rest of us," Eden went on, accentuating the positive, "and everything is clean and neat and new. I want you to enjoy living there, but there are rules. And you need to heed them. First, no smoking in bed."

"Oh, God's Nostrils! Oh, just because you don't smoke, no one should! You sound just like Gideon."

"Pa never had the sense to tell you that you couldn't smoke in bed. If you smoke in bed, I'll take the cigs away."

"Killjoy. You remind me of Ruth. Worse, Afton. You, too, would deny me the teensiest little pleasure in life? After everything I've lost? Your dear, dear pa departing this life just last year." She seemed to pause, seeking something else. "And Tootsie in 1919. He died the same day Teddy Roosevelt died and no one cared 'cept me."

"No smoking in bed. No ashtrays in the bedroom. No overfilled ashtrays. And most of all," she added carefully, "I want you to get along with Matt's family, his mother and uncle. They live there, too. I want you to be respectful. You know what I mean, don't you?"

"No. I'm sure I do not."

"You know that Matt's uncle was once, a long time ago, Ernest March."

"Oh yes! Oh, Eden, why didn't you tell me before! I didn't believe my eyes, when I met him. I mean, he's changed, of course, but all those years ago when I met him in the Pilgrim for *Gold of the Yukon,* I felt certain that we should meet again. Oh, Eden, now I know why you were led by an all-knowing God to marry Matt. So that at last, Ernest March and I might consume our love!"

"That isn't why I married Matt. I forbid you to pester Ernesto."

"I love him!"

"Oh God, Ma! Just use the rag and mop up rain, will you?"

Kitty mopped the ragtop roof of the convertible. "I do no disremembrance to the memory of your own dear pa, Eden, though Gideon could try a woman. I know you think your pa was a Saint, and a wonderful man—and he was, of course. But sometimes I wished he was less of a Saint, and more of an ordinary man. All those bleeding Timetables and the ink and the ruler and whatever else he needed to dance angels on the heads of pins! And then, he gets over that, and he went after the ancestors and genealogy so he could be baptizing for the dead! I feel sorry for the dead. Leave them in peace, Gideon, I used to say, but the Mormons don't know the meaning of peace. All their prayers and pumpsucking talk. I'm trying to listen to *Amos 'n' Andy,* but Pa just prayed away with the ward teachers, happy as if he had sense."

"We're not talking about Pa. We're talking about Ernesto. You must not—"

"*Ernesto,*" she cooed and trilled and sang a remnant of a little music-hall ditty.

Clearly some other tactic was needed. The windshield wipers scraped across Eden's vision. "Ernesto lives a simple life, and he doesn't need you slavering after him or—"

"Never have I slavered."

"He's just an old fat man now."

"O cruelty, Eden." She sighed. "Time has dealt Ernest March a heavy hand."

"About three hundred pounds of heavy hand."

"Not like me. I have grown into my maturity. I have never lost my looks."

Eden kept her gaze on the road ahead. Kitty's hennaed hair was bright as a new penny, and her bulk filled out an ample housedress. She had new dentures, and her cheeks were plump though crepey. The skin beneath her eyes gathered in little protesting pouches, and deep fleshy parentheses framed her mouth and chin.

"Ma, he's not a screen lover anymore. He hasn't been in a picture since 1929."

"That don't stop him from being my con-summate soul mate."

"Ma. Mind your manners."

"I have ever been a lady. What's Ernesto do now?" She lingered again over his name.

"He cooks. He keeps a record player in the kitchen and he listens to opera and he cooks. He has a garden. He's a sweet man, and I don't want you to make a pest of yourself."

"I have ever been a lady," she repeated.

"And Stella. Do not get in Stella's way. She will be a formidable enemy if you do."

"I didn't 'member Greenwater was so far out here in the country," Kitty said a little dubiously, watching the rolling hillsides, the road winding, the country-side in autumnal hues. "I guess the Helms man don't come by here every day, does he? Nor the ice cream man?"

Eden turned through the big Greenwater gate. "Just remember what I said about minding your manners."

258

* * *

KITTY DOUGLASS MIGHT HAVE BEEN UNEDUCATED, VAIN, SHALLOW, WEAK, often misled, sometimes delusional, but she was not stupid. Clearly, the way to Ernesto's heart was through the kitchen. She put on an apron and declared herself to be his student. His ardent student. Her enthusiasm was not feigned, though she had no particular aptitude. She listened closely.

Ernesto allowed her to watch him work. He sometimes instructed her on some finishing touch. When the dish was made, Kitty rolled her eyes and declared that nothing, nothing was ever that ambroysal. Cooking is a performance art, and Ernesto put on sterling performances. Never had he had such an appreciative audience as Kitty Douglass. He called Kitty Dear Lady, as though she could somehow comprise in her single being all the women who had ever adored him. It had been a long time since he had been adored.

With Kitty as his student, Ernesto never again had to roll up his cuffs and put his hand in greasy water. Ernesto sat solemnly, fingers laced over his full stomach, and listened while Kitty did the washing up with utterly uncharacteristic grace and goodwill. She shared with him her own theatrical past. Ernesto, unaccustomed to much conversation, was happy to listen, to nod while the phonograph rasped out his favorite operas. The music blended with her voice. He drank wine. Sometimes he dozed off, astonished to wake and find her still there. She might have been a dream, not of the wife he never especially wanted, but her adulation assuaged hungers he had almost forgotten.

Ernesto and Dear Lady sat in the lawn swing, her head on his shoulder (the springs groaning under their combined weight) while Kitty described Hummingbird Delight. "I'm just sure I read about it somewhere," she said, thinking that perhaps she hadn't. She might have made it up. "Oh, Ernesto, it was just the most beautiful dessert ever. And tasty! Oh, it suited my fancy."

"What is in it?"

She had no idea. All she knew for certain was that it was pink and green and delightful.

"Then I shall make it for you, Dear Lady."

"Oh, Ernesto! Do you really have a recipe for Hummingbird Delight?"

"No recipes for me. I shall create it for you. I keep all my recipes, my knowledges up here." He tapped his skull meaningfully. "I write nothing down."

"Well, you ought to. Yes, you ought, Ernesto."

He patted her hand, and demurred, without quite saying that his written English was much weaker than his spoken English.

Within two months of her arrival, Kitty and Ernesto were taking long afternoon naps in the little guesthouse. Ernesto never spent the entire night with Kitty, but gently ignored Stella's outrage. Stella called it incest. Kitty took care never to be alone in the same room with Stella.

Stella demanded that Eden put a stop to their affair. Eden, then heavily pregnant with Liza, declined. She said that Kitty and Ernest were old enough to make their own choices.

Stella turned to Matt, insisting he intervene. She was deaf to Matt's charm and scornful of his evasions. She said to him privately, "I do not think you understand what is at stake here. It's Ernesto's immortal soul. I don't expect Eden to understand, but you have the advantage of a Catholic education. Fornication is a sin. Eden's mother will be Ernesto's ruination."

"Kitty's not so bad, Mama. She's good for Ernesto. Look at him. He's happy."

"What about mortal sin? What of going to hell?" Stella persisted. "Kitty is a bad influence. She is infecting Ernesto with . . . with . . ." Words failed her.

"Frivolity. Well, maybe a little frivolity will be good for him. For us. It'll be all right. You'll see. There's nothing wrong with a little afternoon nap, Mama."

Stella gathered her innate gravity, and declared, "I will pray for Ernesto. God can do what He likes with Kitty."

Dear Lady never quite learned to love wine as Ernesto did, and he never converted to gin. However, as Ernesto believed that smoking destroyed the ability to savor good food, Kitty gave up her Chesterfields, nearly expiring from the craving for a cigarette. But love conquers all. Even Chesterfields. In the years she lived at Greenwater, Kitty's health improved. Her reliance on gin and fiction diminished. Her perennial sulking discontent vanished, and her native high spirits emerged. Even Annie, determined always to believe the worst of Kitty, had to admit she was a new woman in Ernesto's presence. Love is prodigal.

Their days revolved around one another seasonally. They took long walks. Kitty helped Ernesto in the garden, the first outdoor work she'd ever done, other than hanging up wet clothes. She was astonished that she enjoyed it. When the weather warmed up, they untied the little rowboat and brought it from the shelter of the boathouse. They rowed out on Agua Verde, Kitty equipped with a parasol, Ernesto at the oars. Or they might sit at the end of the long dock, take off their shoes, and hang their feet in the green water, her head on his shoulder.

For his sixty-fourth birthday, in February 1953, Dear Lady gave Ernesto a beautiful Morocco-bound notebook and a chrome fountain pen. She had saved up her allowance, forswearing even gin to be able to buy this present.

"It's so you can write them all down, Ernesto, your recipes," she explained when he opened it and peered at the blank pages. They were alone in the little guesthouse, Ernesto properly dressed after their nap, Kitty in the billowing negligee she favored. "So you will always have them."

"I have them always." He tapped his temples.

"Don't you want to write them down?"

"No."

She looked so downcast, he murmured something to the effect that he knew too much and it would take too long.

"You could tell me. I'll write everything down. Just your word for word, I will."

"I could not ask such sacrifice of you."

Kitty laughed and sat on the floor beside him, her head upon his knee. "There's no sacrifice I wouldn't do for you, duck. I am your paramour. I've always wanted to say that word to someone," said Kitty, looking up at him. "Don't you think it's just the grandest word of all?"

The project took years. A few days a week, they sat at the table in the kitchen, Kitty with the pen, Ernesto thoughtfully reciting his recipes, techniques, ingredients, and in the manner of the self-taught, a sense of their proportions, rather than the exact measurements. Kitty rendered it slowly but faithfully, all in her rounded Bubble and Squeak hand. It was, for her, an achievement on the scale of the Great Timetable, of genealogical charts to connect the living with the dead.

And in some ways, that was the effect this little book had in Eden's life. When, years after their deaths, Eden found it, she held it close, weeping, knowing that Kitty and Ernesto had somehow conspired to give her the tools, the instructions to begin her life anew. They had reveled in their moment together, and then picked up the pen and preserved that moment, passed Ernesto's skill to Eden, reached across time with their handwritten testament to both hunger and fulfillment.

# Peppers Ernesto

*A winter favorite at the Café Eden*

Roast your red and yellow peppers on a grill or directly on the burner, turning till charred. More red than yellow. They hold their color better. Put them in a bag and leave for a while in a colander in the sink or on a dish.

Peel the charred layer from your peppers. Do not slice, but cut them in half gently.

In a big bowl mix together some ricotta, some fresh grated parmigiana, some pepper, a dash of salt. To this add some parsley and a tiny bit of rosemary cut together and mixed up with a few cloves of roasted garlic. If it is summer, leave out the rosemary and use fresh basil.

Put a dollop of this mixture in the middle of each pepper, roll up, and lay in a single layer in a baking dish. Drizzle all with olive oil and bake at 350 30 minutes or so. Serve hot.

Beautiful.

## THE SHAPE OF GRIEFS TO COME

As long fingers of dusk smeared the April sky, Matt saw the rowboat, over-turned, bobbing toward shore on waters that had stilled, no longer agitated. He jumped from the jeep, crying out, pulling off his boots, hopping and running to the end of the long dock. He dived into the murky lake, flailing, diving under again and again till at last he came upon their bodies.

That night, the sheriff's department trained the headlights of half a dozen cars on the lake. Divers plunged into Agua Verde. Winches began to turn, and one at a time, the bodies of Ernest March and his paramour Kitty Douglass were towed from the green water, pulled to shore before Eden and Matt's very eyes.

Ernesto was buried according to the rites and rituals of the Catholic Church, but the Mormons got Kitty in the end. Afton insisted: Kitty had been baptized in the Mormon Church, and though she had not lived as a Saint, Kitty was theirs. It was perhaps just one more fiction.

Eden's sister Ada blamed Eden for Kitty's death. If Eden hadn't married a Catholic, none of this would have happened. Ada wept into the phone, and blamed Eden some more.

The Los Angeles County Coroner's office blamed no one. They ruled in May 1956 that the deaths were accidental. Possibly one or the other had stood up in the boat, perhaps too swiftly, the boat capsizing under the sudden shift in weight when they had lurched toward each other, arms outstretched. Alcohol was a factor.

Matt blamed Kitty for Ernesto's death. When his raw shock subsided, Matt brooded. With his grief grew his grievance: Kitty's drinking had killed Ernesto. Ernesto had reached for her, and she had killed him. If Kitty hadn't moved to Greenwater, Ernesto would still be alive instead of suffering a watery death. Like a slick corrosive pool, Matt's bitterness against Kitty Douglass seeped under the door of his marriage to Eden.

Eden's grief softened over time into nugget of nostalgia for both Kitty and Ernesto. At least they had loved each other. At least Kitty had found and ful-filled the great love she bore for Ernest March. Eden missed Ernest, but he was never a vivid personality. She missed his cooking. But Kitty? Oh, Eden missed Kitty. Without Kitty Douglass, the world seemed grayer. Eden missed Kitty's *la di dah* irreverence, her sentimentality, her music-hall tunes, her romantic enthusiasms, and all the little irritating vanities that she clung to in a world that would not acknowledge them.

Stella's sense of loss was soothed by her devout Catholic faith, though she again donned black garb for Ernesto, and wore it for the rest of her life.

Months passed, and Matt's grief did not abate. He had no appetite, not for work or food or sex, the three elements in life that had always animated him. He became secretive. He would spend long hours alone at the lake. He would sometimes take Ernesto's Chrysler and leave with no word to anyone. The great dark circles beneath Matt's eyes deepened. He grew, indeed, he remained, listless, grim. He picked fights with his wife. Not even his daughters, three-year-old Liza and the toddler, Stellina, could pull him from his pool of despond. If he had occasional uproarious episodes, playing with the children, once the little girls went to bed, Matt went upstairs and closed the door of his study, refusing to answer Eden's knock.

He turned his wife into a moth fluttering around the flame of his grief.

Stella allied with Eden in trying to ease Matt's pain. She told Matt he must be happy for Ernesto. Ernesto was in heaven with Nico, but Matt reminded her that she herself had said Kitty would be Ernesto's ruination. Matt even took from Stella the scrap of her own faith. Matt insisted Ernesto had died in a state of sin. Ernesto was in hell.

As the months passed, Eden floundered, unequal to this volcanic grief. Eden lost sleep and weight, trying to fathom Matt's uncertain moods, and carrying the responsibilities that Matt abdicated in the fullness of his grief. Eden best knew men like the undemonstrative Gideon Douglass, the monosyllabic Tom Lance, the utterly reserved Logan Smith. This side of Matt was a shock. Eden turned to Afton. Afton could be relied upon for strength, wisdom.

Afton came to Greenwater in the summer of 1956 and stayed two weeks. To the chaos in this house, Afton Lance brought her usual remedies, unequal parts of energy and faith. Afton counseled Matt, who listened without hearing. She cooked huge meals and cleaned up, washed, ironed, and in the process, earned Stella's begrudging respect. Afton saw to the children. She hired a local man to save Ernesto's garden from neglect. She hired Matt's friend

Marinda Reynolds as a full-time housekeeper. Juan had died of lung cancer in 1954. Marinda moved into Kitty's vacant guest cottage and walked to work.

Afton Lance set everything to rights. Except Matt. Matt's misery finally defeated even Afton. She could not pull him from the slough of his own despond.

As she stood beside Eden on the platform at Union Station awaiting the train back to St. Elmo, Afton said, Just remember God does not send us burdens we cannot bear.

Then God must be very optimistic, replied Eden.

Afton was thoughtful, unduly pensive. She said, Be careful, Eden. I fear a man this passionate. I fear his grief. Grief like this isn't natural. There's some deeper weakness in Matt we haven't seen. Some deeper darkness. I don't say this to be critical or mean. If I did not warn you, I would not be doing my duty. Matt has abandoned you, Eden.

He hasn't. He hasn't left me.

He might as well have. He's wallowing in sorrow, with no thought for you or the children, or his mother. No thought for anyone but himself. You will undermine your own health and well-being if he goes on like this.

I don't know how to stop him.

Neither do I. I'm sorry. You asked me to come to end his suffering and I have failed.

You have not failed me. You have never failed me.

Afton Lance made no reply.

Six months after the accident, Matt March emerged from despair like light flooding a once-darkened plain. His old buoyancy returned as if utterly untarnished. Wretchedness fled when word came to the Marches that their joint creation, *The Lariat Lawman*, would be seen by audiences across America on ABC. Brought to you by Scoop Peanut Butter: *Scoop—Bread's Best Friend.*

Beginning in February 1957 you could tune in on Tuesday nights at 8:30 and see Rex Hogan starring as Lance Kidd, the Lariat Lawman, the lawman with the outlaw past. You could see Spud Babbitt as his deputy and sidekick. You could see the young blonde, buxom Lois Bonner, as the schoolteacher.

Not perhaps the John Ford–rivaling Western Matt dreamed of, but *The Lariat Lawman* (1957–61) still testifies to Matt March's ambition beyond mere horse opera, those TV oaters of the fifties. It did not transcend genre, but

*Lariat's* story and cast were nonstandard, and the town of Lariat not simply an alabaster bastion of bonnet-clad white matrons, white moppets, and white men wearing guns. Actors of every hue had reason to be grateful to Matt March for the work. In Matt's *Lariat,* black and Mexican and Asian actors had developed roles in the series; they had dialogue not played for laughs or stereotypes. Matt March would not have called it diversity. He would not have recognized the word. He called it authenticity.

He wanted to create a Western true to the sweat and stench, the dust and dry endeavor of everyday life. When the horses dropped great grassy turds on the streets of Lariat, they were not immediately cleaned up. Other TV Westerns might allow painted screens to suffice for barnyards; a wire tumbleweed and a wagon wheel might signify a campsite; barehanded men removed "hot" coffeepots from "campfires." Matt March would not tolerate such patent falsity. Matt liked to see, for the camera and the audience to see, flies on the horses' butts. He liked the wind to blow men's hats from their heads. He had the forge fired up so that sweat beaded on the face of Lariat's blacksmith, and sparks flew out as he brought his hammer down on the anvil again and again, creating the authentic rhythm of the west Matt loved, a West true to the people who had lived and died there.

# PART TWO

# Loaves and Fishes

1959

THEY WERE A SMALL BUT SURLY CROWD, MEN AND women, some carrying babes in arms, or holding the hands of small children, gathered in front of the sheriff's office, a solidly brick building befitting a bastion of justice. An armed man stood on the wooden porch, legs apart, barring the door against the people of Lariat: a town set in a west so indefinite it had no state, no territory, no geography or history outside Matt March's imagination.

"All right! Step back!" said the armed man, Deputy Spud Babbitt, in a gravelly voice. He was hefty, his jowls clean shaven, his hat tilted back on his head; a snarly expression wreathed his face, which was otherwise benign, doughy, with droopy eyes and a slack mouth. Spud held a rifle, pointing up. "We ain't had a lynching in Lariat in twenty years, and we ain't a-gonna start now."

Just then the door opened, and the lawman of Lariat stepped out and raised his arms high. He was handcuffed to two prisoners. "There'll be no lynching in my town," said the Lariat Lawman, Lance Kidd. He wore high-heeled boots, and still he wasn't as tall as Spud. But the Lariat Lawman, the actor Rex Hogan, had the bulk of an aging athlete, a square jaw, curly hair he kept dyed jet black, and the squint of the nearsighted. On-screen, the squint made him look more fearsome, as though he were always sizing up a man's mettle or a woman's bust size. The prisoners to whom he was chained shambled, looked this way and that, and managed to look both cowardly and dastardly. "These men will get a fair trial in Lariat," declared Sheriff Lance Kidd. "I took an oath."

"He killed my daddy," shouted Liza, unbidden from deep in the crowd. At seven, Liza often played sunbonnet-clad moppets in town scenes, and she often piped up, whining or snuffling, never quite the bit of silent set decoration she was supposed to be. Stellina, age four, beside her remained quiet.

The Lawman of Lariat told the townspeople if they wanted to lynch his prisoners, they'd have to lynch him, too. They stepped back.

Down the street, the schoolteacher, Carrie Dunne, ran toward the crowd, or ran as best the long dress and tight corset would allow. The neckline was buttoned up, demure, but the dress fit up and over her breasts, close as paint. Crescent sweat stains darkened her armpits. Her eyebrows were exquisitely arched, her lips full, and her blond hair was piled high, bouffant, with little spit-curls framing her face. She arrived at the edges of the crowd just as the lawman parted the waters of humanity, chained to his prisoners, and pulled them down the broad, treeless street. Spud Babbitt, rifle still in hand, walked backward. The hostile crowd, following, stirred dust. The July heat was merciless.

Tethered horses whinnied, and blinkered horses stood patiently before an empty stagecoach. The graveyard where no one was buried at the edge of town was without shade. Behind the town of Lariat, rugged hills loomed, strewn with rock formations, and beyond, distant mountains foreshortened the horizon. The lawman, shackled to the evildoers, walked in front of the herd of humanity, finally crossing the threshold into the general store, where the trial would take place. Lariat had no courthouse as yet.

"Doesn't anyone ever clean this shit up," cried Lois Bonner, seeing soft green horse dung on her shoes and the hem of her long skirt. "Where's wardrobe?"

"Cut!" Matt cried.

"Change shoes on your won time, Lois," said Eden, checking her clipboard. "Now we have to reshoot this."

"I can't help it."

"You're supposed to watch where you're going, Lois."

"Take a break, everyone," said Matt. "Five minutes."

Anita, the flamboyant wardrobe woman, motioned Lois toward wardrobe's trailer. Actors and extras drifted toward the water trucks set at some distance. The men went up behind one set of boulders to pee, and a few of the women toward another set.

"Hey Matt," one of the young actresses called out, "when are you going to get an authentic toilet in Lariat?"

"You're using it!" he called back. He turned to his wife, threw an easy arm over her shoulders, slid his hand down her bare arm. "Where are we?"

"Behind schedule." Eden's job at Greenwater could be fairly described as the guy with the clipboard counting cowpies. And in answer to the producer's long-ago question, *You think somebody actually writes this shit?* Eden now knew the answer was, well, sort of.

*The Lariat Lawman* and other Westerns reminded Eden of Sister Thorsen's hundred-year-old sourdough starter, or the covered stoneware crock that always sat in its own place in Afton's kitchen. When Afton went to make biscuits, she would lift the lid, flinch a bit at the powerful odor, and slap some sourdough into a bowl, add flour, salt, a little grease, or lard, or butter, and whatever else she had on hand, and with a little beating and pummeling, she could turn out bread or biscuits from this unchanging chemistry. In a Western, the written lines mattered less than the basic recipe.

Here is the recipe: The Good Guy was a masterful rider, wrangler, and shot. As *The Lariat Lawman* aired at night, an adult Western, the Good Guy might drink, he might even smoke, but he was never drunken or cruel. He was loyal to his Horse and Sidekick, respectful to women, certainly not lecherous. His weaknesses were his strengths. See above. Though he sometimes stood outside the law, the Good Guy protected citizens' legal and moral rights. Lariat's Lawman, Sheriff Lance Kidd, had a secret past: he had once been an outlaw. This did not fundamentally alter the recipe, but it did allow for a certain amount of spice. Anyone who knew of Lance Kidd's past could threaten his present position as the much respected, even feared Lariat Lawman. This notion of an outlaw past for the Lariat Lawman was Matt's idea. The name, Lance Kidd was Eden's idea, in honor of Tom and Afton.

Keeping to the ingredients, each Good Guy must have his Horse and his Sidekick. The horse always had a name indelibly associated with the Good Guy, like Roy Rogers's Trigger or the Cisco Kid's Diablo. Lance Kidd's horse was named Cheyenne. This was Les Doyle's idea. The Sidekick, usually wooly and wisecracking, was loyal, but stupid; he was often played for laughs and sometimes got the Good Guy into trouble. (Tonto proving the exception to this rule.)

Rex's sidekick and deputy, Spud Babbitt, was not an exception. Even Spud's name was intentionally comic. Spud Babbitt had been a sidekick in Westerns for almost thirty years.

The Good Guy, his Sidekick and Horse, came into conflict with Bad Guys. They were always plural, often mustachioed, and dumb as sheep. They sometimes ran in cowardly packs, little mobs. Anyone on-screen seen mistreating a horse was of course Bad. Sometimes they were led by a Truly Bad Guy who often wore suits and a string tie, clothes more dandified than others to indicate he was not a true son of the sagebrush. And of course there was the Girl.

The *Lariat Lawman*'s Girl was the schoolteacher, Carrie Dunne. Like most Girls in Westerns, Carrie Dunne could trace her genealogy from the heroine of *The Virginian*. But neither Matt nor Eden wanted to see another round-eyed ninny who cowered in the corner, fist to her lips while the men duked it out. Teacher Carrie Dunne was a lively advocate for justice, education, women's rights in the Old West, and an adroit horsewoman.

Lois Bonner, the actress who played the role, did not, Eden believed, altogether fulfill Carrie Dunne's destiny. Lois was bosomy, blond, and beautiful, but she could be difficult on set. She had been a student at Pasadena City College and studied acting at the Pasadena Playhouse. She was a princess in the court of the Rose Queen for the Rose Parade in 1952, but she couldn't even sit atop a horse, much less ride.

Ordinarily this would not have been a problem. All the young actresses offered parts in Westerns swore they could ride. They wanted the work. Usually Les Doyle took these young women to the back lot and in a few hours—how long depended on the production schedule, which was followed like Holy Writ—he taught them how to *look* like they could ride. Lois Bonner was Les's one notable failure. Lois's scenes were altered so that none of Carrie's lines had to be delivered from horseback.

For an adroit horsewoman, they had Ginny Doyle. Ginny had genius. Ginny could take a fall, or a running dismount, or cling to the saddle and use her six-shooter around the horse's neck at frantic gallop; she could stand on one leg on the saddle, swing around, and do a handstand while the horse tore ahead. Ginny Brothers Doyle had a sad, cinnamon-colored face; she kept her hair as short as a man's so she could wear the wigs obliged of Western heroines. Her muscles were ropy and strong; she was all fiber, no frill, and in this she seemed ageless. With Annie Douglass, she was Eden's best friend, her only friend really on *Lariat*. Eden's job was not conducive to friendship.

Eden handled the straightforward stuff: what and who was supposed to be where and when. And if they weren't where they should be, then they answered to her, and Eden made damn sure it didn't happen again. Anything requiring tact, finesse, or charm fell to Matt. Matt could settle the differences among the dour and the sunny, the beautiful and the plain, and he often, to Eden's mind, wasted a lot of time waxing charm on people who didn't deserve it.

Eden ambled over to the porch of the Lariat bank where Liza was patting the nose of a horse tethered there. Stellina sat beside her, playing with the rag doll they'd given her for a prop. Both girls wore their hair in pigtails in honor of TV's Annie Oakley, whom they idolized. "Hey, don't you girls want to go get some water with the others?"

"We're okay," said Liza, and her sister did not contest.

Eden knelt, pushed back Liza's sunbonnet, and smoothed her dark hair tenderly. Liza had the look of her father. "Hey, peach, you piped up again today, didn't you? You're not supposed to say anything in these scenes, just stand there and look like a little girl. Which you are."

"Sorry," said Liza, though Eden could tell she wasn't the least bit sorry. "I'll be quiet in the courtroom scene. I'm in the scene, ain't I?"

"Aren't I."

"I didn't say nothing at all," said Stellina.

"Didn't say anything." The company of cowboys sometimes had its drawbacks.

"Tonight's the big party, right?" asked Liza. "And we get to wear our *Lariat* outfits."

"Yes, but you can't stay up too late."

"I'm a cowgirl," said Liza, "I can stay up."

"Me too," said Stellina.

"You are not a cowgirl," Liza corrected her. "Daddy got me my own horse, Dasher, and Ginny's teaching me to ride. You can't ride a horse."

"Oh, Liza," Eden chided her gently, "why do you always have to win?"

Eden picked Stellina up in her arms, took Liza's hand, and walked back to the reconvening crowd scene. In her little daughters, Eden caught glimpses of herself and Matt. Stellina lacked Liza's drive, but she had a sweetness Liza could never replicate and probably wouldn't want to. In Stellina, Eden could see what Matt must have been like as a child: obedient, implicitly trustful of others, willing to be moved about in accord with adult wishes, sunny and charming. In Liza, on the other hand, Eden too-well saw herself: headstrong, confident, bullying, the eldest, the most favored grandchild, who naturally deserved the adulation everyone accorded her.

They all took their places, Liza and Stellina beside the actresses dressed as their frontier mothers, and the clapper went down. Carrie Dunne ran up to the Lariat Lawman and Spud, who were keeping the crowd at bay, walking backward toward the general store. The judge, a lean old actor, turned to Lance Kidd and uttered words suggesting he, too, was all for the summary hanging of the Bad Guys. The Lariat Lawman would never countenance injustice.

Matt motioned for the camera to move in for a closeup on Rex Hogan's face with its stern, thoughtful expression. Nearby a horse whinnied and Eden waited for Lois to come forward and stand up to the judge. But instead Lois turned to Matt. "What's Carrie thinking? What's her motivation?"

"Just say the goddamned line," said Eden evenly. "This isn't *Streetcar Named Desire*. It's a TV Western."

"I trained as an actress, and I need to understand the character I'm supposed to play."

Eden was about to reply when Matt interrupted.

"Let's talk over here for a moment, Lois."

He led her just out of earshot. Eden and everyone else waited restlessly, perspiring in the summer heat, while he conferred seriously with Lois about Carrie Dunne's motivations. While Matt often had to soothe small uproars usually among the younger actresses sensitive to salty language—stupidly sensitive, Eden thought—no one but Lois Bonner merited this kind of coddling. Eden found her pretensions insufferable. Eden was all for saying, *Adios, Lois, there's no room for the stuffy, the coy, or the difficult on the set.* Everyone was here to make a living. In TV the pay might be lousy, but it was regular, worth having, and for the most part, the actors were professionals. Those who weren't didn't last long. Except for Lois. Matt seemed to think her wonderfully gifted and worth encouraging. Eden thought Lois was both vacuous and preening; the combination was almost intolerable.

Matt returned with Lois, gave her an encouraging nod, and she said her lines. The judge responded. The Bad Guys looked cowardly and unmanned. The lawman held up his hands, still shackled to them, and said a few words on behalf of fair trials.

God's in his heaven, all's right with the world, thought Eden, as the scene finished and they broke for lunch. Everyone headed to the jeeps and pickups that would carry them to the same picnic grove where seven years before an overeager stuntman had somehow smacked Eden into her future. The recollection always made her smile. Even when they disagreed, the marriage of Matt and Eden March was its own force field. They communicated along a wordless connecting current. After seven years of marriage, Matt could still make her tingle; a certain touch, a certain look, or a grin during the day's work, and Eden knew it would be a good night. The Marches were an unbeatable combination, Matt's charm, Eden's energy, Matt's vision, Eden's attention to detail.

Eden got in line at the water spigot, to pour cold water over her short hair. She wore a sleeveless blouse, tied at the waist, capris, and protective sneakers on her feet. She came up from the spigot, cooled, and called Liza and Stellina to ride with her. She slid her clipboard under the seat of the springless jeep.

"You're too hard on Lois," Matt said to Eden, leading his horse, Dancer, over to her. Matt, true to the authentic Western director, rode Dancer to locations whenever he could. "If you were nicer, we'd get more out of her. In less time."

"Or we could find another love interest for Rex Hogan," she suggested. "Lois Bonner's picture isn't on a million lunch boxes."

"Time isn't always money," he replied. "You don't have to always think like a bookkeeper."

"I'm not a bookkeeper anymore. Martin Fletcher does that now. Bea Fletcher runs the front office. I'm the one on site. The clipboard and the cow-pies, remember? I make sure things stay on schedule and move smoothly. Lois gets in the way of all that. She's not worth what she brings to the show."

"She's beautiful."

"So?" Eden shrugged, directing Liza and Stellina to the backseat. "Find an-other princess from the Rose Queen's court. Pretty girls are everywhere. In case you hadn't noticed," she added.

Matt genuinely liked women. For all his cowboy boots and enthusiasm for the Western, Matt March was more comfortable in the company of women than men. He liked being surrounded by his wife, his mother, his daughters; he en-joyed Ginny Doyle's lively company, and he extended his affectionate regard and charm to the young actresses on the set, to the girls in the Greenwater of-fice, to Marinda, the housekeeper. He took unfailing notice of the lowliest young *Lariat* extras, and they rewarded him with hard work.

"I want to ride with Daddy," cried Liza.

Just then Ginny cantered up on a palomino quarter horse, the golden Cody. Cody had a flaxen coat and a silver tail; he was high stepping, high spirited, good for Ginny Doyle, dangerous for anyone else. "You wanna ride with me to the picnic grounds, Short Stuff?" she said to Liza, who stood on the seat, her arms upraised. Ginny's sun-lined face always lit to see Liza. Ginny was child-less; she doted on Liza like her own daughter.

"I know you're teaching Liza to ride western," said Matt. "But I want her to ride English. It's more refined."

"Why the hell would she want to be refined?" Ginny laughed as she hoisted Liza up. "Why would you want her to ride with a broom up her butt?"

"She's going to Stanford. The girls there are refined."

"Don't bet it on it. Besides, Matt, this little girl is a hoyden on horseback."

"Just like Annie Oakley," Liza offered.

"I guess I can't win with any of my women," Matt laughed, as Ginny and Liza galloped off.

"Can I ride with you, Daddy?" asked Stellina.

"Sure, baby. Get on up here. You coming to lunch, Eden?"

"I need to go back to the house first and make sure everything's getting ready for the party tonight. Three seasons, Matt. That's an achievement."

"You wait, Eden. You're going to be so surprised!" He took Stellina in his arms. "It's only a beginning. Lariat is going to make history tonight."

# Ginny Doyle's Cowgirl Chili

Think of this as a recipe in twos.

Two pounds dried red beans, washed and cooked, or two cans same, drained.

Two pounds pork or beef, cut into small bite-sized cubes. Can be stew meat if you wish. It will soften in the cooking. In a big cast iron fry pan, brown the meat quickly in some oil, working in batches. When browned, put in a Dutch oven, or a big heavy-bottom kettle.

Then brown up 2 onions, one red, one white, chopped. Add a couple of garlic cloves, chopped; several long, bright green anaheim chilis, seeded and chopped; and some jalapeños, also seeded and chopped. (At least 3 or 4 jalapeños, more for the brave or foolhardy.) When done, and all these are soft, add to the pan with the meat.

Drain 1 big can crushed tomatoes, or small cut tomatoes. Set tomato juice aside. Put tomatoes in with the meat.

Put the tomato juice in your big cast iron fry pan, and perhaps 1 or maybe 1½ cup rich stock. Bring to a boil and let flavors intensify while you scrape up all the bits from the pan. To this add 1 tablespoon each cumin, chili powder, and salt. Or to taste. The truly brave or foolhardy might also want some cayenne pepper. Lower the heat to medium and let simmer for a bit, stirring now and then to combine the whole.

Throw this in with the meat. Mix well and cook on a low heat, lid slightly askew, for about an hour. Add beans, mix well, keep on low heat, lid still askew, stirring now and then for another hour. Remove from heat. In the middle of the chili put 2 squares unsweetened chocolate. Cover. Let the chocolate melt. Mix thoroughly. Ripens up best after 24 hours. Reheat very slowly.

Mama, with this chili, your babies will all grow up to be cowgirls.

### THE CHAMPION

In her rough-and-tumble rodeo youth Ginny Brothers chose her horses with more care than she chose her men. She named all her horses Cody so they seemed a continuous equine lineage. She called all her men Bucko, so she could cry out, *Whoa! Bucko! What a ride!* untroubled by their individuality. Ginny's natural balance and athletic poise amounted to rodeo genius; her feats surpassed the skills of many cowboys, and on the circuit she raised a lot of jealousy tumbled up with lust. Ginny was untroubled by the ambiguity. She proved herself always fearless, adroit, and immune to hazard. Almost immune.

In 1937, not yet twenty years old, Ginny Brothers won the ladies' bronc riding title at Cheyenne Frontier Days. She went on to perform the same feat the next year at Madison Square Garden, where she won a sterling silver belt buckle. She won a silver-pommeled saddle in Sydney, Australia, where she outrode the men. In Calgary, not for the competition, but for the entertainment, she bulldogged a steer from the running board of a moving car. This became a standard Ginny Brothers feat. Any car with a running board would do. Her trick-riding brought international audiences to their feet, especially her famous Suicide Drag. She invented the Suicide Drag.

Applause—like thunder funneled through mountain passes, echoing across prairie skies—roared in Ginny Brothers's ears, swirled around her in arenas from Boston to San Francisco, from London to Oregon, from Houston to Calgary. Ginny had straight black hair always worn man-short. She was rangy, muscled, with a loping walk, and had the broad forehead, high cheekbones, and the unsentimental gaze of generations who had stared out over empty plains and lived by their wits and skills anyhow. Her mother, the Prairie Fern, hand beaded all her Western shirts.

Ginny performed and competed even through rodeo's lean years during the war. In fact, she cleaned up during the war when the young men were all called up for active duty, and gas rationing kept the old cowboys at home. Ginny Brothers lit up these diminished wartime shows, and took on new challenges, rope tricks, and a few broncs, in addition to her standard feats. In a world of rugged men, and even more rugged women, Ginny wore silver spurs, a fringed leather jacket, and strode into the arena with the aplomb of an acknowledged champion.

She sent half her prize money and all her trophies to her mother in Butte, Montana, where they joined the blue ribbons she had won as a kid. When, as the legendary returning champion, Ginny Brothers played Butte, she dazzled the locals with a free display of the Suicide Drag, standing tall on the back of her horse and tearing down the main street, arms wide, hair blowing, wind-blistered lips apart. Then she executed a move at once so swift, so graceful, so terrifying as she fell—it looked like a fall—down, backward, her body draped over the animal's hindquarters, her face terrifying close to Cody's thundering hooves. When she finished, she reined Cody in and announced to the clapping, gape-mouthed townsfolk, If you want to see the rest of the act, you'll have to pay up and come to the show.

The smell of rodeo was a tonic to Ginny Brothers: hides and animal hair, hay and oats, and straw, dung, dust, rain, the slurp of hooves in mud, the groan of engines moving out in the night, horses whinnying in protest, metal sounds of bits and spurs, boot heels catching in stirrups, the crinkle of cigarette papers in leathery hands, the scratch of wooden matches on belt buckles, men and women who smelled of beer and dried sweat and coffee, who were precise, knowledgeable, reliable with their animals, and full of bullshit everywhere else.

Ginny was third-generation rodeo. Her parents, the Prairie Fern and Bill Brothers, were truly Americans, Native Americans, though not native. They were both born in London, near Earl's Court, where Buffalo Bill's Wild West Show had their headquarters and played for packed audiences nightly, recreating the Wild West for the Brits. Bill Brothers and the Prairie Fern grew up in front of audiences, pretending to be who they were, Sioux Indians. The Prairie Fern performed a ceremonial Indian dance before King Edward VII when she was just a child.

Bill Brothers's father named him for Buffalo Bill Cody. The Prairie Fern's father, White Ghost Dog, named her for nostalgia. They married young, in 1914, in South Dakota. They joined Tex Jones Wild West All-Stars, the Prairie Fern doing ceremonial Indian dances, Bill Brothers busting already defeated broncs and trick riding. Drinking heavily. Their son was killed at twenty months when he fell off the back of Bill's horse; the baby was part of his father's act. They had two daughters, Kathleen and Virginia. They too were part of the act, Ginny known as Little Miss Wrangler from the time she could walk.

In August 1924, Tex Jones Wild West All-Stars played Butte. Bill Brothers took the family car one night and went for cigarettes. He never came back. Bill and his bouts of rage were not such a loss, but the car? Without the car to pull their trailer, the Prairie Fern got left when Tex and the All-Stars caravan moved on. She and her two daughters stood in the gathering twilight and watched the All-Stars drive west, their dust dissolving. Ginny was almost seven. Kathleen was eight. They had never been to school longer than a couple of months.

The Prairie Fern boarded the horse, Cody, and sold the trailer. She moved with the girls into a small apartment at the back of Raymond's Hotel. They kept chickens behind the garage. For the next ten years the three of them did laundry, made beds, cleaned rooms for commercial travelers, and clerked the front desk. Raymond moved away.

Little Miss Wrangler won every childhood competition she ever entered. The Prairie Fern pinned the blue ribbons to the apartment walls. They fluttered there, bleaching in the sunlight, after Ginny left home at seventeen when Tex and the Wild West All-Stars limped back into Butte. When they left for Spokane, Ginny left with them. The Prairie Fern did not try to stop her. Ginny promised to return for her mother, promised one day they would have their own place, and never again be obliged to change the sheets of strangers.

Ginny Brothers—later Ginny Doyle, the greatest stuntwoman in the history of Horse Opera, movies, and television, and the Grand Marshall of the 1957 Rose Parade as well as winner of many national championships—gave the Tex Jones the only immortality he would ever have. Tex Jones liked to tell the lachrymose story of Bill Brothers deserting his family and the All-Stars in '24. In cowboy bars all over the west, Tex would wax eloquent about seven-year-old Ginny, Little Miss Wrangler, thanking Tex, personally, for all she had learned from him. Tex would get all misty, recounting the tableau in his rearview mirror as the All-Stars rode into the sunset—seeing there, alone, little Ginny, little Kathleen, their proud, embittered mother, and the horse stranded beside the trailer. Another drink and Tex would perk right up with the Happy Ending. Ten years later, Ginny rejoined the All-Stars just so she could work some more with Tex. This was bullshit, but it never failed to buy Tex drinks. Everyone in cowboy bars loved stories of Ginny Brothers. Everyone knew that she collected lovers in boots and lovers in suits, raked in prize money, titles, trophies, broke broncs and hearts with almost no injuries. Until that day in 1947 at Madison Square Garden.

Standing upright on the saddle, arms outstretched, as Cody galloped headlong around the Garden perimeter, Ginny calculated one more pass around the arena before she executed her trademark Suicide Drag. Cody picked up speed, tearing forward; Ginny poised for her faux fall in the saddle, about to drop down and backward, when suddenly her grandfather's ghost erupted over the rail: White Ghost Dog flew, fluttered across their path, spooking Cody. Cody stopped abruptly, twisted, flinging Ginny to the side, where she dangled helplessly as Cody swung around and slammed her head into the concrete wall. Cody dragged her, bouncing on the arena floor, before the stunned crowd until two other riders brought him to a halt. White Ghost Dog had not materialized. An admirer had thrown a white mink coat over the rail in front of the horse and rider. A gift.

Two weeks after the accident, Ginny woke up in her mother's apartment in Raymond's Hotel, Butte, Montana. She did not know how she had got there. Her jaw was wired shut and her vertebrae were fractured, eight ribs and right shoulder broken, a foot crushed and a leg broken. Everyone, except the Prairie Fern, thought she would die. If she didn't die, they said she wouldn't walk; if she walked, they said she wouldn't ride. Ginny Brothers was not a woman to succumb to the word *never*, and she'd sooner drink from a trough than walk with a crutch. The accident and recovery became fodder for her legend.

The accident and recovery, however, had indelible consequences. Ginny experienced little hollows in her broken vertebrae, and in the Montana winters these interstices froze and would not thaw. She would never have children. Her recovery took almost three years, much of it sitting behind the desk at the hotel listening to her bones mend. She was thirty. With some bitterness, she deliberated her uncertain future. Her mother suggested the old ceremonial Indian dance with Tex and the Wild West All-Stars. Ginny said, Sure, right after she shat silver dollars, she'd sign up for that.

In the autumn of 1949, Raymond's Hotel burned to the ground. The hotel had been failing for a long time; the building was insured, and the suspected arson was never proved. Raymond collected, but the Brothers women were destitute. Ginny's famous silver-pommeled saddle and sterling silver belt buckle were saved from the conflagration, along with her pistol and a handful of showy, hand-beaded Western outfits, because they were in the garage. Ginny took the saddle and the belt buckle and traded them to a cowboy for a twenty-year-old Dodge truck. She called him Bucko, and gave him a roll in the sack, because she was leaving the next day.

Ginny and the Prairie Fern trundled down toward Missoula, and across the Idaho panhandle, through Wallace and Fairwell, where Gideon Douglass taught high school. They camped at a fishing ground near Lake Coeur d'Alene, with a bar in a fish-shingled building, where a lackluster band played "How High the Moon," except for the cornet player; he stood on a chair and played his heart out. The next day they crossed the wide, dry plains of eastern Washington, and glimpsed the broad Columbia. Finally the Dodge made it up the steep Cascades, overheating half a dozen times. They made a campfire, and slept on the ground, Ginny with her pistol beneath the pillow.

The next day, they went down the long pass into Seattle, and on to Tumwater, where Kathleen lived with her husband. He worked in a plant where they smoked fish. He smelled of smoked fish and smoked Pall Malls. Ginny, herself, preferred Lucky Strikes.

Kathleen, her husband, Ginny, and the Prairie Fern sat at supper that night while wind whipped blackberry brambles that scraped along uncurtained windowpanes. Kathleen said how nice it would be to have Mother stay here in Tumwater. Kathleen had no children. No company during the day. Kathleen put supper on the table: a thick, pale pudding-like mass on each plate, a jar of molasses nearby, a baked potato each, and a cup of black coffee. Kathleen said her husband had the dyspepsia and there was little he could eat. This was a recipe of his mother's.

Ginny listened to the ping of forks and spoons, the thump of mugs, the grunts and gastric bubbles, chairs scraping on linoleum, the intermittent hum of a flickering overhead light fixture, the meandering stupidity of Kathleen's husband's talk. How could Kathleen endure this? How could Ginny condemn her mother to a life here? What choice had she? No money, no prospects, no horse, no saddle.

Kathleen cleared the dishes and said she hoped they'd all saved room for dessert. The husband excused himself. In the living room he turned on the radio, and laughed at *Amos 'n' Andy.* Kathleen explained his delicate stomach couldn't tolerate pie.

Kathleen brought forth a blackberry pie she had made just that morning, and just for them. Little inky pools of blackberry leaked through the golden crust, and though the pie had cooled, the smell of September sunshine wafted from it, wrapping the three women in its olfactory embrace. Kathleen sliced the pie, which stood proud and purple between its flaky crusts, and gave a piece to her mother and sister, as though each were a beribboned gift.

Which it was. Ginny understood that. The Prairie Fern started to cry. Ginny started to cry. Kathleen wept. All those years, and all that skill and muscle and sweat, all those men and horses, all that labor, and practice in the saddle, making the beds of a thousand strangers, and this was all they had. All they might ever have.

Ginny said this blackberry pie was the best thing she had ever tasted. Kathleen flushed with pleasure at the compliment. She said the secret was to make the pie while the berries were still warm from the sun. They all dried their eyes.

The next day Ginny sold the Dodge. Keeping bus fare, and some money for food and cigarettes, she gave the rest to her mother. I'll send for you, Ginny promised. I won't abandon you here. We'll have a place of our own.

Ginny Brothers rode the bus to Stockton, California, and went looking for the rodeo honchos. She was ready to sign up, though she had no horse. In a bar she met a wrangler named Les Doyle. Ginny did not offer her own name. He offered her a Lucky Strike. Ginny bought her own beer.

Les Doyle was in Stockton to see an old army buddy. Originally from Texas, he'd come to California leading a string of horses for Howard Hawks's *Red River.* Les had been a stunt double ever since, trick riding, roping, jumping on and falling off horses, plunging down cliffs, and fording deep rivers. He'd worked for all the Poverty Row producers, for B westerns and serials, horse operas, Saturday matinee fare. Les Doyle stunt-doubled for the calvary and the Indians both, for the singing cowboys, for Hoppy and Cisco, and the Sons of the Sagebrush, the Three Mesquiteers. For handsome actors who didn't know a turd from a Baby Ruth.

Les himself was not handsome. He had a sunshine squint and dusty hair, and his face had prematurely furrowed. But Ginny liked his blue eyes, his clean hands. She said, I'm Ginny Brothers.

Les Doyle stared. They said you'd never walk again.

Ginny shrugged. They said Dewey won too. I don't have my own horse anymore, but you'll see, I'll ride. I'll win too. I'm looking for a rodeo.

Les said rodeo work was for suckers. If all you had to do was fall off your goddamned horse, why not do it for the movies? And television. Ever hear of television?

Sure. But Ginny had only seen a television in display windows. Dull stuff.

Don't be so quick to judge, Les suggested. Television audiences, all those little buckaroos, love westerns. Stunt work was plentiful for a good rider. The pay ain't great, but a champ like Ginny Brothers would never want for work. Ginny Brothers invented the Suicide Drag!

What about applause? asked Ginny. What about the thrill of the audience?

How long can that last? How much applause did you hear after the guy threw the white mink coat over the rail?

Ginny sipped her beer.

Les said, I'm driving back to Los Angeles tonight if you want a ride. We'll go to Poverty Row tomorrow. Hell, Ginny, I'll find you a horse. A good horse. You can call him Cody.

Ginny regarded Les with more interest.

Besides, Les added, how many cowboys you know who live on the road and die there, too?

Ginny thought of Little Miss Wrangler, and watching the All-Stars caravan pull into the sunset; she thought of all the rides and ribbons, the miles and men, the hard work and horses between Butte, Montana, and Madison Square Garden, where the ghost of her grandfather rose up, flew before her, the last thing she saw before the coming of the concrete wall. She thought of her promise to her mother: a place of their own. She thanked Les Doyle. She said she'd take the ride to Los Angeles, the offer of the horse, but she slept with whom she pleased, not whom she owed. He said he understood that. She did not call him Bucko.

Ever.

THE MARCH KITCHEN WAS AWASH IN PREPARATION for the season wrap-up celebration, a reliable *Lariat* tradition. There might be as many as a hundred people here tonight, including network and Scoop Peanut Butter executives.

The Marches had cupboards full of Scoop Peanut Butter, Bread's Best Friend. On these jars there were pictures of Rex Hogan, handsome, clean-shaven, teeth-gleaming, in his *Lariat Lawman* hat, along with the logo of the series and sometimes a picture of Spud Babbitt in the background. Some Scoop jars also had the Lawman's horse, Cheyenne. Reproductions of the Lariat Lawman, his horse, and his sidekick were also plastered on lunch boxes, on towels, on bedside lamps, on breakfast foods, kids' pajamas and cowboy outfits, boots and badges, hats and gun-and-holster sets. The Marches' accountant told them the word for this undertaking: *merchandising*. A word worth millions. Just ask Hopalong Cassidy, or the people who merchandised the Davy Crockett coonskin caps a few years before.

But to Eden, who had grown up scrounging the house for quarters to buy a pail of beans and tortillas, the shower of money from these sales was astonishing. The merchandising largesse brought the Marches new cars, new televisions, new appliances, a new grand piano. Investing back in Greenwater, they refitted and expanded the old barn and brought authentic reproductions of stagecoaches and buckboards, more animals so that Greenwater would not need to import anything. They finished off Greenwater's Mexican village-and-the-cantina set that had long languished; they planted it all around with cacti so it looked like the Rosarita Beach Hotel. On seeing it, Matt and Eden both had the same idea: a second honeymoon in Mexico. For Christmas 1958, Liza got her first horse, Dasher, a fine little mare for a child. Matt bought a horse for himself, Dancer, named after his childhood companion. From Greenwater's main gate, they paved the road that led to the hacienda, and lined it with Eden's favorite trees, skinny crepe myrtle trees that in the summer shimmered pink, papery blossoms. They repaired the hacienda's leaking roof, shored up the balcony, repaired the wiring, and put in a new pool, not on the old site where Ernesto's garden still stood, but nearer the house so that Matt and Eden could entertain long into the evening.

They paid a staff to look after the animals and maintain the gardens. Marinda Reynolds cooked and oversaw the running of the house, freeing Stella to dote on the little girls and soothe herself with the ironing. Marinda Reynolds was a fine cook and a friend to Stella. Marinda needed the Marches, too. She liked to feed people.

For the party tonight, the main attraction was Marinda's famous, ¡Ole! Mole, thick, rich, smooth; the taste of chili and chocolate and peanut would chase one another around your mouth. The peanut butter was Scoop, naturally. Marinda baked the chickens slowly in ¡Ole! Mole, and always had extra to serve with the rice. There would be whole Matterhorns of fluffy white rice, and a couple of vats of Ginny's Cowgirl Chili, which she had made in the March kitchen two nights before. It needed twenty-four hours to reach maximum pitch. Beyond these Greenwater specialties, Oasis provided hams, roast beefs, and leg of lamb cooked according to Annie's own secret recipe, like no one else's leg of lamb ever, as if it wore a silken scarf of mint and lemon and garlic.

When Eden got back to the house, the garden and patio were full of Oasis people who were readying the appetizers, setting up tables and chairs on the patio and the back lawn.

"So," Eden asked, coming into the crowded kitchen, where Marinda and Stella oversaw preparations, "are we ready to feed the five hundred?"

Marinda shooed Eden away from the stove. "You are underfoot here! Get something to eat and go outside! Here." She handed Eden a small plate and heaped it with Annie's truly deviled eggs made with hot-pepper vinegar, fans of salami and sliced cucumbers, and some French bread.

"Take some of my caponata," Stella urged her. "Bitter loves salt."

Eden smiled, patted Stella's shoulder. She sometimes wondered how Stella and Matt could be mother and son. Bitter loves salt might have been the story of Stella's life. Stella was a born pessimist, and Matt the eternal optimist, always ebullient, his plans and dreams energized by impossibility. Everyone knew that Warner Bros. had cornered the market on TV Westerns, but Matt, undaunted by the formidable power of Warner Bros., had even been able to lure some of their talent to *Lariat*. Warner Bros. underpaid everyone and ran their productions like a factory. Matt had a gift for making the work feel important, small screen Horse Opera or not; on the set he was less director, and more conductor.

Eden took her plate and went outside. On the patio, long tables were set up to serve as buffets and a makeshift bar, too. Dotting the lawn were small round tables and chairs, each with an outdoor candle to be lit when darkness fell. Eden wandered to the pool in a bright unshaded patch of ground. She took off her shoes and socks and sat on the edge, her feet dangling, and let contentment overwhelm her. Light twinkled off the turquoise water, and shadows mottled along the bottom. The children's bright plastic toys bobbed like volitionless sea creatures among currents that melded, shattered, recombined, and drifted elsewhere, fleeting, futile unions of light and water.

WHEN MATT CAME HOME, EDEN WAS IN THE SHOWER. HE TURNED THE lock on the door of their bedroom suite and joined her. By the time she sailed downstairs to feed the five hundred, Eden March wore a smile and a deep blue halter-top sundress, cinched at the waist, full skirted, and high-heeled sandals. Her legs were bare and her short hair was still damp. Emerald stud earrings, a surprise present for their fifth anniversary, complemented the emerald pendant and her eyes.

"You look booful, Mommy!" cried Stellina, meeting her on the stairs. She wore her Lariat regalia, complete with hat and holster. All the children here tonight wore their Lariat outfits. Stellina returned her mother's hug, her kiss, then squirmed out of Eden's embrace and ran to join Liza and her cousins, Annie and Ernest's kids, playing noisy cowboys and bad guys in the front where stagecoaches, buckboards, and buggies were bringing the guests. Eden went to the open door to greet people. Everyone, from Rex Hogan to the lowliest gaffer, parked his car down by the gates. All guests were ferried to the season finale party in an authentic western vehicle driven by Greenwater wranglers. Then the old conveyances turned around and went back down the crepe-myrtle-lined drive to the gate.

"Gives me new respect for the real pioneers," said a Scoop executive after he helped his wife out of the stagecoach. The Scoop and network men all had crewcuts and wore sportcoats. Their wives wore straight skirts; their buttocks were constrained, almost visibly, by girdles. "I can't imagine crossing miles of desert in one of those," he added, stretching his neck.

Eden suddenly remembered that the long drive from the gate to the house was mostly unlit, and by the time people left, it would night. Maybe the authentic touch wasn't such a good idea after all. She should say something to Matt.

"Carrie Dunne must have been a sap to travel in one of these," Lois Bonner chimed in, stepping down.

"You're Lois Bonner!" cried the Scoop man's wife.

Lois basked in their admiration and signed an autograph on the spot. Unburdened of her wig and corset, Lois was still curvaceous, a good deal shorter than Eden and more fleshy. There was a succulent quality about Lois that she exuded along with her Shalimar perfume. Lois's longtime boyfriend, Joey something, Eden could never remember his name, asked for an ashtray. He was a heavily Brylcreemed young actor. Eden fanned away the smoke from his cigarette and remarked on the heat.

"What do you expect?" laughed Lois, her bright red lips framing her mouth like a flower. "It's July! So what'll you do, Eden, now that *Lariat*'s finished?"

"My work is never done. Thank God everyone is making TV Westerns. Matt will be busy finishing up *Lariat*, but I'll still be here working locations."

"Someone has to do the clipboard and the cowpies," said Lois.

The phrase, so indelibly Matt's, struck Eden as intimate, but Stella came up and said Matt wanted her to join him on the patio.

Eden made her way slowly through people who stopped her to say how delighted they were to be part of such a winning venture. Three seasons! And more to come! Oasis waiters circuited through the patio, the pool area, the garden, and from the living room Eden could hear that someone had opened up the new grand piano, and a jazzy tune floated through the house on the thin blue cloud of cigarette smoke, and meandered outside. Eden smiled. "Body and Soul."

She found Matt in the patio, where Oasis tended a lavish bar. He came to her, holding a silvery glass. "Gin and tonic. Made just the way you like, honey." He passed his arm around her waist, drew her near. She fit perfectly against his shoulder. Matt lit up any room he entered, but to Eden he shone always in a single beam.

"These are the Baxters, honey. Gus, Beverly, my wife, Eden. They're investors, and they really believe in what we're doing here! Imagination in an investor is more rare than money."

Eden shook their hands cordially. They were a sleek, well-heeled couple. Gus Baxter, perhaps forty, a big, pale man, wore a nubbly sportcoat, expensive shoes, and a silk tie. He had blond thinning hair and cold blue eyes. The droopy jowls and fleshy mouth gave him an indolent air. His much younger wife was cool and beautifully coiffed, her pageboy framing a tanned face, perfect lips, and eyebrows that looked to have been drawn by a maestro.

"Congratulations on another season of *Lariat Lawman,*" said Beverly.

Gus offered cigarettes all around. His wife took one, and leaned in to the flame he offered with his lighter.

"Not for me," said Matt, with an affectionate tug on Eden. "She made me quit. It was tough, but I did it."

"You still smoke a pipe sometimes," Eden reminded him.

"Hey, a man has to have some vices."

Christmas lights draped under the patio roof twinkled as sunset came on, the table candles were lit, and and the tiki torches around the garden smoked, flared as the summer dusk fell. As they ate and drank, Matt rose, and offered a toast to all the daughters and sons of the sagebrush present. Matt waxed eloquent, thanking everyone, singling out even the most minor doe-eyed ingenue who flushed at being included. Everyone sitting at the small white tables dotted around the garden applauded.

One by one, people rose to make appreciative speeches (some slurred) lauding Matt and Eden for producing a TV Western unlike any other. Les Doyle said a few words on behalf of the stuntmen and -women. People refilled their glasses and listened as Rex Hogan stood up thanked Matt and Eden and Greenwater for the opportunity to expand his career in the role of Lance Kidd. But Rex's career was not expanding; his aging, chiseled face was suited only for Westerns now. That he could actually ride a horse helped as well. His new young girlfriend beamed at him. He had a new young girlfriend every season.

Spud Babbitt rose. "I just wanna say, I haven't worked this regular since I was good-looking." And on the laugh that got him, with an actor's sense of timing, he sat down.

"I want to especially thank Matt for his faith in me as an actress," said Lois when her moment came. She went on in a voice at once lively and intimate. "Next month I start rehearsals for *Streetcar Named Desire* at the Pasadena Playhouse. In spite of what some people may think," she glanced toward Eden, "I can play roles other than Carrie Dunne."

"The Old West never had it so good, Carrie!" cried a young wrangler just before he tumbled into the pool and had to be fished out.

Eden went to find Liza and Stellina, who had tucked themselves on the lawn swing, on either side of their grandmother. Stella nodded toward Lois, held up two hands, fingers crossed, against the Evil Eye. Stella believed in the Evil Eye. Fingers crossed was one way to ward it off. Eden laughed to see her stern expression, then turned back to see Lois kiss Matt's cheek, leaving a great cherry-colored stain there.

Later, the Sons of the Sagebrush got out their instruments and played, but the real attraction was out at the pool. Perhaps forty people, and all the children clad in *Lariat* hats, ringed the pool. On the diving board, Ginny Doyle stood, doing rope tricks. Ginny's bronzed face was alight with concentration and pride, and the rope twirled and flashed and reflected over the water, and the lights in the pool played the audience, and smoke from the tiki torches wafted over the blue water. The crowd went *ooh* and *ahh,* and Eden, standing at the back, joined in. I will remember this forever, she vowed silently, watching as Matt held Liza in his arms for a better view and Stellina sat on Les Doyle's shoulders, applauding, both little girls with rapt faces. How have I been so fortunate, she thought. The applause of their friends. The flush of their success. The bright gift that their marriage was to each of them. A place to live and work that rewarded effort and where she could watch all things grow, fruit trees, children, crepe myrtles lining the long drive from the gate. I will keep this moment, these people, somehow preserved, she vowed, as though I could stop the ripples over light, over time and water.

Marinda touched her elbow. "The cake is here."

"What cake?"

"That's what I told them. We ordered no cake, but they are here with it. And it's huge. Took two men to bring it in. They want to be paid. Maybe someone else knows about it."

"Like who?"

Marinda nodded across the pool to Matt.

"Oh, don't bother Matt." She threw an arm around Marinda's shoulder. "Let's go see what this is about."

In the kitchen two young black men waited, frowning, their faces damp with sweat. They wore white uniforms with a logo from a Beverly Hills bakery, the same fancy lettering on the top of the cake box, which was some four feet long. Eden went to open the box, but the young man stopped her, and showed her a paper that said COD, and a delivery time some five hours earlier.

"We'd have been here earlier, but who could find the place? We been driving for hours. Days, it feels like. No checks, ma'am. They told us no checks. This was ordered over the phone. Special order, and it has to be cash."

Eden explained, "I'm sorry, but there's been a mistake."

He pointed to the name on the COD order: *Matt March, Greenwater*

Eden snipped the tape and lifted the cake box lid. Inside, across a vast canvas of frosting, there was fashioned in sugar an antique train, the shining locomotive, number 646, complete with cowcatcher, a big lamp, and a brass bell. Everything was rendered in immaculate detail, the brass fittings shone, created in transparent caramel. The locomotive pulled a train—coal car, cattle car, passenger car, caboose—each elaborately finished, details perfect, the shades in the passenger car windows a butterscotch color, the cars themselves a dark green. Lettered in red frosting along their sides, she read, GREENWATER RAILWAY. A plume of meringue, blackened to replicate smoke, billowed from the locomotive and rose, dwindling into gray across a blue sugared sky.

"TONIGHT WE MAKE HISTORY!" CRIED MATT, STANDING BESIDE THE CAKE, which had been carried, four men to do the job, out to the patio. There, beneath the twinkling Christmas lights under the patio roof with everyone circled around him, the guests, worse for wear and drink and the late hour, Matt cried out, "This is the beginning of the Greenwater Railway!" He lifted the silver-plated cake knife as he kissed Eden's cheek. Everyone cheered. "What did I tell you?" said Matt, pulling Eden close to him, his voice low, rough, urgent with excitement. "I told you we'd make history tonight."

Eden consciously kept her expression neutral as she looked over the crowd, who applauded as Matt talked about laying steel rails, about grading railbeds, and track fastened with double-angle joints, about having found, abandoned, just the sweetest little coal-burner locomotive, Engine 646, portrayed here in frosting.

"And a depot for the town of Lariat," he went on, "a hundred times better than the train depot in *High Noon*." There was a short, respectful silence, as there always was when anyone mentioned *High Noon*, or John Ford. "I'm negotiating with the Santa Fe to buy the Marisol depot. It just sits there by the track now in a little beach town. All closed down. I'm going to have it dismantled and moved here to serve the people of Lariat!" He turned to Eden, his face rapt with happiness. "What a surprise, huh, honey? Happy anniversary."

"It is a surprise," said Eden.

"A little early, I know—our anniversary's really next month—but, hey." Matt turned again to the crowd for validation, and got it. He waved to the Sons of the Sagebrush. "Hey, how about a little 'Anniversary Waltz' for seven years of marriage, two kids, a TV Western, and now—" he pointed with the silver knife to the sugary evocation of Engine 646, "a new beginning! Lariat will make history with this train!" He went on joyfully about the Greenwater Railway, complete with depot in the frontier town, and track that would loop around the whole four hundred acres, where on weekends people would come and pay money to ride the train, just as it might have been in the 1880s, when the railroad brought money and opportunity and thousands of people to Southern California.

"Like the train at Disneyland!" Liza piped up.

Her father beamed down at her, picked her up. "Only better. This will be the real thing. Pretty soon we'll have herds of buffalo and wild mustangs. People will come to Greenwater to watch the buffalo roam, to experience the west. This locomotive, this railroad will connect Lariat with the world!" He put the cake knife in Liza's small hand and she sliced through the thick blue frosting and into the soft white cake below. She swooped her index finger across the smokestack, leaving a great dark swath across the cake, and blackening her lips.


IN THE WEE HOURS, EVERYONE GONE AT LAST—THE STAGECOACHES OUT TO the main gates had indeed been a very bad idea—Matt and Eden climbed the stairs. He reached for her, ran an appreciative hand up her thigh, but for once Eden wasn't in the mood. She stopped and leaned against the rail. "How could you make these plans and not tell me? How could you do all this behind my back?"

"What is this 'behind my back' stuff? It was a surprise, baby! Hey, I thought you'd be happy. The cake and everything! Our anniversary."

"Our anniversary is next month."

Matt continued to trudge up the stairs.

Eden followed, carping at him, flailing away at his obvious betrayal. Matt denied everything. They went into their bedroom and closed the door. The

French doors were open to the balcony; the night was still warm. Matt went into the bathroom. Eden followed him.

"Can't I at least take a leak without you nagging me?" he said.

"I'm asking questions. I'm entitled to some answers."

"Ask later. I'm damned tired." He slammed the bathroom door in her face, turned on the faucet and flushed the toilet to drown out her voice.

Eden could not remember his ever having slammed the door—any door— on her. Not in all their years together. A hard lump gathered in her throat. Night sounds drifted in with the dry breeze. She went to the mirror, took out her emerald earrings, removed her pendant. Matt was the person Eden most trusted, the man with whom she had a life, a career, children, a home, an indelible connection. It was a marriage. Not flawless, but strong, enduring. Oh, sometimes, sure, he'd say he was meeting someone about *Lariat,* but he'd come home with tickets from losing horses at Santa Anita, confetti in his pockets. Once he'd ordered a bouquet for a network executive's wife, who he swore was in the hospital. And it turned out she was. One day he'd left Greenwater in one of the jeeps and returned home in a Cadillac. Now he had a new Cadillac every year. But how could he buy a locomotive without a word to his wife? She turned and regarded the bed, still rumpled from this afternoon. Bits and flecks of saffron tobacco threads from his pipe lay here and there.

Finally he emerged, sat on the bed. He pulled off his cowboy boots and flung them across the room. "That's your problem, Eden, you never do anything spontaneous."

"This wasn't spontaneous, Matt. You must have been working on this for months! Years without telling me a thing."

He ignored the observation, took off his pants and shirt, dropped them on the floor, and lay back on the bed, rattling all the while about the railroad that would bring Lariat into the future, about progress and growth. Now they could have train robberies, and not just stagecoach holdups. He was going to hire Chinese to lay the track, put them in costume and film them while they worked, and use the footage for *The Lariat Lawman.* While the track was being laid, Matt planned to have the cars built, smaller, to scale, as they did everything on the sets so that short actors like Rex Hogan might fill up doorways and seem more physically imposing.

"Matt," she finally interrupted him, "Lariat does not need to be brought into the future. Lariat is not a real town. Spud and Rex and Lois are actors, they are not really deputies and lawmen and teachers. Ginny and Les are stunt doubles. Stunt doubles fall down. They don't get fractured skulls. No one's buried up in the cemetery! No one gets hung down by the lake. No one pumps water into the trough, or kills the chickens with their bare hands, or dies of tetanus, or gunshot wounds. The people who come and go from Lariat are just characters. It's not a real community and it doesn't need a train. There is no progress in Lariat. Lariat . . ." she sought some other word, but found none, "is static. It exists only to be filmed. Then everyone gets paid. And everyone goes home. No one lives there."

"I live there! Look into my eyes." He took her face in his hands, pulled her close. "I've always planned to have a railroad! You know what this means to me! Don't you?"

"I know you love the notion of the railroad—"

"It's not a notion. It's an authentic 1887 coal burner."

"How could you do all this in secret? Without telling me. What's next? A secret herd of buffalo?"

"Where's your faith in me?"

"What did you use for money?"

He gave a short, harsh laugh and released her. "The money from a million lunch boxes, baby! Rex's face on a million jars of peanut butter! The eleventh commandment: control your own licenses. Wasn't that Hopalong Cassidy's best advice to the tykes? Imagine Walt Disney in bed, rubbing his coonskin cap up and down?" Matt gave a great guffaw. "Two out of three kids in this country have Lariat Lawman hats and holsters. Scoop loves us. I know they've sold more damned peanut butter through us than they ever dreamed of. We control our own licenses, baby! We're going places! On the train! Don't you see, Eden? You're thinking small. I have vision. I see it all in VistaVision!"

"You once promised me no more surprises."

"I never said that," he snapped. "I said you were the only girl I ever wanted to marry. Listen, Eden." He softened his tone. "I can't live like some goddamned clerk, every day like the one before or the one to come. If you're not growing, you're dying. You know that. You know me."

"You keep telling me that I know you, Matt, and then you keep this huge secret from me."

"Okay, so now it's not a secret. What of it?"

"Maybe I don't know you at all."

"Come on." He pulled her down to him. "You and I . . ."

"Where is this engine now?"

He rolled onto his back, hands beneath his head, and grinned. "Wait'll you see it, honey! The sweetest little locomotive. Just needs some spit and shine and paint, and a few repairs. They would have scrapped it during the war, along with all other old coal burners, but they lost it! Imagine, losing a locomotive. They had a whole line of track that washed out every other year with the floods, and finally they just abandoned the line in 1916, tore up the track, and left the locomotive in a shed down in San Diego County, Temecula Canyon. They forgot it! I saved it from destruction!"

"Have you seen it?"

"Of course I've seen it! I wouldn't buy a train sight unseen."

"But you wouldn't tell me?"

"It was a surprise."

"Who else knows about this surprise?"

Matt rolled away from her, sat up, fumbled for his pipe on the bedside stand. "No one."

"No one."

He tamped some tobacco down. "Well, I might have told Gus and Beverly Baxter."

"You'd tell the Baxters and not me! Who are they? You just met them. Didn't you? Where did you meet them?"

"At the track. Santa Anita."

"You'd tell a couple of strangers you met at Santa Anita and not me?"

"They're not strangers. They're investors. They think it's a great idea."

"Who else? Did Lois Bonner know?"

"Lois? Why would she know?"

Eden blurted out, "She might if you were sleeping with her."

"What makes you think that? Lois has a boyfriend."

"You have a wife and two kids."

"You're too hard on her."

"I suppose you are, too."

That took him a minute. "You're my wife. I love you."

"You don't deny it?"

"Deny what? You're my girl. You, Liza, Stellina. Hey, Sweetpea, I love you."

"But I first hear of this train in front of a hundred people you don't love? You've shattered my trust in you, Matt."

"You're accusing me of sleeping with Lois because of the train? That's rich. What next?"

This was a question Eden could not quite face. She had long suspected him of having an affair with Lois, but to say so would be to give voice to weakness, worry, suspicions of other women. Suspicion could cloud your day, but you couldn't let it destroy your whole life. If she insisted on the fight over Lois now, tonight, would she lose the locomotive fight? Maybe she had already lost it.

"It's foolhardy, Matt. We can't build track. We don't need a train."

"We do need it! Don't you see, this train will make money! Tons of money! Greenwater Movie Ranch Park! Liza's right, like Disneyland!" He struck a match without lighting the tobacco, and added dreamily till the flame burned down to his fingers, "On weekends, we'd open the place to visitors, take them all over Greenwater on the train to see all the Western sets, and the mustangs, and when they come back through Lariat, we could get a couple of actors to fake a shootout on the main street. Ginny and Les can do some trick riding, standing up on the horses while they gallop down the street! Ginny can do the Suicide Drag. The train pulls in, blow the steam whistle! It's 1887, the authentic Old West! People can ride through the past!"

"You've lost your mind! Lariat isn't Disneyland."

"But it can be *like* Disneyland! Disneyland only opened in fifty-five, four years ago! Look at the money rolling in there! Hell, look at that little wart in the road, Knott's Berry Farm, right nearby. Last time we took the girls to Knott's Berry Farm, I walked around, and I thought, What the hell do they have? Get your picture taken with the wooden Indians? Buy a jar of their goddamned berry jam? Eden, Eden, we got the real thing here! Real cowboys. Real Indians, if you think about Ginny and the Prairie Fern. Didn't the Prairie Fern used to do some kind of ceremonial dance with the rodeo?"

"Oh God, Matt! Are you crazy?"

Matt's expression darkened. "You lousy Mormons have lived so long, scrabbling along with nothing, the only thing you see is the mule's ass pulling the plow."

"What? Are you talking about my family?"

"I've seen how Tom and Afton Lance live. I remember your rotten mother!"

"My family's got nothing to do with this!" Eden jumped off the bed, shouting at him. "How dare you say that about my family! We're not talking about my family. They're not part of this!"

"That's right. My father and uncle built this place!"

"I got you the loan!"

"You did the paperwork. It's my land."

Eden stiffened, her jaw tight. She felt as if her cheek blazed with a blow from his hand. She spoke very carefully, harnessing her words and her voice. "You have lied to me about something I should have shared. If you had asked me, I would have told you then, I don't want it. Not the train. Not the depot."

"God! You're blind, aren't you? You can't see progress. You don't know anything!"

"You can't just do whatever you damn want. We're a partnership. We work together. We have to be able to trust each other. You should have asked me, and I'd have said no."

They heard a child crying, and feet padding along the hall. Eden opened the door to find Liza there in her *Lariat Lawman* pajamas, rubbing tears from her eyes, asking why they were fighting.

"We're not fighting, baby." Eden knelt, stroked her sweet face.

Matt swung his feet off the bed. "This little locomotive is the last authentic thing of the Old West. You'll see it like I do one day, Eden."

"I don't want to see it. At all. Ever." Eden took Liza's hand, and started down the hall.

But Liza balked. "I want Daddy."

Matt stood, pulled on his pants. And his boots. He flung a T-shirt over his head, and picked Liza up. He crooned to her as he took her back to her bed. Eden closed the bedroom door. Twenty minutes later, she heard his boots walk past their bedroom, down the stairs, out of the house. His Cadillac started up. Eden ran to the open French door, stood on the balcony, and watched the taillights burning red holes in the night as he sped away.

He did not come home for two days. And when he did, he reeked of Shalimar and cigarettes.

# Stella's Oyster Sandwiches

Wash your oysters (they can be any size) and pat dry. Dredge the oysters in flour that has been lightly seasoned with salt and pepper. Fry quickly in hot oil or a bit of butter and only till just golden in the fry pan. Drizzle with the juice of $1/2$ lemon.

You need sturdy, thick bread for these sandwiches, or dense French rolls. Warm your rolls while you fry the oysters. Drizzle your bread with a little olive oil and again, a few drops of lemon juice, a dash of pepper. Put your hot oysters on the roll and top with a sprinkling of fresh parsley. Serve immediately. However, they will keep for a while to take on a picnic or journey. They are especially good with Stella's potato salad.

These can also be made with chicken. Bone your chicken breasts. (Throw bones in a small pot with some water and herbs, simmer for stock, à la Afton's Back Burner.) Place waxed paper over your chicken and use a rolling pin over it till the pieces are thin. Cut up the pieces if they are too big. Fry quickly as above with the oysters. Thick bread or rolls. Lemon juice and parsley as above.

### THE PHANTOM OF THE DEPOT

The Surf Line ran from Los Angeles to San Diego: 126 miles of track through oil fields and orange groves. It reached the coast at San Juan Capistrano and rattled south along cliffs and beaches.

In the silent heyday of *The Green Goddess, Gold of the Yukon, The General, Ben-Hur,* and *The Iron Horse,* glamourous people like Ernest March and Blanche Randall and John Kent took this train in the summer to the Del Mar racetrack, which was separated from the beach and the sea, by a big stagnant lagoon.

Before the talkies intervened, young Matt March rode this train every summer. Leaving Greenwater before dawn, the March men drove into Los Angeles, arriving finally at the domed Damascus-type splendor of the La Grande station on First Street. Stella did not go. Stella did not hold with gambling in any form: Life itself was a gamble, why throw dice when you didn't have to? She packed them oyster sandwiches for the journey.

For Matt the train would always be indelibly allied to childhood: the scent of perfumed women and cigarette smoke in first class, the snap of cards as Ernesto and his father and a few others played to while away the journey, the odor of wood varnish on the inlay, and the prickly feel of the green plush seats. The clink and clack of the train over the tracks sent a vaguely pleasant hum through the boy's body, the fried oyster sandwiches his mother always made for the trip, slightly soggy by then, the softened texture of the oysters eloquent on his tongue. The boy sat by the window, eating slowly, watching the dry, austere beauty of the landscape, the vast austere expanse of the Pacific, the waves, rolling in, the train moving on before they could roll out. Like a theatre where the film never ended.

Ernesto, Nico, and Matt usually stayed a few nights at the Stratford Hotel in Del Mar. Then they got back on the train, went farther south, to San Diego, and stayed in the Hotel del Coronado. Money meant little to Ernesto. So what, he and Nico came home, their pockets stuffed with torn tickets from losing horses? The boy got to run on the beach and they all three had a fine time. Matt came home utterly happy and exhausted, his hair blown awry, sand in his shoes, all his clothes stiff with dried salt water.

The Surf Line to San Diego was an express. It did not stop at every little station, like the small seaside town of Marisol, California, north of Del Mar. Still, Marisol had a station, a sturdy structure, built around 1900 but looking older with its pointy roof, long, narrow windows, and deeply shaded overhang for protection against the sun.

Nailed to the outside wall of the station, a timetable noted when the north- and southbound trains would pass. Beside this, hanging from a hook, was a white flag on a stick. If a passenger wanted to board at Marisol, he listened for the distant train, and took the white flag and stood on the track and waved it like hell. There's no record of how many people jumped off the track before the train shrieked past, not heeding the would-be passenger wildly waving. Someone might have taken a tumble into the weeds, but no one was ever killed.

But the last time Matt, his father, and his uncle made this journey, in September 1929, the Marisol station was deserted, locked, barred, and shuttered. Still, little Matt March put his hand up in greeting, as though some phantom figure, behind the dusty windows, still waved the flag, waiting to be rescued from oblivion.

## CHAPTER THREE

THE MONOLITHIC IMAGES OF SCREEN WESTERNS, however beloved, bear scant and only emblematic witness to a more variegated truth. The real west, the sheer geology of the earth, testifies to erosion and endurance. The land, once acted upon by weather, by scarcity and abundance, by natural disaster—to say nothing of volatile combinations of human greed, desperation, or mere discontent—offers up myriad stories, of deprivation, unremitting toil, surrender, people whose fates might be propelled by dreams, but destined for obscurity. However, Matt March was right about the railroad. That plume of black smoke and white steam, once it billowed against the sky, left the landscape changed forever. Certainly St. Elmo, California, was changed forever in 1887 when the California Southern Railway established its main yards and terminus there. The railroad put St. Elmo on the map, saved it from being a mere backwater, with occasional shootouts among hard-drinking Gentiles, hardworking Mormons, and forays of Mexican cattle thieves down from the canyons.

Building that railroad required the skilled hands, the labor, the backs and brains of many, men who remained, stayed, in St. Elmo. Everywhere the railroad went, progress, prosperity followed. This was Matt's steadfast contention against Eden's equally unwavering objections. And then, in February 1960, the Santa Fe sent Greenwater Pictures a bill for eighteen hundred dollars.

The Marches' accountant paid the eighteen hundred dollars and sent the letter along to Matt and Eden, who were still fighting over the Greenwater Railroad Railway and all it implied. The accountant circled the paragraph that said that the Santa Fe would continue to charge two hundred dollars a month rent until the locomotive was moved. That Engine 646 had sat abandoned in a shed since 1916 mattered not. The Santa Fe urged Mr. March to move it at his earliest convenience. The bill, the prospect of paying two hundred a month almost sent Eden into premature labor.

Eden had not even realized at first that she was pregnant. All through September she thought it was the flu. At forty, she thought it unlikely she'd get pregnant again. As their daytime quarrels over the railroad continued, Matt and Eden had turned to each other every night, their physicality rekindled, as if to assure each other that their unresolved differences did not impair their intimacy, or touch their love. And Eden had not forgotten the night of the party, the night he left home and did not return for two days. He had apologized, but never explained. Eden was determined not to lose him, but she hadn't counted on another child.

Matt was pleased about the new baby. Stella was pleased. They both hoped for a boy. For a girl Eden wanted to name her Katherine Afton, but she could not quite bring herself to mention Kitty. So Eden, too, hoped for a boy. Stellina, just starting kindergarten, had no interest in a baby brother or sister. Liza was horse crazy, and too busy with piano lessons, diving lessons, ballet lessons, and riding over Greenwater with Ginny or her dad to care about anything else.

Boy or girl, this baby was an unruly tenant. The pregnancy took its toll not just on Eden's body, but her whole life. Early on, she had been riotously sick, puking her guts out day and night, exhausted continually. Unlike her two other pregnancies, as the months passed, she was swollen with edema, miserable with backache and headache, cross, ill tempered, easily moved to tears; she knew she wasn't thinking straight. Just about the time the bill from the Santa Fe arrived, she began to spot, and the doctor put her on bed rest.

She had long since given up the clipboard, unable to bear bouncing around Greenwater in a jeep, and now she was out of a job, and Matt's working life went on without her. She imagined, believed all sorts of things of her husband, and sometimes she feared her spiraling fears needed to be punched down like a loaf rising all out of proportion. She wondered how Afton Lance had borne eight children and remained stoic, even cheerful, uncomplaining. But then, Afton Lance's husband probably didn't come home, still glowing, from other women's beds and other women's arms.

Matt won the locomotive argument by default. Rather than pay two hundred a month, Engine 646 would be delivered to Lariat in mid-May 1960, with no track laid.

Where and how the track would run was still, as far as Matt was concerned, under discussion. And he discussed it with anyone who cared to come into the dining room and look at the expensive model he had commissioned. The dining room was the only room big enough to contain it. Under the central chandelier, the size of a billiard table and mounted on six sturdy legs, stood the to-scale Greenwater, all four hundred acres. Matt would walk around and point out the tiny, meticulously replicated frontier town, the ranch house and Indian village, the fort and Mexican village, the hideout and cave, a mirror in the shape of the Agua Verde lake. Over the whole there were three potential track loops, laid out in red, blue, and yellow. On these the model locomotive, complete with bell and whistle, and pulling a half-dozen cars, ran on electric current. With the flip of a switch, the train could be moved from loop to loop. Eventually Matt intended to build all three, red, blue, and yellow, but which first? That was the question. Matt foresaw Greenwater Railway carrying paying visitors on prescripted tours. He envisioned the railway and the depot, both better than *High Noon,* better than John Ford's great silent in 1924, *The Iron Horse,* and a hell of a lot better than the lousy 1947 *Union Pacific.* He would turn to anyone present, grin, and say, "Knott's Berry Farm, eat your heart out!"

LIZA WAS UNPREPARED FOR THE GENERAL FAMILY DEFECTION IN NICKY'S favor. Her father, her mother, her grandmother, Ginny and Les, even Marinda couldn't get enough of the drooling, burbling Nicolas Ernesto March who made his squalling appearance in April 1960. Of these defections, the hardest for Liza to bear was her father's. Liza redoubled her efforts on horseback, in school, at the piano, diving lessons, but none of her achievements merited the applause that Nicky could get just rolling over. Like a little dog, thought Liza. At seven Liza had stubs where her big adult teeth were coming in. Her legs were skinny and her knees were always dirty. Liza was going into her long larval

Ugly Stage, from which she would not emerge for another twelve or thirteen years.

"Liza is just a little fireball," said Ginny as she and Eden ambled one May afternoon toward the Greenwater gates. "I never saw a kid so eager to be the best at everything." Ginny led Dasher and Cody, both bearing western saddles. Matt had given up on English riding because there were no local competitions for Liza to show off. There were, however, several nearby junior rodeos, and she had already won blue ribbons in two events.

"No one needs to be the best at everything," Eden replied. "Liza should slow down, enjoy things more." Eden pushed the baby Nicky in his buggy. They were going to meet the school bus. "All this striving for applause, it's like, well . . ." It was rather like Kitty, but Eden did not want to say so. Liza had more of Ruth and Afton and Eden's drive in her, but the need to bathe in praise, oh, that was straight from the Lark of Liverpool, flighty as she might have been.

"Well, her daddy's applause really matters to her."

"Yours, too," Eden reminded her.

"On horseback, sure. But Matt could watch her peeling potatoes, and Liza would made sure she was the best."

"Matt applauds, but he doesn't give Liza a chance to savor what she's accomplished."

"Well, it doesn't seem to have hurt her."

"Maybe not. But every time Liza does something great, Daddy has a new goal for her. She learned to read before she went to school, so now he wants her to read at fifth-grade level. The other kids are doing addition, but Matt's teaching Liza the multiplication tables. Every piece she learns on the piano, she hardly has it plinked out on the keyboard before he wants her to take on something she's not equal to. The piano teacher finally had it out with him."

"Really? Mrs. Klein?"

"Yes, you know Mrs. Klein with her thick German accent, she tells him: Mr. March either I am the teacher of piano, or you are. If you are, please, be my guest, but if you are not, you will please to butt out."

"Mrs. Klein said that? Butt out?"

"She did." Eden smiled at the recollection. "Matt backed down. At least for the moment."

The bright yellow school bus pulled up to the gate; doors hissed open and a dozen kids tumbled out and ran in every direction, calling out to one another. Every time Eden saw her own children jump off the school bus amid their boisterous friends, she wondered how different Matt March would be if, as a boy, he had just gone to Agua Verde Elementary with other ordinary kids—head lice or not. Over the years, as she had heard him speak of St. Ignatius, there was no doubt that he had been well educated, but he knew so little of compromise, or of planning for the unforeseen. There was no unforeseen in the cloistered halls of St. Ignatius. The bells ring and you go where you're supposed to. At St. Ignatius, Matt had never had a friend to whom he had confided the truth. He had wrapped himself in lies about being the great actor's son, and delivered the lies in an aura of charm, high spirits, and good looks, which had sufficed for truth. That still sufficed.

"Hey, Ginny! Hey, Mom!" Liza jumped off the school bus, and ran to them, handed Eden her *Lariat Lawman* lunch box, and nuzzled Dasher's nose. Ginny gave her a sugar cube, furry with lint, for the horse. "I want to ride Cody," said Liza, as Ginny hoisted her onto Dasher.

"You're a fast learner, cowgirl, but not that fast," said Ginny, mounting her horse. As if to underscore, Cody pawed at the ground, and she had to rein him in.

"Don't you want to change your clothes, Liza?" Eden called after them, but they trotted away. The baby fussed, and Eden lifted him out of the carriage and held him close to her. He was a sweet baby, endlessly delightful, even at six weeks. She brought her lips down to his cheek, and kissed him. She adored him.

The school bus pulled away, leaving the grainy taste of exhaust in the air. Stellina waved till it was out of sight, then she put her *Lariat Lawman* lunch box in the baby buggy.

"I invited everyone to the choo-choo party on Saturday. Rebecca Gomez and Miss Oglethorpe are the only ones who believe me that I have my own choo-choo."

"Rebecca is your best friend. Of course she believes you."

"Miss Oglethorpe believes me because she loves Rex Hogan. She watches *Lariat* every Tuesday night. Miss Oglethorpe's awfully pretty. Maybe the Lariat Lawman could fall in love with her. Maybe she could be the schoolteacher instead of Lois."

"I'd love for Miss Oglethorpe to be Carrie Dunne. She's a real teacher after all."

Eden put Nick back in his carriage, wheeled it around, and they started back up the drive. The thin crepe myrtle trees lining either side of the road unfurled little fists of dainty spring green. A strange sound fluttered overhead, a whirring. Eden looked up to see a plane, a small private plane, but noisy nonetheless. It seemed to be circling over Greenwater. "What are they doing up there?" Some amateur pilot, she thought. There was nothing she could do. Whom to complain to? The sky was the sky. But you couldn't have airplane sounds overhead in a Western; any scene being shot right now would be ruined. It would have to be reshot, and would take time and screw up the schedule, and inevitably cost more. She could imagine the tempers fraying on location, the swearing, producers insisting the plane was Greenwater's fault. A Western movie ranch with a plane problem was in big trouble.

Stellina skipped ahead, and then back, ignoring the plane. She handed her mother a painting she had done in school. A train. "I think the Greenwater Railway ought to go on the yellow loop, but Liza thinks the blue. What do you think, Mommy?"

"I can't say," Eden replied truthfully. She would not opt for any of the three colors because Eden didn't want the train here at all. The idea of turning a movie ranch into a public attraction and charging money was ridiculous. The building of a railroad would upset production at Greenwater, probably for a year, never mind Matt's mad idea to put the workers in period costume and film them. Even without laying any track, the locomotive had already incurred enormous expenses, never mind the rent bill. To avoid the rent and bring Engine 646 from Temecula Canyon, they had to hire a flatbed truck, cranes, winches, and crews, and secure permits. Eden had resigned herself to the locomotive at Greenwater, even to the party to celebrate, but she wouldn't give in on building the track.

"Liza says if I call her Your Highness for a week, she'll let me ride up front with her."

Eden watched the airplane swoop off to the east, slowly sputter out earshot. "You don't have to call Liza Your Highness."

A car pulled alongside them, and slowed to a stop, a long Lincoln convertible. Gus Baxter was at the wheel wearing a sporty panama hat. Beverly waved and asked if they'd like a ride up to the house. Eden said no, they would walk. The Lincoln pulled away. Stellina coughed in the exhaust.

By the time Eden got back to the house, fed Nicky, and put him down for his nap, she could hear the model train's whistle coming from the dining room, and Matt's voice, ripe with enthusiasm. He and the Baxters stood before the huge Greenwater model: all four hundred acres, every location and landmark extant, fashioned of sculpted plaster, painted painstakingly as a fresco. The model train shrieked along the red line.

"People stood up in the theatres and screamed. That's how powerful that avalanche scene was! I just about peed my pants the first time I saw the train wreck! Oh, Eden," Matt smiled to see her, "I was just telling Beverly about *Gold of the Yukon.*"

"Wasn't that the train wreck where the actor was killed?" asked Gus.

"Not the actor," said Matt. "But the stunt double died. He slipped, and went down between the two colliding cars, and BANG!"

"Bang?" asked Beverly. She moved to a chair, sat, and lit up.

Matt seemed grave. "They used the footage in the film. That's why people just screamed. You could see what was going to happen."

"I remember *Gold of the Yukon* like it was yesterday. I was just a kid." Gus glanced at his much younger wife. He suggested moving the model train to the yellow loop. "Do you remember *Gold of the Yukon,* Eden?"

"I remember being scared to death by the avalanche and the train wreck."

"It was a real avalanche," said Matt. "They shot it up in Washington. My uncle almost died. The director just about killed them all with that avalanche."

"And the train?" asked Beverly.

"Oh yes, the train was real. You don't have an accident like that unless it's real. And after all that, the stuntman's death, the whole cast just about dying in an avalanche, the picture was a flop. The only flop of Ernesto's career."

As he spoke of failure, the death of the stuntman, of Ernesto, Matt looked suddenly very vulnerable. Eden moved protectively closer to him, between Matt and the Baxters. She could not share his enthusiasm for this pair, but it was certainly true that they had lots of time and money they were willing to part with, invest. Privately Matt joked about the Baxters, describing them as Gus and Beverly Greenbacks.

"Are you coming to the party?" Eden said to the Baxters. "Next Saturday."

"We wouldn't miss it," said Gus. "What time?"

"Afternoon," said Eden. "Maybe two. Come hungry. We'll be feeding everyone."

"We always come here hungry," said Beverly.

"A great day for Lariat," Matt beamed. "I told the girls to invite their teachers and classmates and their parents. People will remember this day for the rest of their lives. They'll witness something historic. The railroad will connect Lariat to the world."

"How much track did you finally build for the locomotive?" asked Gus.

"Not finally," Matt flipped another switch and sent the model train ripping along the blue line, "but there's maybe a quarter of a mile laid, just here beside the platform. Just enough for Engine 646 to sit on. For now." He shot another look to Eden. They still had not settled this. She had not given in, and he had not given up.

"You and Eden feel like going to Pierino's tonight?" asked Gus.

"Great idea!"

"We can't, Matt. Liza's piano recital is tonight. You're the one who insisted she learn *Für Elise*. It was very hard for her. You can't miss the recital. You promised."

Matt put his arm around Eden, and winked at Gus. "My little Liza is her mama all over again. If I break my promise, she'll never let me forget it."

"I wish I'd seen *Gold of the Yukon*," Beverly mused, "but I wasn't even born till 1931."

"It was a good story," Gus offered. "Two brothers in love with the same girl. Lust, greed, peril."

"It was a good story," Matt conceded.

"A remake could be great, all in Technicolor and VistaVision. Done right, it could be a great success. Surprise everyone after all these years."

"It was a melodrama," said Eden.

"So was *Ben-Hur*," said Beverly. "Look what the remake of that did. That chariot race!"

"*Gold of the Yukon* had plenty of action," said Gus. "Imagine Robert Mitchum and William Holden, real Western actors, as the male leads."

"I'd watch Mitchum and Holden recite the phone book," said Beverly.

"It's the kind of picture you could do right, Matt. Make your uncle proud."

"We couldn't do it at all," said Eden with a rueful laugh. "We don't have snow. What would we do? Sift down cornstarch and turn on the fans? Matt likes to be authentic."

Matt reflected as the model train whistled and zipped over the painted foothills, near the lake, the hanging tree, past the ranch house and tiny cattle dotting the range. "*Ben-Hur* was a great remake."

"*Ben-Hur* was a great picture, a success the first time around," Eden said. "*Gold of the Yukon* wasn't."

"Yes, but if Elmer Bernstein wrote the music. Like he did for *Magnificent Seven*," said Matt with a brilliant smile. *The Magnificent Seven* had joined *High Noon*, *The Iron Horse*, and *Stagecoach* in his pantheon. He looked into the distance. "If Edith Head did the costumes."

"*Gold of the Yukon* is way too old-fashioned," Eden protested. "No one would go to see a picture like that now. People want some complexity in a Western."

"How complicated is *Magnificent Seven*?" asked Gus. "There were good guys and bad guys and peons. The good guys won. Some died. The peons endured."

"But what fantastic good guys they were!" said Matt. "And the music made you proud to be an American."

"It took place in Mexico," said Eden.

Beverly's nylon stockings rasped audibly as she uncrossed her legs and stubbed out her cigarette. "What happened to your deal for the Marisol depot?"

Matt shrugged. "Fell through. They're just going to let it sit there by the track and rot in the sun. Too bad, but I'll build my own depot. See, here on the model, near the cemetery." He pointed to the station, with its steep roof and long windows, like the Marisol depot he remembered. There were hog and cattle pens, and tiny wires and poles for the telegraph.

"We'll miss you at dinner," said Gus, taking Beverly's arm. "By the way, did I ever tell you what a beautiful model this is? Really a perfect picture of the whole place, all of Greenwater."

"Yes." Matt's gaze fell benevolently across the sculpted reproduction with its minutely detailed renditions, including the cemetery where no one was buried. Each little headstone perfectly rendered in plaster, painted to look faded, sun-worn, perishable.

# Gold of the Yukon Potatoes

Pour some oil onto a cookie sheet and tilt every which way to cover. Put in the oven and preheat to 350.

Take your fresh Yukon Gold potatoes, or small red potatoes or fingerling potatoes, wash and slice thin. If you're using fingerlings, you probably just need to halve them. When the sheet is hot, spread your potatoes over the whole. If they double up here and there, that's fine. They will shrink a lot. Salt and pepper.

Bake. After about 15 minutes, use your spatula and turn. Then turn frequently, as often as you baste the chicken. This is especially good with Eden's Weekday Chicken, basted to a nice rich mahogany color with sauce compounded of soy sauce, a bit of oil, and a few good shakes of Tabasco to taste. Potatoes and a whole chicken will take just about as long to cook well and crisp, perhaps an hour and a half.

These potatoes are not good for a crowd. Just for a family. The potatoes will shrink and you will have much less than you thought you had.

# SNAPSHOT

## VIEW AND VISION

Matt liked the sounds of the saddle, the feel of the heat and wind, the taste of the dust. Matt on Dancer, Liza on Dasher, they rode hard all over Greenwater, tearing on horseback, galloping over the golden hills. They went often and early in the day. Sometimes taking a lunch, sometimes just a couple of canteens, water for a few hours.

They would draw their horses to a halt on the knoll overlooking the lake and dismount. The hanging tree provided shade. Liza lifted her canteen off Dasher, took a long swig, then another short one. She spat the last out, quickly, from the side of her mouth with as much expertise as Spud Babbitt might have shot a wad of baccy. Her mother would have been appalled. She handed the canteen to her father, like they were Hero and Sidekick. She loved being his sidekick.

Matt told Liza all his old youthful escapades, the summers he had spent envisioning everything he was going to bring to pass. He told her the deep feelings he had for the stories he would wrest out of old myths. The American stories: men and women putting their pasts out of sight, out of reach, making mere tracks, and then wide trails, then vast tracts across the west in search of place and promise. People enduring loss and privation. Shackling themselves to hard work and the unknown. Meeting each day with much-tested courage. Compounding their fears with their strengths, their energy with fatalism to accomplish something important, to root themselves. Then sadly, ironically, even heroically, to find themselves rooted, finally, only in shallow graves and oblivion. Matt shared his vistas and his vision, his conviction that he could link these myths and stories to the land itself, that he could loop longing and fulfillment, knotting the past ineluctably to the future.

Liza listened uncritically; Liza looked where Matt looked, and saw what he saw.

And to achieve all this, all he needed was not-so-mythic money. Greenbacks for Greenwater.

Matt took the canteen from his daughter. Thanked her. He tilted his head back and took a long gulp. Bringing the canteen down, Matt looked eastward across the rims of the nearby rolling hills, to the rugged distant mountains, mottled and rocky against blue sky. He remarked to Liza that he could not even count the number of times he had seen hangings enacted here, but they never failed to send a shiver up his spine. The victim on horseback, the thick rope gnarled around his neck, scanning the horizon, hoping for rescue while awaiting the inevitable slap on the horse's rump that would send his vision spinning and his dreams out into the wild sky of morning.

Cut.

She held her infant son, Nick, in her arms, a little blue baby bonnet on his head protecting him from the sunshine. Stellina and Rebecca Gomez, their hair in pigtails, their *Lariat* badges flashing, stood hand in hand by Eden's side with the crowds at the Greenwater gate, everyone straining to hear the sounds of sirens or air horns. But before the train arrived on the flatbed, an ice cream truck toodled up to Greenwater, a high, tinny "Oh do you remember Sweet Betsy from Pike" playing over and over as it drove in. Eden told the driver to take the road to the frontier town, and wait there.

Ginny, Les, Liza, and a quartet of *Lariat* wranglers were on horseback, directing traffic as people arrived to celebrate the arrival of Engine 646. Sleek, expensive cars with big tail fins and battered pickup trucks were all parked to one side of the gate. Matt had invited the constellation of crewcut Scoop and network executives to witness Greenwater's great day, as well as the whole of Agua Verde Elementary, teachers, janitors, kids, and their parents. There was a huge contingent from the

Douglass tribe: Annie and Ernest came with their three kids, Connie and Victor and their children, Alma and Walter Epps and their sons, a few of Bessie kids, along with Tom and Afton and Lil. *Lariat Lawman* propmen, cameramen, costume people, electricians, drivers, their wives and families, and all the minor actors came, as well as Spud Babbitt, Lois Bonner, and—to Miss Oglethorpe's delight—Rex Hogan. The Prairie Fern stood near Marinda and Stella; Frankie Pierino, his wife and kids, the Baxters, and Bea and Barbara from the Greenwater office milled nearby.

"I hear it!" cried Liza, galloping to the gate, Dasher raising a cloud of dust. Liza was the image of Annie Oakley, except for her *Lariat* holster and toy gun. "They're coming!"

"Stay here, Liza," cried Eden. "You stick with Ginny. You promised!"

The sirens wailed from afar, and the Greenwater staff asked everyone to step back from the gates. Once off the main thoroughfare, the eighteen-wheeler bearing the locomotive drew toward the gate escorted by two sheriff's cars, sirens blaring. They were followed by half a dozen pickups bearing the crew that would put the engine in place. They had begun this journey at Temecula Canyon at dawn, arriving at last, late this afternoon, at Greenwater.

The truck driver pulled long and hard on his air horn. Bystanders scattered in the caravan's wake. Liza, her head down, galloped in circles before the truck, took off her cowboy hat, and cried, "Whoopee!" bringing a cheer from the throng. Matt, waving wildly from the cab, all but jumped out the window.

"So, there it is," Eden remarked to Afton as the huge eighteen-wheeler heaved through the gate with Engine 646 secured to the bed. The locomotive was a heap of dust-caked, rusted metal, windows gone, front light cracked, straw caught in the cow catcher, bell swathed in mothy burlap, and yet she felt a tremor of excitement. "This is the story of my life since last July. That train and this baby." The baby squirmed in her arms.

"I might have misjudged Matt," said Afton. "I'm proud of him. Of you, too, Eden. All of you, Liza and Stellina. You are a family of doers, not like your poor mother, nor poor Gideon either for that matter. For all his work on the Great Timetable, what did he really accomplish? Nothing. No. You and Matt make me proud."

Eden thanked her, shocked that Afton Lance would admit to having misjudged anything.

The eighteen-wheeler again blew its air horn, drowning out her thoughts as it came to a halt in a flurry of dust and exhaust. Matt leaped down from the cab. He took long strides toward Eden, took her in arms, gave her a great kiss on the mouth, a smooch for the baby, Nick. He picked Stellina up in his arms. Then he turned to the rest of them. "All right, everybody, you kids especially," he called out, "now you know the meaning of the phrase *feast your eyes!*" He threw his cowboy hat in the air.

Matt saw the locomotive in its 1887 splendor, three thousand pounds of shining steel, greased metal, glittering copper, oil gleaming on the gears and wheels, lamp polished, brass bell, and the numbers 646 brilliant in the sunshine. He saw the engine stoked with coal, and a fine, fat, thick plume of smoke and steam, rising from the black stack, dissipating into shadows on the hillsides. Matt all but heard its whistle. Maybe, for that moment, others did, too. Even Eden.

He placed Stellina on the flatbed beside Engine 646.

"No," Eden cried, "it's dangerous!"

"Hold on tight, Stellina!" He turned to Eden. "She'll be fine."

In answer to the unrelenting tug on his pants, Matt lifted Rebecca Gomez up beside Stellina. These two, the chosen children, rode with Engine 646, gripping the chains with one hand, waving with the other like beauty queens in something as tame as the Rose Parade. Everyone else scrambled back into their cars and trucks and followed in a caravan, bumping, bundling down the dirt road behind the big flatbed.

The dirt roads crumbled, protested the weight of the eighteen-wheeler and the locomotive; new ruts joined the old ones. The flatbed and caravan made slow progress till at last Engine 646 made its first stop at the town of Lariat. The driver positioned the eighteen-wheeler carefully beside the platform. The crew, perhaps a dozen men in overalls, strapped on toolbelts. Wranglers and the deputies kept the crowd back as slowly, carefully, and in a concerted team effort using powerful winches, they backed the locomotive from the flatbed, down a ramp, and onto the extant track beside the platform. Little stakes with flags marked where the depot, the hog and cattle pens would be built.

High noon had long passed by the time the locomotive stood in its new home. It cast a long shadow toward the town of Lariat, where, on the shady side of the street, trestle tables billowed with paper tablecloths. Oasis workers had set big grills on the street, and from these wafted the smoke of barbecue fires. On the Lariat Hotel porch there were big washtubs filled with ice and Coca-Cola and Dr Pepper and Nehi orange sodas, cold beers. Pitchers of Marinda's famous hibiscus iced tea gleamed garnet on the tables, and splashed scarlet on the paper cloths. Marinda called it Agua Fresca. Call it what you will, it was wonderful, refreshing, with or without a hit of tequila slipped into your glass. Miss Oglethorpe accepted a glass, with tequila, from Rex Hogan.

Matt walked over to the ice cream truck and turned off the ignition. "Sweet Betsy" died, the last notes settling in the dust. Matt called out, "I ask you all to raise your glasses, or bottles, and toast to Engine 646! The last authentic steam locomotive in the west! And the beginning of a great new future!"

Everyone obliged. Matt turned to Eden, and his beer bottle clinked against hers. The happiness on his face was unequaled, save perhaps the day Liza was born. "Congratulations, Matt," said Eden. "It's a beauty."

"You really like it, Eden?" His face lit.

"I really do. And you saved it."

"I did. I saved it from destruction or oblivion. Which is worse?"

"It doesn't matter. You saved it." Eden brushed his cheek with her lips. "You did a fine thing to save it."

Matt beamed. He put the beer down, walked to the platform where at one end there were many boxes stacked. Then he had a long, serious look through the crowds of children gathered on the platform, and he chose a third-grade boy who said his name was Gary Anderson. Matt gave Gary a silver dollar and instructions to clamber up to the bell on top of the locomotive and untie the burlap bag. Everyone watched; the crowd was quiet except for the cries of a few babies, as the boy flung the burlap down. "Now ring that bell," Matt cried. "Ring it like it's just come into town. Like your life depended on it!"

The boy rang the bell. He rang it again and again. Like his life depended on it.

Through all the cheers and hurrahs, Eden's included, she felt a tightening in her throat, a quickening at the heart, as though, unbidden, tears might come.

"And now," said Matt, "for every kid here who doesn't have one, I want you to go over to those boxes and get a *Lariat Lawman* hat, holster and gun set! But you can't bring them to school. Miss Carrie Dunne would never allow it! And parents, don't worry. The only bullet for these guns," he turned to Stellina, standing beside him, "is what?"

"Bang, bang!" said Stellina.

The children stampeded toward the boxes and the adults moved to the tables and grills that were manned by Oasis people.

Matt and Eden paid Oasis for the setup and the cleanup, and staples, hams, condiments, and the like but the feast for this day was donated by the people who came. Scoop Peanut Butter—Bread's Best Friend donated nearly three hundred peanut butter cookies; and the Scoop wives brought salads and one-dish casseroles with no peanut butter at all. Alma Epps brought a raft of chicken wings, baked and gleaming in her own Famous All the Way to Memphis

Barbecue Sauce, and they got tossed on the grill for a final bit of flavor. (Alma, too, had taken Sally's recipe and made it her own.) Ginny dished out dripping ladles of Cowgirl Chili, studded with beans and chunks of meat. She gave Liza an extra helping. Liza was a cowgirl after all. Connie's 7-Up salad mottled, and succumbed to the heat. Afton had made vats of Rice Salad, bright with green onion, parsley, cherry tomatoes, and pimento, which disappeared more swiftly than Stella's Eggplant Caponata, which was not for the faint of heart, eggplant in a wine-rich dressing. Annie's mother, Shushan Agajanian, handed out dark grape leaves swimming in sauce and bursting with rice, meat, and tomato. Frankie Pierino donated great trays of the restaurant's famous three-cheese, five-layer lasagna. Marinda's capable hands held warm, golden tortillas into which she spooned baked chunks of fish. Over each she put a great dollop of her jewel-colored corn salsa, the orange and pepper shining in it. All sorts of offerings lay on the tables, some great, some small, from the *Lariat* cast and crew, from Agua Verde Elementary families, including one that tasted to Eden very like Emotional Cornbread. Miss Oglethorpe brought her mother's famous Strawberry Pie. She had not brought her mother.

But she had brought a camera. "Let me take your picture," Miss Oglethorpe said to Eden. "In front of the train. You and Mr. March."

So Eden handed the baby to the Prairie Fern and stood with Matt, smiling.

"Just a minute!" Matt called out. "Liza, Stellina, Mama! Come here!" When they assembled, he squared his shoulders, lifted his chin. "Now. Take our picture with the 646. Me, and my remarkable women. Come on, smile, Mama, you can do it. You know you can."

Stella smiled, and Matt and Eden both laughed. Miss Oglethorpe snapped her shutter.

"Will you take one of me and Ginny?" asked Liza. "Just us and our horses?"

"Sure," said Miss Oglethorpe. "I brought another whole roll of film. I just knew this would be a great day."

Miss Oglethorpe's photographic genius was in full bloom that day as she took pictures, snapshots freezing forever in fading grainy black-and-white, everyone, young and old, standing in front of the rescued locomotive. Ginny and Liza. Rex, Spud, and Lois. Afton, Tom, Eden, and the children. Stella, Marinda, and the Prairie Fern. Ginny, Les, the Prairie Fern, Matt, and Eden. Annie, her parents, her children, and Ernest. The Douglass women: Afton, Alma, Connie and her daughters, Annie and her daughters, Eden and Liza and Stellina, the latter two waving toy guns in one hand, ice cream bars in the other.

As the shutter clicked on this snapshot, Eden heard a baby's squall, and recognized Nicky's cry. She excused herself and found him in the arms of the Prairie Fern.

"I was just coming to get you," she said. "He's hungry."

Eden bounced the fussy Nick in her arms and took him down the street, away from the immediate celebration. On the porch in front of the barbershop she saw a rocking chair. She soothed her baby son, opened the buttons on her blouse, and put him to her breast, enjoying his greedy slurps, and the insistent tug at her body, this elemental connection to all life, the sustenance that the mother offers her child. She crooned to him, the same song the ice cream truck endlessly tinkled out from a short distance, "Oh do you remember Sweet Betsy from Pike," as she rocked back and forth over the uneven surface of the porch.

She looked up from the smooth orb of the baby's head down the street to the late afternoon party winding down. Spud and Rex, the actors, wranglers, old cowboys, were getting frisky with drink, high spirits and hijinks, while various parents called out the names of schoolchildren, rounding the kids up in Spanish and English. The Agua Verde principal chatted with her teachers. Stella and the Prairie Fern, Marinda, Afton, Lil, and some of the other old women, their chairs clustered together, nodding, shrugging, fanning themselves; the Baxters and Matt were deep in conversation. Ginny and Les sat with their feet up on a rail, rolling cigarettes, talking with the Pierinos and a couple of Scoop executives and their wives. Tom Lance sat on the saloon steps discussing, literally, chicken feed, with a Mr. Washington, who operated a small chicken ranch nearby. Lois Bonner was flirting mercilessly with a network executive, his wife standing right there. Miss Oglethorpe and some of the other teachers laughed with the actors and extras. All these cries and voices mingled extravagantly in the dusk, the drifting smoke.

Eden closed her eyes momentarily, and when she opened them, for all its patent falsity, its existing here in May 1960, she could imagine a town like Lariat, a long-ago Lariat. And people like these, communally celebrating the prosperity assured by this locomotive. She looked at the parti-colored crowd and wondered how had they all gotten here from somewhere else. She tried to imagine the people they had come from, all those anonymous lives. She thought about her father and his Great Timetables reconciling history, his genealogy charts reconciling lives, all waving from the walls, uncoiling, all those names and dates, begets and begats. Each of us, she thought, has someone from our past, begot and begat from someone whose bone and sinew, whose bad temper or blue eyes we yet share, someone desperate, restless, unhappy, someone—what was Margaret Thorsen's phrase all those years ago?—someone with good health and bad prospects. Someone who left the place where God had dropped them. Their backs to every Babylon, their eyes on a new Zion.

We wouldn't be Californians, Americans at all, Eden thought, if there hadn't been someone, forced or fooled, beaten, hoodwinked, or blackmailed, out of one way of life and into another, across the sea or the land. Or both. Some in steerage. Some in chains. They birthed and deathed along the way, abandoned mortal remains to the sea or the sky, and moved on. They were cast off, torn from the arms of people they had loved and would never forget, however distant or unmarked the graves. If they had books and bureaus, harmoniums, they cast those off too, cast off what could not be carried in their arms or on their backs. But the heart? Mind? Memory? These were the really capacious containers. In these you could carry everything. Each heart and mind and memory uniquely its own, and yet in converging, did they become community? Was that Matt's great gift? Collecting hearts and minds and memories, converging them on an experience like this?

She heard Liza's voice above everyone else's, whooping, as she galloped on Dasher, out beyond the cemetery where no one was buried, whirling around, as though those headstones were obstacles in a barrel race. Her pigtails were flying. She had lost her hat.

Eden wanted to go to Matt, to take him away from the Baxters. She wanted to tell him about the living and the dead, the forces that had combined, even combusted, to bring all these people to this place, and where they might go from here, not just to their homes, but into what futures? When this—the present— became the past, drifted, unraveled, dissolved, would this day be the sole connecting thread among all these lives? She wanted to share with Matt the solar plexus certainty she felt, that in all our long, unknown genealogical histories, there was an ongoing lump of starter that could be passed from one nameless hand to another, and yet remain authentic, creative, and treasured. She wanted Matt to know that she recognized how remarkable he was, and how she admired what he had wrought, that she believed in what he could yet achieve. He should not confine himself to those red, blue, and yellow loops encircling Greenwater, endless, repetitive as "Sweet Betsy From Pike" tinkling still from the ice cream truck. Matt should make the films that had always inspired him, tales of people with their backs to every Babylon and their hopes on Zion, but their eyes not daring to look too far ahead for fear of what they might see. Matt should bring his insistent authenticity to these many braided fates, use his gifts and energies to create community on the screen: audiences would recognize their own pasts, their own people. *Lariat Lawman* was an achievement, unique among television Westerns, but Matt had vision for a larger story. Matt should leave *Lariat,* and make the films he had described to her the very first day he brought her to Greenwater, when he had, even then, heard the train whistle, and felt the thunder of buffalo, and watched the wild mustangs from afar in his imagination. Eden stroked her baby son's sweet cheek. "Oh, Nicky," she whispered, "your Daddy really does have VistaVision."

# Marinda's Parti-Colored Salsa

Chop fine one red onion and a couple of cloves of garlic. Put in a big bowl. Then peel a couple of large, fresh oranges with moist skin. Pick off as much of the white as you can, but you needn't be persnickety. Separate the sections and cut each into thirds. Add to bowl. Chop fine a couple of tomatoes, one bunch cilantro, one red or green pepper. To this add to taste one or more washed, peeled, seeded jalapeño, anaheim, and serrano chilis. Strip a couple of ears of cooked corn and add to the dish. Frozen corn, cooked quickly, drained and cooled is fine too. Salt and pepper to taste. Over all squeeze the juice of one fresh lime. Cover. Set aside at least for an hour.

This salsa is especially good with fish tacos.

However, it is extraordinary for baked fish.

Put a layer of this salsa in a baking dish and put on top a sturdy fish, like halibut steaks, nothing flimsy like sole. Put a layer of salsa on top. Cover with foil. Bake at 350 till done. Maybe 20 minutes, depends on the thickness of your fish steaks. Cook your rice and warm your black beans while the fish bakes.

To serve, gently lift your fish and salsa from the baking dish, place in the center of a large oval or round platter. Surround with a ring of freshly cooked white rice and a ring of black beans. Have extra salsa on the table.

# SNAPSHOT

## THE COMPETITION

Liza Ruth March—BA, MA, PhD, Vassar, London School of Economics, and yes, Stanford, eventually Full Professor of Communications, Chair of Media Studies at the Annenberg School of Communications at the University of Southern California in Los Angeles—stayed away from Mexican food and Italian food altogether. Too close to home. Her old home. Her old way of life. The adult Liza preferred tofu, bean sprouts, and miso soup. She did not cook unless compelled to. She never ate desserts. Certainly not that anyone ever saw.

The adult Liza remained fit. She exercised daily, lifting weights in her home gym. Well and good, except that Liza remained, all her life, a fierce competitor, and frankly, the treadmill did not satisfy her need to win. However, physical limitations incurred in a childhood accident kept her from playing golf or tennis or racquetball. After 1960 she never again went near a horse.

That summer, fiercely jealous over the family's doting attention on a mere bundle of pee-pee and poo-poo, which is to say the baby boy, Nicky, Liza set out to prove herself a true cowgirl forever. The hoyden on horseback. She would show Daddy. Show Ginny, too. Show them all that she was the best, better than any boy. Liza would ride Cody, Ginny Doyle's headstrong palomino.

Cody threw Liza in about ten minutes.

These were, however, the most memorable ten minutes in all of Liza's life. These ten minutes gave her more glory, more pleasure, more sheer exhilaration than anything else that life later offered her: grades, graduations, grants, travel, fellowships, academic titles, tenure, brilliant reviews, fawning colleagues, obsequious students, vanquished academic adversaries. More memorable even than her lovers, her two husbands, than her children. These ten minutes were more intensely physical than sex, than childbirth itself.

Nothing ever tarnished the memory of those elated ten minutes of heightened vitality, clutching the mane of the golden palomino, her young cheek close to Cody's neck, her pigtails flying, watching the dry hills fly by, the blazing sunflowers and wild mustard swirling into a streak of yellow, until Cody bolted, and Liza tumbled to the ground, and the horse galloped away.

She broke her ankle, elbow, and collarbone. Confined to what amounted to a body cast after the accident, Liza could not even go up the stairs. They made up a bed for her in the dining room across from the model of Greenwater. Everyone felt sorry for her. No one, not even Ginny, chided her for recklessness.

Ginny visited every day; when she started to walk again, Ginny spent hours exercising her limbs, helping Liza with crutches, telling inspiring stories of her own recovery when Liza cried or balked. Marinda made everything Liza liked to eat. Stella clucked and fussed, and read to her whenever she asked. Stellina gave up her favorite rag doll for Liza to sleep with. Mom was soothing, sympathetic, endlessly attentive. Mom said that Liza had learned her lesson the hard way. Liza wasn't sure what lesson this was, and didn't feel she could ask. Daddy, though, seemed distracted, and once he knew Liza would mend, he was content with a few perfunctory visits to her dining-room bedside, sometimes with a gift. Whatever the gift, it wasn't the present Liza wanted.

One night on her rollaway bed in the dining room, Liza wakened to the sound of harsh sobs coming from the kitchen. She could not move, or tiptoe out to see, because her cast would clunk on the wooden floor. But she lay very still and listened.

The bawling and blubbering were her father's. Her mother's voice was quaking and uncertain, and in between lurching bits of comfort, Mom kept asking, They said what? What? When? Mom's words, too, strangled in little gasps and sobs.

And that's when Liza first knew that the golden era of the TV Western was over. The Western itself went into eclipse. The network had canceled *The Lariat Lawman.*

In 1964, four years after Engine 646 had been brought to Greenwater in a blaze of glory, the Santa Fe bought it back. Matt March had saved it from the scrap heap, but the engine had never been fired up. Never whistled. No track. No depot. No cattle and hog pens. No prosperity. When the Santa Fe came to collect the locomotive, and move it to a museum far away, they, too, brought many men and a flatbed truck. A crew winched Engine 646 on board. No one from Greenwater came to watch. There were no buckets of iced pop and beer, no barbecue smoke, no laughter and voices, no fish tacos, no ice cream truck, and no one remembered Sweet Betsy from Pike at all.

# PART THREE

# Revel and Preserve

1962

WITH THE CANCELLATION OF *THE LARIAT LAWMAN,* Matt stepped out of his obsession with tracks and trains with the ease of a man shedding an old pair of pants. He stepped, in a manner of speaking, into the equivalent of a parka. The remake of *Gold of the Yukon,* like many another masterpiece, remained incomplete, and very much less than the sum of its parts. It floated, suspended in some amniotic daydream where its creator responded to applause so vivid that it might have been remembered rather than imagined. Edith Head did not do the costumes. Elmer Bernstein did not write the music. William Holden and Robert Mitchum did not play the male leads. Two virile-looking unknowns were signed to play the brothers. Lois Bonner accepted the female lead, the role once played by the angel-faced, foul-mouthed Blanche Randall. Though the original silent film had long since disappeared or been destroyed, the story was easily reconstructed. It followed the old recipe: equal parts greed and peril stirred well with lust. Add snow liberally.

To Eden, the old arguments over the train now seemed benign. Engine 646, cleaned up, polished, yet sat, trackless, beside the platform and without a depot. The scale model of Greenwater had been dismantled, and Matt had sold it to the Baxters. The dining room table was back beneath the chandelier, as though nothing had changed. But something had. The marriage of Eden and Matt, their intimacy—physical, emotional, familial—waned, and the central core of their long partnership shriveled with distrust and withered with recrimination. Matt grew testy, secretive, unpredictable; he would pick quarrels seemingly just so he could stalk out of the house.

Moreover, Matt maintained he could not concentrate at Greenwater. Too many interruptions. Too many phones. The Baxters, who were helping him produce *Gold of the Yukon,* had a phoneless guesthouse behind their ocean-view mansion in Malibu. Matt went there every day to work. His schedule was not Eden's schedule. Nor his children's. Eden managed the Greenwater locations, rising before dawn to be out and about when work began, and often she went to bed before Matt came home. Went to bed alone. Sometimes she woke up alone, too.

Eden remembered returning to Greenwater after her Mexican wedding, remembered hearing that Matt had a first wife, a bright barb of doubt puncturing her happiness. The truth had crashed upon her, and though he was divorced, the seismic underrumble remained: Matt could withhold an important truth. Now, years later, she recognized that withholding important truths was in his nature.

Though Matt and Eden fought, Eden knew she would never share his volatile temperament. Rather, she recognized in herself both her grandmother's steely reserve, and her mother's retreat into fiction. She simply would not allow herself or her marriage to be destroyed. That simply would not happen. But she hated *Gold of the Yukon* the more, because Lois Bonner was a part of the picture. Lois Bonner was a fixture in Matt's life. Indeed, Matt had two lives: one with Eden and the family at Greenwater, and one with Lois and the Baxters and *Gold of the Yukon* in Malibu. Jealousy consumed Eden, ugly old green and unrelenting jealousy. She persevered. She ignored. She struggled with Matt and within herself.

Other insoluble problems confronted the Marches. *The Lariat Lawman* wasn't the only Western axed. Only a few TV horse operas limped into the sixties, and the old cheap-to-make B Western Saturday-matinee serials, those too were a thing of the past. The New Frontier might be on everyone's lips, but the Old West was ho-hum. There were fewer and fewer calls for location shoots.

The money that had rolled in with *Lariat* lunch boxes suddenly dried up. While Eden watched their income dwindle, Matt's plans and hopes expanded.

Stella, in her lugubrious way, pointed out how all this reminded her of the talkies. Stella and Eden were shelling almonds, and the crack and splinter grated on Matt's nerves.

"All the more reason to branch out," said Matt, in response to Stella's grim analogy.

"Ernesto hated *Gold of the Yukon,*" Stella grumbled. "The stuntman died."

"No one will die," said Matt.

"It's bad luck," said Stella. "The Evil Eye."

"Don't be so old country, Mama. The Evil Eye doesn't exist."

"Ha."

"Why remake a flop?" said Eden.

"Why are you so against me!"

"I'm not against you, Matt. I'm your wife. I'm against this picture. Your obsession with this picture."

"You'll thank me one day. The kids will thank me. We'll send Liza and Stellina and Nick, all of them, to Stanford on what this film will make. The world will thank me," he added, popping an almond and crunching on it.

"You've already squandered money and time—"

"It is not squandering! How many times do I have to tell you? You don't believe in me. You never have."

Eden recognized the turning point of their every argument: He turned her objections into personal rejections. Matt would deny their long past together, and any attempt to remind him of her ongoing faith in him sounded like abject whining. Her pride intervened, and she would not do that anymore. She cracked another almond, and gave a sidelong glance to Stella's stony face. "Why make a picture with snow? There's no snow here."

"Snow can be found."

"Snow in films is always bad luck," said Stella. "Ernesto always said so. Everyone does."

"Superstitious rubbish," said Matt. "I'm going to make this right." His wife and mother were silent, terse. Matt crunched on an almond, then another. "You don't know what this means to me."

"Then tell me."

"I have! I've told you a thousand times. Why should I again? You never listen."

"Why not do something original? Why remake a flop."

"Stop calling it flop! You don't even want to know what it means to me. You don't give a damn."

"And Lois does? What does she know that I don't?"

Stella left the room. Matt left the house. Eden did not regret the question. She went on cracking almonds till her hands hurt.


In June 1962, Matt traded in Eden's workhorse Dodge (not his own Cadillac) and came home driving a brand-new Ford station wagon, a Conestoga of a car, wider than a king-size bed. "Pack your duds, chickadees. You, too, Mama!" he cried as they all tumbled out to see it. "We're off to see the west. The real thing! Before it vanishes."

He pulled Eden into his arms and twirled her around. "I've made reservations at Grayson's, the old skiing lodge in the Washington mountains where they filmed *Gold of the Yukon*! And we're taking the long leisurely route. All of us!"

"Oh, Matt!" Practical objections sprouted like wildflowers in her mind, but she dismissed them all. The long leisurely route indeed. Eden would have him to herself, even if it meant sharing him with his mother and three kids. "That sounds wonderful!"

"The deserts! The canyons! The mountains! We're going to camp out. Look here!" He opened up the back of the station wagon, and the children hopped in and out of it as their father unloaded a six-person tent. The tent was in a huge plastic bag, but the picture on the front showed one big square "room" with two wings. "We're going experience the real west. The deserts ringed by mountains. The buttes of Zion. The streams and quaking aspens! The Cascades!"

He had bought as well sleeping bags for everyone, including Stella. He bought duffel bags for their clothes, a Coleman stove, a half-dozen lanterns, tin plates and cups, a massive aluminum ice chest, and a transistor radio for Liza.

Their route was surely long, but not leisurely. They had to hitch a horse trailer to carry all their camping gear for three children and three adults. Matt was determined to take them to Monument Valley first; they would stay at Goulding's Trading Post, where John Ford's company had stayed when they filmed *Stagecoach*. However, after crossing the desert in midday, and nearly expiring from the heat, they stopped in Vegas. They stayed for several days. They took rooms in a hotel with a huge pool and a slide, an all-you-can-eat buffet where the food dried under heat lamps, and color television in the rooms. Stella watched the brand-new color TV mesmerized. The children swam and played while Eden sat by the pool and read. Matt lost money to the slots, to blackjack, and to the craps tables.

From Vegas they meandered to southern Utah, Zion National Park, which Matt declared, was almost as good as Monument Valley. "Now," Matt called to the backseat over Nicky's wails, "you'll find out what those old cowboys really knew, how they really felt. We'll sleep under the stars and have a campfire." He registered them for a numbered campsite. Liza's transistor radio lost reception as they followed roads cut through strange formations of earth and red rock.

The campsite was shadeless, and the heat, oddly humid, ricocheted off the red canyons of Zion, oppressive and enervating. They drank from the water bag that hung on the front of the Ford. The water tasted like the engine smelled. Matt unhooked the horse trailer and hauled the tent and sleeping bags out. The tent resisted, and they struggled to get the huge canvas wad out of its plastic sack. Matt and Eden and Liza and Stellina then spread it upon the ground, where it gave up the smell of starch and something weird. Stella walked around the concrete picnic table, crooning to Nick, who fussed and cried, and twisted in her arms.

Matt confessed that he had never put up a tent. "Have you, Eden?"

"I can't say that I have."

"Didn't your family make that pioneering journey to Idaho?"

"Yes, Matt, but we really did sleep under the stars. On the ground. Like the pioneers."

He turned to the girls. "This tent will be up in no time. We'll all work together, and this'll be an authentic adventure." Matt handed the instruction booklet to Stellina. "Okay, read them out loud."

Stellina began, " 'Lay the tent on the ground. The door flaps must be facing the—' "

"We've done that," snapped her father. "You can see we've done that."

She scanned the page. " 'Put peg A into ring A accor . . . ding to the dia . . . gram, and hammer it into the ground. The same for pegs B, C, D, E, F, G, H—' "

"Shit. Did someone bring a hammer? Eden? Anyone?"

"We didn't know we needed one," Eden said. "No one read the directions."

"What'll we do, Daddy?" asked Liza.

"You better get this tent up," said Stella. Nicky was squirming and screaming in her arms. "There's going to be rain."

"There's not going to be rain, Mama!" Matt barked with scarcely a look overhead. "Those are just a few clouds."

The few clouds erupted about half an hour later after a tremendous clap of thunder, and jagged bolts of lightning as the rain coursed down. The tent still lay spread flat upon the ground. Thunder rolled and echoed, caught in the canyons, and rumbled the earth loose from its foundations as the rain poured down in sheets. Red mud bubbled around them, first in rivulets, then in rivers. Then the hillside itself began to slide; oozing red chunks of mud sludged toward them, slurping at the edges of the outstretched canvas, lapping at the tent, as Matt, Eden, and the girls tried to roll it back into its original ball. The canvas tent evolved into a living creature, antediluvian, roaring, resistant, the flaps like scales. Their hands and feet and clothes and hair dripping rain and stained with red mud, they fought, till Matt turned and saw the whole hillside shifting slightly, the earth flowing down toward them.

"Give it up!" he cried. "Forget the tent. Let's get out of here. Get in the car, girls! Mama! Get behind the wheel, Eden!

Matt heaved the sleeping bags, soaked through with water, mud, and heavy as bales of bricks, back into the horse trailer. Rain obscuring his vision, he reconnected the hitch, then jumped into the passenger seat. Eden hit the gas pedal and the engine heaved them forward, but she felt a torque, a jolt as the horse trailer twisted in its hitch, swerved. She stopped.

"You put it in wrong, Matt. It's—"

But Matt was already out the door, splashing to the back of the station wagon, where he yanked the pin, and they left the horse trailer, the tent, and the sleeping bags there for Zion to reclaim, and drove away, darkness falling, red rain defeating their windshield wipers.

As they limped toward Cedar City, Eden suddenly started to laugh.

"What is so goddamned funny?" Matt asked over Nicky's shrieks from the backseat.

"Our backs are to Zion," she said. "It's supposed to be the other way around."

"Why is that funny? Tell me."

"Oh, Matt," Eden laughed again, peering into the darkness lit by headlights, "I look forward to Babylon."

He flung his arm across the seat and red mud dripped, but his hand on her shoulder sent warmth penetrating to her very marrow.

They stayed in a Cedar City motel for three days to recover. All six in a room with a kitchenette. The motel room had a picture of Joseph Smith being martyred in the Carthage jail, and a Bible and a Book of Mormon. Eden half feared that the Mormons would knock on the motel door and snatch her for the backslider she was. All day long the adults watched a lot of black-and-white televison. Liza and Stellina splashed in the ill-kept pool. Nicky jumped on the beds. The red mud streaking their car, their clothes, their hair, and their hands never quite washed out for weeks. The station wagon kept its rusty glow. Matt sulked, and though he continued to watch television, he complained about losing time. Monument Valley was out. They would go north to Washington, to Grayson's Lodge and Mount Baker, the original location for *Gold of the Yukon.*

Past and present seemed to Eden to weave and braid as they drove north into Idaho. Little had significantly changed along this route from the 1930s and her family's long trek to Fairwell. Sometimes, there flitted at her peripheral vision a face, a fleeting figure by the roadside, the lost Gideon or Kitty, the gangly boy her brother had been, the dim but sweet sister from whom she was forever estranged. Ada still blamed Eden for Kitty's drowning. Their exchanges had dwindled to a yearly Christmas card. Eden said none of this as the station wagon moved north, but the current that connected her to Matt must have carried something of these thoughts. They were perhaps twenty miles into Idaho and he asked if she'd like to go to Fairwell.

"We could meet your sister for the first time," he added.

"You don't want to meet my sister."

"Why not?"

"Believe me, you can live without meeting Ada and Melvin Brewster."

"What's wrong with them?"

"Oh, Matt. Nothing's wrong with them. This is our vacation. Don't waste it."

"Are you ashamed of us?"

Eden recognized the edge in his voice, prelude to a sniping quarrel. She looked out the window and he insisted, asking again.

"What are you talking about? Don't be ridiculous."

"Are the wop Marches not good enough for the Saints? You know how the Mormons look down at us mackerel snappers." He glanced in the rearview mirror at his mother, who glared at him. "You know what I mean."

"What do you mean?" Eden retorted. "Why would I think that? Why are you picking this stupid fight, Matt? There's nothing in Fairwell and we're not going there. Don't be stupid."

Tempers and the station wagon overheated as they wound through the mountains, and Matt took the curves with more abandon and more speed than he needed to. Stella, in the backseat, wrung her hands, prayed to St. Christopher to spare them death on the highway. Matt told her to shut up, which hurt her feelings. Then he pushed his point with Eden to a full-tilt quarrel, heaping abuse on the Douglasses till she nearly cried. Stellina announced that she was going to throw up, and did so.

Twelve difficult days after they left California, the Marches' station-wagon-train stopped in front of Grayson's Lodge at the foot of Mount Baker in the Cascades. Eden and Matt were scarcely speaking. The girls were hostile. The toddler, Nick, who had not slept well the whole time, was cranky and wouldn't eat. Stella was more somber than ever. And yet, as they got out of the car, Eden's natural equanimity reasserted itself. The mountain meadows were awash with wildflowers, the snow-clad old volcano, Mount Baker, glittered in the background; the weather was cool and sunny and a bright, refreshing wind blew through the cedars.

Grayson's Lodge had little changed since the 1920s, the stout timbers, local stone just as they had appeared in *Gold of the Yukon*, though the owner now was a Mr. Alvin Denning, a balding man who wore jeans and a flannel shirt with sweat stains and flecks of ketchup on it. Mr. Denning had room for them, but he had no record of a reservation. In fact, they seemed to be the only guests. He led them upstairs to the three rooms, all near the bathroom at the end of the hall: one each for Eden and Matt, Stellina and Liza, Stella and Nicky. The rooms were small, close, poorly ventilated, and had low ceilings. Denning had to work hard to open the windows.

The second floor was more like a gallery that overlooked the big central room. Eden could instantly see why the lodge had served as a set. The main floor was dominated by a massive stone fireplace in the center, with tables of assorted shapes and off-balance wooden chairs around the room. In each corner was a woodburning stove. Eden and Stella exchanged alarmed looks to see rubber rats in the windowsills.

"Just for fun," Mr. Denning assured them.

When he learned of Matt's plans to remake *Gold of the Yukon*, Alvin Denning's plump face lit. He could supply—he could guarantee—an avalanche if that's what Matt wanted. At the kitchen grill, Denning introduced his wife, Zelda. The kitchen was not cut off from this big central dining room; the grill faced a bar, and cabinets lined the walls behind, a few old fridges hummed. Zelda, too, was enthusiastic about a remake of Grayson's only claim to fame. Snow was unstable. It would crumble in an icy wall.

Bored, the girls ran outside, and Stella took Nicky upstairs for a nap.

Alvin led Matt and Eden around the main floor, pointing out framed photographs hung haphazardly, snapshots of Blanche Randall, Ernest March, John Kent, and Lesley Markowitz as they had lounged about the lodge when it provided locations for *Gold of the Yukon*. Alvin offered Matt and Eden beers. On the house.

As the men talked avalanche at the kitchen bar, Eden watched spellbound as Zelda made what she said was Thousand Island dressing, emptying vats, equal parts of ketchup, mayo, and hot dog relish, into a big bowl and mixing it with a spatula. On the grill, Eden noticed with a sickening thump, there were little scatterings of prints in the congealed grease, streaks of something moving fast across this surface.

Eden disengaged Matt from Mr. Denning. "We're not eating here. I think we should leave tomorrow."

"Why?"

"The place is a pigsty. Look over there at the grill. You want your mother and three kids to get sick? Food poisoning, or worse."

"It's not that bad. Besides," he added, "I thought you were the one with the pioneer family."

"Give me the keys. We passed a little store, and I'm going back for some groceries."

Taking Stellina with her, Eden drove to a crossroads some three miles back where there was a small store with a sign that advertised beer and ice cream. With its wooden porch, and tin awning, it might have come out of Lariat, except that the shingles were thick, positively spongy with moss. The place was dim and, like Grayson's Lodge, smelled of damp. Eden collected a few things, milk, eggs, bread, and some cans, and took them to the counter. There, lined up in small baskets, were strawberries, smaller than the California strawberries Eden was used to, softer-looking, their color darker and uniform, not with a green rim around the stems.

"Try one, little lady." He smiled at Stellina. He was a bearded man, perhaps forty, clad in a flannel shirt. "You're not from around here, are you? These strawberries will be a revelation to you. Just picked, down in Skagit." He held the box up for Eden.

The strawberries were, in truth, their own little revelation, more fragile than any she had ever tasted. Eden said she'd take three boxes.

"We're staying with the rubber rats," Stellina piped up. "Mr. Denning said I could have one."

The man broke into resonant, good-natured laughter. "No wonder you're buying groceries. Alvin and Zelda, well." He cleared his throat, and resumed in a serious, almost clerical fashion. "I have your salvation, lady. Copper River out back."

He beckoned Eden and Stellina to follow him through the back storeroom, which smelled of cheese and burlap and melting ice, down the steps to a small, tightly enclosed shed. Refrigeration hummed inside, and there, on cold, waist-high counters, lay whole trays of shining fish, their eyes black and sightless, their scales gleaming even in the low fluorescent light.

"My brother fishes up in Alaska. You ever been to Alaska, ma'am? No? God's country. Like nuthin' you never seen. These here fish, wild caught, never frozen, from those very waters. My brother just got in last night. I'll sell you one of these." He paused and flopped through the fish; they were huge. "Ten bucks. I'll cut it up, too, so the little lady don't have to look at that nasty old fish head."

"Ten bucks is a lot of money for a fish."

"But not for salvation."

"I don't have anything to cook a fish that size."

"You don't need to cook this fish, lady. You just whisper over it. Talk nice to it. You take this fish, a little corn on the cob. That, a couple of cold beers, your husband, and go on up to Artist's Lake."

Eden bought the fish, the corn, the strawberries, the cold beer, some foil, a pot, some kindling, and he threw in some logs. That afternoon the Marches drove from Grayson's to Artist's Lake, a rambling expanse of water encircled by low hills, mountains silhouetted in the distance. The water picked up the color of the sky. Stone barbecues and tables scarred with initials clustered not far from shore. Matt managed to light the stone barbecue. Wood smoke plumed. He and Stella took the children down to the lake while Eden considered the fish. How best to talk nice to it?

She put the water on to boil for the corn. As she shucked the corn, piled them on the table, she watched Stella and Matt and the children down at the lake, hearing their laughter. Matt plunged in, playing dolphin with Stellina; Stella, barefoot, though still clad in her black dress, waded with Nicky. Ten-year-old Liza slid through the water in long, lovely butterfly strokes, calling out for her daddy to watch her.

Their voices carried over water, and Eden felt a profound peace she realized only then that she had long missed. Wood smoke from the stone grill scented the air around her, and a breeze rustled through trees, upturning the pale under-sides of their dark leaves like dancers' petticoats. Eden sat with her beer, looking out over the lake. The light was altogether different from the light at Greenwa-ter, and the days much longer. This far north, midsummer, dusk would not even begin before nine. The air was cooler and cleaner, and the trees encircling the lake were green unto black, the pines and cedars like sharp painted spikes. Little cabins, sunk in shade, dotted the opposite shores, and Eden wondered who lived there, as she plucked the stems out of strawberries. No need even to cut the berries, they were so small and sweet.

When the food had cooked, she called the family back from the lake. Matt bounded up, and she took his towel and rubbed his face and chest. She put a strawberry between his lips. He smiled.

They ate at the decrepit picnic table that Eden had covered with a blue-checked cloth. The children, swathed in damp towels, their hair wet and lank, their skin fresh and pink, were hungry and happy. The corn, salmon, and straw-berries all vanished, and Eden remarked that the clerk had been right about the revelation and salvation.

"Revelation and salvation are not for fish," remarked Stella, but she added, "though this is very, very good, Eden."

"Excellent." Matt pushed his plate away and began to light his pipe. "I don't think I ever ate so fine a fish. I don't think Ernesto ever cooked so fine a fish. I don't think anyone ever did in the whole history of fish."

The children agreed, and Eden's happiness expanded, bloomed under their applause. They lingered companionably while the trees, the lake steeped in shadow, then darkness, though the sky overhead remained light, and streaks of pink and flame and bronze underlit long wispy clouds.

The children ran and shrieked, playing cowboys and Indians in the brush with two boys whose family was picnicking nearby. Their parents joined the Marches around the fire while the children exuberantly reenacted the deathless Western classic lines.

"Smile when you say my name, you varmint!" they heard Liza snarl at a hapless boy.

"I'm an Indian!" cried the boy. "You can't say that to me."

Matt remarked to the boys' parents that Liza and Stellina knew real cowboys and real Indians, but the couple confused *The Lariat Lawman* with *Gunsmoke,* which nettled Matt since *Gunsmoke* had not gotten axed. They said how much they liked *Rawhide,* and *Bonanza,* which also had not gotten axed. Eden experienced Matt's ire wordlessly, and to put an end to TV talk, she asked where they were from. Skagit County, they said, huge alluvial flats of farmland on the Puget Sound. They lived near a town called La Conner. They rattled on happily about the charms of La Conner, the Skagit flats, the hills and lakes to the east, the Puget Sound, the islands to the west. Eden breathed more easily.

Eden and Matt made love that night in the lumpy bed. They savored one another as they used to; they rediscovered the old intensity and gratified one another with a new tenderness. Matt relaxed into her embrace. She held him, stroking his back, her cheek against his chest. When he spoke, she could feel his voice rumble through his ribs and flesh. The rumble was comforting, the words less so, since he was talking about the avalanche scene and how Denning was taking him out there tomorrow.

"Honey, Denning is using you. He doesn't know anything about that old silent film, except for the snapshots he's got hanging up. He's stringing you along. Oh, Matt . . . why are you so set on this?"

"It's going to be a masterpiece. It's a great story, and no one else has thought of it."

"It's a remake, Matt. Someone else thought of it."

Matt rolled off her. "I'm creating something authentic here, and you can't see it."

"Here? In this dump? Is it authentic because nearly forty years ago Lesley Markowitz hauled a company of actors up here and froze their backsides and killed a stuntman? It's a remake of an obscure silent film, for God's sake! It's not authentic even to begin with, any more than Lariat was a real town, or the Indian village is a real village."

"Prairie Fern told me the Indian village looks real."

"Matt, Prairie Fern was born in London with the Wild West Show. The Indian villages she knew were created by Buffalo Bill." He did not answer and she felt his muscles tighten with suppressed tension. She brought her face up so she could see his eyes, the dark circles were deeper, and crow's-feet radiated up to his temples. He was still beautiful to Eden, but his mouth was set in a hard line. "Matt, just help me to understand this, will you. I want to. Help me. Tell me what I need to know."

"It's too late."

"Does Lois understand?"

"Leave Lois out of this."

"Why should I? You haven't."

"She believes in me. She's given up a lot to play the lead."

"Who's paying her rent in the meantime?"

Matt turned his back to her. "I'm making *Gold of the Yukon* with or without you."

Late as it was, the sky was still a creamy blue and moonlight shuffled the shadows around their tiny room. Eden lay in the silence and stared at the ceiling. She remembered all those years ago, trundling into Fairwell, the family's hopes all pinned to insubstantial claims. A fool's errand, her mother had said, at the behest of a knave. "You should just call this movie *Fool's Errand* and be done with it."

"Shut up."

Eden got out of bed, slid her feet into sandals, wrapped a robe around her, and went out onto the landing. Below, in the central room, she saw Stella, sitting alone at a table, a votive candle lit before her, a rosary in hand. Pray away, thought Eden, going downstairs, God knows we need it.

Lit from the votive and the moonlight, Eden could see the young woman Stella must have been, a chiseled beauty before mistrust and religion hardened into saturnine wariness. Stella's skin was threaded with very fine wrinkles and she had the same pouches under her eyes, the heavy lids of her son, and a discernible mustache delicately edged her upper lip. All her years of *mater dolorosa* had endowed her with a sadness that was almost voluptuous.

"We need to leave," Stella said as Eden sat down across from her. "Little Nicky does not travel well. He wants his own home, his own little bed. This place is disgusting. These people . . ."

"I know." The spell of Artist's Lake, the voices carrying across water, the woodsmoke, the salmon and strawberries all dissolved.

"This *Gold of the Yukon*," Stella shook her head. "Ernesto detested *Gold of the Yukon*."

"At least it was his only failure."

"He did not hate it for the failure. Ernesto thought he would die here filming that picture. They made a real avalanche. With dynamite. Markowitz, that bully, he orders the actors, bundle up and go out there, and pretend they were dying. They thought they were. The cameras froze. The snow blinding everywhere. You could not see for the white. Blinded. Cold as the tomb."

In spite of the June night, Eden shivered.

"Eden," said Stella. "I fear for Matt. He is blind with ambition. His health," she touched her head and heart, "suffers. You know?"

Ordinarily Eden might have steered Stella toward some brighter topic, but she didn't. The smoke wafted between them, and in the frail light from the wall sconces pooling with the moonlight on the floor, Eden saw a flash and scurry. Were there rubber rats to scare off the real ones?

"When talkies come, and we know Ernesto can never act no more . . ." Stella held her rosary tighter, "Ernesto wanted to die. Nico found him, gun to his head. That's when they filled in the pool. They left the gun there at the bottom. The gun is buried under the garden. You mustn't tell Matt. He doesn't know this."

Matt did know this, but Eden did not say so. She took Stella's hand in hers. "Don't be afraid, Stella."

"But I am. I have so many fears, they wake me in the night."

"What? Tell me."

"I fear that you will leave him and take the children away. I know about that *putina,* Lois. It's more than a wife can bear. And you are not Catholic."

"The women in my family," Eden replied in a slow, reassuring voice, "have walked from Iowa to Utah. They do not give up. I was not raised a Mormon girl for nothing. I took vows, even if they were in Spanish. Matt is my husband, and I love him. I will never give up on him. You must not worry that I will leave him. I love him still. No matter what. His children adore him, Stella. They adore you. How could I take them from their daddy and their grandmother? No. That will never happen. I will fight Lois Bonner for him, and I will win."

"And *Gold of the Yukon?*"

Eden considered. "That, I may not win."

EDEN WON THE BATTLE AT GRAYSON'S, AND THEY LEFT THE NEXT DAY, BUT Matt's search for snow did not cease. She could not talk sense to a man surfeited with ambition, delusion, and conviction.

That autumn, Matt found a great, snowy location at Mt. Baldy, between Los Angeles and St. Elmo. He was dazzled by the rugged terrain and by the lodge, so reminiscent of Grayson's. One night when his family was gathered for dinner, he announced he would begin filming there in January 1963.

Eden told him then, plainly, though not in front of Stella or the children, she was divorcing *Gold of the Yukon.* She would not leave him, but *Gold of the Yukon* could go to hell or Mt. Baldy, whichever came first.

On schedule, late in January 1963, Matt and Lois in his Cadillac led the Greenwater caravan—men, women, animals, equipment, vehicles, trailers—up the narrow mountain road. Mt. Baldy Lodge was built with timbers and local stone, the same era as Grayson's. Little outlying tourist cabins backed up to a broad, rocky river, swift and shallow by any but Southern California standards. Falling snow speckled the stones. In Technicolor the snowy river would look lustrous, almost pink. Plumes of smoke from the cabin chimneys brushed like calligraphy against the clouds. The weather cooperated, which is to say, it was terrible. "The worse the weather is, the better I like it," Matt said to Lois as he closed their cabin door behind him. His complexion was pink from the cold and excitement.

The ten-day shoot went badly. Matt could not say to Lois, to anyone, how he missed his wife. Or why he missed her. Eden made things work, and work well. She took on the detailed jobs he did not want to do, the thankless but essential cowpie counting. Doing Eden's job Matt had Gus Baxter's nephew, Troy. Even the kid's name grated on him, but he agreed to give Troy a chance. Matt was much indebted to the Baxters, and he could not yank Troy even when he proved hopeless. The weather worsened, and Matt liked to think this, too, was Troy's fault.

Despite the falling snow, the cold temperatures, they worked on, in the interest of authenticity. They lost time. If someone less skilled than Les Doyle had been the rider, they would surely have lost a horse. Matt wanted to do the scene again, and Les said he would. Once more. Ginny got a blanket and flung it over her husband's shoulders while she swore under her breath at Matt. Matt threatened to replace them. Les and Ginny left the set. Matt called a break.

He did not replace Les or Ginny, but production remained dogged with errors and false starts and misunderstandings that Matt blamed wholly on Troy. The schedule suffered, and not till early February did the *Gold of the Yukon* caravan start down the mountain, minus one truck that would not start in the brutal cold. The temperature had dropped yet again in the night, the wind had come up, and the snow was blowing. They left the truck at Mt. Baldy Lodge and Matt hitched the horse trailer to his Cadillac to follow Les and Ginny down the mountain.

Snow funneled in their vision. In the ashen light, only the taillights of Les and Ginny's horse trailer ahead gleamed. Matt followed the red lights like pinprick beacons. Matt thought, unaccountably, of the hammer he had not brought to secure the tent the summer before. He had not read the directions. He should have. Unused to snow, a novice at driving on ice, he had the same vague feeling of imminent failure. But he did not say this to Lois. She joked about the avalanche, about their getting it at last. Matt laughed without taking his eyes from the road swallowed in snow. At a steep turn he lost sight of the Doyles' taillights. Matt speeded up to be able to follow them through the snow. The Cadillac slid on the ice. Compensating quickly, Matt hit the brakes. He felt a jolt as the horse trailer twisted in its hitch, swerved, and he remembered leaving Zion and the mud and horse trailer, the lurch and the rain. He hit the brakes, but he did not merely skid as he would have in the rain. The tires spun out, lost traction, so he hit the brakes again, and again, and the car spun around, plunging off the road and down an incline. He heard the hitch snap and saw Lois's blue eyes widen, her mouth open in a scream as they pitched downhill, taking out saplings, careening into a steep ravine. The horse trailer wrenched, fell on its side, the animals helpless inside, bellowing, as the Cadillac crashed, came to rest at last against an ancient pine. Steam from the smashed engine collided with the cold air and rose in vast gauzy fronds up through the falling snow.

NOT UNTIL THAT AFTERNOON DID THE PHONE RING AT THE MARCH HOUSE. Ginny said to Liza, "Annie is on her way to your house. She'll be there. Don't let your mother leave the house till Annie gets there. Annie will drive her." Ginny's voice was reined in, without affect or emotion. "Your grandmother must stay there with you kids. Now put Eden on the phone."

"Why? What's wrong? What's happened, Ginny? Don't lie to me."

"I have not lied to you, Liza." Behind Ginny, voices sounded watery, echoing, calling for doctors. "Just put Eden on the phone and don't ask me any more questions."

By the time Eden and Annie got to Pomona Valley Hospital, Matt had been in surgery for an hour. Afton and Tom were already there, seated beside Ginny and Les. Annie and Eden joined them in the waiting room. Afton took her hand and said she'd been praying for Matt to live.

The thought of a world without Matt March made Eden reel; her brain shrank away from her skull, and her heart simultaneously burst with longing, despair, and forgiveness.

A sheriff's deputy found the family huddled there. He asked to see Les's permit for the firearm he had used to shoot the horses that been pinned in the trailer, smashed to pieces when it had rolled over. And over. Eden listened, her mouth slack with horror.

"No permit." Les Doyle braced, stubbed out his cigarette, and sat up straight.

"I know who you are, Mr. Doyle. I know how good you are. I know that what you did must have been necessary. Merciful. But you have no permit, and well, I have to cite you," said the deputy, scribbling on a pad. He tore it off, and added, "I don't think I made a duplicate on this. Damn." He nodded to the family group and left.

Eden licked her lips and turned to Ginny. "You didn't mention horses. That horses had been killed."

"It's already so bad, what difference did the horses make?" said Ginny.

And that's when Eden knew she had not yet fully absorbed what had happened.

# Copper River Salmon with Strawberry Lemon Sauce

*Café Eden, Skagit Valley, Washington*

Copper River salmon from Alaska is the monarch of salmon, with a short season, perhaps six weeks, mid-May through June. The end of this season in Washington State corresponds with the advent of local strawberries. At the Café Eden, Eden's combination of fresh salmon and fresh strawberries was an annual spectacular success. But never did this taste as good as it did that evening at Artist's Lake. Sometimes what you have on hand is so perishable, so fragile and fleeting, that re-creation is futile. You can revel, but not preserve.

Take your whole salmon, leaving the bones in. (Bones and skin peel off easily once it's cooked.) Open your salmon and salt and pepper central cavity. Then place there a handful of oregano, thyme, parsley, and one lemon sliced thin. Put in your fish poacher and using a liquid, two parts water to one part white wine, a couple of bay leaves, poach as you ordinarily would. Remember that this fish needs only to be spoken to nicely.

Do not try this with farmed salmon; you'll miss the magic and blame the recipe.

Strawberry Lemon Sauce: Take a small box of strawberries, ripe, not pale and wan. Crush with a potato masher. Put in a small pan and add to this four or five leaves basil (if you can find it fresh, if not substitute parsley) chopped, maybe ½ cup fine chopped red bell pepper and one small lemon, washed, thin sliced, cut in half, then cut into quarters. Put these in the pan, too, with a hit of white wine and a hit of balsamic vinegar, maybe a little water if you think you need it. Bring to boil, reduce heat, swirl, stir till it reduces and thickens somewhat.

On each plate, spoon this sauce in small half-moons beside the fish. Serve on long June nights with a salad of cut-up watermelon, and sliced, peeled English cucumbers.

Welcome, summertime.

### LIZA'S KITE

Once there was a happy childhood with a perfect father who loved Liza best.

This is the story Liza Ruth March told over and over again. She told it to friends, colleagues, to all her lovers, to her husbands, to her own two children. She told it so often, it came to have a frame, a tensile structure, tender, papery words-made-flesh, like a kite, graceful, buoyed aloft and tethered to the teller by a slender thread.

Liza wore cowboy boots like Daddy, and, like him, Liza subscribed to a code of conduct she was sure he invented, or at least discovered. This code required that you be true and, above all, valiant. It helped to be beautiful, of course, but beauty without valor was a poor thing. Liza had valor and proved herself. Again and again. In everything she did.

Daddy never missed Liza's events in the youth rodeos or swim meets. He applauded Liza's every blue ribbon and plastic trophy, her every piece in a ballet or piano recital. Daddy took the whole family, and Stellina's pesky friend Rebecca Gomez, to Disneyland and Knott's Berry Farm at least twice a year. Daddy loved to play uproarious games with all the children, and gave extravagant presents. Every kid who came to the party for Engine 646 got *Lariat* hats and holsters. Daddy donated whole cases of Scoop Peanut Butter to Agua Verde Elementary. Liza tweaked slightly the story of her fall from Cody; she did it to prove she had valor, not that she was jealous of a baby. In the kite-story, Daddy stayed by Liza's side when she was recovering.

As the kite rose, and reveled in the high wind, this happy childhood also had a big hacienda full of people who, along with Daddy, adored Liza: grandparents, Marinda Reynolds, Les and Ginny Doyle, the Prairie Fern, and Mom, of course. And lots of others who adored her: Aunt Afton, Aunt Annie, Aunt Connie, Aunt Alma, tribes, oh, hordes of cousins, as well as her sister, Stellina, and baby brother, Nick. There was a whole big cast of cowboys, too, Rex Hogan, Spud Babbitt, the Sons of the Sagebrush. Lois Bonner did not figure in the story.

As a little girl, Liza had riding lessons from Ginny Doyle, the greatest stuntwoman who ever lived. Liza had her own horse, Dasher. She rode all over Greenwater with her father. She was his sidekick. Other kids might drape blankets over chairs and pretend to have a tepee or a fort. Not Liza. Liza had a real fort, real tepees, a lake, a hanging tree, and a frontier town. She had had a career as a child actor, appearing in more than twenty episodes of *The Lariat Lawman*. She was a wonderful success.

Then came the phone call about *The Lariat Lawman* being canceled. Was that a phone call? Liza was never sure. She blamed the phone anyway.

Subsequent events seemed always to transpire under a thin cloud canopy, so high did the kite dance. Marinda left Greenwater and went to live with her daughter. Everyone cried. With Marinda gone, there was a lot more work. Endless domestic chores. Sometimes Liza's mother and grandmother got angry with her when she failed to do some stupid small task, wash the dishes, or fold the laundry. Daddy always intervened. When he as home, anyway. Daddy said, never mind the dishes and the laundry, Liza had to read and study and go to Stanford. You keep excelling, Daddy told her. Excel at everything. Make me proud of you.

For vacations, Daddy took the family (and the pesky Rebecca) to stay for a month in the Baxters' Malibu mansion while Gus and Beverly went yachting to Hawaii. Daddy asked if Liza wanted to bring a friend, but there was no one Liza liked that well. One vacation Daddy took them all (no Rebecca) camping in the real west. Never mind, he didn't read the instructions for the tent, and that they had nearly been buried in oozing red mud. Who cared that Grayson's and the rubber rats were disgusting? Liza left that out. Liza fashioned her story of Artist's Lake where she, too, had experienced something of what Eden felt: contentment so intense that it felt ominous. She did not say that. Too personal.

The following February, the phone rang again. Ginny calling from Pomona Valley Hospital. An accident. The snow. Another disaster wrought by the telephone.

Then, the newspapers. The headlines. Her grandmother insisted Liza and Stellina stay home from school, so they wouldn't have to answer ugly questions. But they saw the ugly pictures.

The Los Angeles newspapers carried the accident on the front page: one dead, one in critical condition. There were pictures of the smashed Cadillac, and glamorous professional photos of Lois Bonner. Her bouffant hair shone in a halo of light, her spit-curls perfect, her firm round shoulders bare, a white fur draped across her breasts, her lips parted, and her gaze sultry. She was a beauty. No doubt of that.

On the local television, networks too, beautiful Lois Bonner's picture filled up the TV screen. On channel 5, the announcer, George Putnam, got downright misty. George Putnam said her death was a great tragedy, her promising career cut short. He said Lois Bonner had been a princess in the 1952 Rose Queen Court, and played important parts at the Pasadena Playhouse. She made many B Westerns before landing the starring role as Carrie Dunne, the schoolteacher on the series *The Lariat Lawman,* which some of you may remember from a few years ago.

CHOCOLATE AT NIGHT. WELL, NOT NIGHT. PREDAWN. Darkness at the windows, lights on, Eden working alone in the kitchen, the tangerines spilled across the table. China saucers were stacked near a bowl of fresh-cut mint, and on the stove, melting chocolate released its essence. Eden poured honey into a small bowl, where it landed with an audible *plop*. She severed the long golden thread between the bowl and the honey jar with her finger. She sucked on the finger. She was making one of Matt's favorite desserts, a concoction of her own creation. These Chocolate Tangerines would be ready when he came home today from the hospital.

Matt had survived the surgery, the broken ribs, punctured lung, lacerated spleen, the internal bleeding, and the concussion. The same steering wheel that had broken off his top front teeth when he went forward probably saved his life. At least he hadn't gone through the windshield. Lois Bonner had gone through the windshield, her face and body shattered and torn. She had been propelled beyond the car, and found limp on some rocks.

But Matt was coming home.

Eden would be ready. Not just with the food and friends and family he loved. Eden was ready to put behind her, put away forever, blame, guilt, everything that had separated them. She would make it right. Not perfect, perhaps; she did not require perfect. Right and new. Their marriage right and new. The old Babylons behind them. Their eyes on a new Zion.

Eden had been days getting ready for this feast. Her Chocolate Tangerines were the last thing for her to prepare before she left for the hospital. Soon the kitchen would fill up with everyone coming to welcome Matt home after nearly two weeks in the hospital. Annie, Afton, Lil, Alma, Ginny, and their husbands, everyone wanted be part of this homecoming. It was never exactly a plan to have everyone there; they had wanted to help out, and Eden hadn't said no. Now she realized what a crowd they would be. Maybe too much for Matt. Well, at least he would be cheered to know he was so loved.

She brought the pan of melted chocolate to the table, beside the bowl of honey. She had made up this dessert one winter evening when Ginny and Les unexpectedly came to dinner. She had tangerines on the tree and bittersweet chocolate in the cupboard. She smiled to herself: You take what's on hand and apply to that a little imagination, a sense of timing, to make those ingredients yield what you want. Matt had loved the Chocolate Tangerines. In fact, Matt responded happily to all her cooking. Even in their worst of times, Matt was always a man of appetites. No more worst of times, Eden vowed, picking up a tangerine.

Until Marinda left, Eden had spent little time in the kitchen. Eden had reserved her cooking skills for special occasions. Someone else had always done the stoke-the-fires daily cooking, the endless obligatory meals. First Ernesto, and his willing student, Kitty, Stella, the talented Marinda Reynolds. But then the network canceled *Lariat,* and the Western itself fell out of fashion; but if Eden now had less money, she had more time. The task that began as mere necessity became a pleasure. The kitchen became not just Eden's domain but her favorite room. The perishable events of everyday life transpired here, and time slid transparently beneath Liza and Stellina as they did their homework at night on the kitchen table, as Nicky played on the floor, banging pots and pans. Stella liked to join them, to talk, to do any little task that would keep her off her feet. Her feet bothered her. The kitchen was the place of endless processes, cook, eat, clean up; Eden did not see these simply as a round of necessary, thankless tasks. Rather, they seemed to her deeply sensory, soothing, even comforting. The kitchen table, like a wheel, held them all together amid the daily flux, pulled them back into the orbit of their love for one another.

Moreover, Eden was astonished at the immediate pleasures that cooking afforded her. She had always had her sights on other goals. Often on long-term goals with long-term rewards. Compared to almost any other undertaking in life, the rewards from cooking were absolutely immediate. Of course, so were the failures. You could create and concoct and then, *hmmm,* often before you brought it to the table, you knew if you had succeeded. Or not. And even success and failure weren't mutually exclusive possibilities. Eden had created dishes that might taste good but did not look all that appealing. And vice versa. Anyway, if the people you were feeding were hungry enough, complete failure was impossible.

She peeled the tangerine, plucking the membrane from it, and while the citrus scent still dampened her fingers, she held it gingerly, and swirled and turned it over in the honey, and put it on a saucer. Then she took a spoonful of warm, melted chocolate and placed it on the tangerine where it flowed over the gleaming honey.

"What are you doing?" Liza came into the kitchen, rubbing her eyes.

"Oh! You startled me. I'm making these for Daddy. It's his big day to come home. Where are your slippers? Why are you awake so early? You need to sleep."

"I smelled the chocolate."

"You did? All the way up in your room?"

"I can always smell chocolate."

"You want to help me?"

"Yes."

"You can give the tangerines each a little sprig of mint. Are you cold?"

"Yes."

"Wait here, tuck your feet up and sit on the chair and I'll go get your bathrobe for you." Eden smoothed Liza's dark hair and moved toward the door.

"Will he be well?"

"Of course. That's why they kept him so long at the hospital, so we're certain he'll be well."

"Will he be the same?"

"The same as what?"

"As ever."

"He will be better, Liza."

"He looks awful with his two front teeth broken off."

"They can be fixed. He will be better than ever."

EDEN HALTED THE STATION WAGON IN FRONT OF THE POMONA VALLEY Hospital. She checked her lipstick and her hair in the rearview mirror and smoothed her skirt. She wore an outfit that she had just bought; she had chosen it to speak for, to underscore, all her good intentions, a chic, light wool suit in a creamy pale rose color that flattered her complexion. It had a slightly raised waistline and the fashionable bell skirt Jackie Kennedy had made popular. Eden had been growing her hair out since Artist's Lake, and it was smooth, curled, no longer unruly.

She walked through the hospital doors and up to the desk where a girl with a red bow clipped to a lacquered bouffant hairdo sat chewing a pen and reading a list.

"My husband is being released today," she said. "Matt March."

"Oh, yes. Let me see. Yes. You wait here. We'll bring him down in a wheelchair."

"A wheelchair? He can walk. Can't he?" she added, her throat tightening.

"Policy. Such a tragedy, Mrs. March. Poor Lois Bonner. Such a beauty. And so young."

"Yes," said Eden. "It is very sad."

To the funeral of Lois Bonner, and in the name of the March family, Eden had sent extravagant flowers and a card with conventional sentiments. It was not her finest moment. She did not know what else to do. Her emotions were too mixed to attend. Her first loyalty was to Matt, and she knew that Lois's friends and family would blame him for her death. Matt blamed himself. From the moment he had emerged from surgery and the worst of the painkillers, his grief, his capacity for grief, was further compounded by guilt. They did not even tell him Lois had died for two days. That sad task fell to Eden. He raged against himself till he had to be sedated. Eden stayed by his side daily, but she was as inadequate to his passions now as she had been in 1956 when Ernesto drowned. An accident. Just like this. But for Matt, the blame always had to go somewhere. Eden blamed the snow. Volubly and often, Eden reminded him that snow was always bad luck in film.

"My notes say I'm supposed to ask you about all the flowers," said the girl with the red bow. "People have filled your husband's room with flowers. You want those, too?"

"No. Thank you. You can give these to anyone who might need them."

"That's very nice of you, Mrs. March."

It wasn't very nice, really. In truth, Eden wanted nothing of this accident to come home except Matt himself, certainly not a lot of flowers that would droop, decay, and die. She wanted to bring him home free of the past. If, as Afton always told her, there is a recipe for everything in life, then there must surely be one for making everything new and better. Eden took a seat in the lobby where she could watch the elevators.

They wheeled Matt out, and Eden bent to kiss him. His lips were chapped, but they met hers with warmth. He smiled, and the holes where his teeth should have been were terrible to see. Though he was freshly shaved, he still smelled medicinal and astringent. He reached out and touched her skirt, as if he needed the feel of her.

"You look very beautiful, Sweetpea. More beautiful than I have any right to. I'm ready to go home."

To Eden the simple declaration reverberated with meaning, and a lump rose in her throat.

The nurses handed Eden a large envelope with the doctor's instructions, reminders for the appointments, and another filled with cards people had sent him. They put his few belongings in the backseat and helped Matt settle in the front. They gave him his cane and waved goodbye as Eden turned on the ignition and pulled toward the street.

She glanced at him covertly. His face was lined, his hair salted with gray, and he looked years older than forty-one. The flesh he had acquired in midlife hung on him like an oversized overcoat. He looked penitent and pained. Thoughts tumbled through her mind, but not to her lips. If she said something flip and shallow, she would diminish the moment, but to speak of the truth, of the fear and hope and love that she felt, would be almost unbearable. They had not been alone since the night before he left to drive to Mt. Baldy. They had made passionate love that night. Perhaps you could not call it making love. Coupling, perhaps, reeking of anger, desperation, and lust-streaked longing, the fierce desire to clutch and hold and tear and mend. Struggling against each other even as they held each other.

The silence began to oppress her. "I brought your sunglasses. Just like you wanted. They're in the glove compartment."

"Thank you." He did not look at her.

The February sunshine was wan. "You don't really need sunglasses. It's not that bright."

"I need them for protection." He got them out and put them on.

"Against what?"

They rode a bit in silence; the freeway was not crowded. "I can't bear to see what I've done," he said at last, and Eden tensed for the volley of grief and guilt that must surely come. "I'm sorry, Eden. Sorry for the pain I've caused, sorry for the hurt I've caused, for . . ." He exhaled, and winced; the ribs and punctured lung were still very sore. "I know I've said it before, but it's true. I'm sorry. I don't deserve your love. I don't."

"You do." Eden swallowed hard, and tears came to her eyes. "And I do love you."

"I'm sorry about Lois. I can't believe she's dead. I'll never see her again. She's gone, and I'll never see her again."

Eden was about to repeat that it was an accident, blaming the snow, but she realized he had not uttered words of personal blame, only sorrow and loss. Was love next? Love? He had never said he loved Lois. At least not to Eden. Oh, please, don't let him tell me how much he loved her.

"I loved her. I'm sorry, but I did. Now she's gone, and I'll never see her again." He gasped, racked with sobs that inflamed his wounded ribs and lung, but despite the pain he wept on.

Every time Eden had gone to the hospital these past two weeks, she had heard Afton's remembered voice warning her against a grief as passionate as Matt's, but she, equally resolved, steeled herself: *I'm here, I'm alive, I'm with Matt, and Lois is not.* Perhaps it was a crass personal injunction, but Eden didn't care. Eden had always vowed she would fight Lois Bonner for Matt's love, but at some point she had given up that fight and settled for being his wife. Now Lois was gone forever, and Eden could take no pleasure in her passing, but she was determined to banish her ghost. On her side Eden had vitality, and the vitality of her love for Matt.

She dug in her purse for a Kleenex and handed it to him. "We're not looking back. We're looking forward. We have our work and Greenwater, our children, our lives together, and our love," she added emphatically. "You're coming home. And that's all that matters."

He mopped his face. He waited for the pain in his chest to subside. "I'm sorry for everything. I'm asking you to forgive me, Eden. I need your forgiveness. I just don't think I can go on if I can't believe you'll forgive me for what I've done. To the family. To everyone. I don't deserve to live. It's all my fault."

"Don't say that. I won't let you talk like that." She put her right hand out, across the broad seat, and he took it. She did not let him go.

"Do you forgive me?"

"Of course, we have to be together, and stay together and—"

"I need to hear you say it, Eden. Forgive me."

The literal declaration was more difficult than she would have thought. She wanted to forgive him. She would forgive him, but still the simple words would not quite cross her lips. She, too, blamed him. For the accident and everything that had led to the accident, for needing adoration and keeping secrets, for being reckless and deluded, but mostly for not loving her as much as she loved him.

"You don't have to mean it," he said in the hum of the car, the silence between them. "Just tell me that one day you'll forgive me, won't you?"

"Yes."

"When?"

"I forgive you. I'm your wife," she said simply. "I love you. I have always loved you. I always will love you. Everyone is happy you're coming home. Everyone is there. We've been in the kitchen for days, getting ready for your homecoming. We've got a real feast planned. Afton and Tom and Lil, Alma and Walter all got here early this morning. Before I left. Ginny and Les and the Prairie Fern, Annie and Ernest, they're coming."

Did a frown crinkle his forehead? Well, if they all proved to be too much, he could go upstairs. At least all these would underscore how much he had to live for.

As the hacienda came into view, Eden saw Liza fling open the front door and tear down the steps, and Stellina jumping up and down right behind her, then Nicky, chubby, lovable, and sweet in his sailor suit, and behind him, Stella rushed, her arms outstretched, Ginny and Annie and all the rest of them, Tom, and Les and even stolid Ernest Douglass grinned to see the station wagon. Liza and Stellina wore identical red velvet dresses with white lace collars and lace on their puffed sleeves. They wore matching red velvet bows in their hair, white stockings, and polished Mary Janes. Eden smiled to think how Stella must have labored to keep them so clean and picture-perfect for this moment.

The children were reminded to be gentle with their hugs because of Daddy's fragile taped ribs. The sight of holes where Matt's teeth had broken off shocked poor Nicky, who had not seen his father since the accident, and he burst into tears. So did Liza and Stellina.

"Now, now," he chided them. "I'm getting new teeth. People without teeth look stupid, and I can't have that, can I?" But the sight of the family, and these people who loved him, brought forth the shadow of Matt's old reflexive exuberance. He waved away the use of the cane, motioned Liza and Stellina to his side. "Leaning on my children," Matt squeezed their thin shoulders, "now that's a new sensation."

The kitchen was crowded, and damp with steam, warm with scent. Stella, heedless of his ribs, fell against him weeping. The she straightened up and wiped her eyes. "Today, I am so happy, I am young again, Matt. No Evil Eye can touch me."

Matt lifted the lid on the pan she had been stirring. "Your sauce, Mama. It's always a special occasion with this sauce." The sauce simmered, a rich, vibrant red.

"We used to have this sauce all the time."

"Yes, but I was away at school. So it always seems special to me."

Stella paused, as if considering this thought for the first time.

Into this lapsed conversation stepped Afton Lance, welcoming Matt home. Afton and Tom had visited him in the hospital faithfully, every few days, driving all the way from St. Elmo.

Les Doyle came in through the back door, with Matt's cowboy boots, cleaned and resoled. Matt beamed as he put them on. "Thank you. Thanks to all of you. Now I feel like my old self."

"Come with me, Daddy," said Liza, pulling him toward the dining room, where big red ribbons had been tied to his chair. The leaf had been put in to accommodate nearly twenty chairs, and the girls had cut out red paper hearts, pasted doilies on them, and stuck them in the dining room windows.

"I don't deserve all this," said Matt, speaking to Eden as if they were alone.

Liza tugged at his hand. "I set the table, Daddy, and I'm sitting here beside you."

"And me on the other side," said Stellina, not to be outdone. "I helped. Look at your cards, Daddy. We each made you a card. Mine is a Valentine."

"So is mine," said Liza. "Nicky's is only scribbling,"

Eden stood behind him as Matt studied the cards gravely. He commented on each of the crayon drawings and the poems inside. He kissed the children, pressing their heads against his shoulder as he blinked against tears. "I don't deserve this," he said again, reaching for, holding Eden's hand.

"It's like Christmas, Daddy," said Stellina.

That welcome-home dinner was like a March family Christmas: noisy with children and awash in opulence, with the comfort and contrast of people who had long, warm associations, histories, and sometimes testy connections to one another. The only difference was that Stellina and Liza kept a furtive eye on their father as they ate, as if fearing he might be snatched away again. As Eden looked down the table, she noticed that the china, silverware, even the neatly ironed napkins were an assortment of what had been accumulated over the years. The same might be said of the company, culled from their different pasts, and united here. Was there ever a time in my life when I did not know these people? And then she wondered, Will there ever come a time when I will not know them? When they will not be part of my life? The people who surrounded her seemed permanently grafted to Eden's world and they filled her with a sense of connection to the past, and a surge of hope for the future. She served the amber, onion soup, great ladlefuls from an old tureen that had been Ernesto's.

Matt bent and sniffed at the soup and brought his face up, smiling, his lips self-consciously closed. The broken, sorrowing man he had been in the car was gone and the old, appreciative Matt presided at the table, his color enhanced by the food and the company, his eyes and thoughts on them. He winked at Eden. "They were trying to starve me at that hospital," he said. "Rubber chicken. Beans boiled to extinction. I'd forgotten how much I rely on good food. And good cooks." He raised his wineglass. "To all the good cooks."

The lifted their glasses, and then they passed the wine around along with Nicky, who moved into various welcoming laps.

Afton declined the wine, but took the baby—Nicky would always be the baby, coddled and fussed over, doted on. She fed him little bits of bread and butter, while he nestled close to her. She kissed his forehead, and remarked in a low voice to Ginny, "Eden never has mastered the biscuit. Not even the plain old biscuit, never minding sourdough. Don't tell her I said so. I gave her my recipe, but she just can't seem to follow it. I don't know why. You'll be happy to know that the biscuits today are mine."

"I am happy today," said Ginny. "Very happy."

Eden, nearest the kitchen, rose and went for another bottle of wine. She heard the front doorbell ring. "I'll get it," she called out, though she couldn't think who it would be. Everyone was already here.

She opened the door to Gus and Beverly Baxter, looking cool, coiffed, and smart. "We heard Matt was coming home today and we just dropped by," said Beverly.

People did not drop by Greenwater; it was not on the way to anywhere else. Matt must have told the Baxters he was coming home today. Eden certainly hadn't. Mentally assembling the names of people who, since the accident, had offered Eden condolence, time, effort, food, anything she might need, she could not place the Baxters. They had never called.

Beverly held out an enormous bouquet and pressed the flowers into Eden's arms. They were so fresh from the florist's fridge, they chilled her flesh. The combination of gladiolus and carnations, all pastels, somehow reminded Eden of overdressed, overfed matrons at one of Miss Merton's Events. Gus and Beverly were clearly groomed for an Event. But not this one, Eden decided. Not this event. "We're having a family reunion," she said, blocking the doorway with her body.

"Oh, we wouldn't think of disturbing you," said Beverly. "We're just happy Matt's home."

"We'd just like to say hello to Matt," said Gus, "see how he's getting along."

She paused for a moment, her good manners warring with her instinctive dislike of the Baxters, their connection to *Gold of the Yukon* and the death of Lois Bonner.

Matt's expression brightened when they came into the dining room, and Eden was glad she had given in. Matt liked them. Annie got more plates, and Eden told them where to sit, placing Gus between Afton and Lil. Gus looked around for an ashtray, but there was none. He glanced at Beverly stuck between taciturn Tom Lance and the almost equally phlegmatic Ernest Douglass.

Afton assessed Gus. "I know we've met, but I can't remember your name. Can you remember, Lil?" Afton addressed her sister across Gus's bulk.

"Not if you can't."

"You're something to do with my son-in-law. Eden is really my niece, but her own dear parents are in the Celestial Kingdom, and since I'm still here, I claim her as a daughter. Anyway, I brought her up when she was just little. I taught her all the good things she knows." Afton ordered Gus to try a sourdough biscuit and passed him the plate.

Gus savored the biscuit, its soft texture and tangy taste, and spoke of his role in producing *Gold of the Yukon*.

"Well, perhaps you are the very person I need to talk to!" declared Afton, interrupting him. Like Eden, she was determined to eradicate the immediate past. "I been trying for years to get Matt to see the wisdom of making a movie of the Book of Mormon."

"That would be a long movie." Gus took a forkful of white beans in a creamy artichoke sauce. He closed his eyes to swallow and bent over to smell the slice of pork loin roast on his plate.

"My recipe," said Afton. "Of course, Eden has taken her own liberties with it, and now it's hers. But that's why I don't understand all this eating in courses. At our house, I just put everything out, and what you like, you like, and what you don't, well, don't take it. At least you don't fill up before you get to the good stuff. Don't you agree?"

Gus nodded, sliding a caramelized pearl onion between his lips.

"But you misunderstand me," she went on. "I wasn't thinking of the whole Book of Mormon, just the big battle, that last tremendous battle where the Nephites defeated the Lamanites. Really, the heavens opened up. The Hill of Cumorah is actually in upstate New York, but I'm sure it could be done right here at Greenwater. Now, that would be a wonderful picture! The violence all in a good cause, and none of this *Pillow Talk*."

"My sister's right," said Lil. "She's always right. You just ask her eight kids. And their kids. And Eden, and lots of others. Afton is never wrong."

The leisurely feast finished up with three desserts, though everyone groaned and protested. "No, no we can't possibly eat anything more."

"It wouldn't be a March family celebration if we didn't have three desserts," said Eden, pleased to see Matt happy, smiling, the tension, tears, the dark mood entirely dissipated: Matt returned and restored, not grim, not drained, and not in love with another woman. Matt was the old ebullient host who led a round of applause as Annie's teenage children brought in each dessert: Prairie Fern's Lemon Meringue Pie, a Mexican Chocolate Cheesecake that Eden had adapted from one of Marinda's recipes, and Matt's winter favorite, Chocolate Tangerines sitting in shallow pools of Cointreau with their little caps of chocolate and sprigs of mint. Liza took credit for the mint.

After dessert, the children, all restless, were excused. Afton, Tom, and Lil had a long drive back to St. Elmo, and with Alma and Walter Epps they said their goodbyes. Ernest took his three children and the Prairie Fern home; Annie would catch a ride later with Ginny and Les. Eden brought out coffee and a tray of liqueurs with small glasses for her remaining guests and ashtrays for the smokers. Conversation ambled with the low blue haze of smoke undulating across the cream-colored ceiling. Dusk had fallen, and the wall sconces were turned up. Lighting some candles, Eden tensed as she heard Gus ask if Matt had heard about Rex Hogan. It was a short leap from Rex Hogan to Lois Bonner. Annie interrupted him, asked if he needed some sugar for his coffee.

Gus declined the sugar, and went on. "After *Lariat* was canceled, his career slid downhill. Of course, he wasn't the only one. No one's heard much from Spud Babbitt, have they?"

"Rex wasn't much of an actor in the first place," said Eden quickly before someone mentioned Lois Bonner. She took her place at one end of the table, her view of Matt unimpaired.

"No," Gus agreed, "but at least Rex could really ride a horse."

"In a manner of speaking," Ginny offered idly. "He could get on and off a horse."

"He was no stuntman," Gus went on, "but he looks like a cowboy in Europe."

"Europe?" asked Matt.

"Have you ever heard of a writer called Karl May? No. Well, no wonder, he's a Kraut who wrote Westerns, really fabulously successful Westerns, classics, like *The Virginian*. The Kraut Owen Wister. They've been making pictures from Karl May books for years. Rex Hogan just starred in one, a German-Yugoslavian cardboard cliché, but it's bringing in bucks, and making Rex famous."

"Bringing in deutsche marks," Beverly explained. "We just got back from Europe. We've been there since Christmas. Mostly Rome. All the studios have invested there."

Beverly rattled on about the glories that were Rome, but small sharp shocks of recognition shot through Eden. So the Baxters were not at Baldy, not in the ill-fated caravan. She had always assumed they were.

"I'm glad we came back when we did," said Beverly. "At least we were here for Lois's funeral. The church was packed. Of course, she lived in Pasadena her whole life. Lots of people came from the old *Lariat* days, and the girls who had been Rose Parade Princesses with her. We drove out to the hospital to see Matt right from the church."

To Eden, Matt looked isolated now that Liza and Stellina were gone. He had never mentioned the Baxters' hospital visit to Eden. She played with a bit of chocolate in her plate.

"We're glad we could be here when you need us, Matt," Beverly added.

"What would Matt need you for?" asked Stella, lurking suspicions painted across her brow, and beneath the table, her fingers crossed against the Evil Eye. "He has his family."

"Rome is the next big place," said Gus, lighting up afresh, and pouring a splash of Mexican coffee liqueur into his glass. "They shoot interiors in Rome," Gus went on, "and locations in Spain or Yugoslavia."

"Yugoslavia!" Matt winced, his cracked ribs registering his indignation. "That's not the west."

"On film, a few gunfights, a few horse turds," Gus shrugged, and acknowledged his faux pas to Stella, "it's the Old West. What was *Lariat Lawman*? The same bunch of clichés people have been working with since the first camera turned, but they're American clichés, and the Europeans love them. The Europeans take them for truth. Why not? So all these Krauts and wops and Yugos, or whatever they call themselves, people with names no one can pronounce, they make Westerns and give themselves American names. To look authentic. You see them up there on the screen, think, Well, there are lots of Americans working on this film."

"Lots of Americans are," added Beverly. "You know who else had a part in that film? That colored actor who used to be the blacksmith on *Lariat*. What was his name?"

"James Hayes," said Matt. "A good man."

"Yes, he's doing quite well over there. There's not as much prejudice in Europe."

"And there's a lot of work for ex-cowboys in the toga trade," Gus added.

"What's that?" asked Eden.

"Rome is Hollywood on the Tiber these days. The wops are cranking out the sword-and-sandal pictures, Hercules, Samson, Sodom and Gomorrah, Last Days of Pompeii, that kind of thing. That actor who played the old major in that NBC series, what was it? *Fort Defiance,* he showed up in a picture called *The Colossus of Rhodes.* Not a bad picture, either, if you like that sort of thing. Rory Calhoun starred. Some of these guys, they're living like kings in Europe."

"Living like kings is too much," Beverly remonstrated.

"They're working," Gus qualified, "which they wouldn't be over here. And in Rome a lot of those guys who got blacklisted here in the fifties, left the country, moved to Europe, they're sitting pretty now. Work. Money. Italian wives." He laughed. "Do the Italians care if these guys once kissed a commie? Hell no. In fact, when they were filming the *Ben-Hur* chariot race over there, who do you think the studio turned to for set decoration? Frankie Pierino's older brother."

"That's not Frankie's brother," said Matt gravely. "Paul is Frankie's uncle. His father's much younger brother. Paul got tarred with the commie-pinko brush in the fifties."

"Paul Pierino is a homosexual," said Gus.

"He never worked here again," said Matt.

"Yeah, well, no one asked Paul for a loyalty oath to do *Ben-Hur.* And no one asked who he sleeps with, either. It was Rex Hogan, when we had dinner with him, Rex remembered the Pierinos were great friends of yours. He called Paul, and we all went out to lunch the next day. They both said to tell you hello, and if you're ever in Rome, give a call. I said you'd be there one day." Gus gave Matt a small salute with his glass. "It's the next great place. It's where the next great Westerns will be made."

"In Rome?" Les Doyle grumbled. "That's too far-fetched."

Gus waved away the observation with his cigarette. "The Western is finished here. Here, where it really happened, it's over. You see *The Man Who Shot Liberty Valance?*"

"Of course I saw it," said Matt. "I would never miss a John Ford movie."

"It certainly wasn't *Stagecoach,* was it? Some of those shots looked like they came out of a can. Ford's washed up. It's time for someone new."

"He's had a long, distinguished career," said Eden, defending John Ford because Matt so admired him. She felt adrift, as if she had been picked up by a tide she could not resist.

"When I saw *Liberty Valance,* I thought of you, Matt." Gus tapped his ash. "When that train came on the screen, the telephone, all that civic progress, I thought of you. The train! What the train could accomplish! Oh, sure, Lee Marvin got to mug and snarl, and Jimmy Stewart got to drawl, and John Wayne got to growl, but the picture began and ended with the train."

Eden pictured Engine 646 still stranded with no track and no depot, and the three loops of track on the to-scale model that had once taken up this entire room. If she hadn't opposed the train, the thought came to her with fierce clarity, might she have averted everything that had happened since? Eden wished she had just brought Matt home from the hospital and put him to bed. He sat, both hands around the small glass of Stella's homemade limoncello, studying the tablecloth. He kept his lips tightly closed, no doubt to hide his broken teeth, but he looked grimly pensive.

"*Liberty Valance* was really about legend duking it out with history," Gus observed. "Legend wins. That's what Westerns are all about. That's what Ford's always known. He's just lost his touch. That's all. Go for the truth, and you have to beat your audience. Go for legend, and the audience will stand there at the rail, tongues out."

"Excuse me," said Stella, rising. "No," she put up her dry old hand in an admonishing gesture, "Eden, Annie, Ginny, you stay here. I will begin the dishes."

"Anyway, it was good to see old Rex, wasn't it, baby?" said Gus.

Beverly agreed that it was. "We went on the set with him, too, a huge studio there in Rome. Cinecittà, a city of film."

"How can Rex be in Italian or German movies?" asked Annie. "Rex Hogan can barely read English."

Gus shrugged. "Who cares if you read? Who cares what language you speak? There isn't any script. Some flunky waves his arms at the actors. Everything is mimed out. Like the silent films. Bang bang. The story. Not the script. The script doesn't matter."

"Does anyone really write this shit?" said Matt in a low voice.

Beverly laughed. "The actors can speak any language they want. They dub the voices afterwards. Someone else writes it in English. It's all dubbed in a studio."

"So it's come sort of full circle, hasn't it?" Matt bolted the last of his limoncello and grew contemplative. "My uncle was ruined when the talkies came in because his English was so broken up. And now, in Rome, they're dubbing

American actors to speak Italian in stories about the American west. Ernesto should have lived so long." Matt looked up and gave his wife a pained and piercing stare. "He really should have."

Eden wanted to chase Gus and Beverly out with a flyswatter, but she sat very still, almost unmoving, chin raised.

"Well, it's damned ironic," said Gus, "that right when the Western falls on its face here in America, that guys like Rex Hogan are doing great in Europe, because they can get on and off a horse. And these European Westerns, they make them so cheap! The Europeans work for pennies. Pennies! No unions. The shoot goes dawn to dusk, no breaks." He nodded to Annie. "Oasis would be out of business."

"People need to eat," she said.

"Not on the director's time. They work for a fraction of what an American crew would cost you. Actors can be had for a song. Maybe that's where you should be working, Matt. A wop making films in Rome about the American West."

"Your money would go a lot further," said Beverly.

"What money?" snapped Eden. Then she composed herself. She spoke in a voice worthy of Winifred Merton. "I think Matt's getting overtired. It's been a long day." The Event was over.


EDEN TURNED ON THEIR BEDSIDE LAMP AND HELPED HIM UNDRESS. HIS show of strength was ended. He sat on the bed and she pulled off his boots. "Soon you'll be going everywhere in these boots, Matt."

"With no front teeth."

"They can be fixed. Everything can be fixed, Matt."

He eased himself back into the bed. "Stay with me, Eden." He moved so she could sit beside him. "I can't tell you how good it is to be home."

She brushed his hair from his face. "All those people. I shouldn't have—"

"They were fine. It was good to see everybody. I was touched you'd invite Gus and Beverly, I know you don't much like them."

"I don't dislike them," she replied, a tarnished truth if ever there was one.

"They've been good to me, Eden. They're good friends. Good people. I just about cried when they came to the hospital to see me. They lost all that money on *Gold of the Yukon,* but they didn't have one word of recrimination. I said how sorry I was, and they wouldn't hear of it. And you saw them today, real supportive, not like people who've backed a failure. They didn't even mention

*Gold of the Yukon.* They had new ideas. Like they didn't even think I was a failure."

"You're not a failure. Don't say that."

"*Gold of the Yukon* will never get made. It's over."

"Who cares? Forget all that. I won't hear of it." And she meant it. "You're no failure."

He took a shallow breath so as not to tax his ribs. "Oh yes I am. A failure and a liar, and worse, a fake. Me, I'm the one who's always looking for the authentic, and I'm a fake."

"I won't let you say that. It's not true."

"I wish I'd never heard of *Gold of the Yukon.*"

"Oh, Matt." Eden started to cry.

"I don't know what I was thinking. . . ." He held her hand to his lips, and after a while removed it. "Yes, I do. I was thinking that I'd have something that people would point to, and say, Matt March did that. That I would put the American west up on the screen the way I see it in my head, in my heart. Not cardboard characters like the Lariat Lawman, but the stories of flawed men and women who ran from the past to the west and met each day with courage, even if they were afraid, who wrestled with the elements, with violence. That's the real story of the Western, and I was going to tell it," he scoffed, "in Vista-Vision."

"You have VistaVision. You do. Think of *Lariat* for all those years."

"Television trash. Gus was right."

"He's wrong."

"Clichés, all of it, flushed down the television toilet. Rightly so. No one will ever watch it again. I wanted something permanent, Eden. Something that I could point to, a real achievement, that people would remember me, Eden, remember that the Marches created something authentic."

"You have, Matt. You have." But she struggled to keep from blubbering out sobs.

"I've lived a lie since the day I denied my own father at school, since I played at Captain Propaganda, since I thought I could restore a train to life. I'm a liar, a fake, and a failure."

To keep from crying, she brought her face down to his and brushed his lips and murmured that his strength would return, and yes, his vision, his VistaVision, and his spirits. She encouraged and supported and whispered against his ear, though in her heart Eden dreaded his dreams. The ambition she had always admired in him, that she had fostered from the beginning, now seemed to her a quagmire of wasted hope and squandered time and vanished money. The abyss of what they owed, or would owe from the accident, even though they had insurance, yawned before her. The lies Matt had told her, all of them, the secrets he had kept, mocked and hurt and humiliated her, and yet, at this moment, Eden wanted nothing more than to see him grab hold of a new dream, and again illuminate the small firmament in which she and her children and Stella lived. She wanted Matt to be the bright center of Greenwater again. And she wanted all this knowing that when he once lavished himself on this dream, she would be left to look after the mundane, that—as Afton had once said of him—Matt would abandon her, forsake the routine, the temporal, the ordinary, and move beyond or above her, into some rarefied atmosphere where only he could breathe, where she could not. Once Matt came upon, embraced some new dream—and he would—the past would flicker before her like an old play in a new venue. Excess and elation—and their opposites, desolation and despair— were as ingrained in Matt March as his once-punctured lung. They could no more be plucked out than could his heart.

# Chocolate Tangerines

Carefully peel your tangerines. They must be absolutely fresh, with fine fresh skins, not old. If there is white pith on the tangerine, pick it off gently. Set some water on to heat in a double boiler, if you have one. If not, use another pan, or a bowl set in a colander, to melt perhaps $1/3$ cup high-quality bittersweet chocolate (for about 4 tangerines).

In a shallow bowl, pour some fragrant honey. Turn each tangerine over and around in the honey till it is coated. Then place it on the saucer or shallow broad bowl that you will use to serve each. When your chocolate has melted, and keeping it warm, use a soup spoon and ladle the chocolate gently atop the tangerine. It will slide down the sides, but should not cover the fruit. The colorful contrasts are part of the charm. Then, with a toothpick or a very slender knife, "pop" the center of the tangerine so the chocolate will go down inside as well. Put a nice fat, fresh sprig of mint down the center. For any remaining chocolate, use a knife edge to drape or lace in threads and swirls around the saucer.

These can be made the same day you are to serve them. The chocolate will harden into a cap. The honey will slide down the sides of the tangerine and collect in a little pool at the base. To serve, put a dash, a couple of tablespoons, no more, of Cointreau or some other amber liqueur outside the circle of honey. Eat with a knife and fork.

Very festive for a winter meal.

# SNAPSHOT

### College Essay

For her 1971 college entrance application essays, Liza Ruth March described her education in Rome, how she had worn the sweet little smock required of Italian schoolchildren, a big bow at her neck. Liza's college essay said that after three months in Rome when she was eleven years old, she spoke fluent Italian. Certainly better than her sister, Stellina. Actors they met at Cinecittà remarked on how adorable were the March girls—especially Liza—and how apt was her Roman accent. So successful was this beautifully groomed college essay that Liza got a full scholarship to Vassar, her first choice. Liza wanted to go as far east as possible. Liza was sick of the golden west.

Liza's college essay began with her father's difficult recovery from an accident in the snow. It took a whole year. Then he was well and fine and fit again and he went to Rome in January 1964. Paul Pierino, a set decorator who was a longtime friend of the March family, got Daddy a job at Cinecittà writing dubbed English dialogue for sword-and-sandal films, and a couple of Westerns. Cinecittà was lucky to have her father. No one knew the west like Daddy. The rest of the family joined him in February or March, something like that.

Mercifully, the essay didn't have to be that specific.

So Liza could gloss the bit about how her mother had planned that they would go to Rome in June after school was out. They went in February instead because . . . Liza's essay evaded her mother's increasing alarm at Daddy's nearly daily aerogrammes scrawled on tissuey paper. The letters were exuberant and erratic, sometimes dazzled, sometimes despairing. And his phone calls. Daddy's phone calls from Rome made her mother pale, and her grandmother bead-bumble. Liza blamed the phone. Liza detested the phone.

Never mind. Off they went! To Rome! To live in the apartment Daddy had rented on Via Paolo Emilio near the Vatican. Her grandmother was so happy to live near the Vatican, she walked there every day.

When the Roman school term ended, Daddy bought a secondhand Fiat, and they went on a long vacation all over Italy. Daddy's driving was fearless.

Liza's essay read: *Summer 1964, at the age of eleven, I saw the sun rise up out of the blue Adriatic and set in the bronzed Mediterranean. I went to Tuscany, to Poggibonsi, and met people who remembered my grandfather.* For the college admission boards, she waxed eloquent about narrow streets, sunny piazzas, and left out that Poggibonsi was possibly the dullest town on the planet.

## CHAPTER THREE

EDEN ROLLED UP AGAINST MATT, RELISHING THE
warmth they had created between their bodies. Created
effortlessly, and yet it seemed to her actively generated,
and much to be cherished. It was theirs. It would never
be anyone else's. She loved these moments, when she first
opened her eyes and waved goodbye to whatever dream
had enlivened the night, when she became aware of
Matt's bulk and warmth beside her. He pulled her close.

Already cries came up from the street below. Eden
recognized her daughters' voices, and their small, ongoing tiffs. They must be having breakfast on the little hotel terrace that fronted the piazza. Poggibonsi was a
strange, small, utterly insulated town. Few people spoke
English, and tourists seldom came here. Why would you
unless you were on your way somewhere else? In which
case, you wouldn't go to or even through Poggibonsi.
And yet, Matt brought his best self here to dazzle and
impress the locals. They'd been in Poggibonsi a matter
of days, and Matt had won over everyone, from the sour
old vendor to the youngest hotel maid. He trotted out the

stories of his father and uncle and the cousin with the garage apartment. If his Italian wasn't equal to the telling, Matt had Liza tell them. Liza's Italian was remarkable, fluent.

A knock sounded at their door, and Eden flung a light wrap over her gauzy nightgown. "Coming. I'm coming." She'd no sooner opened the door than Nicky bounded in with a whoop, showing off a small wooden Pinocchio doll he said someone had given him. With its red hat and long nose, wide eyes, the little doll spoke to Nicky in his own language.

Stella lumbered in after him and sat down. "Tell the truth, Nicky. She did not give it to you. The vendor, over there, across the piazza," she said to Matt and Eden, "you know the one I mean, Nicky goes over to her, thinking he could just ask her and get it." She wagged her finger at Nicky and said, "You are a very bad boy," though clearly she did not believe it. "The old lady sent him back to me. So I told him, Nicky, you want that toy, you must ask. In Italian." Stella looked immensely pleased with herself.

"Did you ask in Italian?" Matt picked him up and nuzzled his neck. The child cried out with delight.

"He did. Very polite. Carried on a whole conversation," said Stella.

"So, you see," said Eden, more to Matt than to the child, "when Nicky wants something, he really can exert himself. You should make him do more, Matt. Charm won't get you everywhere."

"Why not? We're here, aren't we?" He laughed. "Okay, everyone out! Eden and I are getting dressed and coming downstairs this minute, and we're off to Siena."

"Why we didn't stay in a hotel in Siena, I'll never know," grumbled Stella, rising.

"Mama! Anyone can stay in Siena. You have to belong here to stay in Poggibonsi! They know us here. They know the family!"

"They're pulling your leg, Matt," scoffed Stella. "You spend more money that way."

THE CANVAS AWNINGS OVERHEAD FLAPPED IN THE WIND AS THEY SAT OVER the last of their late lunch. The bread dried on the plate and the shallow bowl of oil was flecked with crumbs. Shadows darkened the rim of the Campo, the great piazza shaped like a sloping saucer down to the building that served as Siena's heart and navel. People milled, some under hats to protect them from the late August sunlight. Two violinists, their cases open at their feet, played well-known pieces, opera mostly, and the thin strains caught in the shell of the piazza and echoed. Nicky, sitting on the slope near his family, played with his Pinocchio, pulling at the arms, making its legs dance while its expression remained unchanged. Not far away, Stellina drew chalk pictures on the rugged old brick. Liza's book was spread out before her; elbow on the table, she read.

Matt reached for Eden's hand, bringing it to his lips. She was startled, but smiled at him appreciatively. He reached across the table for Stella's hand. He beamed at them both. "Well, we've had a great time, haven't we?"

"Except for your driving," said Stella. "Your driving has made an old woman of me."

Eden laughed lightly. Matt's driving was equal to any Italian's, fast, fearless, and full of high spirits. Since they had left Rome and started north, his driving was erratic, but his affection was constant; warmth bubbled up from a spring deep within him and his generous spirit bloomed. With his children he was indulgent. With his mother he was tender. With Eden, there was satisfaction at night and fulfillment by day. To be in Matt's orbit that summer was to feel his vitality splash on you; he was like one of those fountains you need only be near to be suddenly awakened, and to discover you have been heretofore asleep. Any passerby would hear the fountain's simple splash as music, feel its spray as tonic, see its cascade not as falling water but as recurring rainbows. Eden kicked off one espadrille and under the table stroked his leg with her bare foot. She played with her hair, grown out now, pulled away from her face, and lying on her shoulders.

Matt caught the waiter's attention and asked for three coffees and two of whatever was best on the dessert menu.

"I can't eat anything more," said Eden.

"I can! So it's back to Rome from here! And then, back to California. And we'll all be together again when I get home from Spain."

"Spain?" Eden's languid mood evaporated. "Spain? But what about all that work you're doing in Rome?"

"I'm off to Spain to look—just quickly—at the locations that Sergio used for *The Magnificent Stranger*. I'm close, that close," he brought two fingers together, "to putting it all in motion, Eden, everything I've dreamed of. You go home next week, and I'll be right behind you."

Eden glanced at Liza's intense expression; she exchanged looks with Stella who ever since Matt's accident had developed a nervous habit of bumbling nonexistent rosary beads. "Why shouldn't we stay? We can stay in Rome while you go to Spain."

"Because I need to work! This—" he motioned broadly to the ocher canvas overhead, the cinnamon-colored bricks baking in the sunlight, dissolving in the shadow, "is not our real life. Our real life is in California. I will make this movie, and come home to California a hero, and then we'll all come back to Rome for final edits."

"You're already a hero, Daddy," said Liza, closing her book, not marking her place.

Matt gave an enthusiastic chuckle. "Our backs must be to Babylon, princess. You ask your mother. Our eyes on Zion."

"What does that mean?" Liza demanded.

Matt ignored her. He spoke to Eden. "That's where my eyes are. Zion at Cinecittà, Zion in Spain, Zion. A vision! You know, like you always told me, Brigham Young and *This is the place!* This is the place for me. Right now. Not forever, but for now. I need this place. This chance. You go home and I will be right behind you, and when I come home, you'll be proud of me."

"I'm already proud of you, Matt. You don't need to prove yourself to me. To us. You don't need to prove yourself to anyone. Why can't you just stay with us? Come home to California, work at Greenwater, and be a happy man?"

"I am a happy man!"

"Then why are you sending us away?"

"Don't make so much of this, Eden." He pulled her close and kissed her forehead.

Nicky brought his Pinocchio back to the table and crawled into his mother's lap, put his head against her shoulder.

"Here," said Matt, unfurling some lire from his wallet, "Nicky, go give this to the musicians. You must always pay the musicians. Here, Stellina! You too. Take this money. Liza, here."

"Not me," said Liza. "I'm staying."

He watched the two children run down the sloping piazza. He turned to Eden. "I bought your tickets last week. A surprise."

Like your first wife, Eden wanted to say. But Liza knew nothing of that episode in Matt's life, and Eden intended it should stay that way. If Liza had not been there, she might have made other snapping retorts, remarking on Matt's other surprises. Call it surprise, or call it subterfuge. A secret is a secret. Eden March had her own secrets. She had lost her faith in Matt. She did not trust him, though she still loved him. Love lives in strange corners and under strange, deprived conditions, thrives where a less hardy emotion would wither. "We're not leaving you here alone."

"Alone! How can I be alone in Rome!"

"Oh, I have no doubt that you won't be alone," said Eden, keeping her gaze on the Campo. "I have no doubt that you have plenty of friends willing to take our places in your life."

"Please, Eden. No one can take your place. Ever."

"You'd stay here without us, Daddy?" asked Liza.

"For a month. A month or so. I can clean everything up in few months."

"What does that mean, Daddy?"

"I can't explain here." He spread his arm out to the sepia-colored stones as if the Middle Ages were about to commence. "Not now."

"It's not good for you to be alone," declared Stella.

"A man with work is never alone," he replied. "A quick trip to Spain. It's all so cheap! I can't believe it myself! It's just like Gus said. You can make a master-piece here for fifty thousand dollars! Less!"

Eden groaned aloud and gulped down a knot in her throat. Don't ask too much, she reminded herself, or you risk losing everything. She had long since peeled her fingers from the original dream of their joint ventures. *Lariat Lawman* was so far in the past it seemed like a museum piece of her life. The Baxters had replaced her as Matt's partner. And though Eden detested and distrusted them, they had aided in Matt's recovery, and Eden had accepted their help in order to see him well. After the accident, his recovery was re-markable. Matt himself—with characteristic largesse and generosity—credited his swift convalescence to his wife's good cooking, to his mother's prayers, and his children's affection. But the truth, as Eden well knew, lay elsewhere. The truth was that the prospects that the Baxters had unfurled, dangled before him, had invigorated his imagination, galvanized Matt. His eagerness to be part of everything new and exciting about the old Western hastened his recuperation. Eden had wanted him recovered, whole and well. And now she knew she had sown the wind.

Eden kept her chin in her hand, thoughtfully watching Nick and Stellina run over the sunlit stones toward the violinist who stood at the edge of seeping shadows. He grinned to see the children fling money into his case. The music picked up tempo.

"Look at that boy chase the pigeons," Matt said, as Nicky scampered back up the sloping piazza, his arms flying. "Doesn't he ever get tired? He runs them off, but the pigeons will always come back. The pigeons are eternal." He flung his arm across Eden's chair, tousled Liza's dark curly hair, and leaned back with the expansiveness of a man contented in all things.

*  *  *

NOTHING SEEMED TO TOUCH NICKY'S SUNNY'S DISPOSITION, BUT ON THEIR return to Rome, Liza, Stellina, Eden, and Stella were grim, subdued, saddened. Matt's refusal to acknowledge their pain at this parting only deepened it.

Liza had a desperate, flailing tantrum, beating on his chest, crying, accusing him of wanting them gone, of not loving them. Eden watched helplessly as Matt used the same tactic on his child that he had used on his wife, turning Liza's sadness and anxiety into a test of her faith in him: If she really loved Daddy and believed in him, Liza would be brave and set an example to her little sister and brother. She believed in her daddy, didn't she?

As Eden lay beside Matt that night, she spoke into the darkness. "How can you use the love we feel for you as a weapon against us? Against a child? How can you do something so low?"

Matt turned on his side.

The next day Liza started packing her things, ready to leave bravely, because she believed in her father and he was proud of her. Stellina, too. Nicky didn't care where he went, as long as he would be with his mother and grandmother.

The day before they were to leave, Stella returned to the apartment from her morning prayers at St. Peter's and announced that a vision had come to her, a voice. A saint, or an angel. Perhaps the Virgin herself, there in the Vatican. What could be more holy? This voice told her not to leave. She must stay in Rome.

"If I leave now," Stella said, her jaw squared with resolution, "the Virgin, an angel told me, I will not see my son again in this life. I will stay here. The voice, the Virgin, the angel told me to stay here. I heard this voice as clearly as I hear you." She pointed to Matt. "It spoke in English," she added.

Matt fumed and railed, reasoned and roared. He ordered his mother to go, but Stella said his orders were nothing compared to heavenly voices sent to her in the holy precincts of St. Peter's. Stella unpacked, and sat in the chair in her room, arms folded over her breasts, face grim.

Matt stormed out of her room, slamming the door, swearing. The children cowered in the small living room where their suitcases were stacked. He found Eden in their bedroom, adding the last small things to her suitcase.

"You take her with you," Matt ordered. "Whether she wants to go or not. You hear me?"

"This is between you and Stella. Not me. Talk to her."

"But you're my wife!"

"Yes," she replied with the kind of dignity one can sometimes muster in surrender, "and I am leaving. Just as you wanted."

"It is not what I want! It's what's best! It's—"

"Please, Matt," said Eden, looking up, "spare me all that. Don't insult me on top of breaking my heart. Isn't it enough that you're getting rid of us?"

"That's not what's happening. You don't understand! You don't believe!"

"Stop. Please. I can't bear another word."

"You take her with you."

"Who I am to quarrel with saints and angels? You quarrel with them, Matt. I will not."


BUT IT DID NOT HAPPEN AS STELLA'S VISION FORETOLD.

On a September afternoon, Stella and Matt finished lunch, Matt wiped his lips, and proclaimed it a magnificent meal. "The tortellini with your sauce, Mama! That is the best! The wine! Wonderful."

While they lived in Rome, Stella always kept a vat of this sauce ready and on the stove. Matt said he loved it, that it reminded him of special occasions, coming home. And Stella felt the fleeting nip of conscience stir her cooking, as if she could give her son in middle age what she had denied him as a child. She liked cooking for him. When Eden and the children left, Stella missed them, but she enjoyed having Matt to herself. She had never had him to herself.

"I'm off to work. I won't be back till late. Don't wait up."

"You're going to work now? This time of day? Everyone is at home."

"Well, these guys want to make American movies, so they work American hours."

He held her in an exuberant hug, and again applauded her cooking. Even when he was lying, he was extravagant. Stella thanked him with her usual reserve. Even when she was pleased, she held something back.


MATT MARCH LEFT THE APARTMENT, WALKED TO THE CORNER, HAILED A cab, and took it to a dreary suburb. He booked a room and rode the tiny creaking elevator upstairs to the fourth floor. It smelled bad, like dog urine. He stepped out of the elevator to find plastic philodendrons on either side; their leaves were thick with dust and pocked with cigarette burns. The hall was long, dim, deserted. Once in his room, and the door clicked shut behind him, Matt turned the lock. He put the briefcase on the hotel bed, which had a rumpled, rakish look, even though it was made, as if remembered assignations yet lurked in its coils.

IN THE VIA PAOLO EMILIO APARTMENT, STELLA CLEARED THE DISHES AND turned on the television. A children's program played while she washed them. The children's voices were bright, but they made her miss Nicky too much. She turned the television off. She took a nap.

About five-thirty, she woke, rose, left the apartment with a shopping bag and her purse to make her usual rounds, the meat market, the greengrocer, and St. Peter's, though not in that order. She went first to the church. It would be disrespectful to bring raw meat into the church.

MATT SNAPPED HIS BRIEFCASE OPEN. HE TOOK OUT THE FOUNTAIN PEN Eden had given him last Christmas. There was a bureau in the room and a small desk with a telephone. He opened the desk drawer but found no hotel stationery. He sat on the bed, pen in hand, for a long while. Then he called down to the desk and asked for some paper and some ice. The clerk chuckled, and said ice, of course, but paper? Most people did not come to this hotel to write.

"Just bring it up," said Matt in English.

While he waited, he stood at the open window. An uninspired view, a narrow street, laundry hanging over balconies and late sun reflecting on the windows, inchoate noises, a radio, dogs barking, traffic, the smell of exhaust and anonymous cooking. A children's program played on a nearby TV.

He closed the window, drew the blinds. He moved to the mirror and met his own reflection: forty-two years old, husband, father of three, dreamer and dilettante, lover and son, an American failure. An authentic American failure. When the ice and paper arrived, he tipped the boy, closed and locked the door. He sat at the desk. He wrote two notes. One to his wife, one to his mother. Perhaps he knew, even then, that there was nothing he could say to his children.

Scrawled notes, rambling, returning always to his love for them, asking only forgiveness. Forgiveness not only for his weakness but for his failures. His love for them was authentic. He wept as he wrote, and his tears splotched the ink, diluted the dream he once had of an American story. The authentic American story. He had to stop writing, walk to the window, breathe deep. He had promised himself he would not tread through those old dreams again. There was no time now to say all that again.

There was no time now to explain that the Baxters were not investors. The Baxters were in real estate. They had time and money. They had been unfailingly generous, allowing Matt always more credit and waving away his protests that he could, he would pay it back. Enormous sums. Unthinkable sums. He did not say that he had secured these loans with the Greenwater Movie Ranch. And that he had defaulted. Paid back nothing. Not even the interest. Sometimes time is not money. Greenwater had been his, deeded to him by Ernesto, his alone, terra firma collateral. He did not write that the Baxters had called in his loans. He did not say that he knew, these past months in Italy, in these weeks that they had watched the sun rise in the blue Adriatic and set in the bronzed Mediterranean, that every day they were together, these were the last good times. He did not say that the Baxters be damned, he had spent thousands and thousands, millions in lire, once he knew what lay ahead. Bankruptcy. Loss. And this. This hotel room. This paper. This pen.

Matt March had promised himself he would write till he ran out of ink. He had not brought more. The flow thinned, and he shook the pen. He began another avowal of love, but the pen ran completely dry. He shook it again and again. There was so much more to say.

Perhaps not.

Between six and seven in the evening of September 6, 1964, Matt March tucked these notes on either side of the oval mirror.

He turned his back on the mirror, walked to the bed, opened the briefcase, took out the gun, sat on the bed, and put the gun in his mouth.

STELLA, CARRYING HER PARCELS, AN ONION'S JAUNTY GOLDEN HEAD ATOP the bag, opened the street door to the Via Paolo Emilio apartment. She was already panting slightly and did not relish the climb up three stories. Still, she never trusted the elevator. She would take her time on the stairs. She looked up the long marble flights. Three of them. She stopped on each landing, catching her breath, exchanging little greetings with young people who dashed up and down the stairwell. She was getting old.

Stella put her key in the apartment door and turned the lock. She heard its mechanisms fall into place, like the careful cocking of the hammer on the pistol. She stepped in and heard the door close behind her, but not the barrel turning. She put her purse and key on the table and walked down the hall, hearing her heels snap on the marble floor, but not the trigger pulled, not the shot, not the gun firing, not the bullet propelling deep into Matt's brain, absolving him of all earthly woe.

This sauce needs to be "built." Start with roasted garlic. Cut off the tops of three or four garlics, and pull away the papery stuff. Set each on a square of foil and drizzle over each a little olive oil, kosher salt, and fresh-ground pepper. Cover with foil. Bake at 350 oven for about an hour. Cool. These can be done days before. Anytime you have the oven on for something else.

In a deep heavy-bottomed pan, heat some olive oil, at least $\frac{1}{4}$ cup. Thin slice a couple of onions. Sauté quickly, then slow cook these onions, lid askew, till they turn a deep golden brown, at least 30 minutes, giving them a stir now and then.

When the onions are golden, add a whole fistful of fresh herbs, chopped, but not minced, heavy on the basil, the parsley, oregano, and the thyme. Strip the thyme quickly, holding them from the top, so you don't get little sticks in your sauce. If the basil is out of season, then just omit. Do not use dried basil. Go light on any rosemary you use. Rosemary is for remembrance and too powerful.

Squeeze the cloves of garlic from the roasted heads into the herbs and onions. Stir.

To this add six or seven pounds of tomatoes. Peeled are best, but not absolutely essential for taste. Or a few big cans of diced or crushed tomatoes. Then take any red table wine, and splash in. Your sauce at this point will be bright red in color. Slowly simmer the sauce for several hours, adding a little wine, over the first couple of hours, stir, let the sauce absorb. By the time it's done, the sauce should be a rich burgundy color and no longer bright red. Add kosher salt and fresh ground pepper to taste.

At its best, let it rest off heat. Add what you like, sausage, mushrooms, etc., before serving.

This sauce will keep well in the fridge. And live in memory.

# SNAPSHOT

## THE GREENWATER COWBOYS

Greenwater still exists. Even today, from an aerial view, flying west, the terrestrial contours of the four hundred acres are still discernable even under the mosaic of stucco and shingle and asphalt. Greenwater's main, four-lane artery, Baxter Boulevard, is lined with miles of strip malls, dry cleaners, banks and bars, franchise food chains, gas stations, the occasional skateboard shop, and a tattoo parlor. Nothing except the zip code distinguishes the city of Greenwater, California, from any other municipality in the San Fernando Valley. Or anywhere else for that matter.

Unlike the small noisy plane that scouted out Greenwater that day in May 1960, if you flew over now, you would see a landscape studded with turquoise swimming pools strung like beads on long concrete threads that loop through acres of tract homes. The subdivisions are built over the ghosts of the ranch house, the fort and Indian village, the Mexican cantina, over Lariat's school and saloons, over the blacksmith and barbershop, over the cemetery where no one is buried. In the Greenwater, California, subdivisions the streets have names like Sagebrush Drive, Indian Village, Ranch Avenue, Cantina Court. The houses—all sixties' vintage tracts, short driveways, small lawns—simmer in the dust-nubbled smog.

Before these subdivisions could be built, the whole place had to be bulldozed. The town of Lariat was the last to go. The Baxters allowed the Los Angeles County Fire Department to torch it for practice and training. Firemen set the blaze, and fought it by the book, but the wind shifted, and Lariat did not burn as the firefighters had expected a movie set would. These were not mere flimsy structures. False or not, this town—wood, and brick, beam and bolt—had been built to last. While firefighters struggled with the rest of Lariat, flames engulfing the cemetery where no one was buried grew restless. They leaped to the surrounding brush, and the wind blew behind them, whispering, urging them onward, up the hills. Terrified tumbleweeds fled, trailing embers that sparked the dry brush. The exercise went awry. For two days smoke darkened the sky for miles while the firemen and firetrucks and hoses battled the fire. Greenwater Movie Ranch blackened, then smoldered for weeks till at last the bulldozers growled against what was left. The crunch and crumble of Matt March's vision must have been excruciating, but no one heard it. No one remembered Sweet Betsy from Pike.

Nothing in Greenwater, California, is left to testify to Matt March's Vista-Vision, unless you count the Greenwater High School Cowboys. The GHS cheerleaders wear green and white western outfits, slick, short fringed skirts with hats they can toss in the air when the Greenwater Cowboys are victorious. The drill team wears holsters for their batons and flags; the school mascot is a horse. When the Cowboy Marching Band went to the Rose Parade in 2003, they were led by a trick rider, a smiling girl, standing on horseback, waving to the millions of people watching the parade on television. The Cowboy Marching Band wears western outfits, too, hats, boots, green shirts with white fringe.

Greenwater, California, with its zip code and high school, is not that far away from Universal Studios, Hollywood, with its amphitheater and theme park. At Universal trolleys with attractive young tour guides convey paying customers—audiences, really—around Universal's sets where movies are made. *Please keep your arms and legs on the bus at all times. Whoa, pardner, watch out for that special effect!* Universal began these tours in 1964, the same year that Matt March died with his boots on.

Matt's debts might have been forgiven in heaven, but they were not forgiven on earth.

His death opened up the morass of his complicated affairs, tangled agreements signed in secret, secret at least from his wife; his death created a flurry, a storm of legal documents that fell like snow over a long, long winter. An avalanche. The white paper, the black print, the prose all starched and formal and in triplicate, petitioning the court, advising the plaintiffs, passed between attorneys until the Baxters' attorneys proved, finally, and beyond any doubt, that they owned Greenwater Movie Ranch, all four hundred acres. Time is money.

The Baxters settled with Eden March before the whole mess actually came to the courtroom. The Baxters conceded that a tiny morsel—the scrap on which sat the house itself, the garden, the pool—could go to the widow. They offered this as a gift, not a concession of their claims. They then made Eden an immediate offer—through her attorney—to buy the land back. Her attorney wrangled from them that the widow and her family would have six months to vacate the premises. Eden accepted. She never had to see Gus and Beverly.

Eden, Stella, Liza, Stellina, and Nicky packed and vacated the premises. The house came down. Ernesto's gun, uncovered, upturned, was not actually discovered, and fell back to earth. It remains buried under the patio of 3246 Hacienda Drive, a four-bedroom, three-bath plan with adjoining two-car garage.

Other than that, there's nothing left to suggest what Ernest March first saw here in 1927, though bulldozers spared those few old trees that dotted the hills near the lake. These live oaks, including the hanging tree, are ornamental for Agua Verde Golf Course. Low condos surround the golf course, none, however, with a view of the lake itself. In summer, the lake often dries up, retreats from the shore, its muddy lips curling back in disdain.

The vision Ernesto had of Agua Verde, the place that he created, really, from the partnership of the camera and projector, the darkened theatre, the light upon the silent screen, all vanished. All gone. Ernesto's last vista of Agua Verde resounded with Kitty's screams, as they flailed and clung to each other, as the rowboat drifted away, and the green waters closed over their heads.

Late-evening golfers playing the Agua Verde course always remark on hearing muffled laughter, voices. People who live in the golf course condos complain of late night music, thin, simple tunes they cannot place and that, on investigation, seemingly have no source.

People say that sound carries over water. They just don't say what it carries.

MINE! MINE! MINE! THEIR CRIES SPIRALED UP TO Eden, who was in Nicky's room, packing the last of his things. Open suitcases yawned across the bed, and half-empty boxes littered the floor. Eden dashed out into the hall and yelled down the stairs for the girls to quit fighting. The stairwell was strewn with toys, and she maneuvered these quickly as she darted through the rooms, toward the girls' escalating voices. Their voices echoed because the house was almost empty, the rugs, the furniture sold.

Eden found Liza and Stellina struggling over the bathroom door. They each tugged on the handle, this way and that, each crying, "Mine!" Liza had a screwdriver in her hand, and Eden snatched it from her. Stellina clutched a heavy pillowcase that dragged on the floor; Stellina fell over it with her whole body, bursting into tears.

"What are you doing with this? What are you fighting over?"

"Gimme back my screwdriver," said Liza, still kneeling in front of the bathroom door.

"What's in that pillowcase?" Eden demanded. "Let me have it." Stellina got up off the pillowcase and Eden opened it. Doorknobs. Eden glanced around; all the downstairs doorknobs had been removed. The glass doorknobs lay at the bottom of the bag.

"She won't let me have any of them," Stellina wailed. "She's keeping them all."

"Why are you taking off the doorknobs, Liza?" asked Eden.

"Why shouldn't I take them? Why shouldn't I take everything I can? You're letting them tear it all down. They'll tear the house down, they'll burn it just like they burned Lariat." She waved vehemently in the direction of the front door.

The brush fires were out, at last, but the smell of soot still hung heavy in the air, and all the doors and windows were closed. Even so, somewhere earth moved, bulldozers grumbled. The leveling of Greenwater had started some weeks before.

"I'm unscrewing all the doorknobs, and I'm taking them with me, and you can't stop me. You either," Liza snapped at Stellina, who ran away, crying, toward the dining room.

Eden considered this. "Can you share the doorknobs?"

"No. They're mine. They're all I have after you sold out to those Baxters! You gave them everything!" Liza hunched, her arms over her chest, pressing against breasts that were still foreign to her, still felt as though they belonged to someone else, someone she didn't know. Pimples dotted her face, her neck was too long, and her big feet suggested that she would be a tall woman like her mother, but her face was her father's. "You can make me sad," she muttered to no one in particular, "but you can't make me cry."

"Cry," said Eden, kneeling down and enveloping the girl. "Go ahead, baby. You get it out, just cry all you want." Eden pressed her, stroked her hair.

Liza wept till she hiccuped. "It's all your fault."

Eden held her, soothed her, even rocked her while Liza wept and fought and Eden repeated the litany, now nine months old, still without efficacy no matter how many times she repeated, *It's no one's fault, not even Daddy's, there's no one to blame and nothing we could have done differently. We must move, we can't stay here. We will have a whole new adventure in Washington.* These and other phrases spiraled out continually as though Eden were spinning a rope bridge across the abyss of their lives.

She held Liza till her feet started to go to sleep underneath her, then she rose, drew a deep breath, and said in more astringent voice, "Take the doorknobs. I don't care. But do not point that screwdriver or any other tool at your sister again. You understand me, Liza March? Do that again and I will punish you. Answer me."

"I want to take the pool and the trees and the windows and the doors. I want to take it all and I can't."

"That's what your heart is for, Liza. Your heart and mind and memory. You can carry whatever you like there."

"I can't, and I won't, and it is all your fault. You made us leave Daddy there."

"You might like to think that, but you know it's not true."

Liza hung her head, and Eden gave her back the screwdriver and went to look for Stellina in the dining room, where Stella now slept on a rollaway bed. The furniture had all been sold.

Since Stella had returned from Rome in the weeks following Matt's death, she refused to go upstairs anymore. Stella slept in the dining room, indeed stayed there, seldom came out. Eden found her sitting on the bed, the bed made, Stella fully dressed as though awaiting a cab to take her on some penultimate journey.

"Where's Stellina?" Eden asked. "I saw her come this way."

"I sent her to the kitchen."

"You sent her away? You couldn't put your arms around her? You couldn't do that much? Stellina needs you. I need you, we all need you," Eden added when Stella's eyes closed, and her mouth cinched up. "You are not the only one suffering here, Stella. Think of the kids."

"He destroyed us. He is in hell. How can I think of anything but that?"

"You must try. You must."

"I want to die here, and you won't let me. Leave me here. Let them destroy the house around my head."

"July first," Eden said in the same steely tone of voice she had just used with Liza. "We have to be out by July first. As soon as I get everything packed, we're leaving, and you're coming with us." She went to close the door, but found that Liza had already taken the glass knob.

Though Eden's own strength and resolve tattered and frayed, almost daily, she would not permit herself to dissolve. The rest of family might, but not Eden. When she needed to, which was often, she leaned on Ginny and Les, on Annie, and even her stolid brother, Ernest, had stepped in to shoulder any burdens he could share. Eden could not imagine living through the last nine months without them. Stella had crumbled entirely, waited, wanted only to die; she had to be persuaded even to eat. The children, especially the girls, sobbed

themselves into hysterics, and had to be watched continually, to be fed like babies. Ginny Doyle moved a camp bed in Liza's room and stayed there for two
weeks; Annie did the same for Stellina. And then Eden had a burst of genius.
She went out and bought a dog, a black Lab, a big friendly oaf of a dog. She
drove home, opened the door, and let him charge through the house, delighting
the children with his antics, with his unremitting energy and affection. They
named him Buster.

Eden found Buster now, with Nick and Stellina at the kitchen table, Stellina
with her head in her arms, and Nicky sitting quietly beside her, clutching his
Pinocchio doll to his chest. Buster jumped up to see Eden. He barked, and
wagged his tail. Eden touched her children's shoulders. "Let's go outside," she
said. "Let's find Buster's ball."

Buster bounded out, barking playfully. Eden found his ball on the patio and
gave it to Stellina who tossed it; the dog leapt after it, and the children pursued.

The patio furniture was gone, sold, and now there were only a few folding
metal chairs where she sometimes sat at night with Annie and Ernest, with
Ginny and Les. Eden wandered out to the pool, which was filthy. She lifted her
sweaty hair off the back of her neck and stared into the murky water, algae rim-
ming the tiles, dust and soot and leaves floating on the surface, and who knew
what was that stuff at the bottom? When every penny mattered, why pay pool
cleaners? The house itself would come down when they left. In the distance
Eden could hear the sound of heavy machinery. Bulldozers clanking, earth-
movers groaning.

Liza came to the kitchen door and called out over the patio, "There's a phone
call for you, Mom. It's Auntie Alma." The long cord stretched all the way from
the wall phone to the back door. Liza held out the receiver. "It's bad news, Mom.
More bad news. I'm sorry, Mom. Sorry for everything. I'll be better."

"Hello," said Eden.


When Eden stopped the station wagon in the yard of the Lances'
house, only a single porch light lit up the darkness. She had no sooner turned off
the engine, briefly resting her head on the steering wheel, than she looked up
and the kitchen windows went bright, the door opened, and she thought she
again saw Afton Lance as she had seen her framed in the sunlit doorway at the
Fourth Street School.

But it was Afton's daughter, Alma Epps, who held out her arms to Eden.
Then Alma fell to weeping. Steeling herself against tears, Eden put her hand on

Alma's shoulder, and in doing so she felt she had grown into Ruth Douglass's body and spirit; she was taller than her cousin, fuller, darker, and more vivid. "Why did you wait so long to call me?"

"I woulda told you, Eden. Honest. I wouldn't have kept it from you. But Mother said we couldn't call you, nor tell you, that you, that you had a full banquet of sorrow and didn't need no more."

"When did she find out?"

"A couple of months ago. Four months. Soon as they told Mother and Daddy what it was, Mother just looked over at Daddy and she said, *Connie*. And they knew what was coming. And from that time, Mother just set herself about tidying her life. She wanted to have her house in order."

"And Tom?"

"Daddy hasn't talked for fifty years, why would he now?"

"And Lil?"

Alma's lower lip trembled. "Lil is fragile. She's lived in Mother's shadow all her life. You think Lil can live without Afton Lance?"

"How long has Afton got?"

"Not long."

"Shouldn't she be in the hospital?" asked Eden.

"Won't have it. Says it costs too much, and the result's gonna be the same no matter what. But the visiting nurse comes every day. A very nice Methodist lady," Alma clarified. "And the whole St. Elmo third ward pitched in so's we can rent a hospital bed for her. It's hard for her to lie flat, and with this bed, she don't have to. Come with me, Eden. You must be famished. I'll go check on Mother. She knows you're coming. She's eager to see you, but she's made me promise she won't be a dribbling fool when she talks to you."

"Afton Lance, a dribbling fool?"

"It's the pain medicine, Eden. Morphine." Alma looked sad. "Don't tell Mother. She would not take the medicine if she knew it was so contrary to the Word of Wisdom."

Eden nodded and followed Alma through the back porch, which still had the wringer washing machine. The kitchen looked as it ever did, the oilcloth on the table pale with scrubbing, even the checked curtains that hung around the sink, concealing the pipes, were starched and ironed, though dust gathered in their folds, accentuated by the overhead light. There were pans on the stove, but no stockpot bubbling away. A bowl of lemons on the table rotted gently, going fuzzy and green, but other than that, Afton's house was indeed in order. The dog came up to Eden and sniffed. He seemed like the same old dog they had always had.

"You freshen up. It's a long drive to make so late. I'll go look in on Mother." Alma had many of her mother's mannerisms, but not Afton's sure stride, or the conviction that animated her every gesture.

Eden used the bathroom, washed her face and hands. Coming back into the kitchen, she found Tom sitting at the table, as though he had materialized there, a gathering of atoms rather than a man. His hair was sparse, dry, and gray. His eyes were still blue, though filmy, and the scar across his nose was the more prominent for his having thinned in old age. His hands were the same massive hands, still capable. Tom wore his bleached Sunday-white shirt, short-sleeved in deference to the heat, and light cotton trousers, not work clothes. He tentatively accepted Eden's embrace.

"You should have told me sooner, Tom."

"You had your own trials."

"But she was diagnosed months ago."

"Four months. Just like Connie."

"I can't believe I didn't know. I can't believe she kept it from me."

"You had your own trials," he said again. "And, it's not like it was for Connie. A tragedy. Connie was a young mother. But Afton is ready for this. Nothing gets past Afton Lance. She wants to see you before she goes to join our Heavenly Father in the Celestial Kingdom. That's how I'm thinking of it. Death shall not touch her. Not ever." The muscles in his jaw contracted. He went to the stove and looked into a pot. "There's some leftover mashed potatoes here. Want me to fix you some taters and eggs? I'd like to be doing something. You must be hungry. People have to eat."

"Thank you."

Tom bestirred himself at the stove, heating the fry pan. He took a couple of fresh eggs from the basket on the counter and cracked each separately into a glass. "Don't tell Mother we been using instant mashed potatoes since she got sick. She'd get on us something fierce if she knew. We keep the box hid."

"She never told me she was sick."

"She didn't want to burden you before, not with what you have suffered."

"I haven't heard from her in a few weeks. I should have known there was something wrong. I should have guessed."

"How could you, Eden? With all your trials?" Tom shook his head. "I'm sure, though God don't like what Matt done, that He will forgive a despondent soul."

Eden had not forgiven Matt. She might, in time, but now she felt that she was living in the cauldron and Matt had escaped into the steam. She choked back a burst of tears, not for Matt, not now, not even for Afton, but for herself. She so needed Afton's certainty.

"Afton's refused to let anyone grieve around her, so be careful what you say. She has no fear of dying. She's ordering everyone in to see her, one at a time. Each one of our children, well, each who's here, anyway, them and Micah and Jonah, of course, and the girls."

"Girls?"

"Junior's daughters been living with us these past few years. You know, since, well, since Junior and his wife split up and left St. Elmo. Both of them."

"Yes," Eden intervened, no need to make the old man revisit what was painful.

"Mother calls each one of 'em to her, separate, and she says the same thing to each. She says, *You need to forgive me.* And that person says, Mother, Mother, there's nothing to forgive. That's what they all say."

"I'm sure it's true."

"Then Mother says, I forgive you. Now, you have to forgive me. And they all do, Eden. They all say, I forgive you, Mother, but they all wonder, *What'd I do? What'd I do what needs forgiving?* But when they press her, she says, it's just words that need to be said. So there's been a lot of tears and prayers and soul searching here, Eden. The Bishop himself come for the laying on of hands. Mother told him, You can wish on me God's blessing and forgiveness, but do not ask Him to prolong my mortal life. This chapter is behind me, she says. I sat right there by her side while she told the Bishop his business. Mother and I forgive each other, too, though for the life of me, I can't 'member anything Afton ever did that didn't please me somehow. If not right away, then later. She was always right, you know. Her bones talked to her."

This was the longest conversation that Eden had ever had with Tom Lance. She was astonished at his volubility. Maybe, in all those years, she'd never been alone with Tom. When Alma returned to the kitchen, he retreated into silence. In a family of this many and in a house this small, was anyone ever alone? Maybe that was the point of those huge Mormon families. You were never alone, never solitary; if you wanted a pensive, solitary place, you had to go inside your own head, your own heart to find it.

"Mother's not fit right now, Eden," said Alma, sinking into a kitchen chair. "She's too far under the pain medicine. We have to catch her right between."

"Between what?" asked Eden, thanking Tom for the two fried eggs, sunny-side up, atop the mashed potatoes, pepper flecked on them, salt gleaming.

"Between when this medicine wears off and when she gets the next dose."

Alma consulted the kitchen wall clock. "Dawn, maybe. They say she shouldn't have this medicine but on a certain schedule, but you know," Alma's voice caught, "it's too hard for me to see her in such pain. I sometimes give it to her early."

"Can I just go see her?"

"I think you better wait till she wants to be seen."

The sun rose like a big yolk, already frying in the sky, and dawn painted the walls where Eden lay stretched out on the couch when she felt someone touch her shoulder. Matt. Eden roused from a dream of Matt, a hungry and complex dream of Matt.

"Eden." Alma shook her.

"Yes? What? What?"

"I think Mother's ready. I made her comfortable as I can. She specially said she wanted her mind clear from the drugs when you come, but the pain'll get to be too much. And she might not tell you."

"I won't stay long. I won't tax her strength."

They had moved Afton to the room that had been Ruth's for the last few years of her life. The room that had been Eden's while she lived here and waited for word from Logan Smith. She walked past pictures she recognized from all those lonely nights. Slapped into dime-store frames, the pictures were biblical scenes, cut from calenders or LDS magazines, Great Mormon Moments: the Handcart Brigade, Brigham Young looking over Salt Lake, and declaring, *This is the place!*

Alma went in while Eden stood outside the bedroom door. She could hear the chickens outside clucking around the yard in search of breakfast, and pigeons or doves cooing from under the eaves. She could hear the hall clock, its somber pendulum marking the hours. She could hear the wind ruffling the dusty leaves in tall trees that Tom had planted years ago all along the back of the house to provide shade.

Alma nodded, and Eden followed her in. The floorboards were bare and creaking under their feet. The windows were covered with blankets. A single bedside lamp was lit. There was a long table set up against one wall with bottles and bedpans and basins, all the accoutrements of long-term illness. The smell was overpoweringly awful, medicinal, redolent of rot and pain. Eden breathed through her mouth, trying not to be revolted by the odor of wasted flesh and medicine.

In the hospital bed, angled so as to leave her reclining though not lying flat, lay Afton Lance, gray-faced, shriveled, her salt-and-pepper hair gone white and cut short all over her head. Her lips were pinched and thin. She had lost her solidity, her bulk; loose skin fell in slack folds around her neck. Her breath came in raspy gusts.

Eden had expected, somehow, stupidly, no doubt, but she had thought to find the old Afton here, quieter, maybe altered, but certainly not this withered, diminished figure. She gave herself instructions: You must not seem to be overwhelmed. You must seem to be brave and collected. Seeming to be, as Eden well knew, was the first step toward being brave and collected.

Afton smiled, raised her fingers twice, shorthand to Alma.

"She'll want a sip of water now and then, Eden. Pitcher's on the table over there," said Alma, closing the door behind her.

Eden brought the spindly kitchen chair to the bedside and took Afton's hand, so thin, the bones and veins protruded beneath her skin, the bones pale, the veins blue. They were no longer the hands that could punch down a rising loaf of sourdough, or wring a chicken's neck, or lift a rack of Mason jars from boiling water, or wash an erring child's mouth out with soap.

"It's me, Eden Louise." To this she received a small pressure on her hand. Thank God Tom had told her what to expect, Afton calling everyone to her, demanding and bestowing forgiveness. Eden was braced and ready to extend and accept her forgiveness quickly.

Slowly, measuring out the effort, Afton turned her head to see Eden. Her eyes were dark wells of pain, harrowing to behold. Eden started to cry. So much for being collected.

"Don't cry. You waste time. We haven't got much time." Her voice was thick and gravelly, her speech slightly slurred.

"I can stay as long as you like." Eden swallowed her tears.

"I can't," said Afton.

Again she gestured in a kind of shorthand and Eden rose and went to the table, where she found a clean glass and a pitcher with a cloth over it to keep out the flies. She poured some water and brought it back.

"Straw."

Eden found a straw and put it in the glass. Afton sipped and then spat the straw out.

"Vulgar. To spit. I never let my boys spit."

Eden put the glass on the bedside table.

"There needs to be an infinite atonement, Eden. So says the Word of the Lord as it has come to us, the Golden Tablets given to Joseph Smith."

"I forgive you," Eden blurted out. "Please forgive me."

Afton seemed puzzled. "You don't know what I'm going to say."

"It doesn't matter. Don't tax your strength. We're all forgiven."

"Are we?" She rolled her head back on the pillow, frowning at the ceiling to consider this vexing question. "There needs to be an infinite atonement," she said again, returning her gaze to Eden. "I have no fear of death. I know that my Heavenly Father awaits me with many mansions, that I will be reunited with those I have loved, my son Lucius taken from me by the war, my beloved daughter Connie, my own dear mother, my sister Eden who died so long ago. I know they and I will live for time and all eternity in the Celestial Kingdom amongst the righteous, sealed unto my husband and children for time and all eternity. Death is nothing. Though I must say, I did not think it would be this hard."

Holding Afton's hand, Eden listened while Afton murmured and mumbled, jumbled up the Bible and the Book of Mormon, the Doctrine and Covenants with her own hard cadre of belief. Of course, Eden told herself, religion, the great ballast of Afton Lance's life, would dominate her thoughts now. Eden was prepared to listen to it all, though she wanted badly to interrupt, to ask her own pressing questions: *How shall I live now, Afton? You know everything. You never doubt. Please tell me, what shall I do? What is the recipe for the rest of my life? How shall I live with the burden of Matt's death? How can I serve my children? Can I save them from devastating grief that will color the rest of their lives? And Stella? What can I do for Stella's pain?* And those were just the questions from and of the future. The past? The truly unanswerable past. *How could I have so completely lost Matt to delusion and death? Was there truly nothing I could have done differently to save Matt, myself, my children? Am I right in telling the children it's no one's fault?* Only Afton Lance, on all this earth, might have even fugitive answers to these questions. Afton could be relied upon. And now she was dying, and Eden was bereft.

Eden tears turned to great wrenching sobs, and the words bubbled out: "How can I live? What shall I do? What will my life be like? How can I protect my children from this grief? How could I have so lost him, Afton?"

"I don't know."

This reply was perhaps the most unlooked-for thing Afton Lance could have said. Eden stared at her, astonished.

She gestured again for the water, sipped it. "Listen to me, and don't let me wander off, you understand?"

"Yes, I understand."

"Good. Don't think I'm afraid. I'm not. We but pass through this world to prove ourselves worthy of heaven, the Celestial Kingdom. We test our spirits in bodies, but the flesh is nothing. Nothing," she added, as if to convince herself. "I am not being punished. This is the fate of all mortals. God gives us our bodies that our spirits might be tried."

"God never gives us burdens we cannot carry," Eden repeated by rote.

"Then God must be very optimistic."

Eden wiped her eyes, sat up straight, admonished herself to pay attention.

"I could not die without asking your forgiveness."

"I already told you, I forgive everything—"

"Hush. Hear me out. This is not everything. This is something particular. I cannot die with my conscience unclear. Unclean. I have my house in order. But for this. Now the time has come."

"Please, just rest. I'll sit here with you. You rest."

Afton ignored her. "All those years ago, twenty years ago, after the war, you came here to us, and we was so proud of you, fighting for your country, like Lucius or Ernest or Junior, or any man woulda done. You always had such spirit. I always admired that in you. Of all my girls, I loved you best. You and Connie. I know I shouldn't say such a thing, but it's the truth. I must tell the truth." She paused and closed her eyes. When she opened them, she turned to Eden beseechingly. "I'd already lost Connie. Connie run off and married a man she knew I could never call my own family. Not a bad man, Victor, but she knew I could never love him. She married him to spite me. Connie was gone from me. Lost. I didn't want to lose you, too. I just thought if you could marry a good LDS man, especially right here in St. Elmo, why, I'd have you nearby, and you would be a happy woman. Fulfilled."

"The Parade of Prospective Grooms," Eden murmured, smiling in spite of herself.

"But you already had a prospective groom." Her eyes flickered and met Eden's. "A man in Philadelphia. He wrote you letters. A lawyer. A man already married, who you committed adultery with. A Catholic."

She motioned again for the water, but this time Eden was slow to respond. Her throat closed up, and the blood rushed from her head, and her tongue shriveled into a hard little knot. Her heart clenched, then exploded into rib-pounding thumps. She found the water. Put the straw to Afton's lips. Removed it.

"I disremember his name."

Eden formed the syllables with difficulty. "Logan Smith."

"I found the letters. I picked 'em up in the box down by the gate. I read 'em."

Tendrils of anxiety seized, squeezed Eden's throat shut, though questions bubbled up against her lips. Finally she eked out, "Logan wrote to me?"

"Yes."

"Where are the letters?"

"I only wanted what was best for you," Afton maintained.

"Where are the letters?"

"I burned 'em," she answered at last. "They were shocking. All that . . . lust and longing. He had a hard time of it in the war. A hard time coming back. I could of almost felt sorry for him, but for the lust and adultery. He was going to divorce his wife and marry you."

"He was?"

Afton frowned. "Maybe she already left him."

"She did?"

"No, yes, well, it doesn't matter. Adultery is a terrible sin. My own dear Eden an adulterer. The thought makes reason stare. Go thou and sin no more, Jesus tells us. It was a sin of omission, my not telling you about the letters. I do not excuse myself, nor split hairs with the Lord. But I outright lied, too."

"To me?"

"To him. Water."

Eden put the straw to her cracked lips and then withdrew it.

Afton took a shallow breath. "He telephoned here one afternoon. You were gone. And he said who he was, his name, his name was . . ."

It seemed to Eden that the known world rushed in to fill the silence, the chickens outside, the doves, the dog barking, a toilet flushing. Voices lilting, falling from nowhere into nothing. She said again, "Logan Smith."

"He was calling from Philadelphia and please could he talk to you and I told him, I said, You're too late. Eden Louise has got married. Just last week. You're too late. And he said he was sorry to have troubled me. He said I should wish you and your husband well, or his best. Something like that. It was a long time ago."

"*Sorry to have troubled you?* How could you? How could you do that to me? I loved him!"

Afton gripped Eden's hand with unguessed-at strength. "I wanted a good husband for you, not a divorced Catholic."

"Matt was a divorced Catholic," said Eden.

"Don't think that wasn't lost on me." Afton summoned something of her old snort of righteous derision. "What do they call it?"

Eden's whole body sagged. "Irony."

"Ironing? Ironing? I must be sure the girls are doing the ironing right or they will look like slatterns." She closed her eyes, but she did not loosen her grip on Eden's hand. She held her there.

Reeling, Eden felt time press her in its sieve until her memories of this room, the lying in this bed missing, hungering for Logan, doubting him, all but extruded from her pores. Twenty years ago. Afton daily returning from the mailbox down by the gate with nothing for Eden. And all the while in her apron pocket, there it lay, Eden's best hope of love. The letters read and consigned to the flame. How many letters? Oh God, she thought, as some old shackle on her heart, some old ache suddenly sprang free, he's alive, and he loved me! He did. She wept. Her whole body shook with sobs; she could not speak though she railed against the awful betrayal by this dying old woman, who always believed she was right, and who had denied Eden her own chosen love. The man she would have married. The man who would not have killed himself and left her. She freed her hand.

"Don't blame Tom. It was all my doing." Afton did not open her eyes. "He didn't know. I never told him what I done. Just about the only thing I ever kept from him. I thought I was saving you from sin and sorrow. But you found it anyway. Sorrow. Sin is our common lot as mortals."

"But what you did is not our common lot," said Eden, wiping her face clean of tears and snot and saliva. "What you did was wrong."

"Yes. I was wrong. I ask your forgiveness."

"How could you?" Eden implored. "How could you do that to me?"

"I'm sorry. I don't fear death, but I fear dying without your forgiveness."

Eden closed her eyes, mopped her face with her hands. She had only ever really loved two men, and now they were both brutally lost to her. Both irrevocably in the past, Eden alone to face the future. The long, dry, celibate years lay before her. The loss of Logan Smith was so far in the past, and the loss of Matt March so fresh and raw, that she ached physically, like she had been bombed. Her life was demolished. Indeed, her life seemed to her like one of those London blocks of flats hit by German bombs during the war: the front sheared away, the loo hanging over the sidewalk, connected only by its plumbing, the tub askew, the bedsprings in the front atop the rubble, the clothes now rags, still hung in the closet, the stove upended, the poor dog barking. The homely and domestic exposed by utter destruction. Truly, Eden was evicted from her own life.

"Just say you forgive me. You don't have to mean it," said Afton, her dry lips cracking. "But you'll feel better later that you said it. One day you will forgive me, and you'll feel bad that you didn't say it." Her tongue flicked over her lips and in a whisper of her old indomitable command, she added, "I'm right on this."

The literal declaration of forgiveness. Just what Matt had wanted in the car when she brought him home from the hospital. *Forgive me. Just say it.* To settle it all so swiftly, so finally, with those three words? Why were people always asking Eden's forgiveness? Why was she the one to whom these egregious injustices were done? Why must she absolve others for the wrongs perpetrated against her?

"I don't have much time," said Afton. "Forgive me."

Eden gave a harsh, mirthless laugh. "I've got nothing to look forward to but regret. For the rest of my life."

Afton sought her hand on the bedclothes, squeezed it, and then released it. "You will find some new recipe for happiness. Some new ingredients must surely be at hand, however scanty, sour, or dull. You'll find a way. The Douglass women always find their way. You will, too. It will be hard, Eden, but you've always gone your own way. You always had your own streak of independence. Never thought I'd say it would serve you, but it will. You have good health. That counts for a lot. Don't look back. Look forward."

Oh, God! Eden covered her eyes with both hands, and saw her own life in this unlovely perspective. Oh, God, I am, I will be one of those very people, someone desperate, restless, unhappy, someone with good health and bad prospects. Someone who must leave the place where God had dropped them. "Their backs to every Babylon, their eyes on some new Zion," she mumbled, weeping.

"Did you forgive me?" croaked Afton.

Eden blew out a long breath. She wiped her nose and eyes with the back of her hand. "Yes."

"Good." Afton closed her eyes and turned her face to the ceiling. "I forgive you, too. Now get Alma for me. I need my medicine. Morphine. Never thought I'd look to morphine."

Eden rose from her chair, holding it for ballast. She slowly made her way to the door, and turned around, peered into the unchanging dimness. "Goodbye, Afton."

"Goodbye, Eden."

"Goodbye, Afton." She lingered again on the name.

"Tell them, will you, tell them to turn up the music? Before you leave."

There was no music, only the sound of the wind rustling the leaves on the trees outside, but Eden said she would.

"Goodbye, precious girl." Afton's voice altered, her throat somehow cleansed of grit or mucus. She sounded almost jaunty, much as she had when she stood on the porch, baby on one hip, telling baby Connie, *Wave bye-bye. Bye-bye, wave bye-bye to Eden.*

# EPILOGUE

C
A
F
E D E N

BICENTENNIAL BUNTING DROOPED FROM THE LAMP-posts in the windless heat toasting the bricked storefront. Liza Ruth March pressed her clipboard against her sweaty cotton shirt, eyes closed. She had the height and build of the Douglass women, but she had inherited her father's high, dramatic nose and dark circles under the eyes. At her mother's request, she kept her thick hair in a ponytail while she worked. She stood in the door, directly beneath the café sign, taking a moment's respite. At last the lunchtime rush was over. It had been a hellish day.

One of the fridges had quit working, and everything had to be crammed into the three others. An hour ago, the sous-chef had stupidly sliced across his palm, and Liza had to drive him to the doctor, where she dropped him off. She wasn't about to wait or hold his hand. Either hand. The second lunchtime waiter had called in sick with a boil on his nose. Disgusting. So it was all up to Liza and Nick. Stellina should be here too, dammit, Liza thought. Stellina ought to be right here working her tail off with the rest of us, instead of playing green goddess in the mountains like a goddamned fool. Then Liza remembered her yoga. You couldn't practice yoga when you were cursing your sister. She drew a deep breath and would have held it, but it carried the whiff of low tide. The café and the family apartment overhead had no water view, but they were close to the ship channel. La Conner, Washington, for all its artsy, touristy repute, could get rather rank with very low tides.

A rumble roused her, a car revving in front of the café, a blue Charger with two young men in it. "Hey, Liza!" the driver called out over the passenger's side. "Hey, Liza! It's me, Ricky! I thought you were off to London and the big time."

"I'm already in the big time, Ricky. I'm going to the London School of Economics in the fall."

Ricky revved his engines, confusing, so Liza thought, his prick with his gas pedal. She declined his offer of a date and he sped away. Ricky had been her date to junior prom, and she had rolled around with him in the backseat of his father's car on that occasion. More's the pity, she thought, judging him critically. Liza had been valedictorian, class of 1971, and on to Vassar, where she had graduated magna cum laude. She had chosen Vassar over her father's favorite, Stanford, because Vassar was three thousand miles away from Skagit County and her family. Liza would not have come back to Washington at all, but the Café Eden was the only place she could have a job, free rent, and save for London.

She went back inside, past the specials of the day, done in pastel chalk on a board, Grilled Chicken with Portobello and Sherry Sauce, Steak with Sauce Verte, Marinda's Red Snapper, steamed in corn husks with zucchini, Pasta Pierino, with its seafood and pepper sauce. None of it tempted Liza; she was a tofu-and-miso sort of girl who ate extravagant desserts when no one was looking.

The dining room was nearly empty; the bricked patio outside, altogether vacated. The bricks were fine in April when it held such heat or light as there was, but in the summer? Wisteria, the fountain, the al fresco charm, notwithstanding all that today it was like an oven. Inside the café, high ceiling fans moved slowly, ineffectually. Each table had a bleached white tablecloth and a small vase with bright flowers, a little limp now. The wooden floors were well worn, the chairs an eclectic assortment.

Back in the kitchen, which was like a furnace, despite the high-speed fans, Liza saw her mother sliding a cheesecake into the oven. She always did this with a tenderness that surprised Liza. Like she was putting a troublesome child to sleep.

Eden turned to Liza, lifted her white chef's apron, and mopped the sweat from her forehead. "You can change the dessert special for dinner tonight to Banana Cheesecake. But not right now. If there's no one out there, I need your help. It's just us holding down the fort."

Liza hated that expression. It brought back embarrassing memories of herself in a sunbonnet, the smell of horses, Annie Oakley, and the Lariat general store. She glanced over to the sink, where the pots and pans and dirty dishes were stacked. "I'm not doing the dishes. Where's Mikey?"

"He's outside smoking a cigarette. And he doesn't like to be called Mikey. It's Mike."

"He's a friend of Nicky's, so he's Mikey to me. I didn't think you let him smoke at all."

"I'm his employer, not his mother. No one smokes in the kitchen. On his break, he can do what he wants." She pointed to a pile of oranges and peppers on the central table. "Chop those."

"Where's Nicky, anyway?"

"He went upstairs. He'll be down in a minute."

Liza gave a pronounced harrumph, inherited unknowingly from Afton Lance, and she utilized this fearful noise on behalf of her brother, who, she was quite certain, had gone upstairs to smoke a joint. Mom had no idea what Nicky did. Liza took up the knife, rolled an orange out, and went at it with conviction. "Nicky better get down here. I'm not waiting tables."

"No one asked you to," said Eden, without looking up, "though you do get to share in the tips, don't you?"

This was an ongoing dispute within the Café Eden. The same sort of quarrel had rankled between Kitty and the Chinese waiters at the Pilgrim some fifty years before. Kitty at least enjoyed the job; the same could not be said for Liza.

Eden hoisted a series of saucepans to the sink, dumped out the water and refilled them, put them back on the gas burners and turned up the heat. At fifty-six she was strong, and her short dark hair was shot through with gray, which somehow softened her overall appearance. Two sharp creases etched between her brows and two others framed her mouth. Her figure had amplified over the years, but she did sometimes mistake herself in the mirror for Ruth Douglass, though she remembered Ruth as regal. Eden could not regard herself as regal, more as the mule in harness plowing the daily furrow. Perhaps Ruth had thought the same. Nonetheless, when Eden's life had crashed, she had looked to Ruth—not to Afton with her rock-ribbed certainties, nor to Kitty with her dreamy inanity, not to Stella with her grim suspicions—but to her grandmother who had somehow arranged her life so she answered to no one. She ran a restaurant.

Eden ran a restaurant because, of all the possible avenues open to her after Matt's death, she thought this would keep her so busy that she would be spared all introspection. And she could feed people. She liked to feed people. Feeding people gave her satisfaction. She was good at it. As a cook Eden used her own instincts, imagination, and memory to re-create the fare that had made Napoleon so legendary. In this endeavor she approximated, but never equaled. She used as well the recipes she'd collected and written up for the St. Elmo *Herald*, and the book of Ernesto's recipes and techniques, so carefully copied out in Kitty's hand. Marinda Reynolds generously contributed her own recipes, sent them to Eden with some old snapshots of their Greenwater days. Eden put the photos of Matt underneath her pillow and slept with them for months. In her life with Matt, Eden had eaten at all sorts of restaurants, but when she was planning her own place, she went back to St. Elmo. She borrowed from the Pilgrim, from Bojo's, and Zacateca's, Kee's Red Dragon, eateries where the food was interesting, and the ambience individual, maybe even a little eccentric. Café Eden took no reservations. If you had to wait, you got free hibiscus tea in the summer. Sometimes there seemed to be a party on the street in front of Café Eden as the tourists and locals laughed and exchanged conversation. On Sunday afternoons, Café Eden had local musicians, jazz or classical trios. She paid the musicians. Just like Matt always said.

In the beginning, Eden's unsung eatery limped along, but the work—physical, demanding, detailed—absorbed everyone. Even Stella rose from despond, slowly, with an occasional smile for her grandchildren, and worked almost literally till the day she died in 1971. As the name and reputation of Café Eden brightened, Eden could have moved the family from the cramped overhead apartment, but she didn't. She liked having her children close by even when they weren't working. And she kept them busy in the restaurant kitchen and dining room.

None of that guaranteed your children would love you, respect you. When she looked at her life squarely, Eden knew she had somehow failed her daughters. For Liza and Stellina, Matt's death remained the central impediment they could neither evade nor address. Eden had long since given up trying to make up that loss to her children. She lived with it, as you might live with a heart murmur, an allergy, or a limp. The complex anger Liza and Stellina felt for their father, they visited on Eden. Matt was enshrined in gorgeous memory. Eden was down in the trenches, slogging, flogging her way through the unglamorous everyday. As teenagers Liza and Stellina took up everything they thought would piss their mother off. Eden strove to develop an immunity to their antics. As long as they did their work and excelled in school, she didn't complain about the weird altar in their bedroom window, the chanting, the pine cone sacrifices, the coconut incense.

Liza certainly excelled in school. Eden applauded her achievements, and hid her hurt that Liza had such contempt for her family, for Washington, for the west, indeed for just about everything. Liza's snobbery bothered Eden less than her unremitting need to prove herself to the dead. Liza took up her every endeavor with a clenched-jaw single-mindedness that had drained her of youthful enthusiasm, of some essential spirit or love of life she ought to have had, some wisp of the romantic that one should only lose with age. Liza never had it. And she never would.

And Stellina? Stellina now called herself Saffron, refusing to be anyone's diminutive. Stellina's energies were channeled into everything and anything alternative. After high school she went to an alternative college. Visits home she tried to convert the family to her new zeal. Whatever that zeal might be. Last year, at the age of twenty, Stellina and a like-minded group of Alternative Women moved to an ultrafeminist commune in the Santa Cruz Mountains, called Green Goddess, where they did God knows what and only God knew with whom. When Stellina phoned home, she constantly corrected her mother: not God knows what. Goddess. At least Eden wasn't subject to this didactic criticism very often. Stellina called only when Saffron needed money.

The boy, Nick, at sixteen was his mother's last hope. Would Nick be the child who would grow up and go on loving her? Who would love her at all? Nick didn't seem to share the girls' resentment or long-simmering immersion in the loss of their father. Nick was easygoing, athletic, charming, lazy, shallow, and confident. Eden thought of him as a beautiful blue dragonfly who would touch down on deep waters only to look at his reflection. He was Matt without the manic, and Eden adored him. He had only to put his arm around her shoulder (at sixteen he was six foot one) to melt her every opposition.

The bell from the front door sounded, and Liza wiped the orange from her hands, picked up her clipboard, and went out to the dining room. She plastered on her attractive face an utterly false smile, and greeted a family party of four. She handed them the small menu and pointed out the chalkboard and told them to sit anywhere they liked. The place was all but empty.

Liza plunked down four waters before them. She had long since developed a quick taxonomy for gauging tips. On a descending scale there were the weekday business and professional people, then lovers on dates, then the tourists, ghastly numbers of them in the summer and at tulip time. Weekday evenings at the Café Eden, the boards of the garden club or the art league or Save Our Salmon would meet. There were a bunch of rowdy middle-aged women who all read the same book, and met once a month; they were good tippers. And then the retirees, gents and ladies who lunch. The worst tippers were those wretched family parties, gathering for some birthday or anniversary. Liza thought of them as trundling tribes—the young, the old, the middle-aged, the squalling brats who all shared the familial weak jaw, or buck teeth, and carrying visibly their festering bit of emotional lumbago. The foursome she had just seated? She slotted them swiftly, her judgment final and rigid as an ice cube tray: divorced father making up for years of neglect. Tourists from far away. The girls wore Villager clothes and carried Coach bags. The father's shirt was ironed. The son slouched.

"Your waiter will be right down," she said.

"Down?" said the son, looking aloft at the fans.

"A figure of speech."


NICK WAS INDEED SMOKING A QUICK JOINT. HE HAD CRAWLED OUT HIS bedroom window and was sitting on the roof, his favorite place to enjoy a little weed. The breeze was high and deflected the smoke away from the kitchen vents. His ass would be grass if his mother caught him. The notion of his ass being grass for smoking grass amused him. Everything amused him when he was high. And if he had to be the only waiter today, he might as well be happy. The joint finished, he brushed his teeth and sauntered down the back stairs, happy as a clam, a thought that also amused him. Pasta Pierino was one of his favorites. He looked forward to the Blind Munchies. He sailed into the restaurant kitchen with a full head of smoke.

Eden lifted a lid on the stove and steam roiled out, and, seeing Nick's silly expression, she shook her head. So he had been smoking weed again. Would he ever grow up? "You have work, Nick. Get to it."

He traded a soapy high-five with Mike, who was back at the sink, steam, heat, and water spraying all around him. Mike was a slow learner and thought Nick March walked on water. Nick tied on a Café Eden monogrammed apron and went to the dining room.

"Are you ready to order yet?" Nick believed that weed endowed him with special powers of divination. The vibes at this table were not good. "I'm Nick.

If you need any help," he fastened his gaze and his grin on the older girl, the one he figured to be Liza's age, "just call out my name."

"Like the song," she said. "Like the Carole King song."

"Just like."

Nick had the liquid dark eyes, sensual mouth, wavy hair, perfect brows, and high, aristocratic nose that had made Ernest March the heartthrob of millions of women. His hair was a brown, and he had added a few peroxide streaks of blond. His face was not as chiseled, or his chin as firm, and where Ernest March had wowed women with his smoldering sensuality, Nick effected a cozier charm, more impulsive, with something of the warmth and high spirits of a puppy. He liked women, young as he was, he enjoyed their company and watching them blossom under his attentions. Perhaps all that was to be expected of a boy who had grown up in a household full of women. Nick fell in love, easily and often. Absolutely in love with each new girl. Liza considered him a romantic clod. Stellina, in her rabid feminist stage, accused him of violating every woman he so much as touched. His mother hoped he was still a virgin.

The girl on whom he had bestowed his special smile, Justine, he had caught her name, ordered the Pasta Pierino. Nick grinned. "That's the best. That sauce has been my family secret for years." The younger, thinner girl ordered Cobb salad, boring, and on the menu for the sake of familiarity. In his cheerful state, Nick was glad he'd picked the older girl to flirt with. Nick liked women with appetite. He had found that skinny girls, once in the sack, were always wondering what they looked like naked and not really interested in the roll and tumble.

"It's too hot to eat anything at all," said the son sullenly, mouth and shoulders both drooping.

The son was the image of his father, blue eyes, high forehead, and no doubt when he was the father's age, he, too, would be bald and studious-looking. The girls, Nick noted, had inherited an overbite from someone, not the father. The whole family emanated an air of anxiety.

"Have something to eat. You'll feel better," said the father to the son. "It's just been a long drive."

"And we're not there yet." The son, whose name Nick gathered was Edward, looked to be about eighteen, sporting a goatee to prove it.

"We're on vacation," his father reminded him. "We don't have to be anywhere at any special time."

"We should have stayed in Philly," said the boy. "It's the Bicentennial."

"All the more reason to leave," said the father. "All that hoopla and excess."

The boy turned to Nick. "Here it is, the Bicentennial, the only time Philly is ever going to outshine New York, and my father drags us to the Northwest."

"Well," said Nick, still under the beneficent effects of weed, "the Northwest outshines New York or Philly any day. Try the Steak with Sauce Verte."

"That means green, doesn't it? Why would I eat anything green?"

" 'Cause it's good for you?"

The father shot Nick a fleeting glance of gratitude and ordered the Salmon with Strawberry Lemon Sauce.

Nick doodled happily on his pad. "Summertime specialty of the house. And to drink? We make a mean hibiscus iced tea. From an old Mexican recipe. From an old Mexican friend of the family," he added. The older girl said she'd have that, and Nick ventured another wink. "Save room for dessert. This the best eatery between Seattle and Vancouver. If this was France, we'd have three stars."

After they had been served, Nick went back into the kitchen, gave his mother a hug, and ministered to the Blind Munchies. Liza sat at the front desk on a stool behind the cash register, where she had stashed her dog-eared copy of *Valley of the Dolls*. She had a weakness for steamy best sellers. Two other parties came into the restaurant, and she handed them menus, complete with false smile, and left them to Nick. The new customers were middle-aged, boring, and had come only for dessert. Not big tippers. Nick continued to lavish himself on the family, more particularly, on the older girl, Justine.

"That salmon was the best thing I have ever eaten," said the father when Nick came to collect their plates. "Maybe in all my life. I've never tasted anything like it."

"I'll tell the chef you said so," said Nick. "She'll be pleased. Most everything on the menu, except for stuff like Cobb salad," he added, unable to quell a small sneer, "it's all family recipes, or my mother made them up. How about dessert?" He handed them a small dessert menu. "Where else can you get Rose Raspberry Ripple Ice Cream. Nowhere," he answered his own question.

Edward didn't want anything. Didn't want to be here at all.

"This is our last chance to be together," the father said, "before you go off to Villanova."

"Villanova's in Philly. Anyway," Edward sulked, "we're not together anyway. We live with Mom. You live alone."

Nick, in his weed-heightened sensitivity, felt sorry for the father; some droop of the lip or eye suggested he'd been hurt by the remark.

The father studied his son. "Feel free to go back to the hotel if you want, Edward."

"It's too hot to walk."

Nick wanted to smack Edward.

"Then take the rental car. The girls and I will walk back."

"It's a long way."

"Not that far. Nice day. Nice place. Nice meal. Small town. I don't mind walking."

"Neither do I," declared Justine.

Edward left. Nick didn't know why this should make him so happy, but it did. They had been here for a very long time (time slowing to a proverbial Marijuana Crawl), and now they would stay longer. He had the feeling that he and Justine already knew each other. "Dessert?"

Justine said, "I'll take the Rose Raspberry Ice Cream."

"Rose Raspberry Ripple," he corrected her, caressing those *r*s with his tongue like he'd like to do to that tender little place, just behind the ear. Girls were so much fun. "And for the young lady?" he asked, giving the eye to the sister who was his own age.

"I'll have the ice cream, too."

"Sir?"

The father was frowning over the dessert menu. "What is this? Figs Napoleon?"

"Figs poached in amaretto and served over vanilla ice cream with tiny little leaves of fresh thyme. You'll never taste anything like it. Our Figs Napoleon are legendary."

"How did they come by the name?"

"I don't know. How does anything get its name?" Nick chortled happily until he saw the father go very pale.

"Dad, are you all right?" asked the younger girl.

The father's eyes closed, and he seemed to sway and made a low groaning noise.

"Daddy, what's wrong?" Justine put her hand on his arm. "Daddy, are you ill? Is it food poisoning?"

"Sir?" asked Nick, trying to clear his smoke-filled mind. He might be called upon to do something brave, heroic, something that called for a cool head and quick reflexes.

The father, eyes still closed, pressed his temples, took off his glasses, and then had a sip of the garnet-colored hibiscus tea. His face remained bloodless. He opened his eyes, and regarded Nick as if seeing him for the first time. He turned and looked at Liza for a long time. He said to Nick, "This place is called Café Eden?"

408

"The one and only."

"Why?"

"Well, that's my mother's name."

The man gestured toward the cash register. "And is she your sister?"

"Yeah. What of it?"

"And is your mother the cook to whom you were to convey my compliments? Is she in the kitchen now? As we speak?"

Nick nodded, but unease collected at the back of his throat. He recognized the tone of voice, a lawyerly voice: grave, unswerving, neutral, formal. Nick remembered this voice from the little DWI blot on his juvenile record last spring.

"And her name, your name. Last name."

"March. Eden March."

"And your father?"

The question caught Nick like a slap. That question always rose up and engulfed him with the old grief and fear that made him hide under his bed when he was a child, that made him afraid in the night and sad in the day. Nick March had wet the bed till he was twelve. "My father died."

"How long ago?"

Nick wanted to tell the guy to fuck off, but his mother would never forgive him. "Twelve years ago. September, 1964."

The father pondered the little vase at the center of the table, as though it might suddenly erupt into arcane tongues. He put down his napkin. "Did your mother remarry?"

"No. What's it to you?"

The father turned to his daughters. "Excuse me, please."

Logan Smith rose from his chair and walked through the swinging door marked EMPLOYEES ONLY, and into the steam-swirled kitchen where Mike stood in a spray from the hot water rinsing off the dishes and on the back burner, a stockpot bubbled, and Eden at the counter used a vegetable peeler on a brick of chocolate, long swirls falling into a cold saucer.

"Eden," he said, a little strangle catching in his throat. "Eden Louise Douglass."

She turned and took him in: the blue eyes, the receding hair, the casual but tailored clothes. Age and balding had accentuated his fine bones, but the cool, studious look in the eyes had not changed. She put the brick of chocolate down, but the heat was such that it had melted into her fingers. She stepped toward him. "Logan? You. Is it really you? Logan? How . . . what . . . ?"

"I'm on vacation with my family."

Did her vision betray her? He was still recognizably Logan Smith. No longer young. But then, neither was she. She retreated to the safety of convention. What a surprise and the like, but he brushed all that away.

"Why didn't you write back?"

"Oh, Logan."

"I poured my heart out to you, and you never even replied! How could you do that to me? You never answered my letters!"

"Mike," Eden turned to the dishwasher, "go take a break, will you? Outside."

"You just got married without a word to me!"

"I never expected to see you again," said Eden, suddenly aware of her hair awry, no makeup, sweat beading her upper lip.

"Is that why you never wrote?"

"I waited for you, Logan. Months. You were going to write to me."

"But you got married just the same! No word, no—"

"Logan." She reached as though she might touch his arm, but wiped her chocolaty fingers on her apron instead. "I never saw your letters, Logan. My aunt snatched them before they got to me. She read them, and destroyed them. She knew that you and I were having an adulterous affair. She didn't want me to marry a divorced Catholic."

"You never read them." Less a question than a declaration of disbelief.

"I didn't know they existed. My aunt burned them."

"I called her house, and she told me you were already married. Got married the week before."

"That was a lie."

"You didn't get married?"

"Not then. Not till much later, 1952."

"Fifty-two! You waited that long?"

Eden shrugged. "I didn't meet a man I could truly love till then."

"Like you loved me?"

"Different than I loved you. He was a different kind of man." Eden's lip quivered. "I was at my aunt's for months, Logan, with no word from you. I was devastated. I was beside myself, but I couldn't call or write to you. I had no address. Nothing. I'd left everything to you, and I heard nothing. So pretty soon, I just thought, well, maybe just all the old Philadelphia was too much for you. That, or you never loved me. That you had forsaken me. That I was forsaken, that you were faithless, or dead. I know those words sound silly, but that's how I felt. I had to accept that I would never see you again."

"Oh my God, Eden. How could you think I would have . . ."

"How could I think anything else?"

"You never knew about Frances?"

"What about Frances?"

Logan turned, paced the kitchen. A timer went off.

He turned back to her. "By the time I got home, Frances had fallen in love with someone else, and she wanted a divorce. Catholic or not. Frances took the brunt of the social firestorm. She'd already told her parents she would divorce me. But they told her to wait, not send such terrible news while I was fighting overseas. And then, when I came home, even then she had to wait. After all, I was the returning hero, medals and all. Don't tax the hero with the bad news."

"You mean your wife was already gone?"

"As good as gone."

"Well, why didn't you come looking for me, then? Even if I didn't write back, how could you just let me go? Why didn't you come to California? We could have been happy there."

"Your aunt told me you were married. I had heard nothing from you. I thought you never loved me."

"That wasn't true."

They stared at each other across the years and miles, all insuperable, the lives they might have had unimaginable. Then she remembered the timer. She opened the oven and brought the Banana Cheesecake from the oven, set it on the marble-top table. She mopped the sweat from her face.

Logan lowered himself on a nearby stool, ran his hand over his balding head. "When I finally got back to Philly after the war, I was a wrecked man, a returning hero, yes. Great. But I felt like a cripple and a casualty. These guys who are back from 'Nam, now, they know how terrible. . . . But our war, Eden, well, we won our war, and saved civilization, and then every right-thinking, red-blooded American man was supposed to come home, get married, buy a fridge, buy a car, a house, be pleased with himself, and shut the hell up. I had a medal to testify to my bad luck at getting shot, my good luck at living through it, but I was sick inside. What I'd seen and done. I was sick at my soul. I might as well have been dead."

"Oh, Logan."

"I was such a mess after the war, my father said, Why don't you go west for a while? Go breathe some real air and see some real mountains and get the hell out of Philly."

"The Owen Wister panacea for what ails a young man?" She smiled. "I kept my copy of *The Virginian* for years, the one you gave me."

"Do you remember what I wrote in it?"

"To the Girl of the Golden West."

Logan nodded, moved. "If I had gone west, I would have only thought of you. It was better to bury myself in the firm, in the practice of law. That's what I did. In a few years, I came out of it. And when I did, I was glad you had married someone else. I would have drained your strength. I would have leaned all over you. I would have used up all your fine strength. I would have used up your spirit, all that abundant vitality."

Eden thought of her marriage to Matt. Perhaps the draining of vitality was an inexorable truth of living. Of dying. She stepped closer to Logan. "The war was like living in the refiner's fire. Everything unimportant is burnt away, and you emerge from the experience different from when you went in. It's brilliant and terrible, but I'm glad you were restored. I'm glad you got married again."

"For years I was so sick at heart that I had lost you. Every other woman I met seemed so pale, by comparison, so spiritless . . ."

"What we had, what we did for each other during the war, our love affair was like a beacon, but it wasn't marriage. We had each other, and we had a reason to live when everything around us seemed intent on death, but we would not have stayed lovers, Logan. No one who gets married stays lovers. Marriage is slow, the days and nights grate on you, and shape you slowly. It's like geology, like those plates in the earth grinding and shaping one another. I was married to Matt March for twelve years. And now he's been dead twelve years. I'm not the same woman I was when I knew you. I'd like to meet your wife. You had four lunch orders. Your wife and kids?"

"Just the kids. I'm divorced."

"I'm sorry to hear that."

"Don't be. The marriage was a long time moribund. Ellen and I wanted to get them all through high school before we divorced, but we couldn't make it last that long. Three years ago I moved out. Closer to the city. We were civilized about it. Maybe too civilized. Maybe if there'd been a little more twist and shout, a little more energy expended." His old rueful smile curved his lips, chasing the years that separated them. The Logan smile. "Philadelphia hasn't changed that much. Still subdued. Everyone in their little groove. I was supposed to have the kids two weekends a month, but they had their lives, their friends in Chestnut Hill. To come to stay with Dad on the weekends felt like punishment. These vacations, out of Philly, they're really the only time I get to spend with my kids. And they're not too happy about that," he added. "My son, anyway. I have two daughters and a son."

"So do I. Two daughters and a son."

"The girl has something of you, but they both must take after their father."

"They look like him," she corrected him.

"Café Eden! I just liked the name, but I thought nothing of it really. It was the Figs Napoleon! The waiter handed me the dessert menu, and I thought, No! Not possible. A name like that? I asked him what was Figs Napoleon, and he described them, and I thought, If I close my eyes, when I open them again, I will be a young man, it will be thirty years ago, I will look at Eden Douglass as I did that first night in that little place in Soho, and she will tell me about a Chinese cook, a chef, a magician who fetched up in a railroad town and worked for her grandmother, and could take a few figs and bits of thyme and create magic. You see, I haven't forgotten a thing."

Eden's eyes shone. "And then there were the sirens and everyone went down into the cellar except us because we knew we were invincible, and nothing terrible could touch us. Not that night, anyway."

"I never dreamed I'd see you in thirty years. Have you always lived here in Washington?"

"No. Just since my husband died. I lived in California before that. Near Los Angeles. I married a man named Matt March and we had a place in the San Fernando Valley."

"Did you have a good life with him? I hope so. Was your husband good to you? I hope life has been good to you, Eden. You deserve it. You deserve the best. You're still so beautiful. Your son said you didn't remarry. I asked him. Forgive me if I'm prying, moving too fast. Too many questions. All these years, and I'm still just as dry and legalistic as ever."

"I never thought that of you."

"There's just so much I want to know. I can't believe I've found you again, that your description of Figs Napoleon was so powerful, that thirty years later, I'd know it was you! Forgive me, I'm blathering. But I feel like I've just awoken from thirty years of the legal cloister, the paneled rooms, dry language, and here I am, standing beside you! And a cheesecake!"

They both laughed out loud, impromptu, unforced laughter.

"It smells divine, by the way. What is it?"

"Banana. Sort of an updated version of Afton's Banana Cream Pie."

"When did your aunt tell you she had burned my letters?"

"Twenty years after the fact. Just before she died. She wanted my forgiveness."

"And did you forgive her?"

"I think I've forgiven everybody by now," Eden replied truthfully. "Not all at once. Not maybe when they asked for it, but eventually."

"I should never have believed your aunt that you would marry without a word to me. I must have been mad to have believed her. It shows my state of mind that I just collapsed under the news. But we're supposed to meet again. I'm sure of it. To have this second chance."

"I don't think we can go back, Logan."

"We could go forward." He bent toward her, and spontaneously brushed her lips with his. "There's such a thing as a kiss hello."

"There is," she replied, succumbing to remembered affection, something of the old effect his kiss always had on her. "There is such a kiss. There are fortunate accidents. I can't believe you're here, in my kitchen, that I'm seeing you again! I'll be seeing you. Just like the old song. In all the old familiar places."

"I will be happy with new places, Eden. I'm not asking to make up for lost time. I want to know who you are now."

"Do you still sleep with your watch on?"

Mike shouted from the back door, "I need to get back to work! I wanna leave on time!"

"Can you come back, Logan?"

"I have come back."

"I mean tonight. Later. Say, eight o'clock. I'll close the place up. We don't take reservations, so I can. I'll make dinner for the two of us, and you and I can talk as late as we want."

"Yes. Yes of course. I have time. Lots of time. I'm on vacation."

Eden motioned Mike in, told him to finish up and leave early. Mike clanked away on the dishes, the hiss of the hoses, the water pounding on the stainless steel sink, steamy vapor swirling while Eden and Logan talked and laughed.

Liza burst into the kitchen. "Mom, Nick is out there breaking your rules. He's fraternizing with the customers."

"Liza, this is Logan Smith. Logan is from Philadelphia. We met a long time ago."

"In London," said Logan, beaming, crossing the room to shake Liza's hand. "During the war. The world was falling apart. But look." He cast a delighted look around the unglamorous kitchen. "The world endured. And we're here together. I'm so delighted. I'm delighted to meet you, Liza. And your brother, Nick."

"He's fraternizing with your daughters," retorted Liza, and then she left.

"She's not very flexible," Eden said. "She's a lot like Afton, really."

"I'll be here at eight," he said, returning to Eden's side.

Logan moved as though he would kiss her again, but didn't, and in this Eden recognized his old reserve. So perhaps some things did not change. Perhaps not everything was mutable, perishable. She wondered if anything in herself was still that indelible after thirty years. Some element of character fixed, like the point on a compass. Well, she thought, as she watched him walk back into the dining room, I guess I'll find out.

She glanced up at the kitchen clock. What could she make by eight o'clock that would be worthy of the occasion? Something that would also give her time to take a shower and put on fresh clothes, cologne, and a little makeup, also worthy of the occasion. There must be a recipe for this. There's a recipe for everything. You look to see what you have on hand, and how you can shape those ingredients into what you want. You bring to bear your taste, imagination, impulse, circumstance, and experience. What is a recipe, after all, but a license for invention? Like life.

# Cast of Characters

### Eden Louise Douglass    b. 1920, St. Elmo, California

**Ruth Mason Douglass,**    b. 1865. Owner of the Pilgrim Restaurant.
Grandmother to Eden.
M. 1889 Samuel Douglass in Salt Lake City, Utah Territory
Widowed
Six children: Eden, Gideon, Afton, Lil, Mason, Narcissa

**Gideon Douglass,**    b. 1892, National Falls, Idaho. Oldest son of Ruth Douglass.
M. 1913 **Katherine (Kitty) Tindall,** b. 1894. Mormon convert from
Liverpool, England.
Four children: Tootsie (d. in infancy, 1919 flu epidemic)
**Eden Louise,**    b. 1920
**Ada Ruth,**    b. 1922
**Ernest Fred,**    b. 1924

**Afton Douglass Lance,**    b. 1893, National Falls, Idaho. Oldest living
daughter of Ruth Douglass.
M. 1911 **Tom Lance,** b. 1889. Railroad worker, later a
small-time rancher.
Eight children: Bessie, Alma, Lucius, Connie, Junior, Samuel,
William, Douglass

**Lily Douglass Lance Walsh,**    b. 1895, National Falls, Idaho. Sister to Afton
Lance.
M. 1st Willie Lance, Tom Lance's brother
M. 2nd Mr. Walsh
Three children

**Constance Lance Levy,**    b. 1925. Youngest daughter of Tom and Afton Lance.
M. 1944 **Victor Levy,** b. 1908. Managing editor of the St. Elmo *Herald*.
Four children (two from Victor's first marriage; two of their own)

**Alma Lance Epps,** b. 1916. Middle daughter of Tom and Afton Lance.
 M. 1940 **Walter Epps Junior** from a tribe of Arkansas Baptists, migrants to
 California, who, for a time, camped in the same groves where they picked
 fruit.
 Four sons

**Napoleon,** b. c. 1885, Shanghai, China. Superlative chef at the Pilgrim
 Restaurant, 1915–36.
 Never married as far as is known

**Gloria Trujillo Patterson,** b. 1886, St. Elmo County, California.
 Invented the take-out meal. From her back door, she sold small buckets of
 beans and meat, studded with jalapeños and hand-ground spices, tamales,
 husked forever in memory.
 M. 1902 **Benjamin Franklin Patterson**
 Seven children

**Naomi Bowers,** also known as Nana Bowers, b. c. 1838, northwestern Missouri.
 Successful matriarch of an enterprising family and a famously good cook.
 1854: Came as the slave of St. Elmo's founder, the Mormon Apostle, Madison Whickham.
 1856: Declared herself a free woman, her contention upheld by the circuit
 court judge.
 M. 1856 Elijah Bowers
 Ten children

**Mabel Harriet Bowers Johnson,** b. 1891, St. Elmo, California. Granddaughter of
 Naomi Bowers.
 Owner of the original Bojo's Café.
 M. 1908 Orlando Johnson
 Five children

**Sojourner Hope Johnson,** b. 1917. Mabel's daughter.
 Owner of the new Bojo's out on Valley Farms Road.
 M. 1934 George Thomas Dawson
 Four children

**Winifred T. Merton,** b. 1882, Amarillo, Texas.
 Editor of the Women's Pages, St. Elmo *Herald.*
 Never married

**Sherman Yamashita,** b. 1897, Kern County, California.
 Owner of Green Goddess Vegetables from 1920 till 1942.
 M. 1918 Maskao Hirata
 Four children

## FAIRWELL, IDAHO

**Mason Douglass,** b. 1898. Only brother of Gideon Douglass. Purveyor of Get Rich Quick Schemes.

**Margaret Thorsen,** b. 1901, Rexburg, Idaho. Devout Saint and legendary baker of gingerbread.
M. 1917
Five children

**Ned Redbourne,** editor of the Fairwell *Enterprise*

**Emjay Gates,** jilted fiancé of Eden Douglass

**Melvin Brewster,** m. 1939 Ada Douglass
Seven children

## EUROPEAN THEATER OF OPERATIONS

**Francis Logan Smith,** b. 1917, Philadelphia, Pennsylvania, to a prominent legal family. A lawyer in civilian life. Captain during the war.
M. 1st 1942 Frances Ann Brown. No children of this union
M. 2nd 1951 Ellen Agnes Martin
Three children

**Dottie Lofgren,** b. 1922, WAC, daughter of a Wichita minister

**Faye Cole,** b. 1923, WAC, daughter of a New Orleans brothel keeper

**Mme. Duque,** English proprietor of a French restaurant in Soho, London

## LOS ANGELES AND GREENWATER, CALIFORNIA

**Walter Brock,** loan officer at Columbia First National Bank; Eden's boss, but not her superior

**Annie Agajanian,** b. 1922 at sea, her Armenian parents emigrating from Constantinople and Piraeus.
M. 1944 **Ernest Douglass,** Los Angeles
Three children: Linda, David, and Susan

**Matt March,** b. 1922, Los Angeles, California.
Owner, Greenwater Movie Ranch. Producer of Westerns, including TV's *Lariat Lawman*.
M. 1952 **Eden Douglass,** Ensenada, Mexico
Three children: **Liza Ruth,** b. 1953
**Stellina Lucia,** b. 1955
**Nicolas Ernesto,** b. 1960

**Stella Curro March,**  b. 1897, New York City.
M. 1915 Nico Marchiani (Nico d. 1944)
One son: Matteo Marchiani (Matt March)

**Ernest March** (Ernesto Marchiani),  b. 1894, Lucca Italy. Brother of Nico and uncle of Matt March.
Smoldering star of the silent screen.
Never married

**Frankie Pierino,**  b. 1924, Los Angeles, California. Youngest son of Joe Pierino.
Restaurateur for thirty years, Pierino's on La Cienega.
Married twice
Three children

**Les Doyle,**  b. 1919, Angel's Camp, California.
Cowboy Hall of Fame. U.S. Champion Rodeo Rider, 1941. U.S. Marine, World War II, Bronze Star. Stuntman in over 300 films and television shows. Nominated for an Oscar in 1969 for Best Supporting Actor.
M. 1950 Virginia Brothers
No children

**Virginia (Ginny) Brothers Doyle,**  b. 1918, Minnehaha County, South Dakota.
Cowgirl Hall of Fame. Three-time National Rodeo Champion. Invented the Suicide Drag. Greatest female rodeo star and stunt double of her generation, acted in 250 films and TV shows.
M. 1950 Les Doyle, Lodi, California
No children

**The Prairie Fern,**  b. 1898, Earls Court, London. Her parents, Sioux Indians, performing with Buffalo Bill's Wild West Show. Prairie Fern was part of the act from the time she could walk.
M. 1915 William Cody Brothers, South Dakota
Two daughters: Virginia and Kathleen. Son killed in infancy

**Marinda Villarreal Reynolds,**  b. 1914, Matamoros, Mexico.
M. 1935 Juan Reynolds, Brownsville, Texas. (Juan, stuntman and rodeo star, d. 1954)
Four children

**Lois Bonner,**  b. 1933, Long Beach, California.
1952 Rose Parade Princess. Actress: stage, film, and TV, played Carrie Dunne on *The Lariat Lawman*.
M. 1954 Reno, Nevada; divorced there too, in 1956
No children

**Rex Hogan,** b. LeeRoy Hogan, dates given variously as 1915, 1920, 1923, etc., Lawton, Oklahoma.

Actor. A minor talent, but scored noir parts in the late 1930s. His star rose during the war when other actors were drafted. Rex was almost legally blind. His squint and rugged good looks made him a regular in postwar Westerns, including bit parts in John Ford's *Fort Apache* and *Rio Grande*. Mostly roles in B Westerns, and matinee serials for Poverty Row producers. Career saved by television: title character in *The Lariat Lawman*. Saved again in the 1960s starring in Euro-Westerns.

M. three or four times, two or three children, depending on Rex's mood and who he was talking to.

**Spud Babbitt,** b. Eustace Babcock, 1918, Elko, Nevada.

Perennial sidekick, renowned for his girth, his gravelly voice, his capacity for alcohol, and his bad luck at cards. Look hard enough and you can see the outline of his hip flask in his many roles, 150 films and TV shows, deputy in *The Lariat Lawman*. On set, he taught Stellina March to count using beans from the Lariat general store.

M. twice, four children

**Gus and Beverly Baxter,** m. 1951, Reno, Nevada (third marriage for Gus; no children)

Beverly, b. 1931

Gus, b. 1916

# Acknowledgments

The author is much indebted to the hospitality, generosity, and good cooking of her friends over many years: Margaret Ann Marchioli, Elizabeth Nybakken, Sandra Thomas, Lucerne Snipes, Paola Rizzoli, Muriel Dance, and Terry Harrington.

Thanks, too, to my sister, Helen K. Johnson, an all-around cowgirl, for her time and expertise. Thanks, too, to Judith F. Brown for her willingness to revisit an old Philadelphia.

Thanks to Jennifer Dobbs of Memphis, Tennessee, and Tess Johnston of Shanghai, China, for their contributions to the long walk to the French Legation.

Especial gratitude to my mother, Peggy Kalpakian Johnson, for her patience, caring, and cooking—and for teaching me that a ham can indeed be beautiful. My sons, Bear and Brendan McCreary, and their many friends have given me a lively, appreciative audience for my cooking, and I cherish our time in the kitchen.

Thanks to Diane Reverand for her astute questions and insightful reading of the manuscript. Thanks to Deborah Schneider for her loyalty and enthusiasm for my work. Thanks to Laura Mathews at *Good Housekeeping* for her support of these characters and ideas.

The University of Washington libraries have been a wonderful resource for me.